Moon of the White Tears

~ the Grandest-Ever Appalachian Do-si-do ~

Books by Mark Warren

Moon of the White Tears
Indigo Heaven
A Tale Twice Told
Last of the Pistoleers
Song of the Horseman
Two Winters in a Tipi
Wyatt Earp, an American Odyssey (a trilogy)
The Long Road to Legend
Born to the Badge
A Law Unto Himself
Secrets of the Forest (4 volumes)
Wild Plants & Survival Lore
Fire-making, Storytelling, & Ceremony
Stalking, Tracking, & Playing Games in the Wild
Archery, Projectiles & Canoeing
Librarians of the West
The Westering Trail Travesties
A Last Serenade for Billy Bonney

For more information
visit: www.SpeakingVolumes.us

Moon of the White Tears

~ the Grandest-Ever Appalachian Do-si-do ~

Mark Warren

SPEAKING VOLUMES, LLC
NAPLES, FLORIDA
2024

Moon of the White Tears

Copyright © 2024 by Mark Warren

All rights reserved. No part of this book may be reproduced or transmitted in any form or by any means without written permission.

ISBN 979-8-89022-048-6

To Ethel Garrett
my other mama

Acknowledgments

With gratitude to the Cherokee people, who knew these mountains as no people will ever know them again.

Katuah

Here at the southern tip of the Appalachians—the place Cherokees called "Katuah"—the deep rocky gorges and dark coves are heavily dressed in wilderness greens. Even in winter the verdant colors persist. Rhododendron and mountain laurel. Hemlock and white pine . . . that latter majestic conifer being the tallest of trees in the Eastern United States.

The forests here are shrouded in the smoky veil of morning mist. At night this world is painted silver by the moon. Visually, it is a masterpiece of many parts making up the whole. But it is more than shapes and colors. There is an anthem of indigenous sounds, too.

From the center of Katuah rises a constant, whispery song from the countless ribbons of water that twist and plunge and foam brilliant white as they race down the rocky slopes of these old mountains. The music is close to your ear. Close to your heart. It is like a thousand pages of old parchment being torn one after the other. And then a thousand more. It goes on unending.

In Katuah, you can stand on a trail fifty feet above a thundering waterfall, and you'll not see the rapids for all the greenery around you. To see it, you must descend into the dark portal below, climb down the steep shoulders of the creek and weave through its thick pelage of trees, shrubs, gangly vines, and lush ferns. Once there at the edge of the creek, you discover that water might possibly manufacture its own light.

The white man drove out the Cherokees—most of them—leaving only the music of their place-names. Words like "Noontootla," "Amicalola," and "Tesnatee." The white man deemed himself more worthy of the land than the Cherokee, and so he took it. He convinced himself that he was its rightful, God-given heir by virtue of his superior race. By putting a celestial name to this covetousness of the land, he purged himself of all traces of guilt. "Manifest Destiny" was the phrase. Just to speak the words aloud, one might think he were delivering a message from God, Himself.

So, what is it that makes the white man more deserving of this land? Are the whites truly endowed with some innate advantage over others that makes them better stewards of montane forests? If they are, we have yet to witness any evidence of the theory.

No man can inhabit Katuah without breathing in the same cool mountain air, without drinking of the same springwater elixir, and without hearing the same duet of water and stone that nourished the Cherokees for all those centuries before the white incursion. Does that not mean that all highlanders are like brothers and sisters who feed from the same mother's breast? Perhaps it should, but the white conquerors are a strange lot.

The new tenants of Katuah claim their narrow valleys and clannish coves and pretend to reside in the land of the free and the home of the brave. Yet they scream at one another over the ridge tops at night like madmen who cannot find a moon at which to howl.

Chapter One

**Chestatee River Basin
Moonless night**

Holding the turtle shell in his lap, the warrior crushed the succulent berries into a paste against the inner curve of the sun-bleached bowl. The night was so black he could not make out the movement of his own hands. All the while, he listened to the rippling and lapping of the dark river as though it were a voice, whispering and intimate, approving his plan.

Blindly, he dabbed a fingertip into the reptilian bowl and painted symbols on his face and chest, rendering the animal shapes that would protect him this night. When finished, he set the shell adrift like a tiny canoe. This was his gift back to the river. The river had nourished the pokeberries on the stalk as well as the turtle when it had swum the calm eddies in search of insect larvae. The Chestatee River was the blood of this valley, and the warrior was one of its blood brothers. One of the last of his kind.

Moving silently in his soft-skin moccasins, feeling his way by instinct, he wove through the trees and returned to the high ground. It was there he had left his trusted Pinto hidden in the brush. Lovingly, he stroked her flank and nickered to her, as though to say: *Rest now . . . regain your strength . . . in a short time we will race away like the wind and be gone.*

She was still cooling down from the hard ride from Frogtown. The Pinto was old and arthritic but still adept at being motionless and quiet. And she still understood the stealth needed for such a night as this. She would be strong again by the time he had finished his work.

After hauling his gear to the side of the road, he knelt before the white man's senseless totem, coaxed a spark into a steady flame, and went to work. Every few seconds he looked up at the structure he had come to destroy, and each time he allowed a vindictive smile. Removing this blight from the land was only the beginning. There would be more.

With the burning complete, the totem fell and crashed into the dirt with a loud whanging sound. After snuffing the flame, he held his breath to listen. No one had heard. No one had seen. It was why he had chosen this night, when the white men and their women held their absurd dance in the town.

"I am *Inâli*," he said aloud, "Black Fox of the Blue clan, come to cleanse the land." His rough-textured voice carried the tone of a proper chant, and the formality of the words was pleasing to him, invoking a sense of ceremony to what he had just accomplished.

Summoning strength from his ancestors, he dragged the totem from the brush and lifted it onto the back of the Pinto, and the old girl stood for it without complaint. The structure was too long to be carried unseen, but, by using a Cherokee incantation, he had willed himself and the Pinto invisible this night. And it was so. Or so he believed.

After wiping out the drag marks and strapping down his gear, he mounted the Pinto but then sat for a moment before starting for home. If he were caught, he knew, he could expect no mercy. Stealing the white man's totem was tantamount to taking a scalp.

"Bah!" he huffed and spat off to one side. "Black Fox is too sly for the white man's dulled senses."

All that was left now was to disappear into the night and dispose of the totem. After a silent prayer to the Thunder Spirits, he turned the key and fired the ignition and the old Ford Pinto engine hummed with its familiar steady purr.

"Hey-*hey*-yah!" he yelled, unleashing his victory call to the starless sky. When he stomped the gas pedal to the floor, the tires spun and spat gravel into the guardrail like a spray of buckshot. Swerving out onto the highway, he headed for the bypass to make good his escape. "Hey-*hey*-yah!" he yelled again.

And then he was gone.

Chapter Two

Sheriff's Benefit Contra-dance
Lumpkin County Farmers' Co-op Warehouse
Monday night

"Circle to the left and smile as you go, then greet your partner with a do-si-do!"

The room was packed, and the dancers wove together like multi-colored yarns gone manic on a loom. These veteran dancers knew all the moves: promenades, sashays, California twirls, and the Georgia Orangutan, which the caller pronounced, "Jaw-juh Rang-a-tang." Beneath the music the thunder of so many feet stomping on the old heart-pine floor made these Georgia farmers feel at home. Such percussion reminded them of cattle bumping through loading chutes . . . and horses banging against stall gates . . . and potatoes tumbling out of a burlap bag—the everyday sounds of a working man's life. And the working woman, too.

The caller was Winslow Mooney, who had been an auctioneer at the tobacco barns back when. That was before cancer had popped its ugly head out of the cigarette industry's bag of tricks and killed the local leaf market. In those days Wins Mooney could rival a pileated woodpecker with his rat-a-tat-tat nasal delivery. At seventy-one, Wins had made the transition to calling dances somewhat smoothly and was pretty good at it. His day job was repairing miniaturized spy equipment. No one had a clue where he had picked up that skill.

The band was from somewhere out of Tennessee. Two violins, an acoustic guitar, a banjo, a mandolin, and a standup bass. They called themselves *Fiddlesticks* and knew how to evoke the good old days with pieces like *Pluck at My Heart Strings* and *Possum on the Run*. They even did a teary waltz rendition of *Miss McMurdy's Parlor*, and you could see in the shining eyes of the leathery old farmers and their wives that they were back in a time that made sense to them—before lawsuits over spilled hot coffee . . . before the Internet . . . and before grown men had begun to impale their body parts with jewelry.

Verdie Rider was there—looking emancipated without her waitress apron. Ernest Dowdie made an appearance with his wife, Lurlene. Ernest was the president of the bank, and Lurlene was the president of Ernest. And Arliss Bodie, the owner of *The Gold Miner's Tavern*, was present. Arliss never went out to anything . . . not even a family funeral. But there he was, romping around on the floor with Big Beulah Babcock, who was mostly deaf and stomped to the rhythm on a two-second delay.

Buster "Never Say Die" Gooch had turned out—he and his gargantuan Adam's apple. Both Buster and his half-swallowed apple bounced feverishly as he played his trump card in his quest for a wife. Buster was to dancing what Daniel Boone was to trail blazing, making up moves on the spot that seemed to fit right in. If ever he was going to find a woman willing to live with him and that bulging throat, it would happen here, where a bedazzled widow might find his snappy footwork compelling enough to overlook the anomalous lump in his tortured throat.

L.T. Voss stood just outside the back door, smoking. This chosen spot under the porch light served as an impromptu office, where he handed out cigars to any man whose land he had an interest in buying.

L.T.'s ex-wife, Eunice, had made her famous sweet potato soufflé. All evening she had hovered near the baked goods table to give the samplers a chance to heap accolades upon her modest protests of having gone to "no trouble at all." It was common knowledge that the way she layered the soufflé with cracker crumbs and melted marshmallows took two days of preparation. She had not whipped up the delicacy in years, but tonight she was celebrating her recent divorce.

L.T. boycotted the soufflé out of principle, so he said. But it was just spite. All the ingredients of Eunice's dish had been paid for by her first alimony check.

Ott Ambrose was there, of course. It was the one social event the sheriff was expected to attend in person. For a man his size—which was mostly girth—Ott was light on his feet. Watching him dance, it was easy to see the little boy in him, even though no one who had known him as a little boy had ever thought of him as anything but the future sheriff. Ott's daddy had been sheriff and his daddy before him. Some things just picked up a momentum in a small town, and this was one of them.

Ott's wife, Bernice, did not dance. Period. But she was there. Mostly to keep an eye on Ott. Last year at this occasion, he had overdone the dancing and had to run the office from his bed for three days as he waited for a knotted calf muscle to loosen up. On top of that, he discovered that he had torn his rotator cuff while dancing with Big Beulah Babcock.

In the aftermath of that injury, Ott had been such a demanding patient that Bernice had neglected her soap operas for three days running, and it took her another three to fill in the holes of the plots and piece together all that she had missed. That was a stressful time for Bernice—all six days. At best, she was a challenge to live with, as Ott was apt to say. Under stress she was nothing short of a long-suffering mission.

The new assistant district attorney had dropped by, too. More than likely she was trying to curry favor with the locals and make a bid for acceptance in her new surroundings. Maria Gunlock was her name. She was an African-American attorney from somewhere up north and possessed smooth, coffee-colored skin, lustrous black hair, a perfect nose arched upward just so, smoldering emerald eyes, and high cheekbones that cast shadows in the hollows of her jaws.

Every man in the room was stealing a peek at her every chance he could. She was something new to Lumpkin County, not because she was a black Yankee working for the county government, but because she looked like she had stepped right from the cover of a New York City fashion magazine.

Only a few of the locals had dared to ask Maria to dance, and those who did were so nervous they forgot their dance steps. She even frightened a few of the men into stepping outside alone to breathe in some fresh air. Her green-glass eyes were so full of fiery focus, they looked as if they could fuse mismatched metals. The rumor was that she was going to make one hell of a prosecutor, if the combination of classical beauty and razor-sharp intimidation could be counted on to unhinge a witness.

Ott, decked out in his best sheriff's uniform, left Bernice clucking with her sister, Dora Lynn, and wandered over to the refreshment table where Maria Gunlock was standing next to Mayor Metcalfe. Ott helped himself to some lime sherbet/ginger ale punch and waited for Maria to glance his way. That was one of the assets to his size. If she happened to turn anywhere from ten to a hundred and ten degrees, Ott was all she was going to see.

"Ott."

Ott turned to the familiar no-nonsense voice of Duffy Hawkins, his chief deputy.

"Well, hey there, Duff." Ott smiled his big what-the-hell're-you-doing-here smile and patted Duffy on the upper arm, as if it were something he did on a daily basis. "Ain't gonna break down and dance for us, are you?"

Duffy pivoted his head to watch the dancers out on the floor. Ott could never tell what was going on behind those black-as-midnight sunglasses, but he knew Duffy well enough to know that something was wrong somewhere out in the county. Else he wouldn't be here.

"Little problem out on highway sixty south o' town. Thought you'd wanna know."

Ott hid his irritation behind his Annual-Sheriff's-Benefit smile. A traffic incident, for God's sake! Was there no respite from a sheriff's duties?

Ott managed a pleasant nod and thought about the new A.D.A. standing behind him. What was that Chinese word that meant both "disaster" and "opportunity?" It didn't matter. What was important was pairing up the two concepts together and capitalizing on it. Like when life gives you a dead skunk, you make a stink bomb.

"Well," Ott said, trying to sound both unfazed and professional, "long as God don' make people perfect, we're gonna have us some fender benders, ain't we?" He smiled his you-see-it-all-when-you're-the-sheriff smile and sipped his punch.

Duffy's expression did not change. It never changed. Watching the dancers, he bided his time like he always did. Duffy was meticulous and thorough and could not be hurried. On any given day, Ott imagined that Duffy Hawkins could give a full report on the daily agenda of any stray dog wandering the county roads.

"That sign that went up this mornin'," Duffy said quietly, "the one with the mayor's name on it? It's gone."

Ott turned quickly and frowned. "Whattaya mean 'gone'?" he said, forfeiting the better part of his savoir-faire.

Duffy flexed the steel-cable tendons in his jaw. "Some jasper's gone and burnt it down and carried it off."

" 'Burnt it down'? Weren't it a metal post?"

Duffy nodded. "Used a blow torch. Thought you might wanna tell the mayor b'fore he drives by there on his way home and sees it ain't there no more."

Ott, never too good with maps or directions, wrestled with the logistics and then frowned. "That sign ain't even on his way home, is it?"

Duffy lifted both eyebrows, a near-Thespian departure from his usually stoic face. "It ain't on nobody's way home, but the mayor's been cruisin' past there all day." The deputy shook his head. "I figure he'll be callin' us up to form a midnight posse or somethin' o' that sort." Duffy tightened his mouth. "You know the mayor, Ott."

Ott knew the mayor, all right. He frowned and watched Arliss Bodie attempt to twirl Big Beulah Babcock, who was three-times his size. It was like a least weasel trying to get a watermelon to spin on end. Arliss, Ott thought, had better have some damned healthy rotator cuffs.

"Why the h—" Ott began and changed course when he remembered that Maria Gunlock was just two feet away. He cleared his throat. "Why in heaven's name would somebody wanna go and burn down a metal sign?"

Duffy offered nothing on that. Judging by the slow turret of his head, he might have been memorizing the faces of the two hundred or so people in the room as a way of eliminating suspects.

"Well," Ott said and sniffed. He knew he needed to say something sheriff-like. "I betcha a dollar 'gainst a dung beetle that sign's gonna be out in the weeds somewhere. Git some o' the boys and set up a search party. Keep at it till you find it."

Duffy turned at this, and Ott tried not to look at those imposing Darth Vader dark glasses trained his way. About six measures of music galloped by as Duffy's face held the inert expression of a shovel blade. Ott had no idea that Duffy was looking past him, admiring the profile of Maria Gunlock's face. She was mostly why Duffy had made this appearance at the dance.

"I already checked the right-a-way down to the river," Duffy reported in a dispassionate monotone. "No prints, no drag marks, no sign," he reported in a chant of practicality.

Ott could never get a sense as to Duffy's grasp on irony or disapproval or derision, though he was pretty sure Duffy employed them all whenever the two of them talked. Ott sniffed again, stuck his free hand into his trouser pocket, and tumbled coins. He gazed down into his lime punch and looked like he wanted to spit. This gave Duffy several uninterrupted seconds to admire Maria Gunlock's profile.

"Well, maybe they threw it out in the river," Ott said.

"River's too shallow there. We'd 'a seen it with our searchlights. I think somebody *wanted* the sign."

"What in the hell would—" Ott caught himself and cleared his throat. "What, pray tell, would somebody want with Byron's sign?"

"Maybe they didn't like it."

Ott's face creased like a worn-out dollar bill. He leaned forward and lowered his voice to a raspy whisper.

"You juss finished sayin' someb'dy wanted the dang thang."

Duffy turned back to the crowded room of dancers. "Might be they didn' want it there 'cause they didn' like it . . . so they wanted it so it wouldn't be there."

Ott was about to complete that spit now, looking for some logical place to deposit it. He almost bumped into Maria Gunlock as she ladled punch into a Dixie cup.

"Well," Ott crooned, changing course as easily as a gnat picked up by a crosswind. "Mizz Gunlock," he said, and put on his I'm-just-the-man-you-want-to-see smile. "I didn' really git a chance to in'erduce myself at the courthouse the other day. I'm Sher'ff Ambrose. People call me 'Ott.' "

Ott could feel Duffy's presence behind him like the smolder of a steady flame. This was a complete solar eclipse that Ott wanted to hold in place as long as he could—Miss Gunlock the sun, Ott the big round moon, and Duffy the Earth in shadow. In this moment Ott realized he had held a lifelong grudge against Duffy's carved-out-of-walnut, rough good looks.

Bubbling up from Ott's memory came that memo he had found in the wastebasket at the office last Christmas. One of the deputies on jail duty had filled the black hole of boredom by typing out a cast of "dream-team" movie stars to portray the staff of the sheriff's department, should Hollywood ever want to immortalize Lumpkin County's peace officers on film. For Duffy it had been "a young Charles Bronson." That ate at Ott for weeks. One of Ott's childhood heroes had been Charles Bronson, and

Ott, grudgingly, had to admit that there was a strong resemblance between the movie star and his deputy.

For playing Ott, it was "John Goodman + 100 pounds," but that entry was crossed out. Written next to it was "Free Willy." Ott didn't know who Free Willy was, but he knew in his gut it couldn't be good.

Maria Gunlock pushed the cordial smile off her face and replaced it with a look of concern. She leaned toward Ott to yell over a swell in the music.

"You were understandably in a hurry, Sheriff. How did that hostage incident get resolved?"

Ott's face paled as he remembered the lame excuse he had offered for leaving the courthouse meeting last Friday afternoon when his gut was about to explode. He had needed a bathroom in the worst way. Using the old pager trick, he had mumbled something about a hostage situation at the north end of the county. It was the best story he'd been able to come up with under the circumstances. He'd left the room like there were only minutes to spare before something tragic was going to happen. Which was true.

He had known for hours about the chicken truck jackknifing up at Hester Gap. The truck had flipped on its side onto the right of way, and chicken cages had sprung open, releasing a stampede of Cornish Broilers into the surrounding forest. The first deputy on the scene had reported the site looking like the results of an epic pillow fight.

It wasn't such a stretch to imagine local motorists stopping to confiscate a little something for Sunday dinner. Hell, it was the poultry "daily double!" Who wouldn't stop? Ott couldn't see why this wouldn't fall under the rubric of "hostage-taking."

Ott's gut had been about to burst. As he had hurried toward the men's room down the hall, he recalled that deadly bowl of Brunswick stew he'd eaten at Crowder Ramp's new barbecue place. Ott had thought the stew questionable from the first bite, a rank taste like swamp gas lurking beneath the spice and tang. But he had been hungry. And Crowder was Dora Lynn's boy, which made him Ott's nephew. Plus, Ott had promised Bernice he would give Crowder some business before the week was out.

Without a doubt, Crowder's place had lived up to its name: *In a Pig's Sty*. On Friday, Ott had spent hours sequestered in that toilet stall at the courthouse and had to find the custodian to let him out of the building when finally, he had emerged from the bathroom around ten o'clock, ashen and spent.

Ott waved off Maria Gunlock's query. "Turned out to be a misc'munication. A chicken truck turned over up on highway nineteen."

Maria looked confused.

Ott chuckled and shrugged. "There was some purty big chickens in that truck. First dep'ty on the scene mistook 'em for ostriches. Time it come over the radio, the dispatcher had got 'ostrich' twisted 'round to 'hostage.'" He shrugged and again offered his you-see-it-all-when-you're-the-sheriff smile. "It happens. Say, you wanna dance?"

But Maria was not listening now. She was standing stock-still, her eyes fixed over the sheriff's shoulder on the swarthy deputy staring out at the crowd. For Maria it felt like a pivotal moment with a soundtrack. Something about the deputy's rough-hewn profile, his infinite calm. She knew him from somewhere. When he turned to look at her, her face flushed hot and cold in the same instant. The muscles behind her knees turned to jelly, and Maria reached for the punch table to steady herself. Ott moved to her and touched her elbow.

"You aw-right there, Missy?"

Maria forced a smile. "Just a little faint. It might be the heat."

Ott poured more punch for her. "There you go. Try a lil' somethin' to cool ya down."

Maria shook her head and kept her grip on the table. "I'm feeling queasy."

Ott worried for a moment that she might have eaten down at Crowder's new barbecue place. "Maybe a little fresh air," Ott suggested, gesturing to the door.

"Just give me a minute, Sheriff." She took in a deep breath and raised her head to try for a smile of reassurance. As though she had no choice in the matter, her eyes were drawn to the place the deputy had been standing. He was gone. Maria closed her eyes and sighed, unsure if she was relieved or disappointed.

Ott, with one hand at the small of her back, looked around for the closest available chair. That was when he caught sight of his wife, Bernice, glowering at him from across the room. Ott's gut tightened, not unlike the cramps he had endured Friday from that near-lethal Brunswick stew.

It was mystifying to Ott—who was the county sheriff, for God's sake—how Bernice maintained this tyrannical hold over him, especially since Ott enjoyed a similar sovereignty over the county and all the people in it. All but Bernice, that is.

Ott knew that the baleful look in Bernice's eye was all about his hand on the new A.D.A.'s back. Bernice was always talking about the ruinous end to her soap opera characters as soon as they gave in to adultery. Both she and Ott knew perfectly well that no woman in her right mind was going to help him be unfaithful to his marriage vows—especially one as stunning as Maria Gunlock—but Bernice understood the prudence of a wife lobbing a shot over the husband's bow in situations like this.

"I'm all right, Sheriff," Maria said, getting her color back. "Please, go enjoy yourself."

"Well, how 'bout that dance then?" Ott said. "Might do you some good."

"Oh, no," Maria replied quickly. "I'm really not up to this kind of dancing. I've never even heard of a contra-dance before tonight." She looked up at the stage and squinted at Wins Mooney. "I can't understand most of what that gentleman is saying. Is he really telling the dancers how to move?"

"Sure as Sunday breakfast," Ott assured her. "There's a pattern to it. That's what he's teachin' right now b'fore the music starts and kicks the dance off official. Once't it's started and he's took 'em through it a time or two, he'll juss lay back and watch it all happ'n. Kindly like typin' up the deputy shifts and then watchin' the copy machine churn 'em out."

"You mean the dancers memorize the pattern?" Maria eyed the locals with awe.

"Oh, yeah," Ott purred. "Ever' dance is diff'rent, but once't you've got through it a coupla three or four times, it ain't too hard to keep it goin'."

Maria started to say something, but the band broke into a lively Celtic piece. One of the violinists had set down her instrument and was now playing a bouncy tune on a small silver flute. As Wins Mooney called the dance, he moved his feet to the music. He was like a puppet, his head stationary in space as his once-limber legs made stiff, economical movements that set his shoes to tapping a complicated rhythm.

"Now allemande left your partner . . . and swing your corner till it's time to go. Now it's allemande right and you leave that one … and you come back home for a do-si-do."

Maria shook her head again and leaned toward Ott. " 'Alley-man right'? 'Dozy-doe'? See, I don't even know what that means. I get lost out there." She drank from her Dixie cup and watched the magic of, what seemed to her, a small-town cult's privileged decoding of an arcane language.

"Now grand right and left and leave 'em all alone . . . till you find your partner and you take 'er back home. Now swing her there both high and low . . . then meet your corner for a do-si-do."

"What *is* that?" Maria said. "That 'dozy doe'? It sounds like a sleepy deer."

Ott set down his punch and, in a courtly manner, took her cup from her hand and set it down next to his. Attempting a balletic pirouette, he pivoted to stand in front of her and lightly placed both hands on the outsides of her shoulders. As he moved past her on the left, he pulled her forward to pass him on his right.

"It's a do-si-do. We juss change places. I go where you were. You go where I was. You can spin 'round while you do it, if you want. Then we come back full circle to where we started." When he was across from her again where they had begun, he smiled his look-how-good-a-dance-teacher-I-am smile. "There you go. Come on. Let's go out there and give it a whirl."

Maria eyed the choreographed movement of the people out on the floor. On the whole, the room of dancers rendered a kind of flowing symmetry—not unlike a child's kaleidoscope held to the eye, flakes of mosaics falling into perfect mirror imagery.

"No, thank you," she said. "I think I'll just watch."

From across the dance floor, the dark energy gathering in Bernice's glare had propelled her into a stoic march. Ott had never seen her this livid outside the privacy of their home. He watched her ominous approach and tried to conjure up his you're-gettin'-all-upset-'bout-nothin' smile, but he was pretty sure he wasn't pulling it off.

"Well, wouldn' you know it?" Ott said, squinting at the blank screen on his pager. "Little trouble out on highway sixty." He shook his head and raised the pager to the approaching juggernaut of Bernice—his standard gesture for an emergency calling him away. "Sher'ff's job is never done, is it?" he said to no one in particular and made for the door at a brisk clip gauged to outdistance Bernice. Halfway to the door, he noticed his damned calf muscle was tightening up.

Chapter Three

Crow Mountain
North Lumpkin County
Late morning, Tuesday

Thirty seconds shy of the three-minute mark, Joey Gallatin paid out a flurry of punches to the big canvas bag—*thwump-ump-ump-ump-ump-ump-ump!* As fast as a drummer's paradiddle. Each blow was jarring and accompanied by a whoosh of exhaled air, so that the two sounds taken together were like a pressurized nail gun with its trigger jammed.

This heavy bag he pummeled wasn't the standard gear of the Atlanta gyms he had grown up with. It was a poor man's bag: a green, army surplus duffel filled with sawdust he'd gotten free from the lumber mill down the road. He roped the bag up over a limb of the oak behind the cabin for each workout and then took it down in case of rain. After only two weeks, with the Southern humidity what it was, the bag was packed as hard as wet sand. But it would do. The harder they are, the bigger they fall. That was Joey's variation on the old saying.

He walked three circles around the oak, shaking out his arms, stretching his neck to one side and then to the other, like a man taking two views of the world. He sat down with his bare back against the tree trunk and listened to the stretch of the rope as the heavy bag continued to swing. Inhaling deeply, Joey took in a river of mountain air, the muscles in his chest expanding. When he exhaled, his breathing quieted, working its way back down to its norm of an even ten inhalations per minute.

He pulled out of one glove and flattened his fingertips to his jugular, not to count, but to feel the surge of the fight announce itself in his quickened pulse. Slipping a spear of asparagus from the open can he'd wedged between two roots, he chewed with a stoic expression. He hated asparagus, but his study of the great fighters of boxing had revealed the secrets of their diets, and asparagus was the common link to all of them. Knowing he could not stomach another, he slid the glove back on and stood to pound the bag some more.

Joey was hell-bent on exorcizing the job interview he had botched this morning. Sweat streaked down his lean torso, darkening the waistband of his nylon shorts from blue to black. The salty rivulets running down his arms soaked into the cracks at the wrists of the leather gloves where he pulled them on with his teeth. The mixed aroma of sweat and leather carried the smell of the dozen gyms in which he had trained since he had been fourteen years old. His hands were moist and hot inside the padded gloves, but the mountaintop air was like springwater dousing his skin.

From the knoll behind the cabin, he had a perfect view of Blood Mountain, the tallest peak visible on the ridgeline. It was pumped up like a flexed biceps above the less muscular mountains sloping off to form this section of the Appalachian spine.

Though fresh from the city, Joey was comfortable inside the rugged swell of these hills. They were kindred spirits—these mountains and he. Both possessed a strength and permanence that had been pulled from their molten cores in what seemed an eon ago. Plus, they shared a common quietness. This mountain vista contained a silence as effortless as his own.

At that moment, the chirr of an insect spiraled out of the valley like a fishing line being reeled in. He stood and walked to the edge of the rock where his mountain dropped away at a dramatic angle. The buzzing call of the insect ended, and he heard the white incision of cascading water far below—less an insinuation of sound than a standard by which to measure the greater silence wrapped around it.

The deep, funnel-shaped valley lay in a blue-haze. It was summer-still and full of an ancient order that was foreign to him and his city ways. He didn't know the mewl of a squirrel from the peep of a tree frog, but he was starting to get interested in the differences.

The race of water far below now sounded to him like a distant tearing of paper. It seemed to be an endless sheet that spooled out from the center of the world. As always, this sound made him think of Angie LaFarge. Her angelic face floated before him now—a face he would have died for from the fourth grade through high school. She would, of course, be his age now—twenty-six—but the image in his mind was always of her at seventeen.

That was the last time he'd seen her . . . at their high school graduation. He had wished her good luck at Auburn, and she had shaken hands with him. Joey had been temporarily paralyzed by her silky touch, trying to construe the handshake as an omen, but as he stood there watching her work her way across the room to her boyfriend, he saw her shake hands with two other boys who stopped her to say goodbye.

He liked thinking of Angie, except that it always led to thinking of his father, and Joey wanted none of that. He jerked the glove off again, marched back to the oak, downed another asparagus, and pushed his hand back into the glove. Then he paced around the tree and popped the gloves together twice, knuckles to knuckles. Out of habit he made a little bouncing head-dodge as the gloves snugged against his fists. Moving back to the heavy bag, he was already shuffling and dancing. A little Ali, a little Evander, but mostly Joey.

Now the bag was his father. The scowling face materialized on the worn, green canvas like a wraith. Joey delivered a sudden burst of brutal punches, putting all his weight into the staggering blows, his entire body tensed with a demonic fury as though he were trying to rupture the duffel and spill the sawdust out onto the yard. After three minutes he was exhausted, and the haunting face that had always unfairly judged him sneered back at his limitations.

A truck clawed its way up the road, whining and wavering in its low gear. Joey lowered his gloves. He knew the truck by sound. It was the old Pinto with its trunk area burned out by a blow torch to accommodate the back half of a metal johnboat bolted in place to serve as the bed of a pickup. That would be Hoke.

Hoke Limberlost was Joey's new landlord and nearest neighbor a half mile down the mountain. Joey was three days late on the rent, but he suspected Hoke had not made the haul up the mountain for that. Hoke was an old-timer going on seventy-five. Maybe eighty-five. It was hard to tell. He lived inside the perplexing body of a long-distance runner half that age, and his face knew only one expression: assiduity. It was as though Hoke were perpetually working his way through a stubborn problem that he could never quite solve. He was a man in motion, but Joey had never seen him do anything faster than crack an egg on the edge of a frying pan.

In front of the cabin the engine shut down, and the Pinto's door squeaked open then slammed shut with a rattle. The homemade tailgate dropped with a bang and a long scraping sound followed.

Somehow Hoke always knew where to come—to the front door or out back. When he rounded the corner of the cabin, he was lugging a big metal sign under one arm, the galvanized post dragging behind him, bumping across roots and rocks. His face was smudged as if he had just crawled out of a narrow chimney caked with purple soot. His shirt was open in front, revealing a wiry torso. With his long gray hair trailing down below his shoulders, Hoke and his unexpected appearance with the sign suggested an Appalachian version of Jesus stopping by for directions to Calvary.

"Well, they gone too damn far now. Juss take a look at this here, would you?" Hoke propped the sign against the oak and spun it around for Joey to see. *Byron T. Metcalfe Intersection,* the sign read. White letters against a green background. Hoke widened his eyes at Joey as though waiting for an editorial remark, but Joey said nothing.

"First, they put a name to the damn bridge over the Chestatee. *Dill W. Raynor, Jr. Bridge*. Like we didn't know it was a bridge or somethin'. And like Dill might'a built the damn thing." He pointed south. "Then there's that *Calvin "Bud" T. Grizzle Parkway*, and you'ens knows they ain't a damn park on that whole stretch o' road, 'less they's countin' that ol' ballfield got swallered up in kudzu." Hoke shook his head. "God knows what they'll name next? Maybe a bend in the road. Or a bump. *Hoke B. Limberlost Bump*. How's that sound?"

There was always an earthy scent to Hoke, a permanent fixture in his presence. Joey had noticed it each time they had met. If he had to put a name to it, Joey would call it "decomposition."

"What are you gonna do with it?" Joey said, nodding to the sign.

"Hell, I don' know." Hoke studied the sign and squinted at the question. "This damn post would make a helluva tomato stake in you'ens' garden." He looked at Joey, and his bushy gray eyebrows floated high above his expectant eyes. "You'ens gonna have a garden?"

"Hadn't planned on it," Joey said.

"Well," Hoke sighed, appraising the sign anew. "Might be I could hammer it out into a duck house. Maybe put it out'n the swamp. Them wood ducks might can put up with staring at Byron's name. I know I cain't."

"How did you get it outta the ground? Don't they pour concrete footings for these signs?"

Hoke almost smiled, but he was not through being indignant at the county bureaucracy. "Took my 'cetylene torch out there t'other night and burnt it off at ground level." He blew a fluttering blast of air from his lips, horse-like. "Only one to miss it'll be ol' Byron."

"Who *is* Byron T. Metcalfe?" Joey asked.

Hoke blew another equine breath from his cheeks and pulled a blue bandana from his hip pocket. Pushing his hair back behind his ears, he twirled the bandana into the shape of a snake and tied it across his lined forehead.

"Byron's the mayor. Was a county commish'ner. The whole lot o' em's wantin' their names on somethin' nowadays."

Joey frowned at the sign. "How many of these do you have?"

"This'n here's the first. Once things cool down a spell, I'll go out'n git more."

"What happens if you get caught?"

Hoke's face went sly with a devilish smile. "That ain't likely. I reckon they'll be arrestin' some wood ducks b'fore they can trace it to me." His smile shifted to a cocky tilde. "I don't leave no sign when I'm in my warrior mood."

Joey was pretty sure that Hoke was not aware of his own pun, so he didn't smile. He stared at the trench Hoke had furrowed across the dirt with the sign's post and decided to say nothing about taking or leaving signs.

Hoke wore tanned, ankle-high moccasins seamed up the middle. His jeans looked as soft as old tissue paper and worn to a faded indigo-blue that was almost white. His unbuttoned shirt was a checkerboard of dark blue and black squares. Joey could see now that the smudges on the old man's face were more illustrative than random.

"What's that on your face, Mr. Limberlost?"

"Totems," Hoke said right away, showing no surprise at the question. "I painted up with pokeberry for the occasion. Mostly wore off now." He craned his neck forward, turned his face to one side, and pointed to his left cheekbone. "That'n there's a lightnin' bolt. That's for bein' quick. And maybe a little thank-you-ma'am to that 'cetylene torch o' mine." He turreted his head the other way. "This'n's a hawk." His eyes narrowed and turned earnest with sage advice. "Strike quiet from an unexpected angle. Don' never let 'em know what hit 'em."

"What about that one on your chest?"

Hoke looked down at himself. Below the loop of his odd necklace was another smear of purple. He hitched his head to one side and began buttoning up his shirt.

" 'Possum," he said in a flat tone.

Joey decided not to ask . . . about the opossum or the strange necklace that looked like part of a dead animal that might have been roadkill. He suspected the necklace had something to do with Hoke's trademark smell-of-death ambience. Joey stared at the smears of purple on Hoke's cheeks and imagined the old man's face lit up at night by the flame of a welder's torch. The lightning bolt he might have guessed after a few tries, but the hawk looked more like a muscular pony wearing a dress. Art was not Hoke's long suit, as anyone who drove past his mailbox could see. His name was hand-lettered in light green paint on the dark green box he had mounted on a giant wood carving of a frog, which was painted with both shades of green. The name on the box was legible only if you knew in advance what was written on it.

Looking off toward Blood Mountain, Hoke propped his fists on his hips and took in a lot of air. "That there's the grandest-ever view a man could ask for." He sauntered toward the back of the clearing. "You can hear old Frogtown Creek right good from up here." He turned to edify Joey. "That was the name of the old Cher'kee town, you know. *Walasi-yi.* That's Cher'kee for 'Frogtown.' "

It was word for word the same little speech Hoke had delivered when he first showed the cabin to Joey. Hoke liked knowing the old names of things and places—especially if bestowed by the Cherokee.

"Cher'kee knew how to name a place, by God!" Hoke declared and shot a renewed look of disdain at the sign leaning against the tree. "And when not to." He turned to Joey. "I'm four-sevenths Cher'kee, you know."

"Yes'r, you told me," Joey said, though—mathematically—he wasn't sure you could be four-sevenths anything. He untied the laces of his gloves with his teeth, pulled off each glove under the opposite armpit, and joined the old man at the overlook. It took a measure of resolve just to stand next to him. On a hot day, Hoke's smell often escalated to "hazardous." Joey wondered if this rank aura was somehow tied into the undefined opossum theme of the war-tattoo.

"How'd you'ens come out on the in'erview?"

Joey eyed Hoke obliquely. "How'd you know I had a job interview? You have ESP?"

Hoke made a face and shook his head. "Naw, I ain't even got a television set, son. Don't believe in 'em. Verdie down at *The Sizzling Skillet*. She told me."

"I ate breakfast down there," Joey said frowning, "but I don't remember mentioning anything about an interview."

Hoke grinned. "Verdie reads all them Sure-lock Homes stories. Fancies herself part-detective. You'ens was wearin' a tie. Verdie said last time she saw a tie on you'ens was the day of a interview over to Gainesv'lle."

Small town gossip was something new to Joey. It seemed to him that the mountain people he had met were individualistic and proud and self-sufficient by varying degrees. He wondered how such folks got around to discussing other people's business so freely. Joey stared at Blood Mountain. Maybe mountain people had a need to make their own mountains out of molehills just to feel that they counted for something amid such grand scenery.

"I didn't get the job," Joey said and watched for the old man's reaction, but Hoke's face showed nothing at all. "I know I'm a couple of days late on the rent money, Mr. Limberlost."

"Aw, hell," Hoke laughed and waved at the air. "I ain't worried 'bout that." Then he turned quickly and fixed Joey with a stare. "Hell, you'ens oughta go to work for *me*."

"Doing what?"

Hoke lifted a grizzled eyebrow. "Lot o' them signs still out there."

Joey looked deeply into his landlord's sharp eyes. "Well, that might not be the best idea. If *you* go to jail, it'd be better with me out here paying rent instead of sharing a cell with you. *When* I start paying the rent, that is."

Hoke pulled at the rough whiskers curling off his chin. "Well, that's true enough." He gave Joey an approving nod. "What kind a work're you'ens lookin' to git?"

As he always did, Joey held back the fundamental word that glowed inside his soul like a sacred dream. Instead, he substituted the more proper label that carried a more refined connotation.

"Security," his mouth said, while his heart whispered, *Bouncer.*

Hoke nodded and narrowed his eyes to the east, as though he had heard a distant job offer come wafting on the breeze from that direction. "What 'bout the chicken plant over to Murrayv'lle? They might be hirin' for the nightshift."

Joey kept his eyes on the mountain and tried not to imagine himself guarding a building full of clucking chickens. "Not that kind of security, Mr. Limberlost."

"Well, what kind then?"

Joey sat down on the rock. "Crowd control," he said, still hedging on the description of his life mission.

"Hell, them chickens are crowded. I reckon they could use some crowd controllin'." Hoke pursed his lips and looked south toward Dahlonega. "Or what 'bout the Walmart? Talk about 'crowd control'! You ever see what happens down there when they's givin' 'way free eatin' samples?"

Joey took in a deep breath, exhaled quietly, and softened his voice as though he were whispering inside a confessional. "I'm a bouncer."

Hoke turned all the way around to appraise the boy's stature. "Like in a bar?"

"Exactly like that," Joey said.

"How much do you'ens weigh, son?"

"Enough," Joey replied.

The old man squinted one eye and tilted his head. "Well, yo're shore built 'bout like a scarred-up axe blade, but you'ens cain't weigh much more'n me."

Joey stared at the great bulk of Blood Mountain. "I *think* heavy."

Hoke's laugh cracked in his throat. "Hell, I hear that, son. That's the warrior talkin' in you'ens." His eyes turned flinty and locked on the ludicrous presence of the sign under the oak. "Think I'll go on to home and hammer out that Byron T. Metcalfe duck house." He looked up at the sky. "Gonna rain early tomorr'. 'Round nine-forty. Then again tomorr' night juss after dark, but that'n'll last less than a minute. "I'll see cain't I give them ducks a place to keep they's feathers dry."

Hoke started for the sign but stopped partway to the tree. "Them's you'ens'?"

Joey turned to see the old man staring down at the open can of asparagus. He decided not to explain the part asparagus played in his training.

"Yes, sir. I eat them pretty regular."

"Used to grow some o' them in my garden," Hoke reminisced. "They's right good out the ground, but I cain't tolerate them canned ones." He laughed. "They turn my damn piss the color of a school bus, and it smells like a burnt boot."

"Well, I like 'em," Joey lied.

Hoke shrugged and heaved the sign to his shoulder. "Take 'er easy, son," he said. "I'll let you'ens git back to trainin'."

Joey remained sitting on the ledge and checked the sky. It was solid blue but for a broken row of wispy white commas to the northwest. He wondered if that was a Cherokee sign for rain. And if it was, what were the percentages for a four-sevenths Indian being right about it raining at nine-forty?

He heard the truck start up and begin bumping back down the road. The bang of the metal sign in the bed of the Pinto finally faded at the bottom of the mountain, and Joey welcomed the return of the quiet. The smell of leaf mold and the late blossoms of rhododendron gathered around him like an affirmation of his aloneness. He felt powerful and capable and confident. Afraid of no one. Needing to prove that to no one.

A hawk spiraled upward on a thermal rising out of the valley, but the bird was still below him, and this perspective served only to boost that upper hand he now held on the world. All he needed was that bouncer job, and he would be complete.

Well . . . except for Angie LaFarge.

From far down in the valley he heard the sharp banging of a hammer. Ten aggressive blows. Then ten more. It rang out like a crazed bull trying to butt open a metal gate. But Joey knew what it meant: Byron T. Metcalfe's legacy was going to the ducks.

Chapter Four

North Chattahoochee Elementary School
Atlanta
September, 1983

Since the fourth grade, Joey Gallatin had loved Angie LaFarge the way Percival felt about the Grail. Now, in his last year of grammar school, Joey had seen that dedication sink its roots into the very center of him. From a safe distance he observed her life, wondering when and if he might be worthy of approaching her with his feelings. Her passion, he knew, was horses. She rode three times a week and worked weekends at a stable for no pay. Joey considered taking riding lessons, but he knew his father would never spring for the fee.

Denny Hayhurst was everything that Joey was not—loud, arrogant, bullying, testing everything as though hell-bent on locating its jugular. He was also not a good student. It was his third year haunting Mrs. Alberton's sixth grade classroom.

Denny told everyone in school that he had kissed Angie and in return for the favor she had pushed her hand down into the front of his jeans and created more special effects than the last *Star Wars* movie. No one who knew either Denny or Angie believed it. Still, there it was. Said enough times, words had a way of checking into a room in the brain and loitering there, rent paid or not. It was like reading a lie in the newspaper—the permanence of ink, the formality of the typeset, and all that.

Angie bided her time and chose her moment for balancing the scales of justice. On a Monday morning she surprised everyone in the class by reading not her report on female rodeo stars as was her chosen assignment . . . but instead a treatise on "the grandiose fabrications of the loud and arrogant pre-adolescent male who struggled with shame and denial in the self-discovery of his own suppressed sexual attraction to livestock." She never mentioned Denny by name. She didn't have to. His bumptious personality leaped off the paper. When she finished reading, the only sound in the room was the tick of expanding metal in the heat vent . . . that and Denny's accelerated breathing.

Several seconds of silence ticked by before anyone dared to look at Denny. He was glaring at a paper clip that he had bent around his little finger into the shape of a crooked ring. He had clamped it down so tight that his fingertip looked like a purple crayon.

Later, in the hallway outside the cafeteria, Denny snatched the paper from Angie and tore it three times and let the pieces flutter to the floor. The ring of mute spectators around them formed a circle so perfectly round and frozen that the event took on the strange semblance of a religious rite. From that day on, the sound of tearing paper would forever transport Joey back to that suspended moment when his adrenaline level spiked enough to make his skin tingle.

Angie's smile hovered somewhere between beatification and vindication and with that smile drew the livid Denny right up to the edge of violence. He hocked up phlegm from deep in his chest, sucked in his cheeks, and stepped toward her. Before he could anoint Angie with the blasphemous load, Joey's usually quiet voice filled the hall like thunder.

"Stay thy insult, false knight!"

Joey hadn't planned this choice of words. He had been reading the Arthurian legend, and the phrase just stuck with him. No one in earshot knew what the words meant, but there was a stunned silence for about three beats. Then, when Denny inhaled deeply through his nose, filling his lungs again to carry out the foul deed toward Angie, Joey sprang forward and took the spat slime in his palm and smeared it across Denny's face. He had to reach up to do it because Denny was a head taller than everyone else in their class.

The circle of onlookers widened like a school of small fish surprised by a pebble tossed into their midst. The stunned Denny wiped the back of his hand across his glistening mouth. For a moment, a long string of mucous swung from his chin like a living thing before attaching leech-like to his neck. His arms were thin but ominous with a tattoo of a snake with bared fangs on one and a blood-dripping dagger on the other. Denny faced Joey and allowed a garish smile to stretch across his mucous-wet face as a sign of what was to come.

"You're dead, Gallatin!" Denny growled in a hard monotone.

If Mrs. Alberton had not stepped from the cafeteria at that moment, the fight would have broken out right there in the hall. Under the teacher's admonishment, Denny was dispatched to the bathroom to clean up, and the crowd dispersed.

After school Denny was waiting, leaning against the chain-link fence by the bus pickup area. He wasn't alone. With the help of two other boys, he pulled Joey to the far end of the ballfield behind the dugout, and there before a crowd of his cohorts, Denny beat Joey with his bony fists until Joey could not tell up from down and so had no way to orient himself for standing. It was a pivotal moment for Joey Gallatin.

When Joey arrived at the dingy, little, rented shack that his father called their "home," his clothes were torn, and his lower lip had burst open like an over-ripe plum. Even after an attempt at cleaning himself at the water fountain near the dugout, Joey's face was still streaked with blood. Wiping his face with his hand, he lingered outside the door and listened.

The dark interior was quiet, but Joey knew his father was inside. The Harley stood in the lawn, the big black machine leaning heavily on its kickstand. The front wheel nodded sleepily to one side, and the gleaming black leather seat soaked up the heat of the sun and gave it back like a hotplate. Joey could only hope his father was asleep, as he usually was whenever he was laid off from construction work.

No such luck. Opening the door, Joey stepped inside and looked through the doorway to the kitchen, where his father peeled an apple with his pocketknife over the sink. The coil of red rind hung down like a flaccid spring. The man kept up the knife work as he frowned at the boy and then laughed with a bounce in his chest.

"What the hell happened to you? You look like you been run over by a bus."

Joey looked down at the floor and awaited further insults.

"Shit," the man hissed and shook his head. Carving the apple blindly now, he dropped slabs of red peeling into the basin, each one thumping like a sound of disapproval. "And them's your good trousers, ain't they." He checked the clock built into the small stove. "And you're a goddamned hour and a half late. You better have something good to tell that Polack Jew if you wanna keep that job."

When the father turned to the sink again, Joey spoke to his back, which was their usual arrangement for conversation. "I missed the bus. I had to walk home."

The man turned to face him and flicked the knife shut. "What . . . you can't step up onto a goddamned bus now?" When Joey reached down and closed the tear in his pants at his knee, the father raised his voice. "Answer my question, you little smart-mouth jackass!" The man took a quick step forward, and that and the tone in his voice made Joey look up.

"I got in a fight," Joey admitted.

"No shit." Earl Gallatin took a big bite out of the apple and chewed as he looked the boy over from the cut above his eye to the grass stains and tear in the boy's pants. A tiny light of amusement turned in Earl's eyes. "Well, did you take part in this fighting or just stand there and let somebody whip your skinny ass?"

When Joey looked down at the floor again, the man swatted the side of his head.

"I'm talking to you, boy. You'll goddamn look at me when I talk to you."

Joey looked at him.

"Nobody ever kicked Earl Gallatin's ass, I can tell you that!" the father crowed. "And any asshole that tried had plenty to show for it."

When Earl took another predatory chomp out of the apple, Joey stared at the floor once again—slate blue linoleum squares mixed in with the tan as though they were slate steppingstones across a bed of quicksand. All he wanted was to cross the kitchen and go into the bathroom where he could clean up.

"You didn't do shit, did you?" Earl taunted.

"I did the best I could. There were three of them. And they were older than me."

Earl stopped chewing. "Who?" he barked. His face was changed now, involved in the story.

"Just some boys at school. Two of them are in the high school."

The man chewed his mouthful of apple and swallowed, staring at Joey all the while. Without telegraphing any warning, he slapped Joey across the face so hard that the boy stumbled back a step. Joey tried not to show anything, but as he looked up at his father, against his will, tears welled in his eyes.

"I bet you cried just like that when they lit into you, didn't you?"

Joey's face hardened. "I didn't cry."

"What are their names?"

When Joey did not answer, Earl raised his hand again. "Ever' goddamn time I have to ask, I'm gonna slap those sissy tears off your face, boy!"

"I don't know the two in high school."

"Well, who *do* you know?"

Joey waited, determined to take the blow without flinching, but instinctively his arm came up to take the brunt of it. His lip tore again, and blood dribbled onto the floor. Cupping a hand under his mouth, he watched his father toss the unfinished apple into the brown paper bag full of crushed beer cans. With his hands freed up, Earl took a more aggressive stance and glared at the boy.

"It was Denny Hayhurst," Joey said. "It was about—"

"I don't give a good goddamn what it was about. Where did this fight take place?"

"At the ballfield."

"He still there?"

When Joey shrugged, Earl thumped the boy hard on the top of his skull with his knuckles.

"Well, where the hell is he?"

"He mostly hangs out with boys from the high school. I don't know where he lives."

Earl marched down the hallway and into the back room. When he returned, his heavy alligator-skin boots set up vibrations down the length of the small house. He came into the kitchen punching his arms through the sleeves of his black leather jacket.

"Go and fetch some o' your money for gas then git your ass out on that motorcycle."

"What about my afternoon job?" Joey asked.

Earl pushed the boy down the hall. "You're takin' a sick day."

They found Denny with four other boys at the far end of the bleachers of the high school football field. The quintet sat halfway up the tiers of sun-grayed plank seats. Denny was leaning back, smoking, his elbows propped on the seat behind him. When the big Harley shut off, all five boys watched the father and son with interest as the two riders took off their helmets. At that point, one of the boys sat erect, his face seeming to pale and wrinkle with lines of uncertainty.

The man led the way, coming at them from the outside lane of the track. Joey followed in the wake of his father's purposeful march, if only not to be dragged across the track. Earl stepped up on the first seat and walked the length of it to the end where the boys were clustered a dozen tiers above him. They watched him climb the seats as if he were the Grim Reaper sent to inform them of the coming of the Apocalypse. Reluctantly, Joey followed his father as if attached by a tether.

When Earl stopped, spread his boots, splayed his hands on either side of his belt beneath the jacket, and gazed down at the wary teenagers, the quintet of toughs appeared to have misplaced their bravado and stopped breathing. The only sound to be heard was a cicada chirring high up in a pine tree.

"Which one o' you assholes is a Hayhurst?" Earl said loud and clear.

After a long five seconds, Denny squirmed on the hard seat and lowered the cigarette by his leg. The other boys seemed to shrink in size. Earl pulled Joey from behind him and pointed at Denny with a thick-knuckled finger that held as level and steady as a sniper's rifle.

"That him?"

Joey nodded.

Earl put on a false smile, returned his gaze to Denny, and began nodding as if affirming some inner thought. When Earl beckoned Denny with a curl of his forefinger, the cowed boy slowly stood, dropped the cigarette, and mashed it out with his boot. He looked back at his friends, but their eyes were fixed on the man in the black leather jacket.

Following Earl, Denny clopped down the stadium seats, trying to keep any fear off his face but failing. When they bottomed out at the track, Earl studied Denny from long greasy hair to scuffed boots. Earl frowned and turned back to Joey with a stare that seethed with disgust.

"He ain't got a goddamn mark on him," Earl said and exhaled a quick breath, meant to be either a censure or a laugh of wonderment. He reached out for a fistful of shirt at the back of Denny's neck. "We're gonna sure as hell change that right now." Then he jerked the boy across the track. "Come on!" Earl barked over his shoulder to Joey.

"Hey!" Denny yelped. "Lemme go!" He looked back at the boys still in the bleachers. They were standing now, considering their options for escape.

With a hand clamped down on the nape of each boy's neck—Denny on the right, Joey on the left—Earl marched them roughly out onto the empty football field. When they had gained the center of the fifty-yard line he turned them each toward the other.

"It's just the two o' you now." Earl shook Joey so hard that the boy's neck made a sound like a knuckle popping. "Now you let him know he's been in a goddamn fight! You let him know he's messed with Earl Gallatin's boy!"

Earl walked back to the bleachers and sat down on the second row. The boys behind him remained standing, watching the two out on the field. Like two lost commuters watching their bus pull away without them, Denny and Joey watched Earl lean back against the seat behind him and stretch his legs to the lower seat, where his boots crossed at the ankles. Had he worn different attire, a fresh shave, and a recent haircut, Earl could have passed for an aristocrat about to watch a private sporting event.

Feeling the safety of distance from this crazed man in leather, Denny scowled at the skinny boy standing before him. "You pussy! I can sue your old man for putting his hands on me like that." He rubbed the back of his neck and looked toward Earl again. "But hell . . . I touch you and he's gonna kick the shit outta me."

Joey weighed his options for about two seconds, and then he threw a roundhouse punch that caught Denny squarely on the nose. Blood poured out of the smashed nostrils and dappled the front of Denny's shirt. For the next two minutes, Denny kept Joey pinned to the earth while he bloodied his face all over again. But for the bulge of his tongue sliding across his teeth, Earl never moved.

When finally, Denny tired of beating on the boy and stood up, he saw the father walking back out onto the field toward him. The man's stiff walk seemed full of anger, but he strode slowly, scuffing his boots in the grass. The boys in the stands were gone. Denny spat on Joey, turned, and ran across the far side of the track, where he disappeared around the corner of the gym.

Earl stood over Joey, slid his hands into his pants pockets, and looked down at his son. Then he shifted his gaze to the clouds piling up in the west. He shook his head, leaned, and spat off to one side.

"Well, you got *one* in, anyway." When Joey touched his fingertips gingerly to his face to appraise the damage, Earl said, "I'll be waiting on you at the bike. You need to get over to your job with the Polack Jew. So much for your sick day."

Chapter Five

The Sizzling Skillet
Dahlonega, Georgia
Wednesday noon

Verdie Rider stood at the back corner table doing her thing with the boys from the Amicalola Power Company. As usual, these boys were launching a salvo of duds against her killer one-liners as she pretended to scrawl their orders on her green pad. She smacked gum in a tempo steady enough to set the clocks of Greenwich, and when she suddenly stopped chewing and flipped the pad shut, every workman was smiling, eyes bright with anticipation, waiting for one of her infamous parting lines.

"*That*, Marvin, is precisely why the only orders I will ever take from you are right here at the restaurant." She delivered this in her usual British accent, the one that had prodded the Amicalola boys into calling Verdie "Your Majesty." No one questioned her dialect. It was all they had known from her since the fifth grade. Before that tender age, she had talked like everybody else in the county, but no one could actually remember it now.

Verdie raised the pad and tapped it with her pencil until the boys caught on to the punch line and burst out laughing. She never disappointed them. They were still laughing, leaning forward to see Marvin's face, when she sashayed off to the kitchen.

When she came back through the swinging doors carrying a tray loaded down with iced teas in tall blue plastic glasses, the sheriff had taken his customary table at the front window. Fielding a few more potshots from the Amicalola boys, Verdie off-loaded the teas and crossed the room, where she clacked down the tray on the empty table next to the sheriff's. After dipping into the front of her apron for her order pad, she smacked her gum. Somehow, she was able to give that gum-smacking a hint of English accent. Ott ignored her.

"I say, Ott, are you hungry again, or are you working up the nerve to ask me to take over the sheriff's office?"

Ott, looking very un-sheriff-like in his dark blue suit, did not give her the satisfaction of acknowledging her wisecrack about his work . . . or lack of it. He managed a weak smile for the sake of his companion across from him. As usual, it was L.T. Voss, the real estate independent, who had purchased most of his holdings on the courthouse steps, where properties with overdue taxes sold for a song.

Voss had bought a farm out from under Verdie's Uncle Tate back in the seventies when a tractor accident had sprung a leak in the family's life savings. Voss smiled up at Verdie as if that water had tumbled over the dam without a single bubble of froth. Still, he knew better than to push it. Opening up a conversation with Verdie was like watching the bomb bay door open on the Enola Gay.

"Oh, I reckon we're holdin' our own, Verdie," Ott quipped in his nasal whine. "But I do thank you for the offer." Now he smiled so broadly, his eyes almost squeezed shut on his porcine face, as though there were not enough room there for his little black-eyed pea eyes and his look-how-gracious-I-can-be smile. "I'll sure keep you in mind next time I git stumped on a case, and we'll see what you can throw into the pot, being as how you read all them cheap detective books."

In fact, Verdie read no detective pulp. She enjoyed Faulkner, Kingsolver, and Cormac McCarthy. And she adored Annie Proulx. But Conan Doyle held a special place in her heart. By her estimation, Sherlock Holmes was the only detective worth his salt. She spurned all the hardboiled, smart aleck brutes that had flooded the mystery genre. It was Holmes's intelligence that had inspired her adopted accent all those years ago, and she fancied herself a formidable acolyte of his deductive reasoning.

Verdie kept her eyes on her pad, pretending to write down Ott's order even before he had declared it. It was Wednesday. She knew he would have the meatloaf.

"You ought to read a book sometime yourself, Ott," Verdie suggested. "You'd be surprised what you can glean from literature."

"That right?" he said, smiling his so-you-think-you-know-everything-even-though-you're-just-a-waitress smile. When she would not look at him, he flattened the menu against his chest and neck. "It's all 'bout observin', Verdie. Betcha a pocketful o' pennies 'gainst a piece a pecan pie you cain't tell me what color tie I got on."

Verdie's eidetic recall snapped on like a two-hundred-watt light bulb, and a mental picture of the tie came into crystal clear focus. Not only did she know the color of the neckpiece, she had also itemized a list of clues about Ott's morning: A brown feline hair curled on his lapel, and a tiny smudge of potting soil showed on his shirt collar. The chain of reasoning flashed in her mind like a priority telegram just arrived from Baker Street in London. Verdie pursed her lips and tilted her head to a pensive angle, exactly as she imagined Sherlock Holmes might do.

"Light blue background with black diamonds," she said, matter-of-factly. "I see Bernice tried to straighten it for you this morning on the front porch."

Ott's smile withered. He let the menu fall and lifted the tail of the blue-with-black-diamonds tie, scowling at it as though it had somehow betrayed him. His eyes, now cautious, angled up to Verdie.

"How the Sam Hill'd you come up with that one?"

Verdie, who never divulged the secrets of her detection and deduction, just smiled. The cat hair on his coat was easy: Bernice was seldom without that brown cat cradled up under her bosom. She even drove the family car with the cat tucked into her ribs, its head out the window. That the cat hair was on Ott could only mean a transfer by way of Bernice. Ott would not touch a cat if it had a burning hundred-dollar bill tied to its tail.

The smear of potting soil was more involved. Bernice had won the blue ribbon at the county fair for her purple orchids. Verdie had been there for the award presentation and stayed for the question-and-answer portion of the program, when the audience could probe the winners about their horticultural secrets. When asked about her techniques with orchids, Bernice revealed that she kept her flowers on the front porch in pots during the summer, and each morning she tested the moisture of the soil with her finger.

It wasn't difficult to piece the story together from there. Ott and Bernice had obviously stood close together on the porch. But why? There was a better chance of the cat making an omelet than Bernice giving Ott a goodbye kiss in the morning. There had to be some other reason for their proximity. The perfect alignment of Ott's tie was the clincher.

"Will you tell me somethin', Verdie?" He raised his fist and tried to straighten a chubby index finger to keep a running tally. "One: Ever'body knows you was born right here in Lum'kin Coun'y." He tried raising another finger but when it would not hold its position, he forced it open with his other hand. "Two: Your mama was raised over to Hightower Bridge and your daddy up on Hogback Mountain." He pushed up a third finger. "Three: You ain't hardly never been outta the state 'xcept maybe to go up and see your brothers in Chatt'nooga." Four fingers now, the array beginning to look like a pack of extra-plump Ball Park franks. "Four: Far's I know, no aliens have ab-ducted you and switched your brain with some far'ner's." Ott leaned his head over to one side to take a new slant on her. "So how is it that ever since grade school you got this fancy-pantsy, Queen-o'-England way o' talkin'?"

"I dare say we are who we choose to be, Ott," Verdie counseled in clipped British economy. She glanced at Voss and considered applying some of that philosophy to his wicked ways, but he was too engrossed in the menu to acknowledge an insult.

"I'm gonna have the meatloaf, Verdie," the sheriff said, getting down to business. "Iced tea. And bring out a basket o' corn muffins." He inspected the little condiment corral herded around the metal napkin dispenser. Tabasco, sugar, fake sugar, A-1, catsup, and salt and pepper. "You got any o' that sourwood honey left?"

"I'll see if I can locate some," Verdie said. She turned for L.T.'s order and waited with her pencil poised above the pad, as if she might write it down. Which she never did. L.T. was studying his choices as though he were deciphering the fine print on a quit-claim document.

The thing about Verdie's order pad is this: She never actually used it. She considered memorizing customer orders to be part of the training of her steel-trap mind. She was certain Sherlock Holmes would have understood the brilliance of it. She looked down at the pad and pretended to write just so that customers would stop asking, *Now, did you get all that?*

"Think I'll have the catfish plate, Verdie," Voss said pleasantly. "Extra tartar sauce."

"Hush puppies or French fries or the deed to some poor family's house or potato chips?" Verdie asked with a straight face.

Voss gave her a quick look. They went through this every time.

"You know I don't eat potato chips, Verdie. I want hush puppies, as you well know."

Verdie held her poker face as she pretended to write. "Of course, sir. And for your other side: cole slaw, carrot salad, cabbage, a mortgage-defaulted acre, or potato chips?"

Voss's head came around again, and his nostrils flared. The pupils of his eyes were like little BBs. Despite all the animosity in his upper face, his mouth worked up a smug smile. This odd combination of upper and lower face made him look as if he had grafted together two different Halloween masks.

"Let me remind you, Verdie," Voss lied, "when I was nine years old, I almost died from a throat laceration because of potato chips!" This piece of fictional drama always seemed to Voss a more reasonable explanation for his aversion to chips. It seemed to evoke more pity than making a case for his acute affliction of psycho-chip-a-phobia. "You might as well just bring me an order of razor blades then!" The sarcasm gave his voice the growl of a disgruntled hog.

"Yes, indeed," Verdie said and pretended to write it down. "Razor blades, it is. And which flavor blades, sir: barbecued, sour cream, vinegar, Cajun, or plain?"

Voss stared at her, but Verdie would not blink. "I'll have the slaw," he said in a flat tone.

"Yes, sir," she said. "Does that mean you won't be having the razor blades?"

Now Voss glared at her, prepared to stare her down if it took all afternoon, but Verdie concentrated on her order pad as she struck an imaginary line through the last imaginary item on the paper. "Cancel . . . razor . . . blades," she mumbled to herself.

"What is it with you and the dang tater chips?" Ott said, grinning at Voss. "You let her git your goat ever' time you order."

Voss pretended not to hear the criticism. Sniffing, he closed his menu and tried to look like the kind of man who was accustomed to getting what he wanted.

"Is the catfish fresh-caught, Verdie?"

Verdie pocketed the pad and picked up the tray behind her. She started up the rhythm on her chewing gum and gave Voss her dead-eyed stare for four snaps.

"As I understand it," she began, "a fish in the river is either fresh or dead. So, L.T., I will assume ours were caught fresh. They simply will not bite when they're dead."

When she walked away, the sound on the linoleum floor made Ott think of Clint Eastwood walking out of a saloon after killing two or three desperados. Ott always wondered how she managed that in her soft-soled waitress shoes.

In a few minutes Verdie dispensed the steaming plates at the Amicalola table, matching up the orders to the customers by a little association trick she had developed in lieu of writing down the customers' choices. For her, it was a Holmesian exercise... an original technique that involved a comparison of customers to animals.

Using this method, she connected the barrel-chested Marvin and his sunny blond hair to a Golden Retriever. Because he had ordered fried chicken, Verdie had painted a mental picture of that dog on point just outside the walls of a monastery as it focused on a chicken dressed in a friar's robe.

Loy Grizzle, with his flaccid jowls, was a bulldog. He'd asked for the pork chops sautéed in pineapple sauce and covered in almonds. For this she had conjured up the image of the University of Georgia mascot delivering a downward karate chop to a Hawaiian pig wearing coveralls.

Eugene Boggs, with his short legs and perky ears, was a Welch corgi, and so, to accommodate his tuna casserole, she had imagined Eugene barking and chasing after a calliope tuner as he rode a carousel. Verdie loved the encryption of it all.

She had not intended to limit her choices to canines, but her correlations always leaned that way whenever a group of men ate together. They were like a kennel. Everyone talked at once until the food was served, and then all words ceased as they leaned forward in unison and shoveled food.

She turned to take an order from an elderly couple next to the sheriff's table. They turned out to be out-of-towners passing through on their way to the mountain fair at Hiawassee.

Verdie's eleven years at *The Sizzling Skillet* had served her well in the art of multi-tasking with her ears. She could flawlessly memorize the most complex custom order from a customer before her while still not missing a word of a conversation at a table behind her. This was what she did now as the woman gave special instructions for her salad with no onions or tomatoes or bell peppers because the acids made her stomach flare up and produce sounds "like a rusted hinge on a gate." Verdie got all that—right down to the rusty gate—but most of her radar was focused on the words floating up from the sheriff's table behind her.

"Someb'dy took off with the new sign down at the intersection." It was Ott talking. He had that you-see-just-about-everything-when-you're-sheriff tone in his voice.

"Which one?" This was L.T. trying to sound interested—which was a lame act. Every now and again, L.T. needed the sheriff's backing on some disputed land claim or eviction notice until the courts could settle it. Verdie had never known Ott to pay for a lunch if L.T. was along.

"The intersection sign," Ott said. "One with Byron's name on it."

"Oh, for Pete's sake!" Voss said. "What would anybody want with that?"

"And I want very cold milk," the woman was saying, her instructions overlapping L.T.'s question. Verdie was getting it all, in front and in back. "If you could wait and bring that with my meal," the woman added. She smiled and nodded as though helping Verdie appreciate her medical problems. "Maybe you could go ahead and pour the milk and put it in the freezer until it's time to bring the meal. The doctor says very cold milk is soothing to my stomach."

Verdie nodded, wondering how that same stomach was going to handle the hot'n spicy chili the woman had ordered. She was a poodle with her sprayed-in-place topiary of curly hair perched on her head. Actually, an Arctic poodle. This was to allow for the "chilly" part of the equation.

"Maybe it ain't what they *wanted*," Ott said, appropriating Duffy Hawkin's sound logic as his own, "but what they *didn'* want."

"I don't follow you," L.T. said.

The woman's husband was wondering if he could have traded over to his salad the extra acidic items his wife had said to leave off hers. Except for the bell pepper, which he said left a bad taste in his mouth and made his scalp itch. He had blue eyes and short stiff gray hair. *Weimaraner*, Verdie thought. This one she pictured in Timothy Leary's den with no telephone. Lots of acid . . . no bell.

"Could be somebody didn' want that sign out there," Ott was saying. "Could be some jasper's got a beef 'gainst Byron." Verdie lifted an eyebrow. Ott sounded strangely coherent . . . as if he had stumbled right into some deductive reasoning.

"Hell," L.T. laughed, "maybe Byron's the one did it. He's prob'ly already got that sign mounted up on his wall like a trophy buck."

"Is the catfish fresh?" the Weimaraner man was asking.

Verdie smiled politely and offered a few geographic coordinates that pinpointed the catfish farm on the other side of Three Sisters Mountain. Even after that spiel, the man said he would have the macaroni. For this Verdie had only to alter her image slightly by having the Weimaraner dance the Macarena.

"It was Byron who wanted that sign out there in the first place," Ott was explaining. "He lobbied for it for a year. Ain't likely he's the one gone and stole the dang thing."

"Well," L.T. mused, "if somebody's gonna be stealing something, that's a helluva thing to be stealing. Must'a took a coupla hours to dig it up."

"Weren't dug up. It was burnt off."

"Burned off?"

"Weldin' torch." Ott was reciting Duffy's assessment word for word. Ott hadn't even been out to the scene of the crime, but Duffy's word was money in the bank.

Verdie nodded approvingly at the selection of orders, and, because the man and his wife were new to the restaurant and would not know to do it, she took their menus and jammed them vertically between the napkin dispenser and the catsup bottle where the couple had found them.

"Don't forget to put my milk in the freezer," the woman reminded.

Verdie smiled to put the poodle-woman at ease. "Indeed, I will, madam. First on my agenda when I repair to the kitchen." Stalling, she took her time closing her pad and pocketing it in her apron along with her pencil.

"I cain't see somebody wanting a sign with Byron's name on it," the sheriff said.

"Maybe it's a joke," L.T. said. "Maybe that sign's gonna show up in front of that bar out on highway nineteen where he loses his money in poker games."

"Or maybe somebody juss don't like the way all these signs are popping up all over the coun'y," Ott said, still quoting Duffy. "Waste o' money, if you ask me. Betcha a gold mine 'gainst a gopher's gall bladder it's gonna turn out to be some tree-huggin' Greenpeace wannabe with too much time on his hands."

Verdie walked back to the kitchen, announced her orders to the cook, poured the woman's milk, and set the glass on top of a box of frozen catfish in the frosty air of the freezer. She went back out to the cashier's counter and punched in numbers on the telephone. Lydelle, the cashier, was busy making change for customers and, by appearances, paid her no mind. But Verdie knew that Lydelle could do the auditory multi-task with the best of them, so Verdie turned away and cupped her hand around the phone's mouthpiece.

"Fanny? It's Verdie at the *Skillet*. Is the alternator under the bonnet of your car operating now? . . . I see. Well, is Theron's truck there? . . . Well, can you drive it? . . . Well, when he gets home can you ask him to motor up to Hoke Limberlost's place and tell him he needs to empty out the back of his truck? . . . Well, I know that, but it's all I can say right now . . . Well, that's what he needs to do . . . Well, I would, but Hoke doesn't have a phone . . . Fanny, it would be better if I didn't have to explain."

Moon of the White Tears

She hung up, returned to the kitchen, and watched the cook fill Ott's and L.T.'s plates. Before carrying them out, to balance out the colors a little bit, she placed a single potato chip on Voss's plate next to the catfish between the slaw and the hush puppies.

Chapter Six

Piedmont Road
Atlanta
Wednesday, late morning

Since he'd made the move to the mountains, Joey was hoping he would not have to commute back to the big city for a job. But here he was . . . sitting in his car on Piedmont Road . . . staring through his rain-dappled windshield at the unlighted marquis of *The Skin Tight Club*. He looked up at the drizzling, gray sky, thinking about his landlord's prediction of rain at nine-forty. Joey checked his watch. It read nine-forty-one.

In daylight, *The Skin Tight Club* looked like one more business that had folded to the fickle economy. But come nightfall every color of Lexus and Beamer would purr at the curb under the hot-pink neon marquis, where valets wrangled cars into the parking lot.

He had been in the club once during that two-month period when he had toured every up-scale bar on the north side of town. In each place, he had followed the same formula: assess the sophistication level of the customers, ferret out the hired muscle and observe from a distance, then get the name of the owner. He never made contact on these initial visits. He preferred to phone later, knowing that his slight stature might preclude a serious interview. He had called *Skin Tight* six times but had never gotten through to the manager.

The waitresses, he remembered, lived up to the club's name, their long legs striding dutifully across the black marble floor, high heels clicking, as they balanced drinks on trays, their tight butts winking beneath microskirts of reflective gold. Their jutting breasts—a tacit requirement for employment—cantilevered to provide a sense of symmetry with their rounded derrieres. All the female employees had been friendly, answering his questions about the club's history of violence . . . or lack of.

He was trying to remember if this was the bar that had the revolving circular stage where a girl danced inside a cylindrical glass cage with glittery stars attached to the glass. There, in a cone of stark light from above, she had pressed her breasts into the glass like fried eggs hitting the frying pan. He flipped open his notebook and studied the entries under "S." When he found *Skin Tight* he reviewed his notes:

Clientele—businessmen, congenial, out of shape

Potential for customer unrest—next to nothing

Owner/manager—Gene DeMarco

Bouncer—big! built like a Kodiak bear, slow moving, but when he does, moves like a cat, leans against back wall next to bar, bartender wouldn't give his name. Moving stage in middle of room.

Yes, it was the club with the sequin-spangled, revolving stage. He remembered now the gargantuan bouncer leaning against the wall, arms folded across his chest, the reflections of light from the turning cage scudding across his patient stillness like a migration of elastic fish that elongated as they made the hard turns at the corners of the room.

Joey had gone home that night and practiced standing in his bedroom, back to the wall, arms crossed comfortably on his chest, his entire body unmoving, relaxed. He lasted an hour and a half, then the beer stinging his bladder finally won out. Joey made a note in his bouncer journal: "No beer twelve hours before a job." He liked that provision. It put being a bouncer right up there with vocations like pilot and surgeon.

It was eleven-thirty in the morning, so he did not bother trying the club's front door. He walked through the light drizzle of rain down the alley to the back parking lot and made his way to the service entrance where two men—one black, one white—were stacking crates onto a hand-truck from the rear of a van. The van's panel read *Burt's Discount Liquor.*

"Gene DeMarco here?" Joey asked.

"Never heard of him," the white one said, never breaking his rhythm with the crates. "Don't know 'im, don't wanna know 'im." His voice was too loud for the proximity, and he never once looked at Joey.

"Might ask somebody inside," the young black man said. "Me and Jerry just delivering."

The black man's arms were thick with muscle, but his voice carried a mosquito-like whine that bordered on obsequious. When he passed another crate to Jerry there was a slip, and the crate almost fell in the transfer.

"Goddamnit, Tyrell! You dumb nigger!" Jerry jerked the box from Tyrell's hands and stacked it roughly, causing the bottles inside to rattle like a rack of billiard balls. "Drop one of these goddamn things and it's coming out of your paycheck, not mine! You got that?"

Tyrell made no reply. His face was unreadable, as though he was accustomed to such diatribes. He dodged back into the shadow of the van and came out with another crate. This one he held a little higher and maintained a sure grip until Jerry, frowning, pulled at it repeatedly.

"Goddamnit, Tyrell! I got it! Let the friggin' thing go!"

"So, who's the manager here now if it's not DeMarco?" Joey asked.

"How the hell would we know?" Jerry barked. "Ask one of the assholes inside." His reply was abrasive and loud, as though addressed to the world. Joey watched the angry man step on the foot bar, lever the handtruck onto its wheels, and heave it forward. Blocking the man's way, Joey stood comfortably in the doorway and waited for Jerry to meet his eyes. Jerry straightened and glared with a menacing scowl that looked like it came right out of Earl Gallatin's playbook.

"You got a problem, squirt?" Jerry challenged. The fine rain gave his slicked-back black hair the sheen of plastic bristles on a whisk broom. His mouth curled with contempt. With the questionable advantage of a beer gut, he probably had fifty pounds on Joey.

A vintage Volkswagen Beetle sputtered around the corner of the building and eased into the parking space next to the van. Joey knew it by sound alone—that unique purr of a VW. But neither Joey nor Jerry broke off his part of the standoff. Tyrell eased back into the van out of the drizzle. When the Beetle's wipers stopped and the engine shut down, the silence was like a spotlight shining down on the two men facing off over the stack of crates.

"I got eleven more deliveries today, asshole! You wanna get outta my way?"

Joey offered a bland smile. "You wanna tell me who the manager is here?"

"I don't know and don't care. Now get outta my goddamn way!"

Joey rested a forearm on a stack of cardboard boxes piled high by the door. He tapped a finger on the cardboard as if he had nothing better to do than mark time. Jerry tilted the hand truck forward to let the crates come to a rattling rest on the landing. With his hands free, he sidestepped and let his arms swell from his sides like a high noon gunfighter.

"Who signs your delivery invoice?" Joey asked, friendly enough.

"What's it to you who signs anything of mine?"

"Guy's name is Benny," Tyrell offered from the van. "Don't know if he's the manager. We just unload and he signs the invoice." Tyrell seemed to wait for Joey to see his conciliatory smile, but Joey's eyes remained on Jerry.

"You don't gotta tell him your goddamn life story, Tyrell," Jerry barked. "You don't gotta tell *him* jack-shit."

In his peripheral vision Joey could see an unmoving shape inside the Volkswagen. Whoever it was made no move to get out, and Joey scored the driver a point for prudence. No sense in walking into trouble like this. Especially a female. He was pretty sure it was a woman—a big woman with her hair flared out over her shoulders. The car was painted orange with large black polka-dots. A ladybug Volkswagen. Had to be a woman.

Jerry puffed out his chest and let his gaze travel up and down Joey's slight frame, taking in the suit and tie and shoes and short, bristly hair. A smirk flickered on and off of Jerry's mouth.

"What's your problem, asshole?" Jerry said, ramping up his bravado.

"Well, Jerry," Joey said canting his head to one side. "Several things. You're loud and obnoxious and demeaning." He nodded into the van. "Do you think Tyrell likes being called a 'nigger'?" He asked this quietly, the way a father might ask his son if he knew why the stars twinkled up in the night sky.

"I call a spade a spade," Jerry said, and snorted at his own cleverness.

"Aw, he don't mean nothin by it, man," Tyrell said. "Hell, sometimes I call him a 'nigger.' Ain't that right, Jerry?" But Jerry was busy trying to flex the tendons in his jowly jaws as he held his baleful stare on Joey.

"That right, Jerry?" Joey asked, letting his eyebrows rise with the question. "You let anybody call you 'a nigger'?"

Jerry sneered. "You gotta be black to be a nigger, asshole!" he said and raised his chin to point at Joey. "But anybody can be an asshole." Jerry shifted his weight from one leg to the other and took a half-step forward. Joey lowered his arm from the boxes and took a slow, casual step toward Jerry. A rook and a knight positioning on the chess board.

The Volkswagen door opened and, when the occupant stepped out, the car visibly buoyed up six or seven inches. The human figure looming in Joey's peripheral vision was enormous standing next to the Beetle. Like a woods bison emerging from a picnic basket. When Tyrell made a little gasping sound in his throat, Jerry turned his head to the driver of the VW, and his testosterone-driven ego deflated as if a valve had sprung a leak in his arms and chest.

"Do we have a problem here, gentlemen?"

It was not so much the words as the tone that turned Joey's eyes to the speaker. Erudite and enunciative, the words had purled off the man's tongue like polished stones rolling across black velvet. Joey recognized

Skin Tight's bouncer. A monolith of muscle, thick shoulders, and the long heavy arms of a gorilla.

The bouncer pulled back the hood of his nylon pullover, and now a shining bullet-shaped skull capped the mountain of his torso. He bounced lightly up the steps with hardly a sound and stopped on the landing to appraise the situation. In one hand he held a book. The other hand scratched languidly at the center of his stomach, his fingernails making a dry scraping sound on the nylon jacket. The giant looked from Joey to Jerry to Tyrell, like a schoolteacher waiting for one student to own up to a prank. The fine mist beaded on his skull like tiny orbs of glass.

"This asshole won't get outta my way," Jerry said, his voice noticeably softened. "It's goddamned raining, and I got eleven deliveries after this one."

The massive man studied Jerry's animated face the way a mastodon might consider a snowflake. Then the tapered head turreted on its tree-trunk neck, and the giant studied Joey. Joey stood relaxed, impassive—a cat sleeping on a windowsill—but his knees remained slightly bent and now his focus had expanded to two possible adversaries.

"And what's your story, Captain America?"

Joey cracked a smile at the metaphor, but his attention held on Jerry. "Looking for Gene DeMarco."

The bouncer cocked his head to one side. "And that would be for—?"

Joey waited three beats, setting his own rhythm to the dialogue. "A conversation," he said, injecting a little melody into his answer.

The bouncer smiled, demonstrating effortless patience. "About?"

Joey smiled and shook his head. "Private."

The big man waited, letting the quiet enfold the loading dock. Then he replicated Joey's shake of the head.

"You're not his wife and you're not his paramour and you're not his lawyer. That eliminates 'private' right there. And that leaves you talking to me . . . not DeMarco."

Joey narrowed one eye. "Oh, really? And why's that?"

The man stood motionless in the drizzle. "I'm his bodyguard."

Joey finally looked at the man and shook his head. "Unh-unh. You're the bouncer here."

The bouncer shrugged, his meaty hands sweeping outward so that Joey caught a glimpse of the book's cover: *The Yin and Yang of Jung*.

"I've branched out," he said. "I'm a man of dual occupations now." He made a subtle smile. The crown of his bald head shone like a newly emerged mushroom glistening with dew.

The two professional pugilists stared at one another, each seemingly comfortable in the strained silence. Jerry, now relegated to spectator status, wiped at the water running into his eyes. His shoulders were dark with rain. Tyrell had inched back onto the carpet of the van and had one hand on the door handle in case he needed to ensconce himself behind locked doors.

"Hey! Fellas!" Jerry said, breaking the silence. "Can I deliver this booze or what? Me and the nigger need to get the hell outta here! We got a full day ahead o' us!" His voice was like a small flying insect trying to be heard above the rumble of an imminent earthquake.

Joey watched the hulking bouncer for a telltale movement of his feet or a shift of weight, something that might telegraph his strategy, but the big man continued to stand flatfooted and aloof. In this lull Joey thought of two mountain elk he had once seen on the Nature Channel—the animals posturing, snorting, and scraping hooves on the rocky ground. The two elk did all they could to settle their dispute by bluff. When, finally, they did lock horns, it was just a pushing contest. No blood. No injury, except to pride.

Smart, Joey thought. *Two professionals. It didn't pay to get hurt when superiority could be established another way.*

The bouncer kept his eyes on Joey and spoke out of the side of his mouth. "Jerry, I want you to stop by a library before your next delivery. Can you do that?"

Jerry frowned at the big man. "Huh? A library?"

The bouncer pivoted his head to look at him. "A library," he repeated. "Can you do that?"

"Sure, sure." Jerry looked at Tyrell. "You know where there's a library around here?"

Tyrell licked his lips but said nothing.

The bouncer raised a thick index finger to point casually at Jerry. "I want you to find a big dictionary and look up the word 'nigger.' Probably the second or third definition."

" 'Nigger'?" Jerry echoed.

The bouncer smiled. "I want you to read it to Tyrell."

Jerry's face tightened with confusion. "What for?"

The bouncer's smile widened by a quarter inch. "Always good to know the meaning of the vocabulary you choose for your lexicon, Jerry."

Jerry's brow lowered. "My what?" He frowned at the van. "Man, I drive a Dodge."

The big man cocked his head slightly and studied Jerry's face. "In giving freedom to the slave, we assure freedom to the free—honorable alike in what we give, and what we preserve. We shall nobly save, or meanly lose, the last, best hope of Earth."

Jerry was like a mannequin as he tried to extract some meaning from these words. Then his mouth formed a small O as he struggled to construct a question.

"Abraham Lincoln," the bouncer said. "It's taken from an annual message to Congress." He kept staring at the confusion on Jerry's face. "The library?"

"Yeah. Sure. Okay. We'll go to the friggin' library."

The bouncer turned back to Joey. "Now, if you'll be kind enough to free up the doorway, let's you and I go have a little causerie in my office." He glanced back at Jerry and Tyrell. "Library closes at noon on Wednesdays, fellas."

Chapter Seven

Frogtown Falls
Spring, 1949

Hoke sat on the big sloping shelf of rock that bordered the pool below the falls. There was always a wind there, an invigorating spray of air and mist stirred up by the falling sheet of white before him. The sound of the water was like the roar of the motor that ran the big saw at the mill where his daddy worked. Trout lilies had sprung up on the banks, and the serviceberry trees were tasseled with spidery white blooms. Leaf buds everywhere were opening, dotting the creek banks with the first hints of green that would soon cover the forest.

With his satchel of books set aside on the rock, Hoke placed in his lap the brown paper sack his mother had packed for his school lunch, and, opening it, he felt the guilt of deceiving her and tried to bury that guilt somewhere in the crashing sound of the water. Fry bread, bacon, and an apple. Not bad rations for a day of playing hooky.

The guilt resurfaced when in the sack he found the little sewn pouch tied by a strip of rawhide and adorned with a hummingbird feather. It was the medicine bundle his mother had put there to help him with the arithmetic test. The test was why he had come here to the falls. Nothing good was going to come out of failing that test. Nothing good was going to come out of playing hooky either, so he had a vague plan of staying here by the falls indefinitely. Maybe forever.

There were otters just downstream, where Frogtown Creek joined Dicks Creek to form the Chestatee River. Why could he not live here like those otters, catching fish, playing in the pellucid waters of summer, dragging leaves from the riverbed to pee on them and mark his territory? He took a small bite of fry bread and tried to compare its taste to the otters' harvest of raw trout. If he could not inure his tongue to the taste of uncooked fish, perhaps he might show these sleek fishers the art of twirling a dry stem of horseweed on a seasoned slab of pawpaw to create fire. *How the Otter Learned to Cook Fish.* It sounded like one of the old Cherokee origin tales. From there, the imagined storyline expanded: his acceptance into the Otter Tribe to form an alliance. They would bring the fish, and he would cook. He pictured half a dozen otters lounging on the sandy beach and basking in the sun as he rotated the spit.

For as long as he could remember, Hoke had dreamed about otters, as if his destiny had somehow become intertwined with these aquatic hunters. Actually, he was fixated on one particular otter, a female who had come to him in his dreams on five different occasions. He had thought of speaking about it to his father to ascertain the hidden meaning of the dreams, but when he had begun awaking with feelings of deep longing and of carnal bliss with this creature, he decided to speak to no one about her. He suspected that, through these dreams, the Thunder Spirits had ushered him into manhood. It was the grandest-ever dream, near-sacred, and surely prophetic. Still, he questioned the morality of it, his paramour in this arrangement being, after all, a member of the weasel family.

In case he did decide never to go home, Hoke wrapped the apple inside the paper bag and stored it inside a large crack under the shelf of the rock. Then he stacked the two fry breads on his thigh and carefully inserted the bacon inside them. After taking a bite of sandwich, he set it down and untied the small cord that cinched up the mouth of the medicine bundle.

With his body hunched over, he upended the pouch over his palm. Several coarse grains of yellow powder dropped into his hand. Touching them to his tongue, he identified the crude powder as cornmeal that his mother had ground inside a stone bowl—a symbol, no doubt, she had intended to represent the breaking down of a problem into its simplest state. Like corn kernels crushed into meal. After lapping up all the grains with his tongue, Hoke crunched the cornmeal with his molars and swallowed.

Probing inside the pouch with a finger, he found a portion of knobby little root that he guessed to be ginseng. His mother had told him how it aids in clear thinking by untying knots in the mind. Biting into it, he felt the sharp taste rile up his tongue as if sending a spark of alertness straight to his brain. He waited several seconds to see if he felt any smarter, but nothing convincing came to mind.

The last item was a flake of quartz no larger than his little fingernail. One edge was sharp, napped to a finely serrate line. This was a shard of broken arrowhead. He could see the way his mother was thinking. She wanted him sharp today for the test.

Working on the sandwich, he watched the water plummet over the beveled face of the cliff above him. He could see it fall in two different ways. If he relaxed his eyes and kept them fixed on the falls as a whole, it fell like a curtain of woven water, an unending spool that broke apart at the bottom where it plunged into the pool.

But if he followed a piece of the falling water with his eyes, the sheet appeared to disintegrate into uncountable droplets that seemed to slow down for the benefit of his watching. It was like seeing all the links of a curtain of chainmail disengaging at once. Using the latter method, he saw that the water looked more complicated. It was no longer a unit. He wondered if he were seeing individual molecules temporarily separated for the free fall, then melting back into liquid to become part of the pool.

"I have a son who looks very much like you'ens," came a man's voice from right behind him.

Hoke jumped so that one piece of fry bread tumbled off his lap into the water, and the contents of the medicine bundle spilled onto the rock. When his heart settled back down into his chest, he hurried to get his wits about him.

"But," his father continued in his familiar, edifying voice, "this son of mine would be in school now."

Juni Limberlost stood in his easy, unassuming pose, holding his cane pole and a jar of wormy soil in his big gentle hands. He eyed the scattered items and the bread floating in the water.

"I love a good story," Juni said. "I'm betting you'ens got one."

Hoke hung his head. "I gotta story 'bout a 'rithmetic test." He began picking up the parts of the bundle and salvaging what food he could. A school of small fish darted at the bread in the water, and the crusty flake bobbed farther out into the current where it picked up speed toward the spillway.

Hoke threw the ginseng root into the water. "I cain't multiply nothin'!" He glared at the pool but then looked up quickly, as if he might have convincing proof. "Juss listen to this. My schoolteacher says if you'ens got a certain number and it gits multiplied by zero, it takes away the number you already got."

When Juni narrowed his eyes at these words, Hoke tried again. "Okay, say you'ens got two pieces o' fry bread. She's sayin': multiply that by zero and you'ens ain't got no fry bread a-tall."

Now his father's eyes fixed on the waterfall. "Sounds like maybe usin' that zero on a piece a fry bread is kindly like eatin' it." He looked at Hoke. "You reckon?"

Hoke wrinkled his brow. "Well, if it is, there ain't nobody ever mentioned it."

" 'Course," Juni continued, "holdin' that fry bread in your belly is better'n holdin' it in your hand. So, I reckon we cain't really say it's gone. It's juss in a better place."

Now *that* was worth pondering, Hoke thought, because it was sounding as if that fry bread was like Grandpa Swimmer Limberlost. When he had died, everybody had told Hoke that the old patriarch had gone to a better place. That made sense. Dying seemed like getting multiplied by zero all right.

"What do you'ens plan to tell your mama 'bout missin' school today, son?"

Hoke looked surprised. "I didn' plan on sayin' nothin'. I's hopin' she wouldn' ask."

Juni nodded, and for a time they watched the water take its plunge over the thirty-foot wall of stone. "You'ens' grandpa use'ta tell me if I planned on things happ'nin' like I was *hopin'* they'd happen . . . 'stead o' the way I knew they might *could* happen . . . I was gonna be a awful lot disappointed in my life."

Hoke had nothing to say to that. He was thinking more seriously about sprouting fur, a tail, and some webbed feet and diving into the pool.

"Here's the other thing," Hoke began again, working up a tone of complaint. "Say you'ens multiply a piece a fry bread by one. You'ens still got 'xactly what you'ens started with." He gave his father a pained expression meant to expose the futility of such logic. "I mean, why even bother multiplyin' if you'ens gonna end up with what you started with?"

His father nodded and sat next to the boy. "Seems to me, you'ens is doin' some pretty sound thinkin' 'bout all them numbers. What happens when you'ens multiplies some fry bread by two?"

"Then you'ens got twice as much as you started with," Hoke calculated.

"How 'bout three times four?" Juni said.

Hoke dipped a finger in the water and painted some wet marks on the rock. The drawing looked like a stand of cornstalks all in a row. He took on the pained expression again, erased the calculations with a smear of his hand, and tried again on a new dry spot.

Juni wet his finger in the pool and drew four circles on the rock. "Okay, here's four fry pans. How 'bout if you'ens cook up three fry breads in each one?"

Hoke dipped his finger again and dabbed three dots of fry bread into each fry pan. "Twelve," he announced with pride.

Juni nodded with a grave expression. "Appears to me you'ens got this fry bread down purty good. Maybe you'ens juss need to think with your stomach. You got pencil and paper there?" He nodded to the satchel on the rock.

Hoke got out his tablet and a yellow number two pencil with a broken point. His father opened his pocketknife one-handedly with his thumbnail and carved neat slivers of wood off the pencil until the dark core protruded like a tiny obsidian spear point.

Hunched over the tablet, Juni Limberlost began a slow parade of etchings on the paper. Hoke watched him and struggled to decipher the old Cherokee syllabary. His mother had been trying to teach it to him, but Hoke could not see the fairness in spending the better part of the day in school then having to sit through more of it at night.

When Juni handed the paper to his son, Hoke stared at it. "What's it say?"

"Says you'ens was helpin' me this mornin' and please to excuse you'ens for bein' late to school."

Hoke looked back at the paper. "How 'xactly was I s'posed to be a-helpin?"

"Well, I got laid off for the day from the lumberyard on account o' the belt broke on the rippin' saw, and they ain't gonna be another'n till Jack Trammel gits back from Gainesv'lle. But his transmission fell outta his truck on the way over there. I came over here to fish and forgot my lunch. I left it at the mill. Hey, you'ens gonna finish that fry bread and bacon?"

Hoke handed the half-sandwich to him. It was a small price to pay for his father's silence that night at home.

"How am I gonna git to school?" Hoke said. "I already missed the bus."

Juni Limberlost gave his son a somber look. "Cher'kee runners use'ta cover seven'y miles in a day an' a night, they say. Juss carried a little bag o' cornmeal for strength."

"But it's eight miles to school!" Hoke protested.

Juni's smile brightened. "Compared to seven'y, you oughta cover that in no time."

Hoke exhaled heavily and gathered his tablet and pencil. He stood and frowned at the trail that led downstream toward town.

"Time I git there, school'll be gittin' over with."

"Well," Juni offered, "least you'ens can ride the bus home. That oughta look 'bout right to your mama."

Hoke shouldered his satchel and trudged away over the rock shelf to the sandy bank, where he began following the trail downstream. He had made the turn at the confluence and was contorting through a thick stand of rhododendron when he remembered the apple. He would need the lunch bag when he arrived at home, or his mother might get suspicious about this whole thing. And besides that, if he had to walk the eight miles, he might need that apple for survival.

When he regained the pool below the falls, his father was nowhere to be seen. He found the crumpled bag and pulled it from the crack in the rock, but it came out too light. He knew before he opened it that the bag was empty. Inside he found the little desiccated stalk that had once connected fruit to limb. Hoke turned and stared at the waterfall. Danged if he hadn't helped his daddy this morning! He'd taught him how to multiply a apple by zero.

Chapter Eight

The Skin Tight Club
Wednesday afternoon

Joey walked in the shadow of the bouncer's broad back and followed him through the club's brightly lighted kitchen. Three Hispanic women and one black man worked at metal sinks, their arms up to their elbows in soapy water. Above them on metal shelves lined by white towels, an endless parade of glasses threw off sharp glints of light from the overhead fluorescents. Shot glasses, long-stemmed wine glasses, wide-mouth cocktail glasses, mugs, tankards, and every other drinking vessel Joey could imagine.

They passed through the dark of the main bar, where chairs were inverted and propped on the table edges as if floodwaters were expected. Around the perimeter of the room, the booths were covered in a shiny, burgundy, vinyl upholstery. The revolving stage was unmoving at the center of the room. In this stillness Joey sensed the room breathing in sanity, steeling itself for the chaos that would arrive with the night's business hours. He pictured himself standing in the corner, arms folded across his chest, his radar on high alert for a rowdy customer.

As they entered a small office, the bouncer pointed to a chair, and Joey sat. The big man walked behind a desk to a ceiling-high bookshelf and slid his book into the only vacant spot. When he slipped the nylon pullover off his massive frame, his sleeveless tee-shirt rode up, briefly revealing a torso as rugged as a boulder field.

The bouncer's physique left no secrets about the man's potential. He was heavily slabbed with muscle: hams bulging at his chest, swollen fire hoses for arms, a washboard stomach. His neck was thickly rooted between his blocky shoulders like an oak wedged between great chunks of granite. From a clothes hanger hooked over a nail in the wall, he took down a spotless white shirt and pushed his big arms into the sleeves. From the same nail, he took down a navy tie. Whistling quietly, he buttoned up and then faced a small wall mirror as he knotted the tie at his collar.

Dressed to his liking, he opened a drawer in the desk, struck a wooden match, and lit a candle perched on a flat, stone base on his desktop. Right away, a strong aromatic scent filled the room. Lowering himself slowly, the bouncer sat on a royal blue floor-cushion and crossed his massive legs beneath him Indian-style. Lifting the rock and candle from the desk, he placed it before him on the floor. Every move he made carried the grace of a ballet dancer.

"Aromatherapy," the big man said, nodding toward the candle. "Lilac and wheat germ combo. Supposed to be centering . . . good for balancing strength and grace."

Not knowing what to say to that, Joey looked around at the walls of the room and frowned at two color movie posters, both framed and pressed behind glass. How he had not noticed them before could only be explained by his attentiveness to the bouncer's preening. Both posters were of Julie Andrews. One was autographed but it was a generic message: *Best wishes, Julie.*

"Okay," the bouncer began, "let's talk about this little vignette in which you just starred out on the loading dock." The big man had softened his voice to show that he could be tolerant of the mistakes of novices. When he leaned his elbows on his thighs, his arms pumped up as big as an ordinary man's legs, the elbows like knees. "Wrong war at the wrong place against the wrong enemy," he said, his breath sending the candle flame into a slow sinuous dance. He looked Joey over from rubber-soled cordovans to buzz-cut. An edifying smile eased onto his beefy face, and he cocked his head. "It's a quote from Omar Bradley, Chairman of the

Joint Chiefs of Staff. That was during the Korean War. He was talking about China."

Joey pursed his lips and nodded, but he had no clue what to say to that. "That your car out there?" he asked, hitching his thumb toward the back of the building.

"The bug? No, that's Lily's. Why?"

Joey shrugged. "Wondered if it was part of the uniform. Fits you skin-tight."

The big man cracked a wry smile and pointed at Joey with a forefinger—a gesture Joey took to be a friendly one.

"Lily works here at night. Goes to school during the day. She lets me use it." He laughed. "You're right. Every time I crawl out of it, I feel like I need a chiropractor."

Joey looked again at the Julie Andrews pictures. The larger poster was from *The Sound of Music*—Julie romping through an Alpine meadow with a covey of happy-faced children. Joey assumed someone else shared the office with this brute.

The bouncer raised an eyebrow at Joey. "Why do I get the feeling you would like to supplant me as disturbance suppressor at *Skin Tight?*" The timbre of his words was like a narrator's voice-over in a PBS special.

"You need any help here?" Joey said.

The man smiled. "Does it look like I need any help?"

Joey conceded the point with a nod. "Maybe Mr. DeMarco has other clubs. He need anybody at one of those?"

The man's big meaty hands came together, the fingers lacing as well as could be expected for digits the size of Polish sausages. "Maybe first we ought to talk about the logic of your affinity for this vocation." He spread his hands appraisingly. "You don't weigh more than . . . what . . . one-fifty-five . . . one-sixty? A lot of rowdies are going to top two hundred. How are you going to escort somebody like that out the door?"

Joey gave him his dead-eyed stare for ten seconds then leaned forward, propping his own elbows on his knees. "With surprise," he replied in a flat voice.

The bouncer nodded, but by his twitch of a smile he appeared unconvinced. "Must be a substantial surprise. What is it?"

Joey returned the twitchy smile. "If I told you, it wouldn't be a surprise."

They stared at one another. The sounds of plates tumbling in water in the kitchen rumbled like distant thunder.

"Okay. Fair enough. What kind of references do you have? Any past experience?"

Joey pushed out one cheek with his tongue and nodded, thinking about the question. "Haven't lost a fight since the sixth grade."

The bouncer's smile ventured a little wider. "And how many might that be?"

Joey shrugged. "Quite a few."

They both waited. That was all Joey was going to give.

"Okay, these fights . . . they in the ring or on the street?"

"Both."

The big man let his head drop. When he looked up, he wore an amused grin.

"You give an interesting interview . . . I'll give you that. You bring a note from every guy you ever bested?" When Joey gave him a look, the bouncer waved at the air between them. "That was rhetorical."

"Here's the deal," Joey said. "Let me work a club. No pay. First time I'm needed, the owner makes his assessment by how I handle it. If he wants to keep me, I get the retro-pay and go from there. If not, I'm history. I won't bother him again."

The bouncer's amused grin widened to a full-voltage smile. "And what if a contentious patron weighs two-seventy-five and decides to sit on you?"

Joey's expression did not change as he shook his head. "Mistake," he said.

The bouncer arched both eyebrows. " 'Mistake'?"

Joey picked at a callus on one palm and shrugged. "In everything there's opportunity. He's offering his most vulnerable area to me. The crown jewels. I plant an elbow deep into his crotch." Joey dipped his head and spread his hands with the obvious. "Mistake," he repeated.

The bouncer's smile dissolved, and his eyes seemed to take a clearer measure of Joey. " 'In everything there's opportunity,' " he echoed, as if analyzing the poetic meter of the line. "You see some opportunity right here? With you and me? I mean, should we fall into discord?"

Joey, thoroughly relaxed, stretched a hand toward the big man's chest. Nothing threatening, just a casual move as if he were going to brush away a speck of lint from the man's shirt. The big man's eyes made a subtle shift to opacity. Joey saw the big, clasped fingers loosen and a barely discernible tightening of muscle beneath the shirt.

"This noose," Joey said, sliding the loose hang of the bouncer's necktie toward himself through two fingers. When he reached the tip end of the material he gathered the tie in a loose twist around his fist and gave it a light, instructive tug. Then he let it drop back to the front of the white shirt. "Almost as good as a lasso at roundup," Joey quipped.

The bouncer looked down at his tie and ironed it against his shirt with the flat of his hand. He dipped his head to one side, seemingly impressed.

"Yippie Ki-Yay," the big man said quietly.

They stared at one another. Then the bouncer mimicked Joey's reach and gently took Joey's necktie between two fingers, letting it slide in the same sensuous glide until he pinched the tip end. When he tugged, the tie's plastic clips plucked from the collar with a soft *tick*. The *Skin Tight* giant froze in this ludicrous pose—the tie swinging between the two men like a limp ripcord that had failed to open a parachute.

Joey smiled. "Surprise!" he whispered.

The bouncer laughed softly and laid the necktie in Joey's lap. "You can call me 'Budge'," he said, and offered to shake. Joey looked at the giant hand for a time and then finally took it. It was like pushing his hand inside a rump roast. He knew the giant could have clamped down, held him in place to show Joey how easy it was to be overpowered by a bigger man. But Joey kept that look in his eye—the one that suggested he might have another surprise.

"Joey Gallatin," he said, completing introductions.

Budge released the hand, and Joey clipped his tie back in place.

"I might have a little work for you," Budge said, taking from the desktop a napkin and pen and setting them on the floor between them. "Write down your phone number for me."

Joey narrowed his eyes. "So, now I'm big enough all of a sudden?"

Budge shrugged. "Let's just call it an instinct on my part." He nodded to the napkin. "Write down your number."

Joey made his own shrug. "Don't have a phone," he said.

Budge eyed him for ten seconds. "No phone," he said in a dull tone.

Joey slid the pen and paper to Budge. "Write yours down. I can call *you*."

Budge closed his eyes and chuckled. "And how will you know when to call?"

"Instinct," Joey said.

"Yeah? Exactly how's that work?"

"I'll call you every day," Joey explained and then his cool eyes went earnest. "I want to be a bouncer, Budge."

Seeing the passion in Joey's face, Budge smiled, pulled the napkin closer, and began writing his phone number. "I believe you do, Captain America."

Chapter Nine

Lumpkin County Courthouse
Wednesday, late afternoon

Chief deputy Duffy Hawkins came out of Judge Ricketts's chambers with the signed warrant that he needed to search the Vanstory brothers' farm. Hawkins and one other deputy had been switching off, staking out the farmhouse every night for two weeks. During the day, whichever officer had not been up all night followed the paper trail of the Vanstorys' purchases at the *Walmart* and *The Home Depot* and the new pharmacy across the intersection from the *Walmart*. With the list of supplies bought from these establishments and the volume of traffic going in and out of the Vanstory farm, it all added up to another meth lab in Lumpkin County.

Hawkins was sick and tired of drug-heads. At first, he believed it could only be newcomers to the mountains: young weirdoes spilling out of Atlanta and spreading their urbane decadence like smallpox. But over the last year it had been not-so-young weirdos probably conceived at Woodstock—diehard hippie types who had migrated all over the country in search of the end of the rainbow and settled for Lumpkin County's rural anonymity as a refuge. Both demographics seemed to believe they might trade the wide net of big city cops for the fly swatter of a country-bumpkin sheriff's department.

Duffy hissed air through his teeth. He could no longer deny that old mountain families were involved in this, too. His argument *had* once been simple: Appalachian folk just weren't that kind of people. Until now. The Vanstorys had proved him wrong. Duffy had irrefutable proof that these three brothers had entered the meth market, and he was bound and determined to stamp out their flame before it infected others with whom he had grown up.

He had first gotten wind of it from the Ledfords, who were one farm over from the Vanstorys. Lonny Ledford had said those Vanstory boys were howling at the moon and shooting off twelve-gauge rounds in a high arc that showered down on the Ledford's chicken houses. And it wasn't liquor fueling these outbursts. Between the salvos and the hailstorm of pellets that fell on the long aluminum roofs, those Vanstory boys were screaming to high heaven in such a way it would put a TV evangelist to shame.

That was the giveaway. Those boys didn't ordinarily talk much. They might start a five-word sentence on Monday and get around to finishing up by Friday. And that was when they were sober. Drunk they were even quieter. It had to be meth.

There'd been Vanstorys in the county since before the land lottery that divvied up the Cherokee holdings. Seven Vanstorys had marched off to Chickamauga in confederate gray, and seven had returned. Story was: those Vanstory boys had been crack shots and hard to kill. After tallying up a roster-full of Yankee dead, they became a county legend.

Not that Duffy Hawkins cared for the Vanstorys any too much. They were a rough bunch—Garland and Haymer and Big Mose. If General Robert E. Lee rose from the grave tomorrow, those boys would be first in line to sign up for the second rising of the South, but Duffy was not sure General Lee would be caught dead with them. Literally.

The Forest Service had caught the brothers shining for deer in the Boggs Creek fields, and Hawkins himself had busted up their cockfighting ring. Either of these offenses were somewhat forgivable, Hawkins allowed. They had tradition attached to them. Hell, the Cherokee used to night-hunt with torches. And cockfighting had been a staple of pioneer Appalachia. The Vanstorys just hadn't caught up to the times. But now they had. Tingling with the rush of home-brewed speed, they had jumped headlong into the twenty-first century and hit the ground running.

"Methamphetamines," Hawkins whispered, employing the same intonation he used to describe a lethal disease. "God Aw-mighty. What's next? Satanic goat worship?"

Last February, Hawkins had engaged in a fistfight with the Vanstorys in the Gold Miner's Tavern. It was about a piece of land the sheriff's department had helped L.T. Voss seize on the sly for unpaid taxes. Duffy didn't care for Ott's methods any more than the Vanstory brothers did, but he couldn't allow the sheriff's office to be tarnished by public aspersions. There had to have been seventy people in the bar, listening to Garland cuss up a blue streak, watching him break glasses and threaten any and all members of county law enforcement.

That's when Arliss Bodie, the tavern owner, had called the sheriff. Predictably, Ott had handed the job to Duffy, who went alone without backup. As Duffy saw it, these Vanstorys needed not just taming. They needed a one-man humbling.

None of the brothers had been drinking. They had come to the bar to complain. When Duffy arrived, the presence of his uniform was enough to touch off the powder keg, and Garland lit into Duffy like a wildfire. To no one's surprise—least of all Duffy's—Mose jumped into the fray. It was why, sitting in the cruiser five minutes earlier outside the bar, Duffy had traded his regulation black brogans for steel-toe work boots.

To Garland's wildfire, Mose was a conflagration. The fight was like a tornado spinning in the middle of the room, picking up chairs and playing cards and beer mugs. Then Haymer—the quiet one, whom Duffy had counted on for fair play—got into the action. That had been a miscalculation on Duffy's part. If he had not laid his hands on Arliss' skullcracker—a three-foot section of hickory axe handle—things could have gone badly for him. As it was, Duffy spent half the night in the emergency room getting his lip sewn up and his eye patched.

When the doctor on duty had finished with him, Duffy drove the physician to the jail, where he tended to Garland's bloodied ear, partially severed tongue, and broken nose. And Mose's swollen testicles. And Haymer's concussion. The only way the doctor would treat the boys was to have them sedated and their cots pushed up against the cell door where he could work on them through the iron bars.

Snapping out of his reminiscences, Hawkins stepped outside from the courthouse to a sky heavily laden with charcoal gray clouds. He pocketed the warrant, fitted his straight-brimmed hat to his head, and forked his sunglasses past his temples just in time to see the sheriff coming up the steps from the parking lot. Ott was taking the steps slowly, listening attentively to the new assistant district attorney who walked at his side. She wore a soft brown outfit that fit her like a suede glove. Next to Maria Gunlock, Ott looked like a bloated bullfrog squatting beside a sleek she-cat cougar in her tawny summer coat.

Hidden by his sunglasses, Duffy watched the A.D.A.'s strong legs scale the steps, and, as he did, he felt a hollow space open up inside his chest. Within that thoracic void, his heart thumped like a bass drum that had been sautéed in adrenaline.

The rumor was that Ms. Gunlock was fresh from the flames of a testy divorce and taking out her vengeance on every male criminal she prosecuted. Hawkins wanted to see the Vanstory brothers stand before this firestorm of female wrath. He also wanted to personally gather as much evidence as he could from the Vanstory farm, so that it was he that she would be interviewing and calling to the witness stand. She would probably need a lot of private time with him to go over his testimony. Juggling these dreams like an infatuated schoolboy, Duffy waited at the top of the steps, his face impassive as he unfolded the warrant.

"We'll tow the car in and have it disassembled," Ott was assuring her. "Soon's the judge okays it." When the sheriff saw Hawkins, he looked relieved. "Oh, hey, Duff. Say, you met Mizz Gunlock yet?"

Hawkins smiled as much as he ever dared to in uniform. Professional, focused, at all times preoccupied with the enforcement of the law . . . that was Duffy Hawkins. Somewhere in the vicinity of his heart thundering inside his chest, he imagined a roasting marshmallow that had just burst into flame.

"Ma'am," Hawkins said and touched the brim of his hat. His voice sounded distant even to himself, as though he were at the far end of the parking lot watching himself through a telescope. Standing within the gravitational pull of Maria Gunlock's radiance, Duffy felt like his feet were leaving the ground, and he considered grabbing the nearby stair rail.

"Duffy here's my chief deputy," Ott said through his you-bet-I-know-how-to-pick-'em smile.

Maria casually clasped the handrail and steadied herself. Here it was again. The ungluing of the muscles in her legs . . . the general feeling of surrender at her core . . . as though her intestines had raised a white flag. She felt strangely exposed in the presence of this lean and ruggedly handsome officer. Something about his manner, his movements with no wasted motion. She couldn't see his eyes behind the dark glasses, but she feared they might be dissecting her like a cryptologist pulling a secret message out of mystic runes. He was both familiar and exotic at once.

Unsure of her voice, she forfeited all the usual greetings she had been using with all the other county officials. Instead, she opted for succinct directness.

"Deputy Duffy," she said with a military snap. Her hand shot out like a pool cue.

"It's Hawkins, ma'am . . . Deputy Hawkins." He took her hand, and she pumped once in a short choppy motion that could have been part of a martial arts routine.

She felt it again. The touch of his hand on hers started up a hundred-volt chain reaction that swirled dizzily in her head and terminated with an electric tingle in her toes. Pulling her hand back quickly, she crossed her forearms over her stomach and diverted her attention to Ott.

"Sheriff, please apprise me when the perpetrator's vehicle is in the compound." She nodded to both men, prayed her legs would function properly, spun on a high heel, and walked into the building as though Al Capone was waiting for her cross-examination. Ott and Duffy watched her through the glass door, Ott smiling at her aggressive stride. Duffy looked down at his own hand—the one that had grasped Maria Gunlock's. It was numb.

"Tell ya what, Duff . . . let's don't you and me never run afoul o' *that* woman." Ott's face was as serious as Duffy had ever seen it. "Keep your files straight and don't never step over the line, son." The sheriff sidled closer to his deputy and lowered his voice to a whisper. "She's nice for lookin' at, but—" Ott shook his head. "Betcha a roll o' quarters 'gainst a rhubarb pie she's gonna put more jaspers b'hind bars than John Wayne and Wyatt Earp combined. Anything on the stole sign yet?"

Hawkins worked on regulating his breathing. He hadn't realized he had been holding his breath to memorize the clicking rhythm of Maria Gunlock's shoes in the hallway. As an answer to Ott, he shook his head. Then he turned the warrant around for Ott to read.

"Judge gave us a green light on the search out at the Vanstory farm. I'm ready to go in today."

Ott scanned the order and massaged his temples. "Well, I ain't had my lunch yet. The *Skillet's* got a barbecue special t'day. You hungry?"

Hawkins took back the warrant and folded it. "I don't wanna lose any more time on this, Ott. I'd hate to miss out on some crucial evidence on account of a barbecue plate."

Ott looked mildly annoyed, but he knew that Duffy was right. He couldn't see Duffy's eyes for the dark glasses, but he knew they would be all-business.

"Well," Ott said, trying to sound magnanimous. "How many men d'you need?"

"As many as you can spare. Four anyway . . . besides me. There's two roads outta there. We'll need a man at each exit and three to go in."

Ott looked out over the parking lot at the gray overcast sky and pulled on his upper lip with his lower one. "Aw-right, git on the radio, and git who you need." Ott checked his wristwatch, shook his head, and frowned, trying for disappointment. "I'd go with you myself but I gotta git over to Gainesv'lle. I got a 'pointment with my chir'practor. Guess I'll have to git that barbecue plate to go." He rubbed his shoulder, recalling that after his last chiropractic visit the doctor had recommended some kind of nutritional supplement that would lubricate his joints. Cartilage from sharks, for God's sake. *Hell,* he thought, *cain't see why cartilage from a pig cain't work juss as good.* He smiled, pleased with the idea of a barbecue plate as just what the doctor ordered.

Chapter Ten

Frogtown Creek
Wednesday night

Fannie called back to the restaurant and told Verdie that Theron couldn't find Hoke Limberlost but had left a note in his mailbox, so Verdie drove the seven miles up to Hester Gap after work. It meant missing the Nova special on forensic evidence, but she couldn't stand to think of Hoke being jerked from his anachronistic lark of a life and landing in the county lockup. Aside from the incongruity of it, there was a survival factor thrown into the equation. The word around town was that the Vanstory brothers were behind bars. Who could survive a jail sentence sharing a cell with those miscreants?

Dropping down into the cool hollows along Frogtown Creek, she crept along the dirt road in her little blue Fairlane, checking each cabin and house, fairly certain she would know Hoke's home when she saw it, even though she had never heard it described, much less visited it. At the turnoff that climbed Crow Mountain, she braked and studied a big green mailbox support of the oddest shape. It appeared to be a large tree trunk hacked out by hatchet, but she hadn't a clue as to what the sculpture was supposed to represent. Her best guess was an earless buffalo sitting on its haunches balancing a mailbox on its head.

She made a checkmark turn to train her headlights on the name painted on the box. The writing was illegible . . . or composed of foreign characters . . . or both. She pulled into the drive and cut off the engine.

The small log house looked about right for Hoke, but it was the truck that cinched it. Nobody else in the county drove an old Pinto with the back burned out by blowtorch and installed with the stern half of a johnboat bolted to the frame. It might have been the only passenger car in the county that had been converted into a pickup. Even from the road she could see the acetylene torch and fuel tank strapped in the Pinto's bed.

The cabin was small, rustic, idiosyncratic, and reminiscent of structures built centuries ago. At the far end of the yard were two hay bales, one stacked atop the other. Pinned to the hay was an enlarged photographic portrait of a face—a fleshy man with a stiff upturned collar, long sideburns, and an arrogant glare at the camera. The picture was liberally perforated with small dark holes about the cheeks and forehead and especially between the eyes, where the paper had been pulverized into a ragged hole about the size of a silver dollar pancake.

She cut her lights, got out, and walked to the Pinto. In addition to the welding gear, she found a sledgehammer and a pair of rubber waders freshly caked with mud.

Early yesterday morning when Hoke had stopped at the restaurant for the pancake special, not seeing his Pinto out front, Verdie had peeked out back and seen the mutant truck hidden behind the Dumpster. A silver galvanized post had been propped up on the tailgate where it protruded from the vehicle's fishing-boat bed. Slipping outside, Verdie had tiptoed to the Pinto and found a boxy shape hidden under a blanket at the end of the post. Lifting one corner of the blanket she had seen an oblong cube hammered out of green sheet metal. When she had leaned in for a closer look, she had made out one word in the shady interior of the cubicle: *Byron*.

In the cool night air of Frogtown valley, Verdie walked the stepping-stones to the cabin. Each rock showed a crude painting, all of them together comprising a menagerie of animal totems that led to the front door. The lintel beam under the small porch roof was fringed with feathers that hung by lengths of beaded strings. Over the green-painted door hung a slab of gray driftwood with dark pictographs burned into it. Taken as a whole, the décor of Hoke's residence appeared to be put together in a rather higgledy-piggledy fashion, but Verdie recognized its underlying Native American motif.

Perhaps better than anyone else, Verdie understood that Hoke's Cherokee heritage nourished him the way food and oxygen fed ordinary men. It was mostly what the two of them spoke of whenever Verdie pushed the waitress-customer dialogue beyond collards and cornbread.

She remembered the time Hoke had tried to learn to speak Cherokee from a tape he had mail-ordered from a magazine. She had loaned him her Walkman and headphones for the project, and for a solid month he had sworn off English entirely to struggle with the guttural sounds of his ancestors. He finally gave it up when, because of the language barrier, Verdie had served him eggplant instead of the pecan pie he had meant to order.

Standing at the door, Verdie knocked three times and waited, listening for any sound that might come from the cabin. Surprising her, the response came as a whisper from a thicket of rhododendron on the other side of the driveway.

"Verdie? That you?"

Hoke parted his way out through the leathery leaves, crouching, a bow and arrow held down beside one leg. Folded into headbands, two bandanas were tied across his forehead —a blue and a red. It took her a few moments to get her heart to sink back down into her chest from her throat. Once he was close enough to her, she wondered why she had not smelled him. There was always a peculiar, earthy odor that seemed to follow Hoke around.

"My word, Hoke. You fairly sent me into a palsy."

"At first, I thought maybe you'ens was Ott."

Her eyes fixed on the bow. "Well, what in the name of St. George were you about to do if it *were* Ott?"

As an answer, Hoke lifted the arrow tip before her. Fixed by duct tape to the end of the shaft was a small plastic vial that had been fitted over the bare wood dowel.

"What, pray tell, is that?" she said, squinting.

"One o' them li'l compliment'ry shampoo bottles from the Moonlight Motel down on highway sixty. They juss throw 'em away." He smiled approvingly at the harmless arrow tip. "Theys fit perfect on my arr'ws." He tapped the blunt, plastic arrow tip against the side panel of his truck, and it made a sound like an acorn banging down on a tin roof. "It's right good at discour'gin' trespassers."

Verdie's eyes cut to the rhododendron, as though there might be a war party of Cherokees back in the shadows awaiting Hoke's signal.

"What brings you'ens out here, Verdie?"

"I presume you got the message I sent out by Theron?"

Hoke let go with a smile that erased a decade from his crusty old face. "I kindly thought it was you'ens done sent it."

Verdie started shaking her head. "Hoke, you must be more careful how you carry things around in your truck for all the world to see. Ott was at the restaurant thinking out loud about what kind a person might be hauling off the county signs."

"That was right sweet o' you'ens to come out here an' warn me."

Verdie looked away quickly and found herself staring at the multi-pierced target. "Who *is* that?" she said, pointing to the photo pinned to the hay bales.

Hoke snorted. "Gen'l Winfield Scott." He pronounced the name the way people referred to a disease that had claimed one of their kin. "He's the one moved the Cher'kee outta here and down the Trail o' Tears." Hoke started to spit into the yard, but out of regard for his female guest he sucked in his cheeks and swallowed.

"I reckon stickin' arr'ws in Gen'l Scott is kindly my way o' deliverin' a Cher'kee do-si-do. Sort o' turnin' the tables on hist'ry." Hoke pointed.

"Got ol' Andy Jackson on t'other side. I need me a picture o' Gov'nor Lum'kin, too. That there's a damned trio of forked-tongued devils if ever they was one."

Verdie checked her wristwatch, but it was too dark to see. She looked up at a smattering of stars through a little opening in the hemlocks, as if she might read the time by a more natural means. In truth, she didn't know the Little Dipper from the lights down at the Walmart.

"I should be getting home," she said. "I've got the breakfast shift in the morrow."

He walked ahead of her to the little blue Fairlane and opened the door. After she got in, he closed the door but remained leaning on it on stiffened arms. She cranked down the window.

"I wanna thank you'ens for drivin' out here to warn me, Verdie. I reckon this means we got us a pact, don't it? Kindly like a secret treaty 'tween the British an' the Cher'kee."

"One if by land, two if by creek," she said. "But, most likely, Ott would come cruising in here in his patrol car, not in a canoe."

Hoke snorted. "Ott could no more fit inside a canoe than a circus elephant could squeeze into you'ens' mailbox."

Verdie's smile faded when her eyes fixed on the mailbox again. "Hoke, might you identify for me the sculpture upon which your mailbox is perched?"

He turned to face the carving, and his eyes glazed with pride. "Pick'rel frog . . . notched it out myself. Painted it, too." Hoke opened his arms to the land around them. "You know, all this here valley was once't Frogtown. *Walasi-yi.* That was what the Cher'kees called it."

"A frog," she said curiously, narrowing her eyes at the sculpture and cocking her head, trying to see the amphibian in the mutilated piece of wood. "Well, I dare say it is interesting. Somewhat cubist, I would say."

Hoke squinted at his handiwork and ran a hand across his mouth. "Well, tell you'ens the truth, Verdie, I ain't all that sure they got pick'rel frogs down there."

Verdie turned her detective eye on Hoke. " 'Down' where?"

Hoke turned his squint on Verdie. "Cuba."

" 'Cuba'?" she echoed with a perplexed wrinkling in her brow. Then the confusion left her face, and she closed eyes. "Never mind," she laughed. "I see."

Now it was Hoke's turn to look confused. "Don't see how, Verdie. You'ens' eyes are closed."

It was different talking to Hoke Limberlost like this, in the dark of the valley, with the ever-present murmur of the creek surrounding them like a private soundtrack of intimacy. The only words that had ever passed between them had been delivered over an order pad or a tray of hot food. In the restaurant she had considered only a fraction of the man. She knew his preference for sorghum over honey and, due to Hoke, she could pronounce a handful of Cherokee words, albeit with a British accent. That had been about the extent of their relationship.

Now she found herself expanding her view of Hoke Limberlost, wondering about his nights in this cabin . . . or what books he might read. She imagined him working for hours with his hands to create the esoteric adornments of his home. She pictured him performing life's prosaic duties: combing his hair, folding clothes, carrying in a load of firewood. Then, surprising herself, she found herself calculating the difference in their ages.

"You have a heart-felt admiration for animals, don't you, Hoke?" she said.

As he looked at her, a great calm came over his face. "Sometimes, Verdie, we plumb forget that all us two-leggeds fall under that same headin'. We're juss one more animal crawlin' 'round, scrapin' out a livin'." He gazed off into the dark of the forest. "Maybe lovin' animals is juss a way o' lovin' our own selfs . . . you know, lovin' the animal that's in us all. Could be that's the best part o' us, Verdie, and maybe it's the simplest things we do that are the best o' who we are. Somethin' as easy as slakin' a parched throat, lettin' some cool springwater be the best part o' you'ens' day. Drinkin' it slow and thoughtful like it had seeped outta the ground juss to become a part o' us."

He cocked his head toward the creek, and they both listened to the steady burble of the water. "Water is simple and precious, Verdie. Drinkin' it's pretty near to a prayer, if'n you'ens was to ask me."

His old mountain way of talking had always been a novelty to her, especially with her having defected over to a British tongue. Even the other waitresses saw Hoke's diehard dialect as a cachet of old Appalachian charm. His backwardness and unexpected viewpoints were emblematic of the solitude he chose by living up here on Frogtown Creek, making out like an Indian. Verdie realized that, for all these years, she had only been scratching the surface of Hoke Limberlost.

"You be careful, Hoke," she said and started her car. "Tallyho!" she sang and pushed on the accelerator to start the climb back up to the gap.

Before the curve in the road would separate them, she looked in her rearview mirror. Hoke was standing stock-still, looking up into the hemlocks, probably investigating some nocturnal sound warbling from the wild. *That Hoke*, she thought, *he was tuned into something, all right*.

Hoke listened until Verdie's car faded from earshot. Then his thoughts returned to the insult of all the damned signs cropping up around the county. It was a blight, pure and simple. What were people thinking these days to clutter up the world with such nonsense? Ernest Gooch Bridge. Ricky Lee Atwater Highway. Otis Smoot Rest Area. Algernon "Bud" Grizzle Parkway, and Byron T. Metcalfe Intersection. It made about as much sense as naming the state after a fellow named "George" who never set foot in the South, not to mention the North American continent.

Hoke's gaze came to rest on the crude, wooden pickerel frog. "What this county needs is a few more sculptures like this'n scattered 'round the countryside."

Walking with a purposeful stride, he made for the workbench attached to the side of his cabin and started rummaging through his box of tools, looking for a bastard mill file. It was time to sharpen his hatchet.

Chapter Eleven

**Etowah River
South Lumpkin County
Summer, 1959**

Stretched out under Castleberry Bridge, Ott had waited for Duffy for over three hours. But that's what Ott was good at—anything that did not require physical effort. For a twelve-year-old boy, he was unusually dedicated to inactivity. Napping might have been Ott's forte, and Duffy—because of his slave-driving father—provided many an opportunity for Ott to perfect this skill.

Ott had slipped a barbed hook through a slug he'd found in a white oak stump and then leaned his formidable weight into a bamboo fishing pole to impale the butt-end into the sand. Hanging onto the pole as it sank, he had imagined himself a pole vaulter, agile and strong, caught in a photograph as he stretched toes to the sky. When he gave out and slid the three inches down the pole to the ground, he just lay there and went to sleep with the line angled downstream in the wimpling current.

Duffy spent the morning at hard labor. Tump Hawkins, Duffy's daddy, was, among other things, a logger. If one of his skidder mules was unfit for work, Tump was not above strapping his son into the traces. Since six daughters and one son comprised the Hawkins progeny, Duffy was well accustomed to the feel of a leather harness wrapped about his wiry frame. It was brutal work. But the worst part of it was the disparagement Duffy sensed from the other draft animals better suited for the task.

The mules were named "Butch," "Cornpone," "Elvis," and "Pea-Brain." It was Pea-Brain who had come up lame, and this did nothing for Duffy's standing among the animals. Possibly the creatures resented him for the front-right position granted Duffy in the harness. That privilege was *never* afforded to Pea-Brain. It was a prestigious placement, or so thought the mules, but Tump had learned through his own experiences as a boy laborer under his father that working *behind* a mule carried risks of a permanent nature. Tump often wondered about the connection between a mule kick he had suffered as a boy and his inability to sire more than one son.

It was Saturday, and Duffy would have worked all day if his father had not been obliged to spend the afternoon at his moonshine still. For Duffy, this meant emancipation. He was never allowed near the still. Tump Hawkins knew how to draw a moral line, if not a merciful one. His only son would never be arrested for whiskey-making. His reasoning for this was sound. If Tump, himself, was thrown into jail, he would need Duffy to take over man-of-the-farm responsibilities.

When Duffy got to the river, he found Ott snoring face down on the beach and a fresh hole pried out of the sand with a drag mark angled downriver toward the water. He had to kick the sole of Ott's shoe three times before Ott woke up.

"Somewhere downstream there's bound to be a pitiful carp dragging 'round your cane pole. I bet if he had any say in it, he'd rather be in your fry pan than hung up forever on a snag till a big ol' snappin' turtle starts a-gnawin' on 'im."

Ott tried to drive the sleep from his face with an odd flex of the muscles around his mouth and nose. Duffy had always thought this performance looked like a dump truck losing its load.

"You finish relievin' the forest of all its trees?" Ott said, and frowned at Duffy's mud-caked bare feet and pitch-stained shirt and jeans. Ott flared his nostrils like a pig that had accidentally rooted into an onion patch. "Damn, Duff, you look 'bout covered up with sap and sweat. What'd you do, rassle the trees down?"

Duffy peered downstream, hoping to relieve that poor carp of its burden, but he knew there would be no time if they were to accomplish their mission today. He checked the angle of the sun.

"I reckon we better git started, Ott. I gotta hoe the corn b'fore dark." He glanced at the paper sack on the sand, but he didn't ask. Duffy never asked.

"You want a ham biscuit?" Ott said right on cue. "I brought you one."

Duffy shrugged. "I don' care," he said, but his eyes remained dedicated to the bag. All he'd had to eat that day was part of a cold tater his mama had divided seven ways for the children. "If you got it to spare," Duffy mumbled, "I could eat one."

Duffy was prepared to eat as they walked, but Ott had other plans. He pulled from his pocket a piece of torn linen sheet and wrapped it around one plump knee on the outside of his trouser leg. That, combined with a make-do walking cane of hickory and a melodramatic limp shamelessly performed by Ott, stopped the first truck to come across the bridge heading west. It was a well-drilling crew from Murrayville that was, miraculously, looking for Old Man Crawford's place.

After the two boys crawled into the truck's bed next to the drilling rig, Duffy just shook his head in wonderment. Ott winked and patted his knee and motioned through the window for the driver to lead on. Ott sat there smiling as if he was the Supreme High Buddha of the Himalayas being carted over the Borasu Pass by a team of loyal Sherpas.

At the turnoff to the Crawford farm, Ott thanked the driver as if he had just collected on a long-standing debt the man had owed him. Even as a young boy, Ott had a way with assuming command over other people. Somehow, before it was over, the driver was thanking Ott, talking like he would never have found the Crawford place had not they lucked into the two boys.

"How's that for some good timing," Ott said, smiling at the truck bumping down the Crawford's entrance road. " 'Bout the time that crew cranks up that dang drill, Old Man Crawford couldn't hear a herd o' cows dancin' on his barn roof. He sure ain't gonna hear us."

"You sure 'bout us doin' this?" Duffy said.

"Carlton said they was in there," Ott reported as if those words were gospel. "I reckon he oughta know."

Duffy looked down the Crawfords' entrance road where it cut a straight line through the weeds. It reminded him of the notch in the rear sight of a rifle.

"I ain't never really trusted Carlton all that much," Duffy mumbled.

Ott smiled his don't-you-worry-'cause-I-know-what-I'm-doing smile. "Carlton's scared of his old man and won't go near the shack. He's gonna pay us to give him some o' whatever we sneak outta there."

"Why is it you want these mag'zines so bad, Ott?" Duffy said. "I cain't see how it's worth gettin' shot at juss for pictures of some women with no clothes on. And these're women you don't even know."

Ott's face scrunched up like a twisted rag, and he laughed. "Well, Duff, why in hell would I wanna see the necked body o' anybody I *do* know?" He laughed again. "Name one female around here you'd wanna see necked! Miss Pirkle? That string bean librarian? Miss Olney? The mule-faced organ player at the Baptist church? Or what 'bout that lady at the hardware store who can lift a tractor tire?"

Duffy still looked doubtful. "But these women in the mag'zines are bound to live wherever they make these mag'zines. You'll never meet 'em."

Ott laughed with a short explosive breath. "I don' wanna marry 'em, Duff. I juss wanna look at 'em. And they don' sell mag'zines like these anywhere in Dahlonega." Ott cocked his head to one side and narrowed his eyes. "Are you tellin' me you wouldn' wanna see the bazoombas on some woman purty enough to be a movie star? Hell, Duff, a thirteen-year-ol' boy wantin' ta see a necked female is no different than a 'possum wantin' ta git in your garbage can. It's a natural urgin'."

Duffy frowned at Ott. "You're only twelve."

Ott leaned in. "That ain't the point, Duff. We gotta right to see what we're up against in this courtin' equation that'll be comin' up for us purty soon."

Duffy sighed. "I got six sisters, Ott. I don' care if I *never* see another female walkin' 'round in her underwear."

Ott smiled his big, toothy, man-what-planet-did-you-drop-off-of smile. "Who said anythin' 'bout 'underwear'? They're gonna be necked as jaybirds, son."

Again, Duffy looked off toward the Crawford Farm. He could hear the drilling team's truck jockeying for position to set the auger over a well site. Chewing on his lip, Duffy shook his head.

"Seems like a awful good chance to get ourselfs shot." He turned quickly back to Ott. "What if one o' us *does* git kilt out here? What's the other'n to do?"

Ott put on his mask of sincerity. The same mask that had convinced their fourth-grade teacher that Ott's father had accidentally used his completed homework as kindling to light the woodstove one morning.

"That's why we gotta make a pact, Duff," Ott said, his face turning as serious as Duffy had ever seen it.

Duffy frowned again. "What kind o' pact?"

Ott's face tried to harden, but his round features could never achieve any sharp angles. "If'n one o' us gets kilt, then neither o' us can talk 'bout what we done out here."

Duffy stared at Ott for about five heartbeats. "Well, that oughta be easy enough for one o' us."

Ott grinned. "I betcha a nickel 'gainst a necked gnat this here's gonna be the best danged adventure we ever had. I seen one o' these mag'zines once't b'fore at the barber shop. I tried to sneak it out, but Old Man Burnett saw it stuffed down my britches when I tried to walk out."

"Did he tell your daddy?" Duffy asked.

Ott chuckled. "Hell, no. He didn' want me tellin' anybody where I seen it. Prob'ly afraid his wife would find out. He even gave me my choice of the comic books he kept for his kid customers. It was a bald-faced bribe, and I took it."

"Well, which one did you choose?" Duffy wanted to know.

"Wonder Woman," Ott said with a smirk. "Only one I could find with some decent bazoombas."

Duffy forked his hands on his hips and let his head hang down as he stared at his dirty bare feet. When his head came up to Ott again, he wore a hopeful look.

"Well, ain't the comic book enough? Cain't you learn all you need from studyin' on Wonder Woman?"

Ott was shaking his head before Duffy finished his questions. "A drawin' ain't the same as a photograph, Duff. Besides, it ain't like they show Wonder Woman gittin' undressed at night to pull on her PJs." He reached out and patted Duffy's upper arm. "Come on, son, buck up and let's do this. I been plannin' it for weeks."

They both knew it was inevitable. Duffy always went along with Ott's wild ideas. Duffy was the ideal foot soldier, and Ott—at least in his own mind—was a born general.

To avoid the coon dogs that Old Man Crawford kept penned up next to his barn, the two boys made a wide arc down by Mooney Creek. When they climbed out of the woods near the corn patch, they could see the roof of the barn over a windrow of juniper trees.

"Daddy said this here lot he's got planted in corn don't even b'long to Old Man Crawford," Ott said in a matter-of-fact tone.

Duffy frowned at the crooked rows of green stalks. He'd never seen illegal corn before. Not while it was in the ground.

"How come your daddy don' arrest him then?"

Ott huffed a jaded breath at the ways of county politics. "Man that owns it lives in Flor'da. Daddy said he don' know 'bout it, and it ain't hurtin' nothin', and, b'sides that, any man who'd buy land here and live in Flor'da is juss beggin' for a squatter."

They heard the engine of the auger start up. It grumbled and then settled down to business, and the hum of the engine and the grind of the bit rose up over the farm like covering fire from an army of commando snipers positioned to hold down the enemy.

"We get caught, let me do the talkin'," Ott said a little louder. As if it would go any other way. Ott could talk his way out of a head cold.

"We get caught," Duffy argued, "you might get time for 'bout three words o' the Lord's Prayer before you get a load a buckshot pepperin' your butt. Anything you want me to say to your mama and daddy, you better tell me now."

Ott seemed not to be troubled by this possibility. "Might be *your* butt, Duff."

Duffy shook his head. "I'm faster'n you. If we have to run for it, I'll be out in front, and you'll be makin' some good cover for me."

Ott had no snappy comeback for that. There were some truths that were just immutable, and there was nothing anyone could do about them. He shrugged.

"Well, Duff, if I gotta die today, would you at least try an' hide one o' them mag'zines in my casket? There might be a waitin' room or somethin' like that at the pearly gates. It'll give me somethin' to do while I wait."

Duffy considered the request. "If there's a waitin' room, Ott, I reckon they'll have plenty o' mag'zines there."

Ott blew through fluttering lips, sounding like a horse. "Oh, yeah! Prob'ly *Weekly Reader* an' *Boy's Life* an *Guidepost* . . . stuff like that."

Duffy squinted. "So yo're purty sure yo're goin' to heaven?"

Ott waved a hand at the air. "Oh, hell yeah! All the Ambroses go to heaven! Look how many sher'ffs we've had in our family. B'sides, I give a quarter ever' Sunday when they pass that plate around in the church."

Duffy's brow tightened with lines. "That's half yore allowance, ain't it?"

Ott shrugged. "I sneak it off my daddy's dresser ever' Sunday mornin' while he's shavin' an' my mama is cookin' breakfast."

Duffy thought hard about that but decided to say nothing. He figured the actual waiting room Ott was headed for might have plenty of magazines with naked women in them.

They wove through the cornfield like Green Berets and approached the small outbuilding from the north. It was just like Carlton Crawford had described it to Ott when he was bragging about the magazine collection. The outside walls of the small shack were covered in black tar paper, and the one window was sealed up by a big diamond-shaped highway sign with a big, curved arrow warning about a sharp bend in a road that wasn't there. The door was secured by a thick silver lock that required a key for opening. The only thing Carlton hadn't mentioned was the fence.

All around the shed somebody had planted newly split locust posts into the earth, each one hardly thicker than a billiard cue. Stretched between these were horizontal lines of silver wire, spaced at six-inch intervals and rising six feet above the grass.

"That ain't much of a fence," Ott laughed. "Hell, anybody could slip through that." He paused just long enough to get the timing right. "'Xcept me, o' course. I'm too big." He eyed Duffy appraisingly. "Looks like you could scoot right under it though, Duff. Dang! Looks like you git to be the one to sneak in."

Duffy was accustomed to this—earning the leading role in some misadventure Ott had dreamed up. He stared at the flimsy barrier, wondering about the white porcelain knobs nailed to the posts.

"What's that buzzin' sound?" Duffy said.

Ott went still and listened, trying to hear something other than the well-drillers' rumble of machinery. He frowned, cocked his head, and began to nod.

"Sounds like a bumblebee tryin' to take off after eatin' too much breakfast. I think it's comin' from the grass somewhere out there. Juss crawl around it, Duff, and keep your mind on the mag'zines."

"What if they ain't in there?" Duffy said.

"They gotta be in there," Ott huffed. "Else why'd Old Man Crawford put up a dang fence 'round a dumb little shack like this?"

Duffy studied the window covered by the yellow highway sign, the place he had decided would be the point of entry. That curved arrow seemed like an omen. A bad one. Anyone who'd ever shot a bow knew that nothing good came from launching a curved arrow.

"Carlton said they're stacked up on the floor along one wall. They're s'posed to be under a old quilt in case Old Man Crawford's wife was ever to go in there."

"Well, how many should I bring out?" Duffy asked, like the model soldier that he was.

Ott pushed out his lower lip and thought about that. "Maybe 'bout a dozen or so. You can decide when you see how many there are. Don't take so many that anyone would notice some missin'. Here, don't forget this." Ott withdrew from his biscuit bag a short pry bar.

Just then the well-drillers' bit had apparently struck rock, and the engine revved into a labored whine. Ott raised his eyebrows at their good fortune.

"Geronimo!" Ott said, encouragingly.

Like a point man on re-con, Duffy advanced out of the corn, crawling on his belly like a snake that had sprouted elbows. Ott, acting on his natural instinct for being in charge of things, held his position in the shade of the waxy green leaves of corn as he kept an eye on the main yard. General Ott and Sergeant Duffy. That's about the way Ott would have doled out rank.

Duffy stopped at the fence and looked back at Ott. "That bumblebee ain't in the grass," he whispered. "Sounds like it's on the fence somewhere."

Ott smiled. "Juss stay low and don't bother it. It'll be fine." Before Duffy could protest, Ott held up three fingers and commenced a countdown by mouthing. *Three!* He lowered one finger. *Two!* He lowered another. *One!* Then Ott's thumb shot straight up from his fist. This he had seen in an old war movie, when a pilot signaled from his cockpit before takeoff. The mission was a go!

As soon as Duffy turned back to the fence, Ott backed deeper into the corn crop, stacked one hand on the other, and propped his chin on top. From his command center, Ott settled in to watch Duffy crawl under the lowest wire.

The jolt came almost immediately. Duffy's entire body stiffened and shuddered as if he had touched off a land mine. Ott almost panicked when he heard Duffy cry out with a little high-pitched chirp. He had never heard Duffy express surprise or pain or anything beyond a stoic acceptance of the ways of the world.

Duffy flattened himself to the earth like he was trying to put a bear hug on the planet. Backing out carefully, he got clear of the fence, turned, and crab-walked back into the corn.

"That fence has gotta 'lectric charge runnin' through it!" Duffy whispered. "Felt like I got struck by lightnin' right b'tween my shoulder blades! It crackled like when the barber turns on his trimmer."

Ott had had his suspicions about an electric fence, but there had been only one way to know for sure. That's why some people were generals and others were sergeants, after all.

"Well," Ott said, "I heard of 'em. Juss ain't never seen one. I guess them little white knobs is what keeps the current from groundin' out down the post."

Duffy's jaws were knotted like he was holding a double wad of bubblegum in both cheeks. Otherwise, his face was as sharp as an axe-blade.

"Didn' nothin' keep it from groundin' out down me. You got any ideas?"

Ott looked back through the corn rows toward the creek. This was the kind of moment, he knew, that could for all time secure his position as supreme commander of their two-man army. He was trying to think like a five-star general now.

"How 'bout that cane patch down at the shoal? We can cut you a long piece o' bamboo, and you can pole vault over the fence."

Duffy turned to frown at Ott.

"Well," Ott argued, "you're practic'lly Cher'kee, ain't you? Your grandma was."

"What the hell has that got a do with pole vaultin'?"

"Look at Jim Thorpe," Ott argued. "He could do all that stuff."

Duffy squinted one eye. "Jim Thorpe weren't no Cher'kee. He was a Sauk."

Ott wrinkled his nose and shook off that poor logic. "It ain't the tribe. It's bein' Injun."

"Well, what if I ain't never pole vaulted before?"

"We can practice down by the creek," Ott assured him, carefully choosing the plural pronoun to cinch their solidarity in this venture.

Chapter Twelve

Wally's Grocery
Dahlonega
Wednesday Night

Joey stopped at the grocery store across from the Sheriff's Department to pick up milk and, if he could find any, some fresh asparagus—though he didn't hold out much hope for that at Wally's.

The thing about asparagus was this: Joey had read in *Fight World* magazine that Joe Louis and Bruce Lee and Muhammad Ali all ate asparagus. A little research had led him to another article in *New Age Nutritional News* in which Joey had gleaned enough information to posit a theory about fighters' preferences for the vegetable. It had to do with pheromones.

He came up with this: The natural chemicals in asparagus must trigger the release of certain pheromones that telegraph to an opponent that he was in the presence of supreme confidence. This idea seemed to be reinforced by the neon yellow of his urine along with the strong scent that wafted up from the toilet after he peed. If the stinking "yellow" was purged from a person, he figured, what was left had to be courage.

Plus, the smell of bright urine was like a pair of old workout socks worn for months without washing. This olfactory association made sense to Joey. Smelly old socks were emblematic of hard, dedicated workouts. Furthermore, he had learned that asparagus becomes poisonous once it has grown beyond the young spear stage. Joey liked that, too. A softer version of eating nails.

Joey was not really a New Age kind of guy, but he chose not to pursue his asparagus research any further. He was afraid that someone's empirical findings might burst his bubble. If Ali and Louis and Lee used it, that was good enough for Joey. Besides, even if the science didn't pan out, he liked the idea of a culinary talisman. It's true, he would have preferred it to be carrots or celery or the like, but it made sense that it was something more esoteric, something a little more challenging to get down. He could live with asparagus.

In the store he found no fresh, so he settled for canned. Heading for the checkout line, he came upon a short round man in a pale blue seersucker coat. The little man was standing in the chips aisle, splay-legged, arms akimbo, staring up at the top shelf. When he heard Joey's cart, he turned hopefully and flashed a distracted smile.

"I don't s'pose you could reach something for me?" He wore black-rimmed glasses and a tan, straw fedora. The stumpy man was hard to look at—his eyebrows too dark, his complexion waxy—a peeled version of *Mr. Potato Head*. Actually, his skin did possess the milky-gray cast of a boiled potato, and his eyes jittered in quick horizontal shifts when he talked, as if he could not decide on which of Joey's eyes to direct his attention.

"What is it you need?"

The man pointed. "Those big bags of *Crispy Cheese Twirls* there. I need two."

Joey lifted down two bags, so light they might have contained scraps of Styrofoam. Behind their cellophane windows the pseudo-food looked like a colony of orange snails that had been deep-fried in psychedelic grease. He glanced at the man's cart. Frozen waffles, frozen pizza, potpies of every denomination, and half a dozen TV dinners.

"I know, I know," the man sighed, carefully opening one of the bags of *Cheese Twirls*. He shook his head at the contents of his cart. "I can't seem to keep a wife," he explained, and then he winked as if this was an inside joke that all men would innately understand. He held up one of the knobby orange snacks to the light. He was like a jeweler examining a precious stone. When he took it in his lips, his incisors kick-started into a mechanical grinding action. The man was like an electric pencil sharpener.

Orange dust rained down over his coat, tie, and shirt. He demolished two more *Twirls* and did not falter as he took in Joey's dozen cans of asparagus. He showed no reaction.

"Have one?" he said offering the bag.

Joey shook his head but was careful not to appear judgmental or dismissive of another man's preferences. *Maybe*, Joey thought, *this little man had found his pheromonal catalyst in Crispy Cheese Twirls. Who knew?*

"Anything else I can reach for you?" Joey offered.

"Oh, no. This will do fine. Thank you kindly."

Joey left him gnawing on another *Cheese Twirl*, oblivious to the orange fallout spreading now to his speckled shoes.

When Joey paid the cashier, he noticed the chubby *Cheese Twirl* man at the other checkout lane. His shirtfront and coat were spotless, but his dark brown shoes now looked made from the skin of a Gila monster. He had not started unloading his cart yet. It was filled with flat boxes and one unopened bag of *Crispy Cheese Twirls*. The side pocket of the man's seersucker coat now bulged, and Joey wondered if an empty *Cheese Twirls* bag was wadded there.

In the parking lot Joey loaded his groceries into the trunk of his car and looked up at the sky. Even with the floodlight shining from its tall pole and with light streaming out of the front windows of the store, he could see more stars up in the sky than he ever had seen in his urban youth. It would be easy to believe that all the celestial lights of the heavens sprang from these mountains and spread out to the rest of the world like fireflies released from a jar.

He pushed his empty cart to the narrow cart corral and heard above him a high-pitched *peehnk! peehnk!* A long-winged bird soared and looped around the light pole, where a horde of flying insects were lit up like confetti swirling in crosswinds. Joey watched as the bird swooped like a fighter pilot and scooped up its meal in its gaping mouth.

"Nighthawk," a voice called behind him. Joey turned to see the squat man pushing his cart into the lot. He, too, was looking up at the feeding frenzy playing out in the cone of light. "Easy pickin's. It's like an all-you-can-eat smorgasbord for that sucker."

"You know birds pretty well?" Joey asked.

The man wrinkled his face as if he had smelled something rank. "My third wife was a real bird freak. We had a streetlight outside our porch, and I used to have to listen to her talk about the damn nighthawk every summer evening. She'd spout off names of birds like she was personal friends with anything that wore feathers." He popped the trunk on a silver Cadillac. "That's about the only thing I got out of that marriage, and God knows I wish I could forget just half of those bird names she buried in my head." He let his breath out in a long sigh and loaded his bags into his car. The bulging coat pocket crinkled with the sound of crushed cellophane.

"I'd like to learn the birds around here," Joey said.

"You can have 'em," the man quipped. He slammed the trunk. "You live on low ground or high?"

"Top of a mountain," Joey replied.

"Well, count your blessings, son. I got a damned whippoorwill outside my window at night that I'd like to introduce to a load of number ten birdshot, but I can never find the damned thing when I go out looking for it."

"What's wrong with a whippoorwill?"

The man spat on the pavement and shook his head. "It's a damned stuck record is what it is. Seems it'll go on for thirty minutes without taking a damned breath. 'Whip-poor-*will!* Whip-poor-*will!* Whip-poor-*will!*' " he mimicked, making an attempt at an avian face as he did. Looking up at the nighthawk, he tightened his mouth into a scowl. "At least that sucker up there doesn't have to be yelling his name half the night."

On cue, the bird cried out again. *Peehnk! Peehnk!* Its thin call was eerie and attenuated, sounding like a long taut wire plucked high above the parking lot.

"I might have heard a whippoorwill down in the valley below my place," Joey said.

"Where is it you live?"

"North of town . . . up on Crow Mountain."

The man's head came around at that. "Oh, yeah?" With a knowing smile he hitched up his belt on his ample waist. "Well, I guess we all got our problems no matter where we live. You must be up somewhere near Limberlost's place."

"Hoke is my landlord."

"Mm-hmm," the man hummed with a little "aha" melody. There seemed to be more said in that one vague reply than in the whole of their earlier conversation. He reached into the inside pocket of his seersucker coat. "Listen, you ever wanna consider getting your own place, you come look me up. My number's right there." He handed Joey a business card and Joey read it: *Appalachian Dreams, Inc., L.T. Voss, Realtor.*

When Joey looked back at the stumpy realtor, L.T. Voss was waiting with his salesman's smile and an open hand. "L.T. Voss," Voss announced.

"Joey Gallatin," Joey replied. They shook hands.

"Nice meeting you, son," Voss said. His grip was both greasy and gritty, no doubt textured by the residue of the *Crispy Cheese Twirls* he had surreptitiously devoured inside the store. His smile revealed tiny orange specks scattered about his teeth like he'd been chewing on a desiccated carrot.

Joey laid a hand on the man's cart. "I'll take this for you."

"No, no," Voss protested with a modest chuckle. "That's mine. I'll get it. I believe in us all doing our part, don't you? You go on now and have a good evening."

The nighthawk *peehnk*ed again, and Voss looked up reflexively. He had started moving his cart but froze in mid-stride.

"Wait a damn minute!" Voss exclaimed. "Somebody's stole my damn sign off the light pole."

Joey looked up at the thirty-foot-tall pole. The only sign on it read: *No Signs!*

"Goddamnit! That was one of my laminated ones. Cost me four and a half bucks." Voss pouted as if he had been robbed of his constitutional rights. "This is a prime advertising spot," he began as if delivering an oration. He waved a hand in an arc to include Wally's. "People are happy when they come out of a grocery store. More inclined to tap into their dreams. Like buying a piece of property to call their own."

He broke out of his speechifying persona long enough to beam with a self-satisfied smile and give Joey a wink. "Got that out of a psychology study." He glared at the pole again, and the smile snapped off. "Damnit! Now I got to come back down here with my ladder." He pointed high up on the pole. "Next time I'll put it up about twelve feet so the grocer can't reach it to tear it down."

Voss channeled his frustration into shoving his empty cart out into the lot to roll on its own. It trundled across the asphalt until it settled on the line between two parking spaces. Reaching for his Caddy door he hesitated, peered over the roof of his car, and called out to Joey.

"You know what? That makes three or four signs that have come up missing in the county over the last week. I wonder if the rascal stealing those signs is the same one who took mine?" He studied the pole again in case he might have missed some bit of incriminating evidence. "Damn thieving vandal," he hissed. He shook his head and got into his car.

When Joey got behind the wheel of his car, he stuck Voss's business card in the glove compartment and clicked into his seatbelt. Before he had the key in the ignition, the Cadillac fired up and lurched in reverse, crashing into the cart Voss had used. The Caddy braked, but the empty buggy rocketed across four parking spaces and T-boned into the side panel of Wally's white delivery van. The sound of impact was like a piano falling from the roof of a building into a Dumpster.

After a moment of silence, the Caddy burned rubber and roared across the lot, swerving left into the street and without a signal turned again right away into the front parking lot of the Sheriff's Department.

A fat raindrop thumped the windshield, and Joey looked up to see the stars were gone. Within seconds, rain hammered the roof of his car. Joey checked his watch. The rain stopped fifty-eight seconds later, and Joey—thinking of his landlord—laughed quietly to himself and shook his head. Inside his mind wafted an image of ducks nestled inside a metallic box.

Steam lifted off the streets of Dahlonega like wisps of torn cotton. So pleasant was the freshly washed night that Joey took a turn around the town square, where the quaint tourist shops slumbered in dark repose. Rounding the old courthouse, he saw a crowd gathering at one corner. A sheriff's car was parked at an angle with its headlights illuminating yellow crime tape that had been stretched in the front of a small office set back behind an awning. The sign above the awning read: *Appalachian Dreams*. Joey slowed.

A deputy was examining the awning posts inside the cordoned area. Three wooden posts appeared to have been mutilated. Joey stopped and rolled down his window, thinking he might tell the deputy that L.T. Voss was at that moment down at the sheriff's office. But there was so much conversation going on, no one noticed him.

"How the hell'd somebody manage this without bein' seen, I'd like to know," said a man in coveralls. Next to him a lean deputy with a serious expression on his face stared at the post. Looking closer at the damage, Joey could see now that these were animal carvings imposed on the wood.

"That ain't no ladybug," one man said. "I know a damn tick when I see one."

"Well, this'n might be a m'skeeter," another said. "And that'n could be a bat."

"This one on the bottom might be a leech," a woman ventured. "And you know what? If you step back and look at each post from a distance, they're like totem poles."

Joey eased away from the square and headed home, all the while thinking about the blood-sucking theme of the carvings he had just seen.

Chapter Thirteen

Crawford Farm
South Lumpkin County
Summer, 1959

At the sandy beach on Mooney Creek, Duffy cut a stout pole and trimmed it with his pocketknife as Ott officiously instructed him in the fine art of carving. For the next hour, Ott, who seemed to know as much about pole vaulting as he knew about spotting electric fences, coached Duffy in the niceties of the high-flying track and field event, which made about as much sense as a blind man teaching lessons at a firing range.

In spite of Ott, Duffy's natural athleticism came through, and he began to show great potential. When Duffy seemed to be flying seven or eight feet off the ground, Ott declared the training complete, and the two boys returned to the cornfield with bamboo pole in tow. There they were heartened to hear the well-drillers still busy at their project.

While Ott assumed his position at his command post, Duffy crawled back to the fence and, using a sharp stick, dug a hole in the ground about the size of a cigar box. After tossing the pry bar over the fence wires, he knew the die was cast. Standing, he boldly paced off the necessary distance from the fence, turned, picked up the bamboo pole, rippled his fingers for a final grip on the shiny green of the cane, and leaned forward slightly, poised for action and deep in concentration. The whites of his eyes burned with an incandescent intensity, as if he were already taking a direct hit from the electric fence.

"Wait a minute!" Duffy said, relaxing from his stance and turning to Ott. "How'm I gonna get out o' there?"

Ott raised both hands, palms up, and shrugged. "Easy! I'll slide the pole in."

Duffy scowled. "But there ain't enough room in there to git to runnin' for the return jump."

Ott pursed his lips and thought about that. It was the one haunting shortcoming he had come to admit about himself. He sometimes didn't allow for what happens down the road. In the now, he was pretty agile in the head; but it was that last phase of a problem that sometimes gave him fits. It's why he didn't play checkers.

"Tell you what," Ott said. "You can climb up on the roof and ride over the fence on the pole that way. You juss gotta 'member to carry the pole back over with you. We might wanna do this again some time, an' we don' wanna leave no clues." Ott shrugged. "Else Old Man Crawford might raise his fence up another six feet to ward off renegade pole vaulters." Ott blew air in an exasperated laugh. "Then we'd have to get Jim Thorpe his-self."

Duffy gave Ott his doubtful look. "Jim Thorpe is dead, Ott."

Ott shrugged that off. "Well . . . whoever. Maybe we could git that feller on the *Wheaties* box."

Duffy took his stance again and focused on the fence. Suddenly he took off sprinting down the corn row and then broke out onto open ground. In the corn he had held the bamboo pole at an upward angle, but now he leveled it before him like a medieval jouster's lance. Planting the end of the pole in the dug hole, he sailed up and over the fence, clearing the top wire with room to spare. From his command post, Ott bared his teeth and pumped a fist in the air.

"Jim-God-Aw-Mighty-Thorpe!" he whispered and realized in the excitement of the moment he had vicariously jerked one leg upward just as Duffy had left the ground. "Ow!" Something pulled in Ott's leg and a jolt of pain shot from his thigh to his groin.

For several minutes Duffy used the pry bar at the edge of the road sign covering the window before finally gaining ingress into the shack. Once he had slithered inside, Ott, who had managed to push his pain aside for the sake of the mission, felt chill bumps rise on his arms and back—not so much at the thrill of success as the sudden vulnerability of being out there in the cornfield all by himself. If Old Man Crawford showed up now, Duffy would be well hidden in the most unlikely place of all, while Ott would be on his own lying in the corn rows, crippled, and unable to run.

Ott was already thinking up a story about tubing down the creek and the tube getting punctured on a sharp rock. He could claim the burst tube launched him like a sputtering balloon and delivered him here to the Crawford Farm a half mile from the creek. Looking down at his dry clothes, Ott immediately saw the flaw in this storyline. Finally, he decided that a half-mile-long streak through the sky ought to provide plenty of drying time. He could claim a hawk carried off the inner tube, mistaking it for a well-fed rat snake.

The well-drillers' engine continued to grind, and nothing changed about the farm. It seemed like an hour had passed, but it had probably been less than ten minutes when Duffy crawled out the opening in the window. Ott limped to the fence and slid the pole under the wires.

"Where're the dang mag'zines?" Ott said.

"There ain't no magazines in there. Lots o' whiskey bottles though. Prob'ly moonshine. It's darker'n a root cellar in there. How come you're limpin'?"

"Got injured durin' the foray," Ott replied vaguely. "Muscle pull."

"Hang on a minute. I think I saw a bottle o' horse liniment in there." Before Ott could protest, Duffy climbed back through the window and quickly returned, his window-snaking proficiency improving with each pass-through. After pulling out a small green glass bottle from his jeans pocket, he carefully pushed the bottle through a gap in the wire. "See if that'll help."

After bending the sign back in place to close up the gap in the window, Duffy used the pole to scale the side of the building. On the roof, he studied the section of the pole available to him at that height. It was thinner than he would have liked, but it was all he had. There was nothing for it but to jump, so he pushed off from the edge of the roof thinking light thoughts.

The pole bent so that he had to pick up his feet to clear the wire. When the bamboo flexed back straight, it shot him twenty-five feet past the fence, and when he hit the ground running, he realized the bamboo was still clutched in one hand. He crashed through the corn and reached the forest before Ott, who was behind him hopping on one leg.

Regrouping in the woods, Duffy dropped the pole and, true friend that he was, took Ott on his back. After traveling only a few yards toward the creek, Ott started talking into Duffy's ear.

"You know what, Duff? They oughta add this to the Olympic decathlon right after the pole vault. Carrying somebody piggyback oughta be in the Olympics, don't you think? 'Course they'd have to change the name 'decathlon' to eleventhlon.'"

Duffy frowned. "Well, wouldn't they have to find people to carry who were all the same exact weight to make it fair?"

Ott thought about that. "They could juss use a backpack full of dumbbells to make the weight the same."

Duffy nodded. When he thought about it, using dumbbells to substitute for Ott would be the perfect choice of material.

"So . . . 'xactly . . . what happened . . . to you?" Duffy said between his huffing and puffing.

"Think I pulled my dang growin' muscle." Ott struggled to hang on as they neared the creek. "It's that muscle up near my privates."

"Well, how'd you pull that one?!" Duffy said a little testily, unable to hide his resentment at piggybacking one hundred eighty pounds through the woods for a half mile. He stopped at the beach and eased Ott to the sand.

Ott's face colored. "Look, Duff, bein' in charge of a military maneuver ain't all as easy as you might think." He channeled his anger into the stubborn bottle top he couldn't budge. He scowled at the label as he read, " '*Harry's Happy Horsey Rub—premium liniment for the common equine charlie-horse.*' " Ott snorted. "Lotta good it does in a bottle ya cain't open! This dang top is rusted. How the hell does somethin' rust to glass?"

Duffy took the bottle and opened it on the first try. "You prob'ly loosened it up for me," Duffy said graciously and handed it back.

Ott raised the bottle to his nose. "Peeee-*yuuuu*!" he whined and quickly jerked the bottle out to arm's length, which caused some of the contents to spill on his hand.

Duffy took a step back. He recognized the smell. Though he himself frowned on using such tricks with wild animals, his daddy had often squirted concentrated deer urine around a small glade where he planned to hunt. The wretched scent was good for luring in bucks, who took offense at interloper males horning in on their territory. Because Duffy was still a little aggravated about having to carry Ott a half mile, he decided to keep a straight face.

"That's some powerful smellin' liniment. I hear *Harry's Happy Horsey Rub* works purty good for a muscle strain."

Ott's face was creased with so many wrinkles, he looked like an albino prune. "It stinks to high heaven! Reminds me of the locker room at the school gym when they found that dead 'possum in the heat vent."

"Well," Duffy said offhandedly, "you know what they say 'bout medicine, Ott. Worst it smells . . . better it works."

Ott balked. "Are you ser'ous?"

Duffy shrugged. "If'n the pull't muscle was mine, I'd prob'ly want some strong liniment on it."

Ott frowned at the creek and thought about it. Duffy's face remained as sober as a preacher's. Everything he had told Ott was true. The only part he had omitted was how Old Man Crawford had chosen a *Harry's Happy Horsey Rub* bottle to store a rank solution of concentrated buck piss.

Ott scowled at the bottle. "Aw, what the hell!" he huffed and poured a small pool of the contents into one hand. Making a disgusted face, he reached down into his trousers and applied the concoction high up on his inner thigh. His plump face took on a fleshy pout. "I cain't b'lieve all we gone through only to end up without even a single mag'zine."

"We got a ways to go, Ott," Duffy reminded. "We better git started."

With Ott limping they slowly backtracked along the creek and surfaced on the dirt road about a mile from the Crawford Farm's entrance. Breathing hard, Ott sat down, pulled out the bottle from his pocket, and studied it again.

"This stuff ain't helpin' a dang bit!" he carped. "All it does is stink!" He gave Duffy his most exasperated frown. "We'll never hitch a ride back. No one would pick up anybody smellin' this bad."

I did, thought Duffy.

"Duff, you might need to go ahead and git one o' your mules and bring it back for me. There ain't no way I can make the walk back."

Duffy toed the dry dust in the road. "I ain't so sure Daddy will let me. He's usin' the mules to haul corn out to his still today."

Ott squinted down the road and pulled in his lips, thinking like a general again. "Aw right, then go git Tinkerboy and bring *him*."

"Tinkerboy!" Duffy huffed. "You think your goat can carry that kind o' weight?"

"I used to ride 'im!" Ott argued.

"Maybe when you was 'bout six," Duffy replied and studied Ott's face for any sign of sanity. "Yore daddy ain't gonna like ownin' a pet goat with a broke back."

"Juss git 'im for me, Duff."

Duffy propped his hands on his hips, checked the position of the sun, and then gazed down the road. "I still gotta lotta chores to git to. How 'bout I send down your little sister with Tinkerboy?"

Grudgingly, Ott nodded. The sound of a snapping twig made a subtle report from the shadows deep in the woods. Duffy peered into the forest, but Ott was too busy feeling miserable to hear it. Duffy saw a movement out there. Two or three, in fact. Next came a wheezing snort that nailed the identity of the stalkers. It was probably a buck in the company of its harem.

"Maybe those well-drillers will pick you up again, Ott. They'll likely smell purty ripe, too, after working all day. They'd prob'ly let you ride in back."

Ott gave Duffy his what-kind-of-snake-poison-have-you-been-drinking smile. "Yeah, or maybe President Dwight D. Eisenhower, his-self, will land in a helicopter right here on the road and gimme a lift into town." He hissed through his teeth and shook his head. "*Dang*, this stuff stinks! Juss go git Tinkerboy, will ya?"

Duffy started down the dirt road in a steady, loping gait, following the serpentine lane as it wound through the picturesque farmlands of the foothills. The powdery, red dust was soft as self-rising flour on his bare feet, and, without Ott's prodigious weight on his back, he felt light as a freshly baked loaf of bread. He couldn't suppress a little smile at the way things had gone. True, they'd confiscated no magazines, but Duffy didn't care any more about pictures of women's anatomy than he did about county politics. Neither one seemed a practical part of his life, being isolated at the Hawkins's remote homestead as he was.

But he *had* learned something about pole vaulting today. He'd always excelled in sports, and now here was one more athletic skill to add a feather to his cap, so to speak. And best of all, perhaps, he was getting Ott's goat for once.

When he reached Ott's house, the little sister, Rosybelle, was seated in the grass in the front yard playing with a set of miniature, plastic dinosaurs. She had corralled them all in a ring of sticks she had stacked in a zigzag pattern like a split rail fence. Outside the fence sat a ragdoll, who must have represented some kind of modified Little Bo Peep with a fondness for giant reptiles.

"Well, hey there, Duffy!" the girl called out, waving as if Duffy had just sailed in from the jungles of the Amazon after a four-year absence. "Ott's not home. He's doin' some kinda volunteer work for the church."

Duffy walked his easy stride into the yard and sat down next to her. "Rosy, can you ride, Tinkerboy?"

She pursed her lips and frowned as she thought. "I rode 'im once't," she recalled, "the time I tried to run away from home."

"How long ago was that?"

She scrunched up her face again and did the math. " 'Bout four years ago. I was only three."

"Why were you runnin' away?"

She cocked her head to one side and gave him her well-ain't-you-the-stupidest-thing-in-Lumpkin-County smile. "Ott," she answered simply.

Duffy looked at Ott's two-story house, a big ornately crafted abode that was ten times the size of the Hawkins's rickety cabin. "Are yore mama and daddy home?"

Rosybelle shook her head. "Mama's gone to play bridge at Beulah Babcock's house, and Daddy is at a sheriff's convention in Macon."

Duffy looked off to the west, in the general direction of the Crawford Farm. He made a knowing smile and thought, *so that's why Ott chose this day*.

"So, who's stayin' with you?" Duffy asked the little girl.

Rosy exhumed her mocking smile and canted her head to one side. "I'm seven, Duffy. I can take care o' myself." Her smile turned coy. "I'll be old enough to date boys purty soon. You might wanna remember that."

Ever courteous, Duffy smiled and nodded. "Rosy, do you reckon you could take Tinkerboy out to the Crawford Farm Road to git Ott. He's stranded out there 'bout a mile this side o' the Crawford place."

"Stranded! Is he on a island? Did he get shanghaied by pirates out there or something?"

"Not 'xactly," Duffy said, "he's juss havin' a hard time walkin'. But it might be a purty grand adventure for you *and* Tinkerboy."

"How's that?" she asked, clearly skeptical.

"Well, two reasons," Duffy said, squinting down the road again. "The first part will be a lot like runnin' away again."

She did not appear convinced. "What about the second part?"

"Well," Duffy said, nodding at a good question, "you'll be like a hero for bringin' yore brother home from bein' stranded. You might even git wrote up in the *Nugget*. They're always lookin' for a good story 'bout a local hero."

Rosy cocked her head again and put on a smug look. "I'd be a *heroine*."

This was the one way that Rosybelle reminded Duffy of Ott. She was always correcting people, showing what she knew that others didn't. But he knew just what to do to bring her back down to earth. She loved a good joke. Duffy was not particularly noted for his humor, but having the advantage of being six years older than Rosybelle, he came up with what he thought was a good one.

"Hey, after you rescue Ott, maybe yore mama and daddy would let you live in the attic. That'll make the newspaper for sure. Maybe even go statewide."

"How come?" she asked, her brow wrinkling with the riddle.

"It'd be big news if people found out that inside the Lum'kin Coun'y sheriff's house there's a heroine attic."

"Hah!" she laughed. "That's a good 'un, Duffy! And Daddy would never get re-elected! Then he wouldn' be gone all the time sheriffin', and he could take me to Paris, France like he's always promisin' he will."

It was all just a lot of nonsense, they knew, but the lighthearted feeling seemed to bring her around. She stood up, cradled the ragdoll in one arm, and brushed off the seat of her jeans with her free hand.

"I'll go get Tinkerboy ready. We might can get back before Mama gets home."

When she started off for the goat pen behind the house, Duffy was struck by a pang of conscience. "Say, Rosy? You might wanna take along a coupla clothes pins off yore dryin' line."

Rosybelle stopped and leveled her hand above her eyes like a visor to shade out the sun. "What for?"

"For yore nose," he called out. "Ott ain't smellin' his best t'day."

She kept staring at Duffy, waiting. "What's the second clothes pin for?"

Duffy shrugged, lifted his arms from his sides a few inches, and let them fall back with a soft slap against his jeans. "The goat," he said. "I reckon even goats got their standards." Before she turned away, he added, "May as well take three. I reckon Ott oughta have one, too."

* * * * *

When the *Nugget* came out a few days later, the article about Ott ran a full column down the front page. It was Saturday morning when Duffy happened to see it, only because his father had brought home a stack of discarded newspapers from the Dumpster behind *The Sizzling Skillet*, where he sometimes foraged for kindling paper for starting fires in the wood stove. Duffy was lighting the stove in the kitchen when the article's title jumped out to him like a kamikaze grasshopper hitting him right between the eyes.

Sheriff's Son Mauled by Herd of Rogue Bucks, it read. The piece went on to explain how the boy's younger sister rescued him by hauling the injured boy home on a makeshift travois she had assembled by using two bamboo poles, a rope of braided goat hair, and the fabric off a junked sofa she'd found near Mooney Creek. The pulling power was supplied by the family goat. The article did not mention whether the boy would survive his wounds, but it announced to readers that the goat's recovery was doubtful after such an epic haul.

Duffy ran three miles to the pay phone at Old Man Shope's Store, and, using one of two dimes he had in his pocket, he called the hospital on Crown Mountain. Ott was not listed as a patient there. Using his last dime, he called the sheriff's home. Ott picked up.

"How bad hurt are you?" Duffy asked tentatively.

Ott sighed. "Well, my growin' muscle must be better. I can lift my leg enough to kick my sister now." Ott's voice sounded more nasal than usual. He twanged like one of the old-time country singers. Jimmie Rogers or Conway Twitty.

"No," Duffy said with some urgency, "I mean from gettin' antlered by them bucks."

Ott took in a large dose of air and then exhaled heavily. "I didn' get antlered a-tall, Duff. And it weren't bucks. It was a heap o' female doe deers, and it was more like sexual assault. Man! Who'd'a thought a bunch o' doe deers would'a gone ape on me like that? It was damned embarrassin', I can tell you that. I juss didn't wanna see anythin' like that in the newspaper, so I paid Rosybelle a dollar to go along with me on the big whopper I fed to the newspaper lady."

"Is it true 'bout yore goat?"

"Which part?" Ott asked.

"Did it die?"

Moon of the White Tears

"Yeah," Ott said with hardly a trace of remorse. "Tinkerboy's done passed over to t'other side. Prob'ly in hero-heaven if they got one o' them for goats."

"Was it juss too much weight for 'im?" Duffy asked in a tender timbre.

"Nah," Ott pronounced, "that goat was strong as hell. He lost his clothes pin 'bout a half mile shy o' our house. He lasted 'bout twen'y more steps, coughed a coupla times, and keeled over dead."

"But yo're okay, right?" Duffy said.

Ott chuckled. "Sittin' here watchin' *Captain Midnight* on the TV an' eatin' a bowl o' *Kix* with some ice cream on top!"

"How come yore voice sounds so different, Ott?"

"Oh . . . yeah . . . I'm still wearin' my clothes pin. It's gonna take a while for that stink to wear off. My daddy won't let me come outta my room, but I didn' plan on goin' nowhere anyway, what with all the deer hangin' 'round outside my window. That was a good idea 'bout the clothes pins, Duff."

"Sorry, it didn't work out for yore goat," Duffy said quietly.

"Yeah," Ott agreed, "I tried to snatch Rosy's pin off her nose so I could give it to Tinkerboy, but I was no match for Rosy that day, not with my pulled muscle and all." He paused a beat. "Hey, I betcha those mag'zines were in Old Man Crawford's barn the whole time. When I git to feelin' better, let's go back an'—"

"Ott," Duffy interrupted, "those deer over at Mooney Creek . . . they ain't likely to forget you."

Ott was quiet for a time. Over the phone Duffy could hear Captain Midnight talking to his home audience about acquiring an official decoder ring.

"Good point, Duff. Maybe I can git that dollar back from Rosy and pay Carlton to steal a few o' the best issues for me. I can loan 'em ta you after I look at 'em. Then I can prob'ly sell one to Buster Gooch for two dollars. That way I'll come out ahead in this adventure, anyway you look at it."

" 'Xcept yo're goatless now," Duffy reminded.

"Yeah," Ott said with a sigh. " 'Xcept for that."

Chapter Fourteen

Concord, Massachusetts
1991

Maria Gunlock Schmidt's husband, Darren, once told her that she carried her childhood memories like a cop carried a spare gun strapped to his ankle. She wasn't sure what that meant, but it did cause her to examine her own history with an analytical eye. At nine years old, Monday through Saturday, she had cleaned houses alongside her mother. At that young age she had had no sense of her worth in the task—not in dollar figures at least. By her calculations whatever work she contributed after school simply got her mother home earlier so she could prepare a meal that Maria and her two sisters and their mother could partake together.

The stepfather was gone. He had been a life insurance salesman. Then it was kitchen tiles. And finally vacuum cleaners, which was apropos for the way he had eventually disappeared and left them in a vacuum. He had run off twice before, each time gone for a month. That was how long it took him to go through the cleaning money he had stolen from her mother.

This time, when after two months they had heard nothing, no one had to put it into words. His absence from their lives just settled over them like a changing season. In spite of being robbed again, Maria's mother was not angry this time. She seemed relieved. Maria's perspective was one of simplification. She could stop wondering exactly what this man *might* do to pull them out of the poverty that had sunk its teeth into her family like a pit bull.

Because she had an affinity for the piano, when Maria was fourteen years old, she added teaching music lessons to her schedule, taking students half her age for one-half-hour lessons in upper-class homes on the wealthy side of town. For this enterprise she had invested in a red print dress and shiny black shoes. The purchase had paid off. As a music teacher she pulled in six times the hourly pay that her mother cleared.

At fifteen she began waiting on tables at the *Skyrocket Café* and folding laundry at *Bert's Cleaners*. This on top of her house cleaning and music lessons. She didn't just advance in life. She expanded, accruing occupations like a bus picking up commuters. By sixteen, she took on three more jobs: manuscript editing, wicker repair, and dog training.

When she was twenty-four, she married. It was no stretch of her capabilities when she agreed to support her new husband, an aspiring writer, while she put herself through law school. His name was Darren Schmidt, but he was considering several pen names for the day when his literary wave might break. "Dylan Royale" was his favorite choice for a *nom de plume*, the first part to honor Dylan Thomas and the second to symbolize the money he hoped to amass from royalties.

As an African American, Darren leaned toward historical novels of black statesmen or celebrities and literary fiction focusing on racism and civil rights. But he was not above black mystery and black sci-fi. Though Maria had never actually seen the rejection letters, Darren spoke regularly and optimistically about the three "almosts" that had been returned with glowing reports on his Eugene "the Black Diamond" Washington manuscript. "The Black Diamond" was the first fictional, Negro detective ever introduced into the setting of New England. Darren claimed that the publishers had turned down his proposal only because his protagonist owned a pure white German shepherd, which suggested a racial metaphor that seemed a slap in the face to white America. They had told Darren, if he would change the dog's coat to any other color, the project was on. But Darren would not budge. It was the principle of the thing.

She had never known anyone like Darren. Though a little pudgy and slow to react to the exigencies of their too-small apartment, he had the go-getter attitude of a young revolutionary. He even grew a Che Guevara mustache.

Darren had a way of talking that spiraled effortlessly into exotic realms and made you forget the subject that had spawned the original conversation. He was full of colorful descriptions and character analyses. Very poetic, or so said Darren's mother. His thoughts shot off at tangential angles that always entertained. With his voice so rich and settling, Maria had often thought him well suited for radio, but he would have none of that. He was married to the written word first. And to Maria, second.

Darren was not the man of her dreams, but Maria had taken a practical view on matrimony. As a writer, Darren would be a stay-at-home husband, where he could oversee any future children they might conceive. That would give her the needed long hours at a law firm once she hired on as an attorney. Plus, Darren would be able to help with the papers she would need to write both as a law student and then as a firm associate.

There was, however, one romantic chink in her armor, because there *was* a man of her dreams. One man in particular. She had seen him only once. As a teenager, while polishing silverware in one of the client's houses on her nightly cleaning circuit, she turned on the television *Movie of the Week*. Whether it was because she had seldom seen a television program or because she had never known the familial strength of a sheltering father or brother, she fell in love in that kitchen with the *Movie of the Week* police detective who was bucking the Chicago mob. It was more than cops and robbers. It was personal. The protagonist had made a solemn vow to bust the drug ring responsible for his sister's death. Maria related to this kind of single-minded determination. She also fell in love on the spot. Nick DePuma, private eye. She would never forget that name.

The homeowner returned before the credits scrolled by, so Maria did not learn the name of the star who played the lead. Whenever she thought about him, she pictured him prowling the streets of Chicago with a confident feline walk that needed no embellishment. Just like his talk. A relaxed purr, unhurried and certain of its delivery. Nick DePuma was the cat's pajamas.

It was not until college that she had found out the name of her Hollywood soul mate. Charles Bronson. She'd walked into a dorm room, where two girls were watching a rerun of *The Magnificent Seven*.

"Isn't he a dreamboat?" one of the girls gushed, as Steve McQueen dismounted from his horse by throwing a leg over the pommel and easing to the ground as nimble as a squirrel. On the wall hung a poster of McQueen with one foot inside a racecar, one arm resting on the roll bar, his tricky little smile angled to one side.

But Maria's eyes remained dedicated to Bronson. Casually, she asked about *his* name, and when it was given, she permanently etched it into her memory in the loving romantic rococo font of a Hallmark card. As far as she was concerned, Maria was watching *The Magnificent One and His Six Side-kicks*.

Darren was no Charles Bronson, but—to be fair—Maria had never known such complete attention from anyone. In Darren's presence, a stage light always shone down on her. Always on the lookout for a good storyline, he was rapt over the details of her life, past and present. Sometimes he jotted down notes during their conversations. His devotion to the historical minutiae of her every day was a force enveloping her, feeding her self-esteem. That's what she told her mother and sisters whenever they visited and were quick to point out that he was not putting food on the table.

On a Tuesday night, in that last month of marriage to Darren, with her last class in criminal law over, Maria reported to Professor Singh's office to type the latest dictation for the book he was working on—*Trial and Error*. The manuscript had begun as a dry rehash of jurisprudence gone awry in a 1967 murder case, but of late it had somehow morphed into a suspenseful novel.

"And not a bad one at dhat," as the professor liked to say in the thick accent of his New Delhi family. Professor Singh was convinced there was room for one more John Grisham or Scott Turow in the bookstores.

Ensconced behind the typewriter, Maria clipped on the earphones that fed her the professor's Indian voice from the tape recorder. As was her habit she jumped in at full tilt, punching the start button and tapping the keys with a virtuosity borrowed from her skills on the piano. She had trained herself to type with a cold ear to the content. To her, a sentence was little more than a contribution to word count, not a pivot on which a story turned. But this night proved different.

Singh had his female character—Tasha Torrence—stooping behind a desk-sized copy machine to pick up her dropped pencil. That was when she overheard two of the law associates conspiring against a client of the firm in order to throw the case against a fellow attorney.

Maria's typing fingers froze at the phrase that came rattling into her ear, as one of the conniving lawyers whispered to the other.

"*. . . Suck a plywood ham persimmon tree.*"

She clicked off the tape, rewound it, and listened again.

"*. . . Suck a plywood ham persimmon tree.*"

Then again, this time holding her breath.

"*. . . Suck a plywood ham persimmon tree.*"

Exasperated, she just frowned at the tape player as if it were withholding evidence. "What the hell is a 'plywood ham persimmon tree'?" she mumbled. "And who would want to suck on it?"

On the fifth replay she finally deciphered the professor's words: "Such a ploy would hamper symmetry." Comparing the two translations syllable by syllable, she burst out laughing and did not stop until the door to the professor's study flew open, and the man, himself, filled its frame with his bearded face set in haughty rebuke.

"What is it?!" he demanded.

Maria tempered her smile to a tight-lipped look of contrition and decided it was best not to broach the New Delhi man's personal struggle with the English language. His secretary had warned her on the day she had answered the ad: Singh was mortified at his speech problem and made every effort to hide it. And, actually, he did rather well until he got all heated up in the thick of the novel's plot.

"Is dar somet'ing wrung wit' da stordy?"

"No, sir," Maria assured him as she looked straight at the paper on the typewriter. "The story's fine."

He glared at her, certain he had somehow made a literary fool of himself. When he marched across the room to her desk, she plucked the earphones from her head and presented as apologetic a countenance as she could manage. He stopped inches from her desk, planted his feet firmly on the carpet and crossed his arms over his sunken chest.

"I em not leafing unless you tell me! I wunt to find out now! I dun't want to hear dis from da pub'isher! Just say it, Madria! I wunt to know!"

"Professor Singh, it's really nothing."

His dark skin grew darker still, and his fierce eyes burned like molten white metal. She had the sudden fear that, by some mystical Indian witchery, he had entered her mind and was reading her thoughts. "I dun't belief you. Now just say it. What's wrung wit' it? W'ere are you in da text?"

Thankful for a question she could answer, she tried to pull together the context of the passage. "Tasha is kneeling in the Xerox room and overhears a conversation. The two partners are talking about sabotaging Ryan's case. But really, sir, I wasn't—"

He waggled his fingers for her to hand over the earphones. "Ledt me hear."

He strapped the headset on, bent his head, crossed his arms again, and cupped one hand under his chin. Turning on the machine, he closed his eyes and pulled at the gray hairs of his carefully groomed beard.

Suddenly, his eyes flew open, and he stopped the machine. He ran it back and listened again. After two more runs, he stared at her so long she felt she was supposed to say something. Wisely, she did not.

"I can see dis passage needs work. It's not convincing, is it? She wouldn't be hiding like dis behind da copier. Is dat it?"

Maria shrugged. "Maybe she needs a better reason to be there. On that specific floor of the building, I mean. She probably has a copier on *her* floor, doesn't she?"

He cut his eyes back to the tape. "Yes, I belief you are d'right." He began nodding. "Dat's good. Maybe she is . . . what ees da word . . . *temping* for anudder lawyer."

Maria smiled encouragingly. He rewound the tape again.

"I need to work on dis more before you type it. Why dun't you take da eef-ning off. Dis will not affect your pay. Your input has been well worth it. T'ank you, Madria."

Which was why at six o'clock on a Tuesday she let herself into the apartment three hours earlier than expected with a sack of Chinese take-out under her arm. Despite the MSG-driven aromas wafting up to her face, she immediately smelled something wrong in the apartment—a scent as sweet and aromatic as an azalea blossom.

The CD player oozed some kind of celestial New Age music that rambled without structure through the rooms. Darren's notebook lay open on the sofa and an unfamiliar backpack sat on the floor.

"Darren?" she called out from the kitchen.

She set the surprise dinner on the counter and walked into the hallway, where she heard the shower running. She cracked the door to let him know that she was home but saw the designer jeans crumpled on the floor next to a pair of suede boots. A raspberry blouse and lace bra hung on the towel rack. Through the pebbled glass she saw a single figure in the stall, but it was wider than Darren and had a mass of long blonde hair on one side.

She waited in the living room, which turned out to be a mistake. She heard everything. If the shower had been a cleanup after the heat of passion, the echoing sounds that followed after the water shut off spoke of a powerful second wind on the part of both parties. She could hear their wet flesh slapping like seals. The girl liked to talk. And the crude phrases she pulled out of Darren had a crippling effect on Maria's self-confidence. It made her feel she knew nothing about pleasing her husband.

So surreal was it all that she conceived a hope that—maybe—it wasn't Darren in there at all. It could be two lovers who had wandered into the wrong apartment. She had almost convinced herself of this, until she heard the paralyzing line that would revisit her every night for years as she lay in bed waiting for sleep. The words reverberated out of the tiled bathroom as if announced over a PA system.

"Wow! If Maria could do that, I might have finished this book six months ago."

Chapter Fifteen

**Waters Creek
Wildlife Management Area
Thursday late afternoon**

"I didn' know what else to do but call you 'bout it, Duff. I'm not gonna bother my people 'bout it till I find out what you wanna do."

Vernon Stubbs led the way, following a little feeder creek that snaked its way through a stand of old growth hemlocks. Duffy had hunted here once about ten years ago and thought he might recognize the very tree where he had waited through the chill of dawn. He remembered the nine-point buck, walking right down the creek like it knew not to leave tracks. What he couldn't remember was why he hadn't shot it.

When the valley opened up into a wetland, he guessed he had bypassed the tree. Here there were only warty maples and sweetgums and hickories and spotty islands of ferns. When the ground softened underfoot, Vernon stopped and pointed deeper into the swamp.

"There they are," Vernon said. "One . . . two . . . three." His arm swiveled as he counted. "This's 'bout as far as we might wanna go. There's copperheads in them ferns."

Duffy appraised the altered signs on their galvanized posts scattered about the swamp. The signs had been shaped into rough cubes with a horizontal gap left in front like wilderness mailboxes awaiting a special delivery of parcels.

"All I can figure," Vernon said, "is they're for duck nestin'. Only . . . our department didn' put 'em up. What d'you think, Duff?"

Hawkins stood with his hands splayed on his hips just above his holster belt. "I didn' even know this swamp was back here."

"Me neither!" Vernon laughed. "And I'm s'posed to know . . . bein' head ranger and all."

Hawkins checked the ground, looking for telltale signs of ingress and egress. The ferns were undisturbed and the muddy areas smooth, except for a set of dog prints. He thought about yesterday morning's rain. Tuesday night would have been a good time to get in and out of here without leaving tracks.

"How'd you find 'em, Vern? I mean, how'd you know to look out here?"

Vernon pointed to the dog tracks. "Old Duster . . . he come out this way a-howlin' t'other mornin. I could hear 'im from the game check station, but I reckon he couldn' hear me a-yellin', so I come out as far as I could in my truck with the window down a-listenin'. Then I walked out here, and old Duster he's just a-standin' here barkin' away at them posts like aliens has just landed."

They were quiet for a time, both men studying the swamp but seeing nothing that helped explain the newly arrived posts. "Byron's name is inside that'n on the left," Vernon said. "I figure these're all those signs you're a-missin', aw-right."

Hawkins nodded. "Wouldn't someone have to drive by your cabin to get back here?"

"Only way *I* know," Vernon admitted. "'Less, o' course, they come in on foot, but that ain't likely. I figure them signs for at least thirty, thirty-five pounds apiece. 'Less, o' course, it was more'n one doin' the haulin'." Vernon canted his head in admiration. "Somebody did a helluva lot a work hammerin' out them signs, too." Vernon nodded at his own assessment as he admired the new, metallic duck houses.

Hawkins nodded to a place deeper in the swamp. "Are there any ducks back in here?"

"I ain't never seen none. But like I said, I didn' even know this swamp was here."

Hawkins took off his sunglasses and slowly swiveled his head, taking in the serenity of the isolated wetland. Had he been born a duck, he might want to live here.

Just ten yards to their right, the ferns exploded with a splash of water and a sharp *who-eek! who-eek!* A dark bottle-shaped creature shot at an angle through the trees. *Wheek! Wheek! Wheek!* The frantic bird flew like a small cannonball in a line arrow-straight where no straight path seemed possible.

"Be damned!" Vernon said. "Wood duck. A female, too."

The two men listened to the duck's persistent cry fade in the deep woods. When the quiet returned, Duffy felt that vague deference toward wild animals that he always experienced whenever his interruptive presence in a place was thrown back at him like an insult.

"I cain't see how we can hammer the signs back out and make 'em presentable," Duffy considered aloud.

"No," Vernon said, "I'd have to agree on that."

Hawkins inhaled deeply and then let the air seep from his nostrils. "They doin' any harm out here far as your concerned, Vern?"

Vernon checked the deputy's face and then looked back at the signs and chewed on the inside of his cheek. "Hell, if I didn' know 'bout the swamp, I couldn' rightly know 'bout them signs, now, could I?"

Hawkins nodded. "Reckon there ain't no need to call the state. This *is* a wildlife management area. Seems to me these duck houses might be part o' that managin'. Purty nice homes, too . . . for a duck." Duffy turned to Vernon. "Whattaya say we juss let 'em be for now. Sorta keep this 'tween us." He turned back to the swamp and stared beyond the wetland to the bigger picture. "I'm pretty sick o' all those signs out on the highway myself."

Chapter Sixteen

**Morgan Falls High School
North Atlanta
Late Autumn, 1984**

Joey knocked on Coach Padgett's door, slipped his book satchel off his shoulder, and waited.

"Yeah?!" came a gruff reply from behind the door.

Joey opened the door, and Coach Padgett looked up from the reel of film he was threading into a projector. "Yeah?" Padgett repeated, already back to work on the film.

"Coach Padgett, I'm in your third period P.E."

Padgett glanced up irritably. "Gattling, right?"

Joey set his satchel on the floor. "It's 'Gallatin.' I'd like to request a boxing match in the gym under your supervision."

Padgett's fingers stopped coaxing the film through the projector. Straightening, he took off his glasses, and squinted at Joey.

"We don't do boxing matches, kid. We don't have a boxing team. That went out with *Brylcreem*." His head turned automatically toward a tall beige locker cabinet. "I don't even think we have gloves anymore."

"I can supply the gloves," Joey said.

Padgett pushed his lips forward. "You wanna challenge somebody? That it?"

"Yes'r."

The coach frowned. "Go to a YMCA and sign up for Golden Gloves. Probably join up at one of the gyms downtown somewhere."

Joey shook his head. "I want to do it here at the school."

The coach sat back in his chair and cocked his head to one side. "Son, you know why schools don't do boxing anymore? Same reason we don't burn up students' fannies with a paddle. Liability. Lawsuits. They're the new sport of the twentieth century."

When Joey wouldn't budge, Padgett jerked open a drawer in his desk and began searching for something. Finding a yellow rubber band, he stretched it around his fingers and tried to look annoyed. "You got a beef with somebody, Gattalin?"

"It's 'Gallatin,' sir. Yes'r, I do. Denny Hayhurst."

Padgett laughed. "Well, I can't argue that. *Somebody* ought to clean his clock for him." He let his eyes run up and down Joey's frame. "Don't think that'll be you though."

"I want to do it here at school," Joey repeated. "He'll *have* to fight me if it's here. He's not going to go off campus with me. Not one on one."

Padgett swiveled his chair and looked out the window at the football field. He orbited his hands inside the elastic rubber band, like gerbils chasing each other in a cage. Joey could see by the coach's eyes that something entertaining was running through his mind. Padgett sniffed and gave Joey a tired stare.

"Listen, son. When two bucks wanna fight, they fight. I can't control what you do every minute of the day. So—" He raised his eyebrows and shrugged. "Do what you gotta do. You know what I mean?"

Joey looked down at his hands. His knuckles were permanently callused from his training. The knuckles were like marbles pushed beneath stretched leather. Five years of hitting the heavy bag and sparring with boys half-again his size and weight at the clubs in that part of Atlanta that the Chamber of Commerce kept swept under the rug. The only white boy to show his face in those establishments, Joey had trained five afternoons a week and swept floors and folded towels on Wednesdays. Saturdays he sparred.

His entitlement to all this came from simply walking into a club by himself when he was eleven years old. At first, he was a novelty to the all-black crowd. Then, when he began to show promise, he was tolerated for his staying power in the ring. After the first six months, he was a fixture—"the skinny white kid who didn't know quit."

Holding a steady gaze on Coach Padgett, Joey kept his voice low, trying not to sound arrogant. "I don't want to hurt him. I want to humiliate him. If I fight him off-campus, I'll have to hurt him."

Padgett smiled at this, but as he stared into the certainty of Joey's eyes, the smile faded. "Why's that?" Padgett said. "Why will you have to hurt him?"

"So people will know he lost."

The coach's smile widened. "So, you already know how this is gonna go, huh? You plan on winning this fight?"

"Yes'r," Joey said. "I figure a knockout in the first fifteen seconds."

Padgett's face was completely sober now. He began to nod. Then he stopped nodding like an actor who had taken the wrong cue. He began shaking his head.

"Hayhurst is a jerk, but he's going to be our starting quarterback next year. He might be a horse's ass, but he's got an arm. Might take us to state."

Joey's expression did not change. "I won't hurt his arm. Just his ego. If you let me fight him here, that is."

Padgett looked out the window and frowned. Joey could see he was considering it. But finally, the man sniffed, dropped the rubber band, and closed the drawer.

"Can't do it, son." He leaned back in his chair. "What's all this animosity between you and Hayhurst about?"

The image of Angie LaFarge's saintly face assembled on the altar of Joey's consciousness. As always when he pictured her, she sat astride a powerful stallion as black as obsidian.

"I'd like to go out for football," Joey said.

Padgett frowned again, this time at the unexpected change of subject. Restraining a smile, he openly measured Joey's slight stature.

"Well, anybody can try out. If I were you, I'd consider beefing up a little. With the right weight-lifting program and diet, you maybe could put on ten, maybe fifteen pounds before next season. You could try out then."

"I want to try out for this season."

Padgett's face screwed into a question. "It's the middle of November, son."

"Yes'r."

"Son, the season is better'n half over. You can't join a team that late. Coach Youngblood would never allow it. Did you play junior varsity?"

Joey shook his head. Padgett's frown deepened.

"You be a senior next year, son?"

Joey nodded.

"Well, like I said, you can try out then. Anybody can try out."

"I'd like to sign up right now," Joey said.

Padgett's eyes narrowed as he studied Joey's cool demeanor. "What? You figure to punish Hayhurst out on the football field? Being on the same team?" He laughed and pointed north out the window. "Maybe you ought to go to North Springs next year. Play for them."

"That would only give me one night with Hayhurst."

Padgett couldn't hold a smile on his face. "You're serious, aren't you?"

"It would be easier to set up a boxing match."

Padgett set his jaw. "Can't do it." He stood and bent over the projector.

Joey slung his satchel over his shoulder. "How do I sign up for football next year?"

Chapter Seventeen

NAACP Regional Symposium
Magnolia Convention Center, Regalia Hotel
Forsyth County
Thursday evening

"You can see the problem here," Budge said, sweeping a catcher's-mitt-sized hand through the air, the movement graceful and fluid, like a wood nymph scattering rose petals over a sylvan pond. "We've got the big room inside plus all this space out here by the pool. And over there by that wall, that's gonna be where the ones selling books and software will ply their trade. One guy will be signing books. You read Delmont Devane? *Race to the Finish*?"

"No," Joey said and watched a blond, pony-tailed teenaged boy in a uniform of gray shorts and gray tee-shirt work his way around the pool with a long-handled skimmer. On the left breast of the boy's shirt the word *Regalia* was embossed in yellow thread. The boy softly whistled as he scooped leaves and dead caterpillars off the surface of the water.

"Pretty good book," Budge reported. "Balanced. Edifying. Offers an insightful perspective on the contemporary black man in the South." Budge pointed to the huge glass doors that opened to the convention room. "Anyway, I figure I'll cover the main room. That's where they're gonna eat, give some awards, talk about future strategies . . . that kind of thing. Most of the crowd will be there. But I can't be in there and out here at the same time. Why I'm paying you to cover the *al fresco* portion."

Joey nodded and surveyed his assigned territory. "And you're expecting trouble?"

Budge buttoned his blazer and smoothed the hang of the material with a sweep of his big hands. "Does us no good to expect otherwise," he said quietly. When he inhaled, his chest expanded. It was like seeing the mainsail of a clipper ship swell with favorable winds. "Thirty years ago, this county had an unofficial motto: 'The sun never sets on a black man in Forsyth County.' 'Course they used a more regional epithet for 'black man.' Used to be enough racist rednecks in this town to form a confederate regiment. Now, I don't know. But I want to be ready."

"You carrying a gun?" Joey asked.

Budge shook his head. "Too many people. If there's a need for guns, there will be cops near enough for that. They'll be in the lobby . . . this at the request of the hotel's convention planner. Mostly we want to dissuade trouble." He made a little shoulder shrug—the kind of subconscious adjustment a boxer makes in the ring just before a fight. "About a dozen years ago the black community from all over the greater Atlanta area decided to march up here. Make a statement. They were organized, permitted, and legal. Lotta whites came up for it, too . . . to support the black cause. Lily was here. Anyway, a brick came sailing out of the crowd of onlookers and sent someone to the hospital."

Budge dug into his pants pocket and pulled out a bright metal coach's whistle. "Here you go. Keep this with you. If pop goes the weasel, use it. I want to know if there's trouble out here." Joey picked up the chrome instrument from Budge's hand. The whistle was heavy for its size. Probably top of the line.

"Okay, here's the protocol," Budge said and unfolded an index finger as he began a count. "One: Somebody looks like trouble, you politely ask his name. Check that with his ID and see if he's on the guest list." Finger two extended alongside the first. "Two: If he's not on the list, you politely ask him to leave." Budge's ring finger joined the first two. "Three: If he balks, you quietly help him leave." Fourth finger. "Four: If he resists, you blow that whistle, and then the two of us politely overpower him and escort him to his vehicle." Thumb. "Five: He gets physical before I can get to you, nip it in the bud. Put him down fast . . . un-politely. But listen. Before you step into the fray, you got to know if he has friends. Don't let yourself get outnumbered."

Budge gave Joey a moment to digest instructions. "Any questions?"

Joey shook his head.

"You and I are going to circulate. If there's going to be trouble, I want us to see it first. Tomorrow the coordinator of this event would like to say that no police intervention was necessary. That will bring in more attendants to the seminar next year."

Joey watched the gangly kid cleaning the pool empty his net of flotsam into the shrubs beneath the crepe myrtles that lined the wall. He figured the boy for a local high schooler with an easy summer job. Probably had an uncle who managed the hotel or the dining room. Joey wondered if the Camaro in the parking lot belonged to the kid. It had a miniature Confederate flag framed inside the front vanity plate.

"Wonder how many generations it will take to cleanse the racism out of the South?" Joey said, talking more to himself than to Budge.

The big man casually palpated the knuckles of his right hand with the thumb of his left—like a physician searching for an abnormality in the bone structure. Budge struck a pose.

" 'I have one great fear, that one day when *they* are turned to loving, they will find *we* are turned to hate.' "

Frowning, Joey looked deeply into Budge's intelligent eyes. "What?"

"Alan Paton," Budge explained. "From *Cry the Beloved Country*."

By eight o'clock the total crowd had swelled to two hundred, with about seven whites attending the conference. Only blacks were swimming in the pool—two men and three women, each a handsome specimen of human anatomy, which, Joey figured, was why they were taking their dip. This quintet had something to show for their time spent in a gym.

Moon of the White Tears

Joey observed the forty or so onlookers around the pool as they sipped drinks, chatted, and eyed the swimmers. All the men spectators, he noticed, studied the female bathers. All the women studied the female bathers, too. Joey thought about this phenomenon as he pondered the intricacies of gender-driven human nature.

So far, the most exciting thing to happen this evening was a "can-opener" performed by one of the men after springing high from the diving board. The spray carried all the way to the grill where the hickory coals hissed and puffed a cloud of steam. The cook had to put on fresh wood chips and squirt lighter fluid over them before relighting.

At 9:05 pm a deep, bubbling thunder erupted from the parking lot beyond the wall. It quieted the crowd in the book signing and sales area under the awning, and right away the silence spread from there out to the pool area. The rumbling sound crescendoed again and then lowered to an idle. Joey recognized the growl of a high-performance engine channeled through a modified glasspack muffler. When the vehicle revved again, the roar was deafening, and everyone around the pool stared toward the archway and wrought iron gate that led to the parking lot.

Joey checked the book-signing area and saw the vendors trying to disregard the interruption with nervous smiles and accelerated sales pitches. In one corner of the lighted patio, the author, Devane, was staring at Joey with three lines creasing his forehead. Joey gave him a reassuring nod, opened the gate, and wandered out through the archway into the lot.

There were two pickup trucks, a red in front and a faded yellow behind it, both shod with oversized, mud-caked tires. The hood of each truck boasted a full-sized confederate "bars and stars" painted in bright colors on the smooth metal finish. Joey noticed the Camaro was gone.

The red truck's windows were tinted, preventing a view inside. The older model truck's windows were open. The man in the driver's seat had a wedge-shaped head shaved clean as a billiard ball. His thick neck and bulging arms threatened to test the black tee shirt stretched across his hefty body. He turned up his radio to release a maelstrom of heavy metal into the lot. Smacking gum, he smiled as though something too delightful to describe had just occurred. When he raised a cigarette to his lips, a swastika tattoo swelled on the curve of his biceps.

Joey casually stepped back to the patio, walked slowly to the grill, and borrowed the can of lighter fluid. After checking to ensure the stem valve was closed, he slipped the can into his blazer pocket and was back through the gate before the next fusillade of engine roars had subsided. The heavy metal music now filled the lot with a sound not unlike an eighteen-wheeler crashing into a bridge abutment.

The driver of the yellow trash heap—a.k.a. "Wedge-head"—held to his savage smile as Joey stepped into the lot, leaned back onto the trunk of an SUV, and crossed his arms over his chest. The muscular driver hocked up a load of phlegm and *thwooped* it from a curled tongue. The mucilaginous glob landed two feet shy of Joey's feet. Then the driver turned back to his companion sitting at shotgun, and from the cab came a yammering laugh that could just be heard above the din of music.

The red truck began to rev and bounce like a predatory creature ready to pounce on its prey. Then the yellow truck responded in kind, snarling and lunging as if snapping at the heels of the red truck in front of it. The lead driver lowered his window and stuck out his head so he could laugh with the second driver. Joey recognized him. The pool cleaner, now out of uniform in a sleeveless tee shirt that bore a shadowy portrait of Hitler's face on the front, laughed like a hyena. Pool boy had a skinny arm with a short blue chain tattooed around the biceps. He now wore a baseball cap backward, which made his loose golden blond hair frizz around his ears like a fallen halo.

"Hey, boy!" Wedge-head called out from the yellow truck. His manic eyes were riveted on Joey. "You with them jigaboos?" He maintained eye contact with Joey as his whisker-stubbled chin started up a slow chewing rhythm as he worked on a stick of gum. When Joey did not deign to answer, Wedge-head sat up straighter in his seat and glared at Joey. "You got a problem, asshole?" he challenged. When he leaned further out his window, his upper arm bulged against the side of the door. The swastika looked like a USDA stamp inked on a ham. Joey could see it was the kind of muscle that came from daily hard labor. Maybe a cinder block mason, a furniture mover, or a steel worker, early twenties, hard-drinking, full of bluster, and accustomed to backing men down.

From a distance, Joey couldn't smell Wedge-head, but he was betting this night's performance was alcohol-fueled. In the bed of the truck, a tool-handle—maybe a shovel—protruded from a pile of hastily loaded lumber. Dried concrete scabbed one of the boards.

Bingo! Joey thought. *A mason.*

When the two engines roared again, the combined sound was deafening—a profane and defiant insult to all within earshot. Joey turned to the spectators peering through the archway.

"Better wait inside, folks," he suggested and smiled reassuringly. "We're just doing the male posturing thing, and it's kind of embarrassing if I know that sane people are watching."

No one laughed. Their eyes could not stay off the two trucks. The author, Devane, was there with that same look of concern. The worry lines appeared permanently etched into his dark face, and Joey imagined this man's life marked by a slew of moments like this one. Joey took a step toward the writer and tossed the chrome whistle to him.

"Do me a favor, sir? Step inside the main room and give that a blow. When a man approaches who looks like he could stunt-double for a rhino, tell him he has an appointment out here in the parking lot."

"Hey, niggers!" Pool-boy called out. "Y'all git your black asses outta our coun'y!" He scowled at the group gathered near the wall.

Wedge-head chimed in with a backup insult. "Don't want no darkies 'round here, 'less we got some cotton needs pickin'."

Again the two trucks' engines roared in unison—dual exclamation marks punctuating their ultimatums.

Joey could see it all like a techni-color movie previewing in his mind: *Joey walking out to the yellow truck, rolling up the right sleeves of his coat and shirt to the elbow. Joey stopping so close to the truck that the driver's flexed arm retracts inside.*

Wedge-head snorting, trying for an amused look. "Whadda you want, asshole?"

Joey positioning his exposed forearm next to the bricklayer's. Joey's arm smaller and paler . . . but hard, compact, and marbled with blue veins. Like a chunk of quartz with streaks of blue amethyst running through the ore.

"You're darker than I am," Joey is saying, staring at Wedge-head as if this observation might be significant.

Wedge-head looking uncertain. "So-fuckin'-what?"

Joey pressing his lips together as if in regret, "I guess you'll be leaving the county soon." Joey checking the western horizon. "Sun's down."

Five beats of silence. Wedge-head squinting, trying to figure out what he's up against. The skin on his forehead hardening with two vertical lines creasing the flesh above the bridge of his nose.

"Why the hell would I leave the coun'y?"

Joey holding his forearm flush against Wedge-head's. "You're darker. Guess that means you're a darky."

Wedge-head hissing a laugh through his teeth as he's opening his door. "What I'm gonna do is step out there and whip your skinny ass."

That's the way it might have gone five years ago, when Joey had put almost as much importance on cleverness as he did his fighting strategy. He was done with all that now. Verbal skirmishes were pointless. They had never felt natural to Joey. Directness fit him better. Directness was like a good sparring glove laced up tightly around his fist. Clicking off the movie in his head, he walked to the yellow truck like a man taking a late-night stroll out to his mailbox.

"Whadda you want, asshole?" Wedge-head said. He took a draw on his cigarette, exhaled, and squinted through the blue skein of smoke rising from the window.

Joey stopped two yards away from the truck, outside the radius of a swiftly opening door but close enough to smell the beer. Now that he could see Wedge-head's riding companion, Joey took a quick measure of this one riding shotgun.

He was skinny as a scarecrow, so Joey tagged him with that sobriquet. Scarecrow's dark hair hung over his forehead in a diagonal waterfall of India ink. He had a beaked nose, thin lips, and pimples on his cheeks. His arms were mere sticks. His tee shirt was expensive but appeared to have been aerated by scissors. His feet, propped on the dashboard, sported brand new running shoes, which Joey knew retailed for over a hundred and thirty dollars.

This boy suddenly laughed with a witchy cackle. No brick mason he. Joey figured video games and an exorbitant allowance for this one. Probably spent most of his time at an arcade. That, or lying on a sofa watching MTV.

"I'm almost ashamed to admit this," Joey said to Wedge-head as if they were old comrades sharing a booth at a bar after a day's work troweling mortar. "I still have these great one-liners running through my head. Comments you'd have a hard time one-upping me on. I never liked that part of the process. I figure you and I could keep it going for a coupla dozen exchanges before one of us pushes the other's button. You know what I mean?"

Joey's voice was earnest, no mocking, no double-meaning. Wedge-head looked like he was trying to translate a Latvian speech with the use of a Spanish to English dictionary.

"So," Joey continued, "let's pare this down to its basics. You've come here to start trouble. You have a problem with African Americans being here in your county. You've told this guy here . . ." He gestured toward

Scarecrow. "... And you've told those guys ..." He nodded his head toward the idling red truck. "... How you're gonna put the fear of God into these black people trespassing on your home turf. How, if they don't heed your threats, you'll beat somebody or somebodies to a pulp."

Joey paused here and touched his fingertips to his clip-on tie. "*I*, however, have been hired to protect the integrity of this peaceful gathering. I have a problem with anyone who wants to upset that." Joey opened his hand toward the confused neo-Nazi, a simple gesture for clarification. "And here you are ... the source of upset. So that makes you and me the two obvious gladiators in this arena."

Wedge-head tried to smile, but there was no room for it on a face filled with so much disbelief. He was the great white shark of the dark depths of Forsyth, and who was this little guppy trying to explain things to him like a family counselor? Wedge-head's eyes began to spark with the prelude to violence.

"You're tellin' me a runt like you is supposed to be the security guy for this nigger-fest?" His laugh was full and resonant. Scarecrow tried to join in, but he was good only for another cackle.

"What I suggest," Joey said patiently, "is that we cut right to it. You and me. I don't think your anemic friend there is up to combat, and your sidekick in the red truck is a joke. So, please step out and let's get started. I need to get back to my post."

Wedge-head clamped his cigarette in a tight V-shaped smile. He nodded to the front windshield, making a big production of how confident he was. But it was all hesitation, Joey knew. Every move Wedge-head made was an affectation. His version of cool. Yet he made no move to get out. He pivoted his head to Joey and tried for a Marlon Brando-esque aloofness.

"I'm going to come out there and whip your ass, prick." The words were mumbled around the bobbing cigarette. As he opened the door with a vicious jerk on the handle, Joey silently lauded himself for expediting the inevitable.

"Thank you," Joey said, taking a step back and cracking a modest smile to match his gratitude.

Wedge-head's face compressed with confusion, and he paused with one silver-studded boot on the asphalt. With the door opened only halfway, Joey breathed a sigh of disappointment. It looked like the preliminaries were going to drag on.

To save face, Wedge-head turned to his buddy, mumbled something derisive, and laughed heartily. Dutifully, Scarecrow added the expected cackle, which was, apparently, all he was capable of contributing to the night.

Joey kicked the door hard against Wedge-head's shin, causing the brute to draw his leg back into the cab. When Joey kicked again, the door slammed shut. When Joey slapped down the lock with the flat of his right hand, Wedge-head recoiled deeper into the cab and then frowned at the trespass of Joey's hand on his truck.

"Ow!" Scarecrow chirped. Wedge-head had braced an elbow on the console between the seats, where Scarecrow's left hand was crushed by his weight. "Get off, Skull!"

Joey couldn't help but chuckle. " 'Skull'? Seriously?"

Trying to exhume control of the confrontation, Wedge-head, or Skull, if you wish, reached out for Joey's tie and pulled hard. The flimsy, clip-on tie flailed in the air like a limp noodle.

Before Skull could form his next word, Joey torqued around the axis of his spine, throwing all his weight into the move, and rocketed a punch through the open window, catching the bridge of Skull's nose at the perfect angle to break bone and cartilage, and rupture blood vessels. It sounded like a carrot snapping.

The cigarette dropped into Skull's lap, and both hands steepled over his nose as if he had taken an urgent prayer break. Blood streaked down his chin and wrists. Scarecrow looked on with horror and pressed his back against the passenger door, trying to distance himself from the blood.

"You shouldn't feel bad about this," Joey said to Skull. "I'm a professional. You're just not up to speed on how to handle this kind of situation. Your mouth is ahead of your talent. And your beefed-up physique has convinced you to be complaisant."

When Joey raised a hand to point at the bleeding nose, Skull jumped back deeper in his seat. "You ought to go get some ice on that," Joey said. "Keep your head forward and down. You don't want to let the blood build up and get sucked into your lungs."

Above Skull's fingertips, raw fury shone in his eyes. He growled something unintelligible and clawed at the door lock, finally popping it up. In a flash, Joey slapped it down again. This time he swung with a left, cracking the nose in the other direction. Wedge-head's scream was like the throaty blare of a cow in labor.

Joey wasn't through. With a hard left jab, he caught Skull on the left eye, and he knew that the neo-Nazi wannabe was now seeing four different colors of fireworks exploding on the dark screen of his retina. Tomorrow he would wear the classic Roman nose that was common among the clientele at the boxing clubs. Skull's eye socket would be the color of a ripe eggplant.

Tears brimmed in his eyes. Skull was done.

When Joey reached inside the cab with his hand flattened, palm-side up, Skull's reflex was to push himself on top of Scarecrow, effectively crushing his sidekick against the passenger door.

"Ow!" Scarecrow whined again.

"I just need my tie," Joey said.

Scarecrow jerked the tie from Skull's grip and threw it at Joey, who deftly caught it and fastened it to his bare collar.

"You goddamn broke my nose, you som'bitch. I think my eye is gone blind."

Joey noticed an aggressive stream of smoke rising from the driver's crotch. He thought about the starter fluid in his pocket but didn't think it necessary now.

"Go home and get some ice on that," Joey said. "If you can cool it down before it swells too much, it will heal faster."

Both boys stared at Joey as if he were a neurosurgeon spelling out their prognoses.

Joey smiled. "By the way, your pants are on fire."

Skull looked down and widened his eyes. The red brick of hot cigarette ash shone brightly against his dark trousers. Like a tiny meteorite that had crashed in his lap. His crotch smoldered red in a circle around his fly. His light blue undershorts could be seen in the spreading hole. Smoke streamed across the cab past Scarecrow, where it flowed outside through his window. Skull slapped at the burning circle and raised himself off the seat. Joey waited patiently until the smolder was extinguished by Scarecrow emptying a beer can into his friend's lap.

Leaning toward the truck, Joey quickly slapped his hands on the roof of the cab. Inside both boys jumped at the hollow, clanging sound. Skull lowered himself to his seat and dropped his right hand to the gearshift knob.

"You goddamn som'bitch!" he growled. Now his voice carried a nasal tone due to the pinch his left thumb and index applied to his gushing nose. After jamming the stick into reverse, he popped the clutch and burned rubber as he backed up, made a checkmark turn, and paused long enough to shift gears again. With tires screaming, the yellow truck tore out of the lot and barreled around the first turn toward the exit. When it reached the highway, the truck roared off like a dragster given the go flag.

Joey walked to the red truck and stopped at the same distance from its door. Pool-boy powered up his tinted window, leaving only an inch for communication. As Joey studied the boy's eyes, a strange image formed in his mind: a Norway rat trying to analyze a painting by Jackson Pollack.

"Your friend has gone for some ice," Joey said through the breach in the window.

" 'Ice'?" Pool-boy echoed weakly.

"Yes," Joey said. "He's bleeding pretty badly, can't see out of one eye, and probably got some heavy-duty bells ringing inside his head. I'm guessing you'd like to go see about him about now."

The engine *vroomed*, and the truck lurched backward, braked, and accelerated forward through the lot in a repeat performance of Skull's speedy departure. But Pool-boy pushed it too hard in the turn and skidded sideways into a Dumpster. After a loud *bang*, the back end of the truck fishtailed as it roared out of the exit.

A sudden applause broke out behind him, and Joey turned to the patio. Every dark face there was beaming with a crescent of startling white teeth as a chorus of clapping hands gave the seminar its most animated moment of the evening. Budge stood in the archway leaning one shoulder against the brick wall. He brought his hands up in front of him and offered his own slow version of applause.

"Excellent. And edifying. You think they'll be back?"

Joey shrugged. "Maybe. Hard to live with that kind of humiliation."

"They come back, they might bring some artillery."

"Might be a good time to park a police car over here by this entrance."

Budge handed Joey the chrome whistle. They stood for a time watching the highway, where cars were streaming in crosscurrents up and down highway 400. Budge pushed his hands into his pants pockets and gazed up at the night sky. There was a low ceiling of clouds, and no stars were visible. He breathed in deeply, then out.

"He was a foe without hate . . . a soldier without cruelty . . . a victor without oppression." He paused for effect. "Benjamin Harvey Hill," Budge said, capping off the quote. "Talking about Robert E. Lee."

Joey's head bounced with a silent laugh. "Perfect," he said and walked back to the grill, where he returned the can of fire starter. The patio was buzzing with conversations.

"Joey?" It was a woman's voice and it cut through the din of the crowd like a razor slicing through a sheet of paper.

Joey turned, his face slack with surprise. When he saw her face, a warm wave washed through him and swirled in his loins. He couldn't speak at first. He could only look at her. When, finally, he spoke her name, his voice was a whisper, as if he were seeing her from a distance and muttering the words to himself.

"Angie LaFarge."

Chapter Eighteen

**Morgan Falls High School
Football Practice Field
Autumn, 1985**

The second-team offense broke out of the huddle and came to the line like a pack of rabid Rottweilers stretched to the ends of their leashes. Standing five yards behind them, hands on his knees, whistle clamped in his teeth, Coach Zubin had as much to prove as these boys who wanted to make first team. Zubin taught English Lit, and Coach Youngblood thought the man better suited to parse a sonnet than to coach football, which is why Zubin was in charge of the offensive wannabees who had not made the first-team cut.

In one hand, Zubin clenched the North Springs playbook, which he had compiled from watching films of recent games. His job was to run North Springs offensive plays against the Morgan Falls first-team defense to get the starting players ready for the game.

On the other side of the scrimmage line, the first-string defense hunkered down with serious motivation. Not only did they want to protect their standings on the elite team, but they were not about to let second-string slag score on them. The defense wore red scrimmage vests. Red was the coveted badge on this field. If you wore red, you were starting Friday night.

Coach Walther—the head defense coach—stood across the line of scrimmage from Zubin and scanned the flank of grass-stained butts staring at him. His job was to turn his elite squad into a brick wall that shut out the North Springs running game. The last thing he wanted to see was a second-team running-back breaking through his line of red, which he had dubbed "the Great Wall of Walther."

The quarterback set an audible shift on the count, and Walther watched his defensive right tackle and guard adjust accordingly. On the snap, his right defensive end sidestepped and followed the tackle into the offensive backfield, which was already moving like a wave in an option left. When the tailback took a quick toss and had two blockers out in front of him, Walther almost bit his metal whistle in half. With his defensive right end committed through the tackle hole, there was nobody to contain the play. The defensive back came up on that side, but the two blockers gave the ball-runner what he needed. Two jukes and he was gone.

Walther didn't look at Zubin, but he could feel the lesser coach's elation from fifteen yards away. Walther blew his whistle as if trying to squeeze something profane out of the instrument, until it popped from his mouth and fell mutely onto the grass.

"Gallatin! Get your butt over here!"

Joey extricated himself from the pile-up behind the line and ran to his coach. Walther slapped a fist on Joey's faceguard and towed him into the end zone, Joey stumbling behind, trying to keep his cleats off the man's heels. Walther spun around and stuck his nose two inches from Joey's face.

"Son, do you know why I put a red shirt on you last week?"

"Yes, sir!" Joey replied.

"Well, why don't you tell me, because, right now, I can't remember!"

"You said I played my heart out to get on this team, sir!" Joey sounded like a marine grunt sounding off with all the appropriate deferential monotone due a drill sergeant.

"Did you play your goddamned brains out, too? You're not supposed to stunt left on that line-up. You're supposed to stay outside and hold your goddamned ground, Gallatin. Contain, goddamnit! Contain! That's your number one job! *Nobody* gets outside you! Do you understand that?"

Walther jerked the faceguard and shook Joey's head like a gourd on a vine. Joey's feet danced beneath the iron grip on the helmet, trying to keep himself upright.

"Maybe Julian would do better in my position, coach. He's a hard hitter, too."

"Oh, he is, is he?"

"Yes, sir!" Joey assured him. "And I could go take his place lining up against our first-team offense."

The veins at Walther's temples looked about to burst. He stripped the red vest off Joey and pushed it into Joey's hands.

"Take that to Julian and tell him to come play for me. Tell Coach Youngblood you're second-string now. You can go run your thick skull into the first offensive team and see how you like that!"

"Yes, sir!" Joey replied and jogged down the field in his smooth unhurried gait, the red vest wadded in one hand.

When he reached the first-string offense scrimmage area, Joey watched Denny Hayhurst take the snap, scramble to the backfield, and set up to pass. His tailback ran a post pattern and outdistanced the defensive backs by ten yards. Hayhurst fired the ball, and the receiver made the catch without breaking stride.

Coach Youngblood stood on the sideline, clipboard in hand, watching the first-team offense get to its feet after slamming its formidable weight into the pseudo-North Springs defenders provided by the second-team defense. Youngblood never got upset like his underling staff. He was a quiet but powerful general, so sunbaked and inured to the coach's life that his arms and neck was as dark and hard as a pigskin football pumped up to regulation pressure. If he spoke at all to a player, it was usually through one of the other coaches.

The elite red shirts walked slowly back to huddle as the routed defense picked themselves up from various parts of the field. The North Springs simulators were spread out like bowling pins that had been fired on by a cannonball. Joey spotted Chris Julian sitting on the grass near the line of scrimmage. He was testing the bend of one knee when Joey knelt beside him.

"Coach Walther wants you down there on first team." Joey handed him the prized vest. "You're with the defensive starters now."

Julian's head came around—mouth open, breathing suspended. "I'm on first team now?" he asked, holding the dazed expression. He had to hear it again. He took Joey's offered hand and hoisted himself up. "For real?"

Joey nodded. "You're taking my place at right defensive end."

Julian wanted to believe it. He was like a stick of dynamite with a fuse too long.

"What happened, Gallatin? You were hitting like a wrecking ball yesterday."

Joey shrugged. "They're mostly running a razorback split. Just remember, when you see the option play, drift wide with the running back no matter what the QB does on the inside. And watch Jacobson's three-point stance. Watch his knuckles on the line. When he points them a little to the outside, it's usually a pitch out to the tailback. If he puts his fingertips down instead, he'll drop back to protect a pass. Hit him quick while he's back-peddling, and he'll go down."

Julian swallowed and wet his lips. "How do you know all that?"

Joey shrugged again. "Just a matter of studying human nature. Go on! Get going, and good luck!"

Julian formed the word "thanks" on his tongue, but Joey was already running toward the ragtag defensive huddle. After tugging on the red vest, Julian looked at Coach Youngblood and pointed downfield as he started sidling away toward the far end of the practice field. When Youngblood nodded once, Julian covered the eighty yards like a gazelle that had jumped the containment fence at a zoo.

Joey squeezed into the huddle to hear the repeat of the defensive play from Truck Truebolt. Through his mouth guard Truck's words sloshed like a washing machine.

"Y'all got it, defensh? Goal-line crunsh! Play it tight! Don't let Hayhursht dive over ush! Make him pash!" Truebolt's eyes found Joey. "What're you doin' here, Gallashin?"

"I'm taking Julian's place."

Truebolt took out his mouthpiece and spat down into the grass. "Well, contain that right side. It's a sieve. They've been running all over us over there. Grubber's been out in front blocking, and he's kicking ass." Truck stuffed the mouth guard back onto his teeth. "Let'sh do thish, boysh!" He clapped his hands for the break, and a few of the others tried to join him in unison, but it came off like a string of dud firecrackers.

Grubber came to the line facing Joey across from his left shoulder. The tight end, Sticky-fingers Stimson, took a position one yard back from the line and right in front of Joey. Hayhurst strutted up to the center and looked over the defense. Joey's head went down, keeping a low profile for the element of surprise.

When the ball was snapped, Joey feinted toward the end and saw Grubber lunge that way for him, elbows wide. Like a matador Joey side-stepped and let Grubber sail past him to crash into Sticky. Through the gap, Joey saw Hayhurst set to hand-off on an end reverse, but Joey knew it was a feint. Hayhurst's grip on the ball was solid, fingertips splayed on the laces, his thumb spread wide to take a fierce hold on the ball. Joey knew he was either going to throw or run.

Joey accelerated through the gap as the right end sprinted behind the quarterback and pretended to take the ball. Still holding the football, Hayhurst pivoted quickly and started for the hole supposedly provided by his offside tackle. He never saw Joey coming.

People down at the defense-end of the field later said they heard the impact. Coach Zubin, embarrassingly, had dropped his clipboard in the grass, thinking a gun had gone off somewhere on the field. Coach Walther would later admit he thought the goal post had fallen and cracked the scoreboard in half.

Those on the sideline with Coach Youngblood had enjoyed the best view of the incident. When Joey Gallatin hit Hayhurst, the surprised quarterback emitted a loud exhalation that sounded like *"koosh"* as he was jackknifed by Joey's shoulder and lifted into the air. Joey drove him nine yards back before completing the rainbow arc of the rise and fall of the quarterback. Hayhurst hit hard on his back, but this time there was no air to "koosh" out. Whistles were chirring like a chorus of manic locusts. Joey stood over Hayhurst's unmoving body and waited for him to open his eyes.

"Angie LaFarge," Joey said quietly. He turned and walked back to his side of the line as the returning offensive players veered around him, stealing sidelong looks at the compact little dynamo who had carried their quarterback like a scud missile that had picked up a sheet from someone's clothesline before crashing to earth.

"Gallatin!" yelled one of the coaches. "Coach Youngblood wants you."

Joey jogged to the sideline and stood before the head coach. Youngblood looked down at his clipboard, his lips pushed forward in thought, his jaws lazily working on an over-chewed wad of gum. His head came up, but he did not look at Joey. He kept his gaze on the players working their way back to their huddles. Hayhurst was still down, with two coaches kneeling beside him.

"Good hit," Youngblood said. "What are you doing up here on the second team?"

"Coach Walther sent me."

Youngblood waited, but Joey offered nothing else.

"Why?" the coach persisted.

Joey shrugged. "Maybe he thought I could help the first-team offense get ready for North Springs."

Youngblood tapped his pen three times on the clipboard. "You mean . . . if you don't kill our quarterback first." He looked down at his play sheet, but his eyes glazed over with an amused inner thought. "How much do you weigh, Gallatin?"

"One forty-nine," Joey reported.

Youngblood looked at Joey for the first time—but only for a glance. Then he turned to the players waiting on the sideline.

"Bobby G, go in at defensive right end for a play. I want to talk to Gallatin." Youngblood watched the boy sprint in, snapping the chinstrap of his helmet on the run. "So . . ." Youngblood began quietly, his voice like the purr of a large cat. "What would've happened if the ball had gone to the end on that reverse?"

When Joey said nothing, Youngblood turned and squared his hard blue eyes on Joey's and held this stony look without blinking. Actually, it was his only look. What counted was where it was aimed.

"I'll tell you what would have happened," the coach said in his calm, collected monotone. "He would have scored, and you'd be back there dancing with the quarterback without any music."

Joey nodded as if this were no surprise. "My bad, Coach."

Hayhurst limped from the huddle to crouch behind his center. As Joey watched Hayhurst, Youngblood studied Joey's profile. The head coach was accustomed to his athletes standing before him in awe, intimidated by his taciturn command over the team. It was clear to him that Gallatin was different, charting his way through life by his own set of rules.

Together they watched the next play. The fullback crashed up the middle and carried three defensive linemen with him for eight yards until they all collapsed, grunting, into a pile of flesh and pads and clacking helmets. Still wobbling from being sacked a minute earlier, Hayhurst walked to one of the backfield coaches and began complaining about something. He lifted his jersey to show his ribs.

"You all right?" Youngblood called to Hayhurst.

Denny frowned, and the effort seemed to make him stagger. " 'Course I'm all right!" Hayhurst yelled, but his voice cracked and suffered from a strange mousy squeak. He tried to march angrily toward the waiting huddle, but he kept veering left from his intended destination.

"Go back in," Youngblood said quietly to Joey. "Take the right linebacker position. Watch your assignment."

Joey joined his huddle and patted Truck on the shoulder pads. "I'm in for you, Truck," Joey informed him. On the other side, Hayhurst barked angry commands inside the offensive huddle.

On the next play the fullback stuffed the ball against his stomach and started off-tackle on the off-side. Joey met him a yard behind the line of scrimmage, rocked him back on his heels and kept driving until they landed on top of the quarterback. The three players hit the ground like a stack of lumber, Hayhurst taking the worst of it beneath his own fullback.

A vicious string of profanity snarled and sputtered from the bottom of the heap. It was the voice Hayhurst used whenever his athletic destiny was not being taken seriously by the gods of football.

"Angie LaFarge," Joey said, as he leaned down to whisper right in Denny's face. Joey pushed up from the wreck of bodies and jogged back to the defensive huddle with a light spring in his step. Denny Hayhurst sat up rubbing his right arm, already complaining to the trainers who were closing in on him.

Youngblood watched it all but finally turned his attention back to Joey and watched the rookie stand relaxed, his hands splayed on his hip pads as he waited for the huddle. Turning to the bench, Youngblood gestured to Truck with his clipboard.

"Truebolt, get back in there as linebacker. Tell Gallatin to take defensive right end." Then he gave a hand signal to Hayhurst, instructing him to run an option left.

When the ball was hiked, all the offense flowed to their left. In near mirror image, the defense swept right. Hayhurst faked a toss out wide to his running back and cut inside just off-tackle. Joey had danced on his toes toward the sideline, staying with the running back as instructed. But when Hayhurst faked the toss, Joey sprang inside, got his head in front of Denny, and hit him broadside with his shoulder, driving hard into the quarterback's ribs. Denny was immediately thrown right, his body folding sideways as if he'd been caught by the wing of a low flying aircraft.

Joey stayed on his feet and churned his legs like a locomotive, his cleats throwing up a spray of dirt clods in his wake. Veering deeper into the backfield, he carried his prey seven yards, leapt two feet off the ground, and came down head-first so hard that Denny erupted with an involuntary scream that sounded more like a cheerleader than a team captain.

"Angie," Joey reminded quietly. He wasn't sure if Denny could hear him, because the boy's eyes were crossed, and his tongue hung out of one side of his mouth. Joey waited until the shell-shocked quarterback could focus on him, and then Joey whispered again, "Angie LaFarge."

On the sideline, Coach Youngblood pursed his lips as he studied the enigmatic Gallatin boy. Then he turned his gaze downfield, where Coach Walther was whipping the defense into shape. Just yesterday, Walther had praised Joey as—pound-for-pound—the toughest kid wearing a jersey on the field. Youngblood frowned. And, now, here was Gallatin bumped down from first-string to second-string defense, and yet he was hitting like a bull dozer running on high octane. It made no sense.

Youngblood turned back to the players waiting on the sidelines and curled a finger, beckoning one of the more intelligent looking players.

"Yes, sir, coach!" said the hopeful athlete as he pulled on his helmet. "You want me to go in?"

Youngblood ignored the question. "Anything personal going on between Gallatin and Hayhurst?"

The boy hesitated only a moment. "Coach, everybody's got a problem with Hayhurst. He's a bully."

The coach nodded as if this were news to him. "Then why doesn't someone like Truck Truebolt put the fear of God into him?"

The boy shrugged. "Coach, Denny doesn't try to bully people like Truck. He only picks on smaller people."

Youngblood gestured out on the field toward Joey. "You think Gallatin would purposely get himself demoted from first-string defense so he could get a chance to knock Hayhurst on his butt in practice?"

The boy shrugged again. "Don't know Joey very well, coach. He's pretty quiet."

Youngblood nodded. Finally, he covered his mouth with his hand and rubbed at the stubble on his chin for as long as it took to erase the smile that had miraculously appeared on his lips.

Chapter Nineteen

Kudzu Cafë
GA Route 20
Forsyth County
Late Friday night

Joey ordered two coffees at the counter and turned to look at Angie LaFarge seated in the booth. She was gazing out the front window, her elbow on the table and her chin propped on her fist. That angle of her face was as familiar to him as the creased photo he had cut out of his yearbook and kept in his wallet. She was as stunning today as she was in high school.

In truth, Angie did look different now. Her face had leaned out, her body trimmer. And there was something in her eyes—a combination of weariness and knowledge . . . as if she had hacked her way through a jungle and come out on the other side with a new understanding about the rules of survival. For certain, Joey saw these outward changes, but he also recognized what was, and always had been, at the core of her: a quiet awareness of self and a loyalty to the integrity of what that self was. It was these qualities that he had most admired in her . . . and admired in her still. If he had been an artist, he believed he could paint her soul.

He took the hot drinks to the table and slid into the seat across from her. She opened an ersatz cream packet and clouded her coffee with it. Then she tore open a packet of sugar and stirred that in. When she raised the mug with both hands, he noticed for the first time that she wore no ring.

"You're not married," he said.

She sipped, set the coffee cup on the table, and stirred again. After she watched the surface of the liquid eddy and then settle, she made a humorless half smile.

"Not now." She looked at the back of her left hand and stiffened her bare fingers. "Divorced."

Looking at Joey, she completed the other half of the smile, but still her eyes hinted of tragedy. Joey sipped his coffee and watched her gather her hands around her mug as if needing its warmth.

"What about you?" she asked.

When he shook his head, she tilted her head to one side. "Smart. I think maybe there ought to be a law about living a decade alone before we are allowed to marry."

"Any children?" Joey asked.

She looked down into her coffee. "No, thank God."

"Tell me about your life," Joey said.

She set down her mug, closed her eyes, and shook her head. "It would not be a pleasant conversation," she advised, sounding clinical about it. "He was abusive. Both physically and emotionally. I'd rather not talk about it."

Joey could see that she was fighting tears. Already he was entertaining thoughts of tracking down the ex-husband to make him a believer in the "what-goes-around-comes-around" adage.

"I didn't mean *that* life. Tell me about your life *now*."

Her face flushed. After a moment she laughed quietly and sank back into her seat.

"Sorry. I suppose I am what the psychologists would call 'self-absorbed' right now."

"Don't apologize. Abuse can bury you. It takes a while to climb out."

The skin around her eyes tightened, and she studied him. "You talk like you know something about that."

Joey drank some coffee. "Do you have a therapist or someone to talk to?"

She picked up her spoon and paddled her coffee again. "I'm talking to you," she whispered and flashed a little, endearing smile that he would have died for a decade and a half ago.

Joey remembered the awkward silences that had been a part of their past—all those high school conversations he had so carefully rehearsed and then botched in Angie's presence. He felt none of that now. They were kindred spirits, each having put in substantial miles on the road of life.

"Are you working?" he asked.

She put down her spoon and nodded. "Do you remember how I rode horses when you knew me?" She made a self-rebuking smile and dipped her head to one side. "When I got married, I gave all that up. Gary needed to spend a lot of social time with his boss. I was expected to be there with him." She exhaled heavily. "It was a law firm. He wanted to make partner." Angie pushed her coffee aside. "I gave up the most important thing in my life. He gave up nothing."

Joey nodded and looked at his hands, thinking about a life without boxing gloves, training, or the dream of becoming a bouncer. The idea came apart in his head like rotted cloth. It was unthinkable.

"So now I'm using a stable a few miles from here." She pointed. "I barter for riding time by teaching some lessons. A girlfriend of mine runs it."

"So if you barter at the stables, how do you make money?"

"My friend also owns a bookstore in Midtown and doesn't like the commute. She inherited the store from her mother. I run it for her." Angie nodded toward the hotel across the highway. "That's why I was at the conference. We arrange for authors to do book signings. We were responsible for getting Delmont Devane there tonight."

"Which bookstore?"

"It's called *'Cover to Cover.'*" She watched him file the information away. "You always listen, don't you, Joey?" she said, tilting her head to look at him from a new angle. "You always paid attention, even when we were kids." She pushed her mouth to one side. "Was I always so self-absorbed?"

He thought about that. "You were always thinking. I liked that about you. If anything was absorbed, it was the people around you. You were like a planet and the rest of us just drifted through the universe until we were drawn into your gravity to orbit. That or burn up in your atmosphere." He sipped his coffee. "I was a well-toasted meteorite."

She blushed and turned her face to the window. When her eyes narrowed with deliberate focus, Joey followed her gaze out into the parking lot. Two pickup trucks—one red, the other yellow—were parked on either side of his car, both facing the diner. The rebel flags painted on the trucks' hoods were brightly lighted under the parking lot security lamp. Cigarette smoke curled from the windows and angled away on the breeze.

"Aren't those the guys who were making trouble at the hotel?"

"Yep," Joey said as he watched the driver of the yellow truck step down to the pavement and set a baseball bat on the hood of Joey's car. Turning his back to the car, Skull hoisted himself over the wheel well by his arms, sat on the hood, pivoted on his butt, and lay back against the windshield with his hands laced behind his head. The bat lay next to him. A wad of bandaging glowed white from each of his nostrils. His burned trousers had been replaced by a well-worn pair of jeans spotted with tiny islands of dried concrete.

From the passenger door of the yellow truck stepped not Scarecrow but a gorilla of a man in camo army pants, black work boots, and a black tank-top stretched like a second skin across his thick V-shaped torso. Like Skull, his pale pate was shaved as clean as a white bowling ball. His arms, heavy with muscle, bounced stiffly by his sides as if they were too tightly strung to straighten. This one stole Joey's pose as he leaned against the front grill of Joey's car and waited, arms folded across his thick chest, legs crossed at the ankles. Pool-boy remained in the red truck like a wide-eyed spectator awaiting the main event at the Roman Coliseum.

"We should call the police," Angie said. She rummaged through her pocketbook and pulled out a cell phone. Joey reached out and gently covered her hand with his.

"Let's wait on that," he suggested and kept his hand on hers. Angie's skin was smooth and silky. He had never before felt such a texture. A warmth coursed through him like a mild electric current.

"Why?" she said.

Joey nodded toward their two cups. "We haven't finished our coffee. And besides, I've wanted to sit and talk with you like this since the fourth grade." He bobbed his head toward the parking lot. "It doesn't seem fair to cut it short just because of these clowns." Releasing her hand, he sat back against his cushion and smiled. "I'm living up in the mountains above Dahlonega. Ever been up around Blood Mountain? It's beautiful country."

Angie tried to appear engaged in his question, but she was having a hard time keeping her eyes off the men in the lot. "Don't you think we should go ahead and call, Joey? What if they do something to your car?"

Joey turned his head to watch the men outside. "You're not going to be able to relax, are you?"

Angie frowned. "How can you be so nonchalant about this?"

"Well," he said, talking into the windowglass, "I pretty much know how this is going to play out with these guys, so—" He shrugged. Returning his smile to Angie, Joey tapped an index finger down on the tabletop. "I'm much more interested in what's going on right here in this booth. Would you like some pie or something?"

He looked up at the menu hand-lettered on a chalkboard above the counter. The first column, in red chalk, covered meats. The second, in green chalk, listed vegetables. The third was in yellow for desserts—

banana pudding and a gamut of pies. He scanned the green column for asparagus but found none. Angie clutched her cell phone and stared at him.

"Joey, I'm scared. Surely, you're not going to go out there, are you? There are four of them. And that big one in the black tank-top looks dangerous."

"Well, I think mostly he *believes* that he looks dangerous. Inside he's probably not too sure. Looks like he might be the big brother of the other bald guy. Most of what he's doing out there is for his friends. He needs an audience to pump himself up." Joey shrugged. "This is an important part of the show for him—letting his friends see how tough he is. But he's probably not accustomed to having to go through with backing up his words. He's counting on me to be so intimidated that I won't meet the challenge."

Angie frowned as if he had spoken in tongues. "How do you know all this?"

"Watch his mouth."

She peered out the window. "What about his mouth?"

"Just keep watching. There you go. See that?"

"Did he yawn?"

"Yeah. He tried to cover it, but you really can't suppress a yawn. It arises from the limbic system, and that overrides your conscious will. Yawning is a form of nervousness or fear, forcing your body to accept plenty of oxygen to be ready for whatever's coming."

"How do you know that? How do you know he's not just sleepy?"

Joey smiled as he watched the big man's mouth struggle with a yammering spasm again. "I know," he assured her. "It's my job to know." He tried to comfort her with his smile. "Sure you don't want some pie?"

"I'd feel better if we called the police." She pulled in her lower lip with her teeth and sized up the parking lot again. "I think I'd like to go home, Joey, but I'm afraid to walk out to my car."

Joey's smile died. Now he turned his head for a more deliberate survey of the situation in the lot.

"Angie, would you give me just three minutes? Wait here until I come back, okay? Maybe finish your coffee? Then I promise we'll leave, if you still want to."

Her eyes widened. "Wait! You're going out there?"

"Sooner this gets resolved, sooner you and I can enjoy the evening."

"What if they have weapons?"

He stood and took off his coat and clip-on tie. "I'll be careful."

Walking out the door, he put all thoughts of Angie on hold. Joey focused on the bald ape leaning on his car and eyed the others peripherally. When Joey stopped halfway across the lot, Big Baldy turned to Skull and produced a machinegun laugh accompanied by a look of incredulity.

"H-h-h-him?" he said jerking a thumb toward Joey. Big Baldy's smile was a mix of mockery and surprised delight. "Y-y-you gotta be k-k-kiddin' me!"

Joey stopped four feet from Big Baldy. "I figure this comes down to you and me," Joey said, looking directly into predatory eyes. "So—" Joey waved him closer to get things underway.

When the brute pushed away from the car, the muscles spreading from his neck to his chest and shoulders rippled, defining themselves for a flash of a moment like a confluence of snakes flexing just under his skin. His skull looked crammed into a pouch of skin too tight for it—like a cantaloupe forced into the finger of a surgical glove.

Joey made a vague gesture toward Skull, who now sat up straighter on the hood. "Your friend there has had his try," Joey said, displaying neither haughtiness nor criticism. "I doubt he wants that nose broken again." Then he canted his head toward the red truck. "And I don't see the pool skimmer wanting in on this. What do you say we skip all the preliminaries and bluster and begin the main event . . . you and I?"

Skull, looking ridiculous with cotton stuffed up his nose, slid to the front of the hood and propped his boot heels on the bumper. Clearly a spectator now, he propped his forearms on his knees and spoke in a muffled, nasal tone.

"See wha' I dold you, Kip? See da way dis asshole dalks?" Skull managed a cocky smile beneath the cotton wadding that expanded his nostrils. He pointed at Joey. "Hey, asshole, afder Kip sdomps your ass in da ground, we'll find oud wha' your smard mouth has da say den."

Kip gathered his body into a combat stance: legs bent, left foot forward, head hunched low, his pumped-up arms weaving before him like two cobras emerging from a basket to engage in a mating dance.

Joey had Kip pegged for the "avalanche" type of fighter—first the showy martial arts pose, then coming hard all at once. In the attack he would either throw what he considered to be a finishing blow, or he would lock Joey up like a wrestler and crush him in the fall.

But it was neither. Kip hocked up phlegm from his chest, made a cannon barrel of his tongue, and shot the glob of mucous at Joey. Not wanting to make an ungainly or undignified move, Joey took his chances and stood his ground, relaxed and confident. The wad of spittle caught him on his left shoulder. Not deigning to look down at the trespass, Joey showed no reaction.

"H-h-how's th-th-at for g-g-gettin' it started, a-asshole?"

Now Joey realized his miscalculation and saw Kip's vocal idiosyncrasy for what it was. The man's habit of wrestling with his gaping mouth hadn't been yawning at all. Kip was one of those linguistically challenged people who had his emergency brake pulled too tight on his vocal cords. He stammered. Like Joey, Kip seemed perfectly at ease. Right away Joey began restructuring his fight strategy into a plan B.

"As an opening shot, that'll do fine," Joey said and took an easy step forward.

Seeming to welcome the approach, Kip produced a confident smile and tightened his fists into chunky boulders. His body shifted into a perfect boxing stance. Kip knew something about fisticuffs.

"Br-br-bring it on, D-Dude."

They began to move in what almost seemed a rehearsed choreography, Joey bobbing and weaving his head, Kip less fluid, tightening like a spring, but showing a sense of timing and control.

"Y'all are damned embarrassin'!" came a new, loud, blaring voice from the red truck. Both fighters were pulled from their rhythm, and they straightened. "Y'all talk too-damn much and juss gen'rally waste time. Juss whip this som'bitch's ass and let's git on home, Kip. I'm hungry!"

"M-m-me f-first, B-Booger," Kip said over his shoulder. "Y-you c-can have l-l-leftovers."

Joey allowed himself a quick glance at Booger, and right away he knew that a "plan C" was in order. The leaf springs of the red truck squealed, and the chassis buoyed up more than a foot. Joey kept his eyes on Kip but watched in his peripheral vision as Booger unlimbered from the bed of the red truck.

Silently reprimanding himself for the oversight, Joey guessed that the new player had been hiding underneath the blue tarp now crumpled in the truck's bed. No, not hiding. He was in the bed because he could not have fit into the cab. The tarp was probably just a cover against dust and mosquitos.

Booger was massive, almost seven feet tall and at least eighty pounds heavier than Kip. He was one of those amorphous rural monstrosities who wore oversized coveralls that must have once been part of a circus tent. He was your typical Southern good old boy raised on biscuits and gravy and fried chicken, all cooked in a lard/steroid concoction. His midsection swayed like a weather balloon filled with oil. His arms were soft and flabby and shook like elongated jellyfish. Rolls of fat stacked up his neck and melded without border into the jowls, which gave no hint of the jawbones hidden beneath. Booger's beady eyes were buried in plump rounded cheeks, and his brow creased like a freshly opened package of overlapping strips of raw bacon. A blue tattoo crowned the top of his head. Joey assumed it might be a swastika. That Joey had not noticed him in the bed of the truck was a major tactical error, but Joey's confidence remained stolid. He liked a good challenge.

"Well, git 'er done then, or I'm goin' inside for somethin' to eat," Booger drawled. When he pointed at the diner, the flaccid flesh hanging from his arm wobbled as if a giant vat of *Jello* was trying to swim out of his T-shirt sleeve. "They make a damn good b'nanner puddin' here."

Joey made a decision—the only one for this situation. One, put Kip down . . . fast! Two, then deal with Booger. The chronological order of his plan was dictated by the simple fact that he could not yet think how to access the vulnerable parts of the well-padded Booger.

Kip opened the play, rushing Joey, who feinted right then dodged left. He turned at the hips and caught the back of Kip's head with a left cross that sent the big man facedown, sprawled in the lot like a paratrooper whose chute had failed to open.

It wasn't the crushing blow Joey had counted on. Kip was fast on his feet, and Joey had not connected as solidly as planned. When Kip pushed up to his knees, three beads of blood formed a dotted line where his cheek had hit the asphalt. Specks of grit and gravel peppered his face from temple to chin. On a professional level, Joey knew that this moment, while Kip was still on his knees, was his opportunity to end phase one of his strategy. One left jab feint and a right cross would do it. But he let Kip get to his feet, and they began to circle again.

Joey danced on his feet, counter-circling, forcing Kip into a side-to-side rocking motion as he turned to follow. Joey's timing was perfect. He insinuated two quick left jabs inside the rhythm of the man's rocking, catching him off-balance. Kip halted his shuffling back-step and straightened, touching his fingertips to his nostrils. When his hand came away with a bright crimson color, he became enraged and lunged at Joey with a roundhouse punch.

It was an easy swing to slip. Kip had abandoned all form and telegraphed the punch in every way. Joey jerked back and followed up the dodge with a back-step retreat as Kip would expect, but then Joey reversed direction and rushed forward to build his own momentum. It was a do-or-die move that he generally did not like to employ with big men, because if it failed, there he was within a bigger opponent's reach. But Joey had no plan to fail. The idea of Booger going inside for pie—and being in the same room with Angie—inspired a swift denouement on this field of battle.

Joey's right fist connected squarely with Kip's Adam's apple, and a wet, choking gasp erupted from Kip's mouth. He went down hard, moaned, and rolled slowly onto his back. There he cradled his throat with both hands and tried to breathe.

Joey turned to face Booger, but the behemoth was practically on top of him, just standing there, unconcerned. He stunk of something so invasive that Joey almost gagged and wondered how this obese man and his stench had gotten so close without Joey detecting him. Joey tried to back away but felt his heels catch on Kip's prostrate body. Right away Kip's hands gripped Joey's ankles like dual vises, and it was clear the situation had flipped with the advantage going to Kip and Booger.

Crouching and then rising, Joey delivered a vicious undercut into the area he judged to be Booger's solar plexus, but his fist seemed to travel endlessly through fat on a path that had no destination. It was as though his hand had been swallowed by a waterbed.

Booger breathed stale beer fumes into Joey's face, canted his head, and pursed pouting lips as though commiserating over Joey's dilemma. Joey paid out two left jabs as a set-up and unleashed the best straight-ahead right he had ever delivered. His fist actually recoiled off Booger's face, like swinging a sledgehammer at a fully inflated car tire.

Booger's smile widened, and one eyebrow arched on his porcine brow. "That all ya got, Pee-wee?" he taunted. He stepped onto Joey's feet, wrapped his gelatinous arms around Joey's shoulders and leaned forward. "Tim-ber!" he sang out in the dutiful warning call of a logger.

There was nothing for it. Nowhere to go but with Booger's downward momentum. Somewhere during the fall Joey had a flash of memory from a high school literature class. Captain Ahab . . . lashed to the underbelly of the great white whale . . . plunging into the depths of a dark ocean that would become his grave.

At impact Joey got a surprise. He had steeled himself for the slam into the asphalt, a bright sear of pain in every vertebra, in every bony edge of his scapulae and pelvis and the back of his skull. Instead, he hit the fleshy landing pad of Kip.

After verifying he was still in one piece, Joey's first concern was air. All reserves of oxygen were closed off to him. Pressing down on him from above was a giant amoeba named "Booger," a mass of stinking, smothering blubber that plunged Joey into darkness. Then, an unexpected sound reached his ears.

Bong-g-g-g-g!!!!

It carried the dulcet resonance of a distant church bell heard in fog. As soon as the faint peal reached Joey's ear, the flaccid mass of Booger went completely limp. Joey tried to identify the sound but abandoned the puzzle when his body signaled more urgent demands for oxygen. He attempted to push the enormous weight off of him, but it was like trying to bench press a thirty-gallon, plastic, garbage bag filled with the bio-hazard throw-away from a liposuction procedure on a pod of elephant seals. Booger was unconscious. Or dead. Joey didn't care which. He needed air.

Then the great inert mass of body above him moved. Not the kind of movement accomplished by internal muscle but more an oozing motion, snail-like and nearly magical. A crack of light opened, and Joey greedily sucked in a lungful of night air. When the space widened, he saw the undercarriage of a car and heard the motor revving. A car was pushing Booger's body off him. It was the unmistakable purr of a Volkswagen.

When Booger's body had rotated about sixty degrees and the car's tires were within an inch of Joey's shoulder, the motion stopped, and the engine shut off. An emergency brake ratcheted tightly, and a door opened. Joey saw a large shoe touch down on the pavement.

"Joey, are you all right?"

It was Angie's voice somewhere behind him. To extricate himself from the sandwich of flesh, Joey gripped the VW's axle and wormed himself free.

Angie stood with her back to Joey and faced off with Pool-boy and Skull who stood frozen side by side at the front of the red truck. Their hands were raised above their ears like outlaws who had been ambushed by a one-woman posse. With a double-fisted grip on a long handled frying pan, Angie stood poised for battle. The pan was as big as a garbage can lid. Her arms were cocked, elbows pointing north and south like a major league heavy hitter.

Booger, still atilt on the front bumper of the VW, was out cold, anaesthetized by the metallic ring of heavy cookware. Kip, still dazed, got to his knees and rolled Booger to his back, which was no mean feat. Then Kip tried to revive Booger by slapping his face, gently at first, then more vigorously.

"B-B-Booger!" Kip called out. "Can you hear me?" He placed a hand on each of Booger's cheeks and applied a viselike pressure as though trying to coax a response from the unconscious redneck. The width of Booger's flaccid face squeezed down to just a few inches, and his lips puckered with a glob of saliva bubbles expanding at the seal of his mouth. Booger looked like a giant, prehistoric manatee sampling a mass of frog eggs.

Desperate, Skull screamed at Kip. "For God's sake, do somethin', man!"

Kip knelt over the fallen giant, pinched Booger's nose, and tilted the shapeless chin up into the CPR position. Kip took a deep breath, stared at Booger's mouth, and reconsidered. Wrinkling his face, Kip exhaled, lowered Booger's head to the asphalt, and turned to Skull.

"Y-Y-You wanna d-do this?" Kip said, his tone defensive now. "He's *your* b-brother!"

Skull stared down at Booger, and his face paled to the color of his cotton nose plugs. When he looked back at Kip, he shook his head.

"He prob'ly ain' all thad bad hurd," Skull mumbled. "Besides, you ain' s'posed da do CPR if your nose is bandaged," he explained. "Ya can die thad way."

At that angle, Joey had a good view of the tattoo on Booger's bald pate. It wasn't a swastika at all. It was, as best Joey could make out, a bowl of banana pudding.

Budge stood coatless in his shirtsleeves, one foot inside the driver's door of the ladybug Volkswagen, his forearms resting on the orange and black-polka-dotted roof. A subtle smile played across his face. Inside the VW a shapely woman with ebony hair and long eyelashes peered out the window at Joey. She was smiling. She looked like the kind of person who liked happy endings.

"You okay, Captain America?" Budge inquired.

Joey rolled his shoulders and tested the arch of his back. "All but my pride."

Budge shrugged. "That'll heal."

Joey pressed his lips into a hard line, nodded, and stared down at his shoes. He knew what was coming.

" 'A man's life,' " Budge began, " 'is interesting primarily when he has failed . . . for it's a sign that he tried to surpass himself.' "

When Joey looked up at Budge, the big bouncer threaded his fingers together on the roof of the car. Joey waited.

"Georges Clemenceau," Budge said, naming the source of the quote.

Joey looked across the highway at the hotel, where they had served as security for the conference and book-signing. "I guess you just happened to be here?"

"Nope," Budge said. "Followed you." He pointed across the parking lot. "Lily and I have been sitting over at the far end of the lot doing the New York Times Sunday crossword puzzle." He nodded toward the two pickup trucks. "Figured these jokers would make a run at you." Budge cocked his head. "Would this be a good time for a critique?"

Joey propped his hands on his hips and let his head sag again. He breathed deeply in and out through his nose and brought up a resigned expression.

"Okay, let's hear it." Grudgingly, Joey pulled a small notebook and pen from his shirt pocket. Flipping open the cover he poised the pen over paper and waited.

Budge crossed his arms over his chest in classic bouncer repose. "Soon as the red-neck, mutant amoeba there—a.k.a. Mr. Booger—made his appearance, you needed to eliminate the Nazi-wannabe—Mr. Kip—posthaste. No rules, no ethics . . . just results. You had two willing and hostile opponents. Taken together they had almost five hundred pounds on you. That's against your one-sixty."

"One-sixty-three," Joey corrected.

Budge conceded the three pounds with a bow of his head. "Still, that's more than three-to-one in the weight department. Not good. You've got to factor in weight. It matters . . . as, I am sure, your recent pile-up here in the parking lot illustrated."

When Joey said nothing, Budge continued. "Your other option was to call the cops." Budge raised his eyebrows and waited for a response. When Joey offered none, the big man pointed across the highway toward the convention center. "Look . . . that was your job site—the hotel. That's where the rules of our profession were relevant." Budge spread his hands to the diner's parking lot in which they stood. "Not here." He tempered his voice with an avuncular tone of understanding. "You've got to learn to think both professionally and unprofessionally." Then he smiled at Angie, who had not relaxed from her Hank Aaron pose. "Lucky for you this lady is not one to sit on the sidelines. That was a helluva headshot. Sounded a little like the bell at Madison Square Gardens. Got *my* adrenaline going."

Joey scribbled notes and ran his tongue across the front of his teeth. "Okay," he admitted, "maybe I hesitated. And I probably should'a called the cops."

Budge spread his hands to the obvious, and together they watched the constant flow of traffic on the highway. A few seconds ticked by, and Joey knew that Budge was browsing through his stockpile of apropos quotes.

" 'On the Plains of Hesitation bleach the bones of countless millions who, at the Dawn of Victory, sat down to wait, and waiting—died.' "

Joey wrote down every word, ballooned his cheeks, and let loose an airy sigh. The quotations were wearing a little thin on him; still, he found himself waiting for Budge to name the author. But the brawny bouncer had directed his attention to the highway again. Cutting through the traffic's steady oceanic roar came the distant whine of a siren. Then another. Paired together they sliced through the night like the cry of seagulls rising above the sound of a heavy surf.

"I called them," Angie said, still holding the giant skillet as though she were ready for an outside fast ball. Her two prisoners remained frozen in time, their hands still up. They stared at her frying pan as if the thing might accidentally go off.

Kip was busy fanning Booger's face, using a flattened-out cardboard carrying container from a six-pack of beer. Each time he fanned, Booger's eyelids fluttered, and a little sigh escaped his fat lips.

"Cops are coming . . . time to vamoose," Budge said and made a snappy drum roll on the roof of the VW. "Follow us around back. We can get through to that *Wendy's* over there and drive out their exit. You pass me and go on out. I might pick up a burger. Haven't eaten since lunch."

Joey walked to Angie and relieved her of the frying pan. Even so, her arms remained in place like a mannequin robbed of its prop. Just a minute away, the police cars sped across the overpass, but Joey took the time to touch Angie's shoulder. Slowly she relaxed.

"I owe you," he said. "Big time."

As she lowered her arms, the two local boys before her lowered theirs in unison. Angie faced Joey, and her nostrils flared. Joey imagined this is what it would feel like to stand before the Queen of the Amazons to ask for a promo photograph as a souvenir. He squeezed her shoulder, smiled, and winked. Pool-boy and Skull took this opportunity to scramble into the cab of the red truck.

"My coat and tie are still inside," Joey said. "Go ahead and get in your car and drive outta here before you have to answer a lotta questions."

Angie pulled the felt-tip pen from Joey's hand, took him by his wrist, and began writing on his palm. When she finished, she capped the pen and inserted it into his pocket.

Joey oriented his hand and read the ten numbers printed in black below his calluses. It was the first time in years he had thought of Sir Percival, but in his mind the image formed: the loyal knight holding the Grail at eye level, studying its elegant lines.

"Call me?" Angie said quietly.

He looked deep into her eyes and soaked up the moment that had been his butterfly dream throughout high school, flitting just out of reach ahead of him in a flower-dappled meadow.

"Is tonight too soon?"

She smiled. "Maybe tomorrow."

He nodded. "Tomorrow."

When Angie pulled away, Joey turned to Kip who now stood uselessly beside Booger's inert mass. "If I were you, I'd think about a quick exit. I don't plan to waste the rest of my night at a police station."

Kip tried to lift Booger, but it was an impossible task. Finally, he produced a mechanic's dolly from the bed of the yellow truck. With Joey's help he managed to roll Booger on top of it. After hooking a heavy-duty chain from the dolly to the trailer hitch of the yellow pickup, Kip slowly hauled Booger toward *Wendy's* in a slow and bizarre procession that brought to mind a Viking funeral gone awry.

Joey returned the frying pan to the diner's kitchen, retrieved his coat and tie, and left a five-dollar tip on the table. By the time he stepped outside to the lot, Angie was gone. When he drove out through *Wendy's*, he spotted the VW waiting in the drive-through lane. Just a few yards away the towing parade had run into trouble at a pothole. Booger was sitting up on the pavement. Using his fingertips, he gingerly tested the swollen knot on the back of his head. Kip struggled to pull one of the back wheels of the dolly out of the hole in the asphalt.

When Budge signaled, Joey pulled between the VW and Booger and stopped. Budge, stuffed behind the VW's steering wheel with his head hunched down under the low roof, leaned over Lily to speak out her window.

"George W. Cecil," Budge said.

Joey frowned. "Huh?"

"The Plains of Hesitation?" the big man reminded.

Lily paid them no mind as she frowned at a folded newspaper held in one hand. With the other hand she tapped a pencil's eraser against her curvaceous lips.

"Anybody know a nine–letter word for 'First tie that binds'?"

Three seconds of silence fell over the two idling cars. At the pickup window, the driver of an open Jeep received a white bag bulging with fast food. A voice blared over a loudspeaker explaining that salt and catsup packets were already in the bag. Beyond the diner, sirens were screaming now, coming hard down the access road.

"Umbilical!" came an unexpected reply. Joey, Lily, and Budge turned as one. It was Booger, looking back at them as if he had won the lottery.

Chapter Twenty

The Sizzling Skillet
Friday noon

When Verdie peeked into the dining room from the kitchen door to keep tabs on the midday crowd, she felt the skin on her forehead tighten with curiosity. She had never known Hoke Limberlost to come into the restaurant for lunch. Around this time of day, if she thought of him at all, she imagined him stewing up a squirrel or turning a trout on a spit in the cool of the forest. But there he was. Sitting at his regular breakfast table.

Hoke wouldn't sit in any other waitress' section but Verdie's. She always took time with him and enjoyed learning about the Cherokees, whose ancient ways Hoke loved to describe. More importantly, Verdie was also the only *Sizzling Skillet* employee willing to brave "Hoke's aura." That's what Verdie called it. Lydelle and the others were more apt to label it "the Limberlost stink of death," and because of that they had begged off from serving him. It was just one more manifestation of Verdie's good heart, and it was proof that growing up on a hog farm—as Verdie had—can widen a person's latitude considerably on what she can tolerate in the way of atmospheric ambience.

Trouble figured into the equation on this day. If Ott was to come in for the Friday Special Chicken Platter—and that was as sure a bet as the county taxes going up to pay for more road signs—there was going to be a serendipitous proximity of outlaw to lawman in the restaurant.

Taking out a tray of iced teas, Verdie took the long way around the room to check on Hoke's truck from the back window. There was nothing incriminating poking out of the Pinto's johnboat bed. She served drinks to the mayor and crossed to the front window as if nothing were out of the ordinary.

"Well, Hoke, I missed you at breakfast this—" Verdie held her breath, leaned in closer, and scrutinized his face. "Hoke, if you paid for that tattoo, I hope you kept the receipt."

Hoke picked up his spoon, wiped it on his shirt pocket and held it before his face like a mirror. "Hell, I plumb forgot."

Verdie squinted at Hoke's smudged cheek. "What is that? An alligator?"

"Beaver," Hoke said, trying to get a profile view of his face in the distended reflection on the spoon. Verdie straightened and worried her eyebrows.

"Why do you want a beaver on your face, Hoke?"

"Verdie, do you'ens know what one word a beaver would wanna say if it could talk the human language?"

"One word? I don't know . . . maybe 'dammit?' "

Hoke frowned and shook his head. Then he cupped a hand beside his mouth and quietly pretended to holler.

"Tim-m-m-m–ber-r-r-r!"

Verdie's gaze remained fixed on Hoke's performance as he scrunched up his face and covered his ears with his hands flattened against the sides of his head. Verdie tilted her head to one side.

"Meaning?"

Hoke leaned forward on his elbows. "Meanin' . . . they's nature's masters at felling very tall structures."

Verdie cocked her head to the other side and considered Hoke. "I hope you don't have any wood shavings in the back of your truck that look like they might have come off an awning post down at L.T. Voss's office."

Hoke smiled and set down the spoon. "Reckon I'll use your restroom and warsh up my face, Verdie." He slid out of the booth. "You can bring me some sweet, iced tea, if you don' mind." He started to walk away but stopped. "Oh, the young feller that rents my cabin is joinin' me for lunch. He'll want iced tea, too. Should be here in a few minutes."

When Hoke came out of the bathroom, his face freshly washed of the pokeberry stains, he saw three things waiting at his table across the room: two glasses of tea and the sheriff. Ott sat there as pretty as he pleased and sipped Hoke's tea.

Verdie managed to intercept an angry Hoke just before he got to the booth, and she practically thrust a glass of tea into his hand before he could speak. "There you are, sir," she said, herding Hoke toward the back of the room. "I have the perfect table for you and your guest right back here, sir."

Because he had no intention of sitting in the back of the room—this being a stigma from his grammar school days—Hoke balked at Verdie's physicality, slipped around her, and dropped into the front booth abutting Ott's. He sat with his back to the sheriff's back, but because Ott's rotund body could turn only a few degrees at most from a seated position, the sheriff didn't see that it was Hoke behind him.

Verdie pressed a stiff index finger against her lips and gave Hoke a stern look of warning. Then she sidestepped to Ott's booth.

"You must'a heard me comin', Verdie," Ott said, raising the iced tea like a toast.

"Will it be the chicken platter, Ott?" she said, flipping open her pad by habit.

Ott gave her one of his wistful looks that always accompanied his attempts at humor. "Does a trout make pee-pee in the creek, Verdie?"

Verdie had mouthed the predictable words with him, but he didn't see her as he gave the menu a perfunctory look-see. He pointed to the empty seat across from him. "Better bring two platters. L.T.'s buyin' today."

Like that was some breaking news. L.T. buying was as sure a thing as that incontinent trout fouling its own stream. Ott wrinkled his nose and looked around the room as much as his inflexible neck would allow.

"Y'all's septic tank back up or somethin'?"

"I think the cook burned the eggplant," Verdie said and flipped the page of her order tablet. "Enjoy your tea, Sheriff. I'll have your platters out here in a few minutes."

When she sidled back to Hoke, she found him working up a look of indignation at being bumped behind Ott in the ordering process. To shush any complaint, Verdie jumped right in.

"All right now . . . where were we, Mr. L? For entrees . . . the fried chicken special, fried chicken livers, chicken-fried steak, catfish, meatloaf, pork chop casserole, Irish stew, and Friday hash. Oh, and burned eggplant." For sides we have collards, fried okra, field peas, stewed corn, fried tomatoes, cinnamon carrots, pole beans, turnip greens, and a baby kale salad." All this was delivered in one British breath, and Hoke stared at Verdie in amazement—not just because of her long-winded recitation of foods but also that she was able to maintain that accent throughout the ordeal. Then, when she pressed a vertical index finger to her lips again, his expression turned questioning.

Just then L.T. Voss appeared and squeezed into Ott's booth across from the sheriff. Verdie watched him make a big presentation of a cigar box that he pushed across the table.

Verdie leaned on Hoke's table and put her English lips close to his ear. "Now listen to me, Hoke Limberlost," she whispered in a no-nonsense tone. "Don't you start bragging about anything you might be doing at night, do you hear me? I know you. It might be amusing to you, but it's going to be something else to him." She jerked her head toward Ott.

Hoke performed a sewing-up-his-lips pantomime, stacked his forearms on the table, and stared at Verdie like a recalcitrant child. He tried to say *yes ma'am* but his stitched lips allowed only a muffled version of the phrase.

"Ymmmg, mmmngm."

Verdie arched one eyebrow as an exclamation point to her ultimatum. She slapped her order pad to the table and bent as if she might actually use it.

"So, what will you have, sir?" Verdie asked, holding a warning in her eyes.

Hoke pointed to his own mouth. His lips were pulled in now, making his mouth a sealed slit. Apparently, his stitches had tightened.

Verdie upped the arch of her eyebrow and winged it. "Yes, sir . . . one chicken special."

Hoke murmured something unintelligible and shook his head.

"Meatloaf?" Verdie suggested.

Hoke shook his head again.

"Pork chops?' she tried.

Hoke's head kept shaking.

When Verdie propped her fists on her hips and glared at Hoke, he just shrugged. "I dare say it's probably time for those stitches to come out, don't you think?"

Hoke shrugged again.

Verdie held up two stiff fingers and spread and closed them like scissors twice. "Dr. Verdie will see you now." Assuming a surgeon's inspecting gaze, she snipped her fingers before his mouth, and right away his lips parted, and Hoke sucked in a chestful of air.

"I'll order once't my tenant gits here, Verdie."

Looking out the window, Verdie saw Joey's car and a sheriff's patrol car pull into the lot in mirror symmetry. Joey got out, spotted Hoke through the window, and came inside. Duffy Hawkins stepped out of his patrol car and propped a boot inside the open door as he talked on his radio. When he finished, he tossed the mouthpiece into his cruiser and walked around Hoke's truck. As he passed the cab he bent from the waist and spent some time at the window.

"Yes, sir," Verdie said. "I'll come back when your guest arrives."

"The guest is already here, Verdie." Hoke jabbed a thumb toward his chest. "Joey's buyin' *me* lunch."

"Very good, sir," Verdie said, and reminded Hoke to be cautious by pressing her index finger against her mouth yet again.

Hoke frowned. "You want me to stitch 'em up again? How'm I gonna eat?"

Verdie closed her eyes and shook her head like a retriever emerging from a pond and flinging water everywhere. Without further ado, she walked off toward the kitchen.

Joey came down the aisle walking a little stiffly. When he slid into the booth with Hoke, his face went stoic as he tried to hide the pain in his joints.

"Mr. Limberlost, I hope you haven't been waiting long."

Hoke waved a hand at the air, dismissing such a thought. "Cher'kees were masters o' waitin', son. Bein' patient, for the old-time Cher'kee, was as nat'ral as breathin' air. Did you'ens know there ain't no word in the old Cher'kee language for waiting too long in a rest'rant?"

Joey frowned but did not comment.

"What I mean is," Hoke continued, "they weren't no word for 'patience.' " He chuckled. "Makes you'ens wonder what a medicine man called his customers, don't it?"

Joey opened his mouth as if he might ask a question, but he didn't.

Hoke smiled. "Juss a old Cher'kee joke, son. Medicine man? Patients? Git it?"

When Joey did not laugh, Hoke lost his smile and leaned in closer.

"You'ens is lookin' a lil' bent, son?"

Joey nodded. "Woke up with a kink in my back. I tried to lift something too heavy last night."

"Well," Hoke said with a twinkle in his eye, "you'ens look like yore spirits got lifted in the bargain. You'ens get a job?"

The picture of Angie's face projected in full color on the screen of Joey's mind's eye. This time the image was not a high school memory. It was Angie wielding a fifteen-pound frying pan, standing radiant on the field of battle. Angie of Arc.

Joey shook his head. "It was a temporary job. But I ran into an old friend last night," he said, opting for supreme understatement.

Hoke laughed and pointed at Joey's flushed face. "I know *that* look. There's a good-lookin' woman some'eres in this story."

Joey smiled and lowered his gaze to his hands on the table. Before Joey could explain, Hoke felt his seat shake as if the first tremor of an earthquake was announcing itself in Lumpkin County.

"That you back there, Hoke?" Ott grunted, trying to turn enough to see for himself but losing that battle.

Hoke said nothing, his mood changed like the sudden spoiling of a fruit by an early frost. Joey watched as Hoke once again went through his sewing-up-the-lips act.

An awkward silence stretched out for several seconds until Joey leaned across the table. "Mr. Limberlost, I've got the rent money for you," he whispered. "And, like I told you, lunch is my treat." He pulled some folded bills from his shirt pocket and slid them across the table. "I want to thank you for your patience." When Joey realized his choice of a word, he made an instant edit. "Or whatever it was you used."

Hoke ignored the money. The back of his seat continued to bump and rumble, making Hoke's head bobble as if he were driving one of the county's worst roads with four flat tires.

When Ott had gotten himself turned part way around with his chubby knees out in the aisle, the shimmying of the booth seat stopped. "How the hell you been, Hoke?" Ott said through his election-day-is-only-a-few-months-away smile. "This your new renter?"

Joey looked from the sheriff to Hoke, but Hoke seemed dedicated to the spoon he was paddling in circles in his tea, his mood as gelid as the ice tinkling in his glass.

"Joey Gallatin," Joey said, by way of introduction.

"I'm Sher'ff Ambrose," Ott said through his a-vote-for-me-means-you-got-a-friend-in-county-politics smile. He cut his eyes to the back of Hoke's head and widened the smile. "Ol' Hoke, he don't much talk to me on account o' my ancestry. Even though I put a pris'nor work detail out there at Hester Gap to clean up that mess o' dead chickens after that chicken truck turned over."

"Yeah, I noticed you'ens got on that right quick," Hoke said, without turning. "Heard you had a big chicken fry over to your place that night."

Ott laughed quietly. "Well, you know the ol' sayin', Hoke. 'When life gives you worms, you go fishin'.'" Ott chuckled. "I think we might'a left you one or two out there by the highway in case you was to do some foragin' o' your own, Hoke. Mr. Gal'tin, anythin' the sher'ff's department can help you with, you come on down to the office and lemme know."

As the booth seat went into spasms again, Joey nodded his thanks and leaned in closer to Hoke. "Who's the sheriff's ancestor?" he whispered.

Hoke hissed through his teeth. "Damn Gen'l Winfield Scott. He's the one run the Cher'kees out the mountains. Made 'em walk all the way out to Oaklyhomer."

"Aw, come on, Hoke," Ott crooned over his shoulder. "It weren't as bad as all that. Betcha a gold mine against a grub worm that was a dandy little trip." Ott took on an impish grin and winked at L.T. "Good scenery. Good climate. Good exercise. And well worth the trip, considerin' all them gamblin' casinos they got out there now. Wouldn' mind goin' out to Okl'homa myself one day . . . try an' get rich off o' blackjack, maybe."

"Say, Hoke," L.T. Voss said pleasantly. "I hear the land taxes are goin' up considerable next year. I'm still interested in that creek frontage should you need to sell off a little land."

Joey recognized the *Crispy Cheese Twirl* man from the grocery. When Ott chuckled, Voss's smile widened, and he winked at the sheriff.

Hoke huffed deep in his throat. "Prob'ly turn it in to another damn circus like you'ens done over on the Etowah," Hoke said loud enough to carry back behind him.

"Just helping folks find their dreams, Hoke," Voss crooned. "That's my job." Holding on to his unctuous smile, Voss winked at Ott and shook his head at Hoke's lack of vision.

Hoke snorted. "Soon's a hunert-year flood comes a-warshin' through there, you gonna help those folks find their furn'ture while it's a-floatin' down to the Gulf?"

Voss chuckled. "Come on now, Hoke. It was up to you, we'd all be living down at the penitentiary in Alto, and the Indians could all come back here to live in our homes."

Ott shot L.T. a look for opening up that can of worms.

"Well, why not?" Hoke barked indignantly. "It's all Cher'kee land that got stole from 'em by the likes o' you!"

Verdie seemed to appear out of thin air. "Here are your chicken platters, gentlemen?" she said cheerily and clacked down plates before Ott and Voss.

Hoke was not through being incensed. He raised his voice to Voss.

"Ask your sheriff-friend there 'bout how his great-granddaddy, Ott Scott—second cousin to ol' Winfield—took over a Cher'kee log cabin at the point of a shotgun. Moved in and ate they's corncakes while they's still hot from the woodstove."

Ott shook his head and muttered, "Here we go!"

When Duffy Hawkins entered the room, Ott noted his purposeful walk, and already he was feeling his gastric juices gathered in vain. Ott held his iced tea with both hands—a sign that he would not easily be pried away from the Friday special.

Hawkins stopped next to Ott and hooked his thumbs over his gun belt. Joey remembered him. It was the deputy on duty at the scene of the awning post mutilation. Joey watched the easy way the deputy stood, relaxed but ready, reminding Joey a little of himself. The deputy gave no indication that he saw L.T. Voss or Hoke or Joey, but something about the deputy's deportment made Joey think that, if asked, he could fill out a seating chart from memory naming everyone in the room. He wore his straight-brimmed hat low over his eyes. Joey thought he looked a little like a young Charles Bronson.

"I tried callin' you, Ott," Duffy said. "Must'a had your radio turned off. Phone, too."

"Must have," Ott quipped and sipped his iced tea. After setting down his glass, he looked up at his deputy and shrugged. "It's lunchtime, Duff. Wanna join us?"

Duffy's expression remained unreadable behind his dark glasses. "We got us a situation out on the highway."

Ott picked up his tea again and started to drink. "What? Pileups?" He almost sipped but changed his mind again. "Listen, Duff, don' be callin' in any tow trucks from outside the coun'y again. That don't help us come election time."

Deputy Hawkins turned his head toward Joey's table. Joey could not be sure where the man's eyes were angled behind those glasses, but he put his money on Hoke.

"Somebody felled four full-sized billboards out on highway four hundred sometime last night. Looks like they burned through the posts with an acetylene torch. Same M.O. as the Metcalfe sign. Took down a subdivision sign on highway sixty, too. One with the golf course."

"Which one?" Ott said, his face wrinkling with an anxious frown.

"*Fields o' Gold*," Hawkins reported flatly.

Voss frowned at Ott. "Isn't that your brother-in-law's development?"

"Damn," Ott said. "Dwayne's gone be madder'n a preacher at a cussin' contest." He looked up at Hawkins. "Four hun'erd is a state-funded highway. I reckon them billboards is the state's business. We can juss concentrate on Dwayne's sign." Ott thought about it and whistled one sliding note. "That one o' Dwayne's was a thirty-footer. Did the dang thing land in the road?"

Hawkins shook his head. "Landed on Dwayne's truck."

Ott's glass stopped partway to his mouth. He eyed Hawkins again. "Dwayne in it?"

"Nope. Only thing in it was a lawnmower in the bed."

"Well, there's some good news," Ott said and drank some more tea.

"Dwayne said his truck's timin' belt is tore up," Duffy explained. "Why he had to leave it out there. Don't matter now. The truck's totaled. Lawnmower, too."

Ott nodded and started to drink again but turned open-mouthed to Duffy. "Wait a minute! What kind o' lawnmower we talkin' 'bout?"

"Ridin' mower. Looked like a Lawn Master 260. Kind o' like that'n o' yores."

Ott lowered the glass to the table and squeezed his eyes shut. "Dammit!" he hissed under his breath. "It weren't 'kind o' like' mine. It *was* mine! I loaned it to Dwayne a coupla months ago."

Chapter Twenty-One

Qualla Boundary, Oconoluftee River basin
Cherokee, North Carolina
Autumn, 1947

Hoke stared out the window of the family DeSoto sedan and could not believe what he saw. On the three-hour trip from Dahlonega into North Carolina, he had quietly tingled with the anticipation of seeing "his people." Now he saw a town crammed with tourist shops and sideshows. It was a circus of enterprises stretched out to fit onto the main street. The thick cloud cover that hung over the valley was like a blanket thrown down by the Elder Fires Above, so that they would not have to witness the sacrilege of the song and dance.

In front of a store selling beaded necklaces, moccasins, and rubber-headed tomahawks, a heavyset man—his face painted red, white, and blue and atop his braided hair a Plains Indian bonnet of fake feathers that trailed down his back—danced on the sidewalk for a crowd of gawking tourists snapping cameras, eating *Nutty-Buddys*, and laughing. A young girl wearing fringed buckskin and a beaded headband beat a drum to help him keep time. She looked bored.

At a street corner next to a drug store, another man wore a chain shackled to his ankle. On the other end of the chain was a fully grown black bear. The spectators formed a cautious ring around this pair and threw peanuts and candy for the bear, who pleased all contributors by lapping up their offerings. No one threw food at the man, but a small girl dressed in buckskins walked around with a coffee can to collect coins from the crowd.

"When the white soldiers drove our People out of the mountains," Hoke's mother explained from the front seat, "the ones who ran away with *Tsali* hid in these hills where the soldiers could not find them. Eventually, those who were left behind settled here. They came to own the land, and now it is Cherokee land. This is why we still have Cherokee people here in Katuah."

" 'Xcept for all the ones with paint on their faces, it looks purty much like Dahlonega," Hoke mumbled into the windowglass. "How come they's dancin' on the street like this?"

Selu Limberlost smiled and looked to her husband to answer this. He was watching the road ahead and seemed to have no interest in the spectacles along the sidewalks.

"This here is what the Cher'kee learnt from the white man," Juni said, his usually soft voice now crusted with a hard edge. "How to turn a dollar by providin' a little cheap entertainment. These here . . . these street actors? Some o' the older Cher'kee don' think too highly o' their ways. Some ridicule 'em. Others feel sorry for 'em. They prob'ly ain't got too much else goin' for 'em, so this is how they scrape out a livin'. I reckon they'll keep on a-doin' this long as the white man is foolish enough to pay for it."

Juni turned his head to look at three men decked out in chicken feathers and opossum skins. They stood around a fire that roared inside a metal garbage can. One man had both arms raised, telling a story to a crowd. The other two, both wielding bows and arrows, acted out the plot.

"This ain't our part o' the town, son. We'll be gittin' to the real part d'rectly."

Selu turned around to face Hoke. "It takes all kinds to make a village, my son. Remember that. There is always room to slip one more flower into the vase."

They rumbled across the wooden bridge over the Oconaluftee and turned upstream on a dirt road that wound along the floodplain of the river. Big hemlocks and birches and sycamores leaned out over the water like vaulted arches. The water looked dark and powerful—like blue-black metal somehow liquefied by the cold. Unpainted cabins were scattered along the stream and splotched with lichen and moss and fit into their surroundings in a way that made the cottage architecture seem more Indian than white. Every house had at least one dog lying out front. Hoke had hoped to see horses, but there were none. At one cabin an old woman swept her bare dirt yard with a straw broom.

When they crossed another bridge, Juni turned up a dirt lane to follow a smaller tributary churning with rapids. "This here is the Raven Fork. All your people on my side lived up here in these coves."

"What about Mama's people?" Hoke asked.

Selu turned and propped her arms across the backrest. Falling in gentle waves all the way to her waist, her hair was the dark amber of maple syrup and did not look Indian at all. But her colorful dress and necklace of tiny carved animals more than compensated. She gave more attention to her heritage than even did Juni, who wore coveralls over a white, J.C. Penney undershirt.

"My family lived down in Bryson City," Selu explained. "My people got all mixed up with Scots and scattered about from Florida to Ohio. My mama and all my aunts and my sisters and cousins . . . they all married Scots. In our courting days your father hitchhiked down to Bryson City at least once every two weeks to make sure I didn't run off with a Scot." She poked Juni's shoulder, but he didn't look at her.

"Why'd they all wanna marry someb'dy named 'Scott'?" Hoke asked.

Selu laughed. "They didn't, silly. They had names like Horace and Wallace and Dunston. They were from Scotland."

Juni rotated his head a degree to talk over his shoulder. "There was this one named Silas. He thought he was gonna marry your mama. Thought he was bound and destined to be with 'er."

Hoke sat forward on the seat. He could detect no smile on his father's face, so he assumed this was a true story.

"What happ'ned?"

Juni cracked a grin and turned his head enough to show his profile. It was a face Hoke loved to admire. Whereas some folks had expressed surprise at Selu's heritage, no one could doubt Juni's with his strong nose and jutting cheekbones. His soot-black hair was coarse and glossy like the mane of a horse. Juni winked at Hoke.

"Juni Limberlost came along . . . is what happened," he said and turned back to watch the road as he allowed his smile to spread into his twinkling eyes. Just as quickly, he grew serious again. "Our people took a likin' to the Scots. They say it's 'cause we're both mountain folks. They called theirselves 'highlanders.' But when it comes down to a woman choosin' 'tween a Cher'kee and a Scotsman, there really ain't no contest. Them Scots got teeny, little twangers underneath them little plaid dresses they wear."

Selu punched Juni's arm. When he didn't flinch, she said, "Silas Manning got rich over in Asheville buying and selling land. Maybe I *should* have married him." She winked at Hoke. "Maybe I could be living in a mansion right now."

Juni nodded thoughtfully. "Well, we can call 'im up from the gas station b'fore we leave and see if it's too late."

Selu punched Juni harder, but her husband remained in character. The car sputtered and lost power for a moment and then lurched forward and settled.

Juni jabbed his thumb back toward Hoke. "If it's all the same to you, I'd like to keep ol' Hoke there and you can have this damned DeSoto. That was one damn poor idea buyin' a car named for that Spanish jaybird."

When the car pulled into a narrow drive that snaked back through a dark stand of hemlock trees, Hoke could sense a change in his parents.

Gone was the light banter, and in its place came an expectant reserve as their eyes peered into the shadows.

"This man livin' here," Juni explained in his no-nonsense voice, "he was a respected healer for a long time—maybe the grandest-ever. But now he's got so old, people ain't too sure 'bout whether he's 'memberin' the plants and the medicines 'xactly right. But I want you to be respectful to him. He was there the night you was born, and he gave the blessin' that got you started on your path."

Hoke stacked his forearms on the driver's seatback. "What's my path?"

Juni exchanged a glance with Selu. "Well, that there's something you and old Mingo can talk 'bout." Juni pointed out the front windshield to a cataract of cascading water. It was partly hidden behind laurels and rhododendron where a side-creek joined with the main fork. "That there's Mingo Falls."

Still in earshot of the falls, they parked the car in front of a shack slapped together with every manner of boards and no discernable method of design. One piece of the siding was a slab of plywood painted yellow and turned on the vertical. Hoke angled his head to make out the stenciled lettering across the middle. *Bridge Out 100 Yards*, it read.

The shack's roof was shingled in cupped sections of tulip tree bark. The individual pieces had warped so badly that Hoke could not imagine the hovel staying dry during a storm. A cap-less stovepipe rose straight out of the roof like a cannon barrel intent on lobbing a suicide shot.

Before they opened the car doors, Juni turned to Hoke with a sober eye. "Son, the proper thing would be for you to call 'im 'Grandfather Mingo.' Now, he ain't your rightful grandfather, but it's the polite thing to do. Do you think you can do that?"

"Yes'r."

The three of them gathered at the cabin's front door, where Juni knocked quietly. For a long time they listened and heard nothing at all, until a voice spoke from outside the house at the corner nearest the creek.

"Been plenty a winter since I seen you, Juni Limberlost. And your good-lookin' woman." His shining eyes fixed on Hoke, and the boy felt himself heat up and then go cold—as if he had stepped from bright sunlight into a waterfall. "And this would be Black Fox," the old man said.

"Well, we mostly call 'im 'Hoke' now," Juni said.

Mostly?! Hoke had never heard the name "Black Fox" in his life. He had the strange feeling that this old Cherokee holy man knew more about him than even his parents did.

The man called "Grandfather Mingo" was tall for a Cherokee. His skin was as dry as snake's scales and his silver-white hair as fine as spider's silk. He wore a two-striped Hudson Bay blanket that had been converted into a capote. Capping the silvery hair was a multi-colored turban just like Hoke had seen in that famous painting of Sequoya smoking his long-stemmed pipe and holding up the Cherokee syllabary he had developed.

"We brung you this pie," Juni announced. "Selu made it. It's persimmon." Juni put his arm around his wife, and she held out the pie wrapped in foil. This she topped with her engaging smile.

The old man nodded. "You two go on inside and heat some water for coffee." Then he lowered his gaze to Hoke. "You and I will walk by the water."

Hoke followed the old man along a river trail, neither of them trying to talk over the rush of water. The river stones cobbled on the beaches were smoother than the ones at home. More symmetrical. Like unsliced, oversized, gray hamburger buns made of rock. The water was clear and dark at once, and the air lifting off its surface felt clean and cool, except when the breeze shifted and brought a disagreeable aroma from somewhere. Hoke tried to ignore it and concentrated on the pristine feel of the valley.

He knew he was walking through history. The Cherokee had been living in harmony with this land for a long time, and it still looked healthy and nurturing—not all used up and eroded like the land that was mined for gold around Dahlonega. He felt the long stifling ride in the car loosen and fall away from him like binding cords that had untied themselves as if by magic.

The old man moved with great care among the rocks and roots and the fiery autumn leaves, but Hoke had to work at keeping up with him. Each time he came abreast of the man, he saw that old Mingo had his eyes closed, and Hoke wondered how he could walk like this without tripping. He also noticed that each time he gained the side of the old man . . . that foul smell intensified.

They stopped at a great hollowed-out sycamore bole that stood on the floodplain like a giant, sturdy, milk-gray washtub right at the edge of a wide pool. The stream was quieter here. Hoke watched the old man step into the circular trunk and sit on its smooth rim. When Hoke climbed in and sat across from Mingo, they were like two strangers soaking their feet in the same tub. Hoke noticed that the offensive aroma that had intermittently wafted to him during their walk was now a permanent scent violating the air. He checked the inside of the cavity for anything dead but found nothing but desiccated leaves.

"What have your mother and father told you about the People?" Grandfather Mingo asked and held his dark liquid eyes on Hoke. They were kind eyes. Eyes that could wait an eternity for an answer.

" 'The People'?" Hoke said.

Grandfather Mingo nodded. "Our People," he said.

Hoke cleared his throat. "Daddy told me 'bout the Little People who live in the woods. The tricksters. And Mama tells the story about *Tsali* a lot. I ain't really all too sure how much they know 'bout any other Ind'ans." Hoke's eyes widened with a memory. "But I read a book 'bout the Cher'kee from the library."

"I don't know that story," old Mingo said.

Hoke frowned. "Which one?"

" 'The Cher'kee from the Library.' Would you tell it to me?"

Hoke's frown deepened. "It's juss a book. It tells 'bout the Cher'kee growin' corn and beans and squash together and makin' a gov'ment and a newspaper and havin' to walk the Trail o' Tears and how *Tsali* escaped and stuff like that."

Mingo looked out over the calm pool and nodded. "*Tsali*," he sighed, as if he might have known the man. "He will always stand as a lodestar for the Cher'kee. We can all learn from his story. Have you ever looked at his name backwards?"

Hoke's eyebrows lowered over the bridge of his nose. "How would I see it if I turned 'round backwards? I'd prob'ly git a crick in my neck tryin'."

"I mean write it down and look at the name from the wrong end?"

When Mingo spelled it for him, Hoke squinted at the old man for several seconds, then picked up a stick and scratched the word in the sand outside the bole. When he had it written—"T-S-A-L-I"—he tried coming at it from the tail end. "I . . . last?" he said.

Mingo smiled. "Sorta like a Cher'kee version of 'Last o' the Mohicans,' ain't it?"

"I guess," Hoke said and stared at the letters again. He thought about it and slowly began to nod. "How come you'ens was to call me 'Black Fox'?"

Mingo's smile softened. "That was the name given to you when you were born." The old man made a dismissive gesture with his hands. "Many of the People who live among the whites use a name more suited for that commingling, but all have a true Cher'kee name—a name of the spirit. Sometimes a shorter, conversational name is used. Like your father's. Has he told you about his full name . . . Junaluska?"

"Who?"

"Junaluska was a great warrior. He saved the life of that forked-tongue snake Andrew Jackson at Horseshoe Bend. If only he had known then how Jackson would betray the People."

"I read 'bout the Battle at Horseshoe Bend," Hoke said proudly. "Cher'kees and the whites ag'in' the Muskogees."

Mingo pushed a harsh breath out of his lungs. "The white devils were clever. Taking advantage of our long-standing enmity with the Muskogee. It was the native people on both sides who fought the bravest. Mostly native blood was spilled that day."

Hoke was getting lost with so much history thrown at him in one sitting. The last thing he had expected today was a school lesson. For lack of anything else to do, he etched the letters of his Cherokee name in the sand beneath *Tsali*'s. Once he had it, he tried reading it backwards. "X . . . of . . . Kcalb," he said, frowning. He looked up at Mingo. "I don' git it."

Mingo swung one leg over and swept away the English words with the toe of his high-top moccasin. "The Cher'kee word for Black Fox is '*Inâli*.' Write that down." He spelled it for Hoke. "I-N-A-L-I."

Hoke scratched out the letters and stared at this new word. He went at it from the back, from the bottom, and from the top. He even tackled it inside out but to no avail.

"I still don' git it."

Mingo stared at the word for a long time. Then he looked off over the creek with a pained expression.

"Yeah, me neither. Sometimes it don't seem to work."

"Who chose that name for me?"

Mingo brought his hand up and pressed it flat against his own chest. "I did." That was when Hoke noticed the odd necklace partially hidden behind Mingo's capote. A flap of something black and hairy strung with rawhide. Two flies kept buzzing around it, but Mingo seemed not to be bothered by them.

Hoke studied his Cherokee name in the sand again. "So how come a fox? Why weren't I a wolf or a mountain lion or a bear or somethin' like that?"

Mingo crossed one leg over the other, clasped his hands over the upper knee and leaned back, settling in for a story. It looked to Hoke like they might be sitting in this tree trunk for a long time—a proposition made worse by the unpleasant odor hovering there.

"Once in a rare moon the mother fox drops a pup that is solid black. As he gets older the tips of some of the hairs will turn silver, but by and large this fox is as dark as a moonless night. The one you will not see. He is the rare one. The black fox."

Hoke waited for more, but the old man's eyes closed and soon his breathing became more pronounced. Hoke was half sure the man had fallen asleep. When Mingo's body began to tilt toward the river, Hoke jumped up and grabbed him by the front of his capote. Mingo's eyes flew open, and he took a grip on the rim of the trunk. Hoke let the man go and peered around his feet. That death-smell was stronger here by Mingo.

"Thank you," Mingo said. "I stayed up very late last night working out that thing about *Tsali*'s name. I thought you would like it."

"You'ens knowed I was comin'?" Hoke asked in a cracked whisper. Grandfather Mingo nodded. "But Daddy said you'ens ain't got no telephone."

As they stared into one another's eyes for several heartbeats, the sound of the rapids upstream seemed to grow in volume, and Hoke began to suspect that there must be ways to send messages other than by telephone. He imagined Grandfather Mingo lowering his ear to the river to pick up communications from anywhere that river went. Because Hoke was good with maps, he could see the route in his mind. His daddy's message would have traveled down the waterfalls of Frogtown Creek, down the rapids of the Chestatee then over the shoals of the Chattahoochee into the slow meander of the Apalachicola, all the way to the Gulf, where it would skip across the salt waves over to the mouth of the Mississippi and travel upstream to take the right fork of the Ohio, another right at the Tennessee River and then across the state of the same name to the Little T, then the Tuckaseegee to the Oconaluftee and finally taking a hard left up the Raven Fork. It was a remarkable path for a message, Hoke calculated, and it didn't cost a cent.

"Daddy said you'ens would show me my path today." Hoke looked back at the trail they had followed along the riverbank and pointed at their tracks in the sand. "Is that it yonder?"

Mingo smiled. "Black Fox, do you feel the Cher'kee blood running through your veins?"

Hoke considered this. "Sometimes, I guess. I make bird calls a lot, and the birds talk back to me. I reckon that means somethin'. I guess maybe I oughta be tryin' to talk with foxes, though. Is that right, Grandfather Mingo?"

"Your father's father was a full-blood. Juni's mother was half. I've never been sure about your mother. That part is complicated. She comes from the Blue Clan, and they got plenty watered down by them Scots, if you can pardon the expression."

Hoke's face lighted up. "I heard o' Scots and water before. It was down at a bar where I had a day job sweeping the floor."

Old Mingo nodded politely, but a look of confusion remained on his face. "Anyway, 'bout your mama . . . she has enough of the blood to put you above the mark of a half-breed. Because you walk in the white world, you are like a shadow of the People reaching into a culture that needs to understand our ways."

Hoke swallowed. "I ain't sure I followed all that. I'm a shadow?"

"If you remember your roots," Mingo continued, "you will find your path among the whites. Your shadow will fall over them, change them. This is your prophecy, Black Fox."

Hoke was lost. He looked down at the roots of the old sycamore and wondered if he was supposed to memorize them. After a few minutes he gave up on the task. It was like that hour of arithmetic in school. He decided to be quiet, soak up what he could, and hope for the best.

"The fox is cunning," Mingo explained. "He is the phantom of the forest. You'll not know he was there but for the pile of feathers he leaves from the grouse or the droppings of scat filled with hair and bone of mouse. Like the black fox, you will blend into the night. That is when you should hunt. But before you go out, learn your territory well. Look for signs."

"What kind o' signs?"

"You will know the answer to that when you need to, Grandson. Remember, the fox is like smoke drifting into the trees, disappearing. Whenever you are unsure what to do, disappear like the fox, go into the deep forest and listen to the real world. The real world will always show you the right thing to do."

They sat in silence, and again Mingo closed his eyes. Hoke kept steady watch over the old man lest he fall asleep and start to tumble toward the water again. A long time went by, most of which Hoke searched for the source of that smell. The sun would soon slide behind the steep mountains to the west. The temperature had already dropped by several degrees, and Hoke hugged his arms to his chest. Finally, Mingo's eyes opened.

"Can we go git some o' that pie now?" Hoke asked. "I been cravin' it all the way up here to North Car'liner."

Grandfather Mingo smiled. "Spoken like a true fox."

No other word was said of paths or foxes or the real world. Hoke and Mingo returned to the cabin, and the four of them ate pie and drank hot coffee by the woodstove. The grown-ups talked of family and deaths and what was going on with the tribal council. Hoke was still trying to identify that smell. It seemed to have followed them into the shack and somehow had grown stronger in the confined space.

In the early evening when Juni and Selu rose to leave, Grandfather Mingo took Hoke aside and said, "I have something for you."

Juni and Selu stepped outside, giving the boy and the old man some privacy. Mingo lifted the necklace over his head and placed it over Hoke's. Right away the rank smell assaulted Hoke's nostrils. The stench nearly made him pass out.

Steeling himself against the odor, Hoke held his breath and lifted the lone talisman to better see it. It was smaller than his hand, triangular, hard and twisted, and covered with black hairs on both sides.

"A fox's ear," Mingo said. He lifted his eyebrows. "A black fox."

Hoke turned it in his hand, thinking all the time how his father was not going to let him take anything that smelled like this into the car. "Where'd you git it?" Hoke asked.

Mingo pointed down the drive. "Down the road at Hootie Deerlope's place. Juss a week ago. It was hung up on some barbed wire. Just a ear . . . all by itself. I was lucky to git to it before Hootie's hogs found it. I think this timin' was meant to be."

The more he thought about it, Hoke could see that this old man had made a sacrifice for him—enduring this odor of the dead for seven days. A warm wave of gratitude washed through Hoke. Whether the necklace was a skunk or a Doberman pincer or a vampire bat, it didn't matter. It was the giving that mattered. It didn't mean he had to wear the stinking thing though . . . he hoped.

"You must always wear this . . . until the day you become complete," Mingo said.

Hoke felt his future collapse under the weight of this smothering stench. "When do I 'become complete'? I feel purty close to bein' who I'm s'posed to be right now."

Mingo closed his eyes and smiled. "You will know."

Hoke figured that the rest of his life would be one long chain of contests in seeing how long he could hold his breath.

"This fox ear has been blessed and touched by the Elder Fires above. It will forever be potent and a source of strength for you."

"What do you'ens mean?" Hoke said, already dreading the answer.

Mingo smiled encouragingly. "Most animal parts dry out and lose their smell." He dabbed his finger at the air, pointing to the necklace. "Not this one. It has big medicine."

Hoke looked down and frowned at the vestige of ear. "There's some excitin' news," he mumbled and followed Mingo out into the waning light of day's end.

Outside the shack they all said the proper words, and the Limberlosts piled into their DeSoto. When Mingo approached, Hoke rolled down his window.

"I will come see you again, Grandfather Mingo."

The old Cherokee nodded. "And I will be waiting."

Hoke marveled at the old man's certainty. "Will you know when I'm coming like you did this time?"

"I will if your father calls down to the gas station again. Ernie Two Pipes works down there. He is my nephew." Mingo raised a finger. "One last thing, Black Fox?"

"Yes, Grandfather."

"Remember, you must always wear the necklace. To remind you who you are."

So much for ever gettin' married, Hoke thought. "So far I ain't never had no trouble 'memberin' who I am."

"You will wear it until you leave the white world and come back to your people."

Mingo stepped back and raised one hand like a holy man bestowing a prayer upon a traveling pilgrim. As the car pulled out on the long winding drive, Hoke knelt backward in his seat, staring out the back window with his chin propped on the backs of his hands. The old man stood as still as a tree on a windless day, and then he was swallowed up by the bend in the road.

Just after Juni made the turn onto the river road, something dark stepped behind the car from the sumacs and stood in the road looking at Hoke. A dog. A medium-sized black dog. As the car sputtered away Hoke made out a dainty muzzle and one ear missing or laid flat. He couldn't tell which. When the animal turned and leaped into the forest, Hoke saw the unmistakable plumed tail of a fox. Hoke raised up his head just enough to let his jaw drop.

He turned and sat, cradling the fox ear in his hand. When he slipped it under his shirt, he felt the dried triangle of skin fall somewhere between his chest and his belly button. He felt proud that he understood the significance of that ear without it having to be explained to him. He must be ever-alert, listening like the fox. He resolved to follow Mingo's orders . . . to never take the necklace off. Not until he became complete. Whatever that meant.

Hoke had never felt more Cherokee in his life. It was one thing to know by mathematics that he was four-sevenths Cherokee. Having an ever-present aromatic reminder was quite another. It was the grandest-ever gift he could imagine.

"Inâli," Hoke whispered. He felt struck by silent lightning. He looked up quickly to the mirror to see if his father had heard him. Their eyes locked on one another in the reflection.

"What the hell is that stink?" Juni said.

Selu looked at Juni a little defensively. "Well, it wasn't me!" She turned to look at Hoke. "I could smell it inside Mingo's cabin, too. What have you got there, Honey?"

"Nothin'." Hoke tried to push the rawhide thong deeper under his collar.

She craned her neck forward and made a face. "Is that a necklace? Is that what smells?"

Hoke had to act fast. He asked the Great Spirit's forgiveness for the lie even as it rolled off his tongue.

"Mingo said if I didn' wear it I'd die for sure b'fore I was thirteen."

Hoke saw his father's eyes bore into him from the mirror. Selu turned back around and waited for Juni to make a judgment on this unexpected forecast, but when he said nothing, she cracked her window and raised her chin to get her nose closer to the top of the glass.

Hoke lay down on the backseat and listened to the hum of the tires in the dark. He thought about his name—a name that was all his. *Inâli*. He worked on the letters in his head and discovered that something of note happened when you flipped the last two letters.

"I . . . nail," he muttered to himself. *Maybe*, he thought, *I'm gonna be a carpenter. That or a manicurist.*

Chapter Twenty-Two

Lumpkin County Courthouse
Roy Earl Ricketts, Sr. Memorial Courtroom
Friday afternoon

Duffy Hawkins slipped his sunglasses back on and was betting that Judge Ricketts was wishing for a pair himself. The Vanstory brothers sat side by side at the defendants' table—all of them in odd-fitting sports coats, white dress shirts, and neckties. One coat was hunter green with a royal crest of some kind on the pocket. Another was metallic blue, and the last coat—the one hanging on Mose Vanstory like a tarp thrown over a refrigerator—was lemon yellow. All of it, individually or taken as a whole, clashed with their clannish red hair. The coats were obviously recent purchases from the Thrift Store, but the effect was like wrapping up a set of rusty tools in fancy Christmas paper and setting one end on fire.

"Your Honor," Marvin Huthwaite whined in his long-suffering oratory voice, "these young men represent a long line of Lum'kin County pi'neers and foundin' fathers, and they have never before been associated with such a charge as this. We ask the court's indulgence in suspending bail, as the absence of these hard-working men from their farm would constitute a great hardship on their livestock."

Marvin Huthwaite could find a reason to mourn over a road-killed rattlesnake.

Judge Roy Earl Ricketts, Jr. looked like he had heard everything at least twice up there on the bench, and Marvin's attempt at livestock appreciation was no exception. The judge knew, like everybody else in the room, that Marvin would not know a Charolais breeding bull from a

Shetland pony, much less what kind of care they would require. The judge didn't blink.

"Before I rule on that," Ricketts growled, "let's hear what the prosecutor has to say." When finally, Marvin pressed his hair flat over his bald spot and sat down, Ricketts turned his tired expression to the A.D.A. "Miss Gunlock?" he intoned with judicial solemnity.

Maria Gunlock stood, and every eye in the room was trained on her. She had already conceded to the "Miss." There would be no "Ms. Gunlock" in Lumpkin County except by dialectic elision or by vocal lethargy.

She wore a smart gray suit and plain white blouse with a high button-up collar. Her lustrous black hair was gathered in back by a blood-red brocade ribbon. Her dark skin looked as smooth as coffee-dyed alabaster. The contrast of colors in her appearance was eye-catching. Her large emerald eyes shone with intelligence, and the planes of her cheeks were set like a splitting maul ready to crack Marvin's defense.

Her presence in the courtroom probably accounted for more than eighty per cent of the hundred or so males in the audience. For an arraignment, this might have been an all-time record. Duffy had never seen anything like it. Of course, she was the reason he was here, too.

"Your Honor, by the size of the laboratory and the volume of illegal product seized on the Vanstory farm, I would estimate that these men were capable of supplying most of north Georgia with methamphetamines. Should any hardship to Vanstory livestock arise from their incarceration—that is to say, if these gentlemen cannot afford to hire overseers, and by all accounts they should have the means—we have already contacted the proper agencies to ensure that care and grooming of the animals will be provided until such time as these men are found guilty, as I am confident they will. At that point, an Animal Dispensation Auction will be organized, the proceeds of which will be returned to the accused less the cost of intervening care, transportation, feed, and the auctioneer's fee."

Ricketts turned a cold eye on Marvin Huthwaite. "Motion denied."

A thunderclap applause filled the room. Maria's face flushed to a very dark shade of scorched red, as she turned at the sudden shuffle of men getting to their feet. The scene startled her. Hands clapping in a masculine fervor, toothy smiles, and all eyes locked on her, the whole crowd standing. Turning to the empty jury box, she tried to compose herself. That was when she noticed Deputy Hawkins.

Also surprised by the courtroom's reaction—the first of its kind in Lumpkin County's halls of justice—Hawkins was crouched with his hand gripping his sidearm and panning it in a slow arc in the general direction of the spectators. Lowering his handgun, he slowly straightened like a snake relaxing from its striking coil.

Amid the deafening applause, Maria stood transfixed and helpless. The déjà vu had hit her again, this time like a blow to the solar plexus. Maria leaned forward on the table and tried to steady herself as she stared down at the yellow legal pad between her flattened hands.

She began a silent mantra: *Don't look at the deputy . . . don't look at the deputy.*

She looked at the deputy. The strong and swarthy officer holstered his gun in a movement so flawless and fluid, Maria felt like raising a score card of ten over her head. Standing there in his uniform and ray-bans and illuminated by the courtroom lights, Duffy Hawkins was, as far as Maria Gunlock was concerned, Lumpkin County's Charles Bronson . . . come to rescue her from the crash and burn divorce that had tried to snuff out all her dreams of a happy-ever-after denouement to her life. At that moment . . . in that courtroom . . . she felt as if she had been thrust into a movie to play the leading lady to Bronson's private investigator, Nick DePuma. All this, but without a script. Maria's mind went blank. She could only stare at the deputy. When their eyes locked on one another, she thought she detected a subtle smile that carved a rock-hard dimple into Hawkins's square chin. A startling chill like ice water trickled down her back and then spread a warmth through her loins. It was like lowering herself into a warm bath of carbonated water.

As the unruly din of male celebration filled the room, Judge Ricketts looked as if his boxer shorts had burst into flames beneath his exalted black robe. His ruddy face turned ruddier, and he whacked his gavel until the spectators sat and the room quieted. All but Mose Vanstory. Mose was trying to duplicate the sound of the gavel with his mouth and, failing that, he segued into a syncopated beat for a rap song. When Mose finally noticed the judge glaring at him, he sat down contrite and silent.

"People," Ricketts warned, slowly sweeping the gavel across the room as if he were considering a target at which to hurl it. "This is not a high school basketball game. This is a court of law. If I hear one more outburst like that, I will court this clear-room."

It was Roy Earl Ricketts's most unfortunate character trait: to scramble his words when he was livid. Whether or not he ever heard it himself, no one knew. But his history of verbal *faux pas* had become so firmly established in the county that the locals automatically made the correction on the spot. It usually took out-of-county attorneys a few days to accustom their ear to the perplexing flip-flop of his words.

Maria Gunlock was seated again, and the room was so quiet that the VCR narration from the driver's license bureau on the floor below could be heard through the heating vents. Maria looked a little flustered as she picked up her glass of water and spilled a dollop on her legal pad. She hurriedly dabbed a tissue at the puddle, knowing that Deputy Hawkins was probably watching her every move.

And, in fact, he was. Duffy noted the various stages of embarrassment as they drained from the prosecutor's face. At one point she had been the same shade as a Fram oil filter. She looked good in orange, Duffy decided. Hell, she would look good in one of the Vanstory's sports coats.

"Roy Earl," Mose Vanstory spoke up, "I wanna say somethin'." Round as a bale of rolled hay, Mose was trying to stand as he swatted at

Marvin Huthwaite's restraining grip on his sleeve. Mose rose in his bright yellow sports coat; and, as if God were flexing His sense of omniscient humor, from somewhere out in the distance a rooster crowed.

Clearly exasperated, Ricketts inhaled deeply through his nose and leaned forward on his elbows. He glanced briefly at Duffy, and Duffy was half-certain that Roy Earl was considering confiscating his sunglasses so that he could look directly at Mose.

"Mr. Vanstory," the judge said in Mose's general direction, "you've been here enough times to know that your attorney speaks on your behalf."

Mose wrinkled his broad brow. "Well, I wanna speak for my other behalf then."

You could hear the smack of a hundred lips opening up to chuckle at this breach of protocol, but Ricketts lifted the gavel again and every tongue turned to stone.

"Mr. Vanstory, you have retained Mr. Huthwaite to speak for you."

"Aw, come on now, Roy Earl. I juss—"

"*And*," Ricketts decreed, cutting him off, "in the event you are required to speak, you will address the officers of the court by their proper names."

"Hell, Roy Earl," Mose said, "you been Roy Earl ever since I first knowed you!"

Garland sprang up beside Mose. "Thang is, Roy Earl, we got us some fine bred horses out on the farm, and they don't take to juss anybody. I know for a fact they's two of 'em won't eat less Mose hand feeds 'em hisself. And they's two others you gotta sing to if'n you want 'em to git up on a trailer ramp. They's all a bit high-strung, and I'd hate to see a man git hurt on account of us not bein' thare to tend to 'em." Garland smiled and showed his meth-ravaged teeth, which did nothing for his hope of acquittal. His incisors and canines looked like they had been regularly stored overnight in battery acid.

"And it ain't juss any ol' song neither," Mose offered in dead earnest. Again he shook off his lawyer's attempt at restraint. "You know that ol' tune 'bout the crow and the sycamore tree?" He cleared his throat, lifted his chin, and snapped a finger four times to set a rhythm.

"Well, it's the same ol' tale that the crow tol' me . . .
Way down yonder by the sycamore tree."

Haymer Vanstory, who had buried his face in his hands, finally looked up. "Mose, you ain't got the brains God give a chigger. You juss told the whole damn world what song to sing to git our horses to step up onto their trailers."

"Mr. Huthwaite," Roy Earl droned, "can you get your clients under control? If not, I can invoke a variation on a gag order."

As Marvin whispered frantic counsel to his clients, Judge Ricketts glanced at his bailiff and at Duffy—this time to put both on notice that the Vanstorys were one word away from being physically quieted. The brothers sat down and lowered their heads like scolded puppies.

"We're sorry, Your Honor," Marvin mewled. "Please continue."

Duffy could see Marvin's problem: These boys were still hyped up on meth. Garland especially, who pumped his leg so fast on the ball of his foot, it set up a vibration in the windowglass across the room.

Duffy turned his attention back to the assistant D.A. Maria Gunlock, who looked like she could walk onto the set of *Law and Order* and bump that lead actress down to the paralegal department. Hawkins did not own a TV, but he had seen the show at his mother's house. It was why he regularly visited his mother on Tuesday nights. Though he'd had a hard time admitting it to himself, he'd developed romantic feelings for that lawyer actress.

It was, he told himself, just a crush. It's not like he thought of that Hollywood star all the time. Just on Tuesdays. Staring at Maria Gunlock now, Duffy was in a mild state of disbelief that he had forgotten the name of that actress. The new A.D.A. eclipsed anything on TV. Maria Gunlock was more than a crush. He thought about her every day. Hell, more like every hour!

Judge Ricketts referred to some papers on his desktop and remained in a pensive pose for several minutes. He appeared to be deliberating over some fine point of the law, and everyone in the room awaited his wise counsel.

From where he stood by the jury box, Duffy could see that the judge was perusing the spring fly-fishing portion of an *L.L. Bean* catalogue. He seemed to come to some decision and closed the magazine.

"Bail is set at ten-thousand each," Ricketts announced and leaned right to leaf through a ledger. "We'll set trial for August twelve at ten o'clock." He raised his eyebrows to Maria Gunlock and then to Marvin Huthwaite. Seeing no protest from either, he banged the gavel and walked out of the room with the L.L. Bean catalogue rolled up in one hand.

Chapter Twenty-Three

County Roads
and
The Home Depot
Friday night

With the Ace Hardware closed after six o'clock, Verdie had driven the six miles up highway 400 to *The Home Depot* to pick up a lock washer to stem the leaky bathroom faucet that had been working its way into her dreams at night. She had read a little Freud. Enough to try her hand at some do-it-yourself dream interpretation. But she had found the analyses disturbing. All of them dwelled upon her biological clock ticking away, leaving her with the dreaded sobriquet of "old maid." It was time to fix that leak. If a gentleman caller happened by for a visit, she could not have dripping water as the background music to their romantic interlude.

Just a mile from home she saw the first felled billboard, one that had advertised to the northbound traffic. It had fallen facedown into the pines above which it had once towered. The big rectangular depression looked like a gigantic footprint pressed down into the trees. Surely, she thought, Hoke had not boosted his sign pranks to this ambitious level.

The billboard's mounted lights still illuminated the front of the sign, causing an eerie luteus glow to escape from beneath the collapsed structure, like a door unexpectedly cracked open to the underworld. She tried to remember what the sign had advertised, but she couldn't pull it up from memory. She made a face. She hated it when her observation skills failed her like this. It was like personally disappointing Sherlock Holmes.

The next three billboards were in a similar state. She imagined Hoke skulking through these hinterlands, backing up his truck to a sign and going to work on the poles. If this was Hoke's doing, it was a risky business. With the rocket-like whoosh of the acetylene flame and the helmet needed by a blow-torch wielder, he would have been deaf and blind to any passerby. Only someone foolish or stupid would try such a stunt, and Hoke was neither. There was a third possibility, however: a loose-cannon eco-warrior. Verdie frowned. That title fit Hoke like a felt glove.

At *The Home Depot*'s huge warehouse store she found the washer she needed and, as long as she had made the trip out here, decided to browse the aisle with the outdoor furniture. Verdie was about two-thirds convinced she wanted to buy a two-seater swing for her front yard, so she decided to try out a wrought iron model the store had hung from a steel girder near the garden center.

Someone with a sense of humor had seated a scarecrow in the swing, and Verdie giggled as she sat next to it and turned to look into its button-eyed face. Secretly, the intimacy thrilled her, for the scarecrow seemed to reinforce her proactive reason for buying a two-seater, which was all about courtship and salvaging what was left of her life. She had finally watched *Field of Dreams* last winter, and, since then, the phrase "build it and he will come" had taken on marked significance for her. Only . . . she didn't want to build it herself. It wouldn't do to have the thing collapse during a swinging tryst.

She didn't like the feel of the ornate metal design pressing into her backside and along her spine. She imagined the iron filigree warmed by the sun of a late August afternoon. She might stand up from the swing with a paisley butt that looked more like a waffle iron than a part of her anatomy. But she gave it a fair shake. She decided to sit awhile to see if her derriere might become accustomed to the feel.

That was when Hoke walked down the aisle right past her. That strange odor that seemed to follow him around had marched right into the store with him and hung in his path like a wake of exhaust from a school bus. She didn't know why she didn't speak to him. Maybe a little embarrassment about sitting next to a scarecrow on a Friday night. Or maybe a remnant of childhood games and the thrill of hiding. When Hoke stopped and started sorting through items on a shelf just fifteen yards away, she decided to wait and speak to him on his return. It would be fun to surprise him.

Hoke took a long time assessing the merits of outdoor candelabras. One in particular had caught his attention. It looked hand forged. The black metal curved and spread in a pattern reminiscent of a great rack of elk antlers. The ends of most tines were cupped for a candle, but some terminated in hook-like points. It reminded Verdie of something else: an apparatus she had once seen the Search and Rescue boys use when the little Colderfield boy had drowned in the Chestatee.

Hoke appeared to be wrestling with the candelabra, hunching over it with a fierce grip and a frightening grimace. He was straining so hard Verdie thought he might tear one of the tines loose. That or a muscle.

A short, stocky man in an orange apron and black, suspendered back-support rounded the corner just then, stopped, and watched speechless until Hoke straightened up, breathing hard like all the oxygen had been sucked out of the warehouse.

"Sir, may I help you with something?" the employee said, his query hardened by his suspicions about a man in spirited combat with a candelabra. He snorted once, as if trying to clear his nose.

Verdie could tell by the tone of the man's voice that what he was really asking was: *Sir, if you're all done wrestling that candelabra, you can take it up front and pay for it!*

Right away the stern expression on the salesman's face changed to uncertainty. "What in hell is that smell?"

Verdie sat stock-still and tried to look like a female scarecrow.

"Where do you'ens keep the rope and paint? Hoke said. "I need some stout rope and red paint."

The stocky man was eyeing the candelabra, looking for signs of damage, no doubt. "Aisle nineteen for the rope," he said tersely. "Center aisle for paints."

Carrying the candelabra in one hand, Hoke walked past the man and then marched right past Verdie. *The Home Depot* salesman snorted again, turned, and watched Hoke for several seconds and then walked to the shelf where he made some minor adjustments to the candelabra display. He came walking up the aisle and had almost passed Verdie when some sixth sense turned his head. He jumped, and then his eyes shrunk from surprise to caution.

"These seats are quite uncomfortable on one's backside," Verdie reported in her finest British accent.

He swallowed, looked toward the candelabras and then quickly back to Verdie. "Uh, are you with the gentleman who was looking at the—"

"I am not!" Verdie replied adamantly.

He turned instantly apologetic, snorted, and pointed to another swing that was packaged in a box. "We have this one here also. It's made of oak. Do you think wood would feel better on your—" He frowned and snorted again. "Would you like wood better than iron?"

"Is it treated? It'll rot if it's not treated, won't it?"

He snorted and started reading the fine print on the box. "I think you're supposed to keep it rubbed down with linseed oil."

Now Verdie snorted. "Do you know what linseed oil can do to a sundress? It ought to be pressure treated."

He looked perplexed. "The sun dress?"

Verdie gave him a look. "I'm talking about the wooden swing."

The salesman surveyed the other models. "I don't think we have any that are treated." He snorted, shrugged, and surprised Verdie with a smile. Jamming his hands into his rear pockets, he rocked back on his heels and lifted both eyebrows. "Are you from England, ma'am? You sound like a Londoner. I lived there for a year."

Verdie beamed and checked the man's name tag. "Spot on, Travis. You have a good ear. But I'm hardly a 'ma'am.' How old do you think I am?!"

Knowing better than to answer that, Travis looked to the scarecrow, as if it might be willing to enter the age-guessing game. When the scarecrow offered nothing, Travis snorted.

Verdie canted her head. If viewed from a certain angle . . . and if the viewer wore ear plugs . . . Travis was not a bad prospect, she considered, now that he was relaxing a bit. But a new trait surfaced now. He showed a habit of licking his lips every few seconds. His tongue darted out with the speed of an iguana checking for facial flies.

And there was that incessant snorting. Now that he was closer to Verdie, it sounded as if he were trying to dislodge a load of gravel from his nasal passages. This unfortunate sound evoked bad memories from Verdie's past, reminding her of the porcine grunts at her daddy's hog farm, and with that soundtrack came all the attendant misery of being dirt-poor.

Tilting her head to the other side, she decided to concentrate on Travis's plus column. Physically solid, he appealed in a kind of protective way, which was no small consideration for a girl whose entire diminutive family had been humiliated by bullies for as long as she could remember. It was unfortunate, however, that Travis's big, rounded shoulders were counterbalanced by a beach ball beer gut.

"Well, I'll just tell you then," Verdie offered. "I'm twenty-nine." She rationalized shaving off ten years from her age by deciding that the first decade of her life—before discovering Arthur Conan Doyle—had been a virtual vacuum. "May I inquire as to your stay in London?"

Travis shrugged. "Yeah, I worked in a bakery there. Made bread, rolls, tortes, scones, eclairs, and croissants . . . things like that. My aunt owned the place."

Verdie perked up at this. "Was it on Baker Street?"

Travis narrowed his eyes and stared at the high ceiling. When he looked back at Verdie, he shrugged again.

"It was a few years ago. I don't remember the street. The shop was called the 'Polly Watson Breads and Desserts Bakery.'"

Verdie's spine froze as if a three-foot icicle had been slipped down the back of her collar. "Watson? Your surname is Watson?"

Travis shook his head. "Mine's 'Kablomawitz.' My aunt is a Watson."

"What do you think of Sherlock Holmes?" Verdie asked, getting to the pith of the matter.

For a time, Travis again searched for an answer in the heat and air ducts above them. "*Sure-Lock* Homes," he said and frowned. "Is that one of those new security systems for private residences? I think we might carry some *Sure-Lock* deadbolts over in hardware."

In the privacy of Verdie's mind, in that frontal lobe courtroom where she passed judgment on potential paramours, husbands, or soulmates, a red flag rose to the top of its pole, snapping in gusts of cerebral winds. Accompanying this visual signal, a deep-throated buzzer sounded its alarm. Its tone was that of a bumblebee in her ear.

"Well, this is really all I need," Verdie said, standing and holding up the single plumbing washer between thumb and index. "Ta ta!" She spun around and walked down the aisle toward the checkout counters. When she glanced back at the man, he was sitting in the swing, his elbows on his knees, his fingers raking through his hair. The scarecrow appeared unsympathetic.

On the ride home Verdie fired up her powers of deduction, hoping to make sense of Hoke trying to bend a candelabra out of shape. As she drove south on 400, while her mind was preoccupied with Hoke, suddenly the contents of the felled billboards came back to her. As she topped the rise where normally the first sign would have come into view, she stared at the gap in the trees and recalled the message. *Elysium Elite, Homes in Pristine Settings, Next Right.* Then, at the next collapsed sign: *Sylvan Retreat,*

Your Permanent Getaway Home. The third was *Gold Fever Estates.* Soon she passed a sign that had not been vandalized: *Cherokee Mists, A Community for Discerning People.*

"Aha!" she breathed in a whisper.

Now she felt better. Sherlock would be proud.

As if to underscore her detective assumptions, a rumble of thunder rolled across the sky, resonant as a giant bowling ball trundling down a wooden alley. Fat raindrops began to thump on the car roof and as the storm built, there was a cleansing sensation as the highway began to glisten from her headlights.

As she pulled into her drive the rain hammered the roof of the car. Verdie shut off the motor and sat for a time to see if the storm might pass, but, when it didn't, it got her thinking about the river rising, which brought her thoughts in a circle back to that day the Colderfield boy had drowned. That was when another memory byte loosened and floated to the surface of her consciousness. The tool the Search and Rescue boys had used—the one that looked like that candelabra. It was a four-pronged grappling hook, with which they had dredged the deep pools in the river in search of a body.

"Aha!" she said again, this time loud enough for the words to hang in the car for a few seconds. "The game is afoot," she said through a sly smile. She found herself longing for her own Watson to chronicle this moment of epiphany. This idea was accompanied by a moderate tremor of near regret.

Thank God, Verdie thought, *that Travis's last name was not 'Watson.'*

Chapter Twenty-Four

**Town Creek Church Road
and
Lumpkin County Elementary
Spring, 1978**

On this particular morning it was an extra half-mile walk from the Rider hog farm to get to the school bus. This was because of the Chestatee flooding at the Town Creek Church Road. The water hadn't actually covered the bridge, but the county was fearful of putting the weight of a bus on it with so much hydraulic power grinding away at the questionable concrete abutments. A crack had appeared in the pilings last winter after a twenty-eight-day hard freeze. That was the month white pines along the floodplain had burst open at unexpected times with explosions as loud as cherry bombs.

The rain had stopped, and the air was filled with the smell of silt and drenched highway asphalt. The world was starting to resurrect its vernal green. Descending the last hill before the bridge, Verdie and her two brothers watched a Cooper's hawk glide down from a pine, cross the road diagonally, and snatch a vole from the weeds in the right-of-way. The hawk tumbled onto its side but held on to its prize. When it flapped away with its limp baggage, Verdie started to say something about predator-prey relationships, just to put a scientific slant on the violence that had fallen across their path. Looking at the boys' jaded eyes, she decided to say nothing. This was the way of the world, well known to underdogs such as they. The "big" always beat hell out of the "little."

Since their mother had died in '73, Verdie had assumed responsibility for the boys' upbringing, but she had not yet figured out exactly how to do that. Nine and ten-year-old boys didn't want a twelve-year-old girl poking into their affairs. The only thing all of them had in common was their stature, or lack of one. The boy's nicknames were "Beanpole" and "Snake," and these sobriquets had worked their way home and become entrenched in family life, which was the boys' own fault for using those names like weapons when they were mad at each other. Which was most of the time.

Verdie's father was widely known as "Edge" because someone had once said he was thinner than a piece of paper turned sideways. But over the years that lean handle had been corrupted to "Age" by sheer laziness of the rural Appalachian tongue. Age Rider. He even signed his name that way . . . or at least he claimed that's what his "X" stood for.

It was one of the great paradoxes of the county that a man so thin as Age Rider raised hogs. His was a small farm, never accommodating more than ten or fifteen hogs, but the aroma rivaled anything a landfill, a skunk, or a two-seater outhouse could offer. The hog pen was directly attached to one side of the house. That was on account of space . . . or lack of it. Age was down to a fifth of an acre after selling off little parcels to the adjoining church property for expanding its cemetery. This was his steadiest income, but it could not last much longer. It was only a matter of time before the burial needs of the church would roll over the Rider property like kudzu . . . that is, unless the old hog pen site proved too violated and too rank to be considered consecrated ground.

Age had been a hog farmer since before he'd married, but he had been whipped so many times by hog poachers on his own property that once, when Snake had a school assignment about parental vocations, he had asked Verdie if their daddy's job was "gittin' beat up by strangers."

People had tried out a few nicknames for Verdie, too. Even though she was as skinny as any of her kin, her sobriquets eventually came from her reading habits: "Nerdy Verdie" and "Wordy Verdie." But when her chest had sprouted moderate but shapely breasts, she earned "Purty

Verdie"—the one name that actually appealed to her, at least on one level. Still, she was the smallest person in the sixth grade, and she knew it would be only a matter of time before someone thought of a more belittling rhyme.

In her classroom, Verdie was still thinking about that fat Cooper's hawk and the dead vole. It didn't seem fair that the hierarchy of success had to be linked to size, but deep down she knew it was the natural order of things. It came down to common sense. Why would a hawk think about diving on something big . . . like a German shepherd or a black bear . . . or a cow? She and her brothers would have to settle for being voles in this world. They'd just have to keep a watchful eye out for the hawks.

The class had lapsed into a deathly quiet, and Verdie—snapping out of her reverie—realized there was a teacher-versus-the-students standoff going on. A question on the history homework was up for grabs, but no hands were up. Mrs. Dowdy still wore her confident smile as she called on her favorite students, but that smile only lasted through four more consecutive shrugs. Her question still unanswered, she conjured up her infamous evil eye and progressed down the rows, determined to elicit a correct answer or, if not that, to shame everyone in the room. The mood of the class darkened.

With Mrs. Dowdy's usually sunny temperament in total eclipse, the exercise quickly became an inquisition. Like an assassin who loved her work, she was taking her time, finishing off each victim with a kill-shot sneer and basking in the metaphorical death of each of her sixth-grade wards. Already she was halfway down the third row, and not a single person had known what the Louisiana Purchase was.

Verdie turned in her desk and glanced across the aisle at Ott, who was next to field the question. Big fat Ott sat anchored in his desk and looking smug, like he was watching a slab of wet concrete dry where he had just immortalized an impression of his chubby hand.

Ott was the sheriff's son and seemed to exist under the illusion that he enjoyed a separate standard of life. No matter how poorly he did in school, the course of his life was charted in indelible terms that would deliver him to the same easy existence that his parents and grandparents had enjoyed. He, too, would probably be sheriff one day. That or mayor. It was a depressing thought to Verdie, even at her tender age.

When gold was discovered down on Yahoola Creek in the 1830's, Copernicus Ambrose, Ott's great-grandfather, was one of the lucky ones. The richest vein in the county ran through the creek bed near his apple orchard. This mother lode was like a long yellow snake partially burrowed into the ground, showing its back in the rock and sand in places.

It had all happened by accident when he had dynamited his fields to divert the water through a new channel, which would better serve the irrigation of the trees. There, exposed in the dry creek bed, lay the windfall bonanza of yellow metal shining in the sun.

When he had finished mining the creek, his land looked like a war zone, where cannonballs had blown a portion of Lumpkin County off the map. Legend had it that when Union soldiers arrived decades later, due to the profligate destruction of the land, they bypassed Dahlonega thinking the war had already come there and gone. Their route actually spawned the path of the modern bypass where the *Walmart* would be built almost a century and a half later.

Ott's grandfather had been a city councilman, mayor, sheriff, county commissioner, and finally a state senator, who had somehow accrued enough money to buy most of the buildings on the square in Dahlonega. When the Depression hit, Senator Aristotle Ambrose practically set up office on the courthouse steps, snatching up cheap land from the hundreds of farmers who found themselves strapped for money and unable to pay property taxes.

By the midpoint of the twentieth century the Ambrose family owned most of Lumpkin County and substantial tracts in two neighboring counties. If the Ambroses possessed a coat of arms, Verdie thought, it should include gold nuggets, a pasty smile, and a portly silhouette.

"Ottoman Ambrose, can *you* enlighten us?" Mrs. Dowdy challenged half-heartedly. The tone of her voice suggested she was just going through the motions with Ott. It was Ott who had once answered "Milton Berle" to the question: "Who is the Father of our country?"

Now Ott pretended to think, as he carefully unfolded a strip of paper held at arm's length on his desk right behind Pinky Shope's shoulder blades. "That's what Thomas Jefferson bought from France for fifteen million dollars and made us a whole lot bigger. It made us stretch way out to the Rocky Mountains."

Interesting, Verdie thought, *how Ott used "us" instead of "America"—as if he considered the rest of the country an extension of the Ambrose holdings.*

Mrs. Dowdy stared at Ott as if he had pulled a grand piano from inside his desk and on the spot performed a Chopin etude in F sharp. "Very good, Ottoman," she said cautiously and started up on the lesson again. But Verdie wasn't listening. She was watching Ott, who pulled a pack of gum from his desk and—defying the limitations of what Verdie thought his obese body was physically capable—stretched an arm back to deliver the gum to Duffy Hawkins, who sat behind him.

After lunch the class went outside for recess, and Verdie took her Conan Doyle detective book out to the trees in the far corner of the playground where a moss patch made a perfect carpet. The moss was still wet from the rain, so she took off her shoes and socks and knelt on her shins and sat on her heels to read.

Her two brothers were playing catch with some other boys, and she watched them for a while before opening her book, wondering where Beanpole had gotten hold of a baseball glove. She hoped it did not involve another unsanctioned "borrowing" like the incident last week with Buster Gooch's pocketknife. Verdie considered keeping an eye on Beanpole and Snake, even though this kind of hegemony did nothing for their bonding as a family. When the two boys saw her in this watchful pose, both brothers rolled their eyes and spat into the dirt of the worn-out playground. She decided to read her book and forget about them for at least as long as recess.

She always read Conan Doyle out loud because she enjoyed rendering the characters' English accents as much as she enjoyed the story. Midway through the first chapter, when a baseball came bumping over the roots toward her, she put a finger on the page to hold her place. Duffy Hawkins came jogging out in his bare feet to retrieve the ball. Verdie watched him pick up the ball and hurl it all the way back to Haymer Vanstory on the far end of the playground. She lowered her eyes to the book and once again transported her inner-self five-thousand miles across an ocean to London of the 1890's, dropping her British voice to a whisper.

"Hey, Verdie."

Verdie looked up to see Duffy Hawkins still standing five paces away, staring at her. "Hello," she said, still holding on to the tightly clipped rhythm of her reading voice. She made a face. "Where, pray tell, are your shoes, Duffy?"

Startled by her accent, Duffy looked down at his dirty feet and made his own face. "Aw, the shoes I got are too big for runnin' in." He noticed Verdie was not wearing her shoes either, but he said nothing about it.

Out of kindness, Verdie did not ask more. The Hawkins were dirt-poor people. Or, rather, they were dirt-rich, she amended, considering how soiled Duffy's feet were. The shoes he wore inside the classroom could have come from anywhere. The dump maybe. Or it could be that Duffy's daddy had bought him extra big shoes that he might grow into over the next few years.

"You and I must have been the only ones to read the history homework last night," Verdie said. Again, Duffy looked down at his feet. "Why do you do that, Duffy? Ott probably got an extra star for that today, and that star could have gone to you."

Duffy stepped forward and splayed his toes in the cushiony moss. "Aw, Ott can use the help sometimes."

"But it's like stealing from you. You know that, don't you?"

"Well, it don't seem like that to me. I mean, he ain't takin'. I'm givin'. B'sides, Ott does some things for me sometimes."

"Like what?"

Duffy pushed his lips to one side as he thought. "Gave me his raisin and carrot salad on Tuesday. Ott can't eat carrots. Said it makes his eyes hurt when he watches the TV."

Verdie wondered about what kind of lunch Duffy's mother might pack for him. "What did you give him for it?"

Duffy shrugged. "Buster Gooch owed me for fixin' his bicycle chain, so he gimme a whole bag o' ginger snaps. I traded that to Ott."

Verdie canted her head in a pose of Holmsian perusal. "You are a thirteen-year-old boy, Duffy. Are you telling me you'd rather eat carrots than cookies?"

Duffy poked his soiled big toe into the tuft of moss. "Well, it was really more 'bout the raisins. Raisins give you more energy than anythin'. It's why they say people who get all excited and kind o' wild are 'raisin-hell.'" Duffy shrugged. "I'm gonna try out for the wrestling team when I get to high school, so I'm tryin' to eat lots o' raisins."

Verdie tempered her voice so as not to sound judgmental. "Where, pray tell, did you pick up that information on raisins?"

Duffy toed the moss again. "Ott," he said. "Ott knows a lot 'bout a lotta stuff."

Verdie nodded but decided not to intercede. She tried examining Duffy Hawkins as Sherlock Holmes might. Those bare feet were a lot dirtier than five minutes at recess could allow. She was betting those shoes saw action only at school in the classroom. His trousers showed horizontal parallel creases from the knees down where they had been frequently rolled up in three-inch sections. This suggested a milieu of creek or mud.

More likely—because a creek is cleansing—it was mud. His hands were callused like a man's, and his arms, though slender, were well-defined, like one of those complicated electric cables that is filled with a lot of other wires. The three clues conjured up a picture of Duffy working a muddy bottomland field with a hoe.

"You like to read, don'cha, Verdie?" Duffy said.

Verdie looked down at her book to hide the roll of her eyes. Duffy's deductions were of a simpler variety. Still, she thought there was more to him than he let on.

"I guess you do, too, Duffy. Else you wouldn't have been able to help Ott look like he has a brain." She was getting comfortable with this public debut of a British accent. Duffy seemed to accept it as easily as a raisin's nutritional value.

"He ain't so bad. You juss gotta git to know 'im some. You want some gum?" Duffy reached forward and offered the unopened pack. She hadn't seen him dig it from a pocket. He must have had it ready when he walked up.

"That would be the gum Ott gave you?"

"Yeah, I don't really want it."

"Why not?" she asked.

Seemingly pained at the question, Duffy squinted off toward town. "Too sweet."

Verdie stood up and stared past Duffy with her mouth agape. Haymer Vanstory was pounding on Beanpole, and a crowd was cheering him on. She took off running, letting the book tumble to the grass. Duffy caught up with her in his effortless glide of a gait. He was carrying her book and shoes and socks in his hands.

"What are you aimin' to do, Verdie?"

"That's my brother getting the stuffing beat out of him!" she exclaimed in her new-found accent.

"I know that. But what are *you* aimin' to do?"

Verdie did not answer. By the time she reached the ring of spectators, Snake had jumped on Haymer's back, and Big Mose Vanstory was pulling him off by his feet. For a moment Snake was parallel to the ground holding onto Haymer's blazing red hair by the fistfuls. Haymer was growling like a crazed bear and taking out the pain of torn follicles on Beanpole's head. Mose sputtered out weird percussive sounds that seemed to echo the violence being dealt out to Verdie's brothers.

Standing with both fists clenched at her sides, Verdie was in tears. Here it was again—the hawk and the vole. Verdie did not think she could witness another beating for her family. She felt like screaming. So she did.

"Leave! . . . my! . . . brothers! . . . alone!"

The sheer force of her shriek should have sufficed to inject a lull into the melee, but the strange British lilt to the demand seemed to take the punch out of it. Some of the onlookers actually giggled. Big Mose glanced at her in open-mouthed curiosity then continued pounding on Snake's back. With each slam of his fist, Mose rendered the sound of it with his mouth.

Thwunk! "Thwunk!" *Slap!* "Slap!" *Thud!* "Thud!"

Frantic now, Verdie rose up on her tiptoes to look for help. Mrs. Dowdy was not on the steps where she usually sat and graded papers. Desperate, Verdie tightened her focus on the students around her. The Vanstorys were big, so her eye was searching for bulk. She marched up to Ott and got right in his face.

"Your father is the sheriff! You should be the one to stop this!"

Ott's face showed equal measures of surprise and dread. He licked his fleshy lips.

"Dang, Verdie, Beanpole spit in Haymer's glove," Ott whined. Then he narrowed his eyes and leaned forward to inspect Verdie's mouth. "Who the Sam Hill is that talkin' out your lips? You sound like the Queen o' England."

"I don't care what Beanpole did! It's not fair, and you know it!"

As a reprieve from the wrath in her eyes, Ott watched the Vanstory boys at work, both straddling their victims and pummeling Beanpole and Snake unmercifully.

"Ott!" Verdie yelled.

Ott winced at the Shakespearean sound of his name. "This is how it works, Verdie. I bet ya a *Tootsie Roll* 'gainst a tangerine that Beanpole ain't gonna be spittin' in nobody's glove ag'in. Them Vanstorys will stop directly. They'll prob'ly tire out." Ott turned his attention back to the fight, but he could feel the scorch of Verdie's eyes on the side of his face. "Verdie, quit lookin' at me that way. Look. It's a simple law o' life. You're gonna git what's owed you." He chewed on his lip the way he did whenever he tried to pull up something buried deep in his memory. "There's a old sayin' goes somethin' like this: Any skunk who ain't got no clue where he's a-headin' is bound to wander back into his own stink sometime. And that's where Beanpole is right now."

Verdie might have spat on Ott at that very moment except that she knew Sherlock Holmes would never do such a thing. Besides that, her mouth was dry. She figured all her body fluids were tied up with the production of the tears pouring down her cheeks. She looked back at the mauling of her kin. The punishment showed no sign of abating. Sobbing, she turned a circle, her hands outstretched like a beggar's.

"Won't somebody help me get those Vanstorys off my brothers?" She stopped spinning when she faced Duffy. She could choke out only one word now. "Please!"

Though Duffy Hawkins did not weigh much more than she did, Verdie's wet eyes bored right into his heart. He could see that she was looking to him as her last hope. Her lips quivered, and her head tilted like the dog in the Victrola phonograph ad.

"Duffy?" she keened. Even crying like she was, the British accent was strong.

Duffy looked down at his feet and shook his head with the certain logic of a bad decision. Then he met her pleading eyes.

"Fightin' one Vanstory is the same as fightin' three, Verdie. And one's bad enough. I could purty near git kilt three-'gainst-one."

Verdie closed her eyes tightly, trying to stem her tears. Then her body convulsed once like an electric current had passed down her backbone.

"Verdie?" Duffy said, making his way to her.

She collapsed and Duffy got to her just in time to ease her to the ground. She sighed, and somehow even the sigh sounded British. Then she was mumbling something that he could not hear for the wailing from her brothers, so he lowered his ear to her mouth.

"Why did God make us Riders so small?" she breathed. "Everybody beats on us."

Duffy had no satisfactory answer for that, so he remained quiet. But the tearful misery in Verdie's plea was like a vise squeezing his heart.

Some of the girls were kneeling beside Verdie now, lifting her head and soothing her with the kind of words girls knew to use amongst themselves. Duffy laid Verdie's book and shoes beside her, stood, and breathed out his own long sigh. Without prelude he kicked Haymer Vanstory in the head to get his attention. When he did the same for Mose, Mose broke off from his vocalizations of his pounding on Snake and took a try at this new sound ringing in his head.

"Ka-whongggg!"

There had been no passion to Duffy's attack. He had moved in a perfunctory manner, as though following an obligatory formula for a last rite before being carted off to the funeral home.

"Who the hell kicked my head?" Haymer said and stood up.

Mose sat upright on Snake and rubbed his temple. "It was 'Half-breed Hawkins'."

Garland arrived on the scene, darting his eyes from brother to brother, eager to throw in with his lot and join the rhapsody of unfettered violence.

Duffy might have laughed at the impossibility of the situation, except that it involved his demise. Garland stepped beside Haymer and Mose, and their eyes filled with bloodlust for their new prey. Mose's mouth was moving, already practicing the sounds he anticipated when beating on Duffy's head.

"There ain't a one o' you Vanstorys ever stood up for a fair fight," Duffy declared.

The Vanstory boys began to spread out. Like wolves approaching a lame deer, sure of their kill but still contemplating the best tactic toward that end.

"There ain't no 'fair' and 'unfair' in fightin', you goddam half-breed squirt!" Garland said. "There's juss fightin'."

In his peripheral vision, Duffy saw four boys help Verdie's brothers up and start them for the building. Verdie was behind them, using two girls as crutches. He glanced at Ott. He wasn't sure why. He couldn't really expect physical help from Ott, but maybe there was a chance Ott could think of the right thing to say. But Ott only gave him a rueful shake of the head.

It was as if Ott were standing glumly on a dock, somberly waving, as Duffy sailed off weaponless to a futile war in a far-off country no one had ever heard of. The three Vanstorys inched toward Duffy in a flank. Duffy's classmates took an involuntary step backward, widening the circle of spectators, as though removing themselves from the potential spray of blood. Ott was already grimacing.

Duffy had a sudden vision in his head: a great hole opening up in the sky, God leaning down from His throne, smiling in all His wisdom, granting Duffy one last earthly question before ascending to heaven.

How the hell did I get into this? was all Duffy could think of.

Chapter Twenty-Five

In a Pig's Sty Barbecue Shack
Dahlonega
Saturday noon

When the door slammed a little too hard, Crowder Ramp looked up from the vat of Brunswick stew he was stirring and felt his bowels relax to the edge of disaster. With his business failing like it was, the last thing he expected was to get robbed. He made three desperate prayers all in the time it took him to swallow . . . so fast that he could now understand that theory about a dying man seeing his whole life flash before him.

Prayer one: that Raynelle would remain in the kitchen out of harm's way. Two: that Uncle Ott or one of his deputies might drop by for lunch again, even though that would mean honoring the tacit tradition of "law enforcement officers eat free," which in Ott's case meant a substantial loss. And three: that the health inspector would not show up should Crowder's sphincter fail. The debacle concerning last week's questionable Brunswick stew had been the second strike against Crowder. One more and he was out.

"Yes, sir?" he said, his voice cracking on each word.

The man approaching the counter wore a blue bandana across his forehead and another red one folded into a triangle and draping down from the bridge of his nose to cover half his face. His forehead was smudged with some kind of purple pigment, and his silver hair sparkled as though he had crawled out of a salt mine. In his left hand was a loaded bow and arrow.

"What's the matter?" the intruder said. "Are your arm joints seized up?"

Crowder did not remember raising his hands. He lowered them to the counter, leaned forward, and squinted. "Is that you, Hoke Limberlost?"

" 'Course it's me. What's the trouble here?"

"What do you mean? What trouble?"

Hoke jabbed a thumb over his shoulder. "That your sign out there?"

Crowder peered out the front window. "The 'help wanted' sign? Sure, it's ours."

"Well?" Hoke said, looking around the room. "What's the problem?"

Crowder's face squeezed into multiple questions. "How come you to be wearin' that mask, Mr. Limberlost? I figured you to be a robber."

"I'm tryin' not to smell you'ens' barbecue, son. I got a powerful weakness for it, and right now I'm followin' a Cher'kee warrior's formula that only allows for eatin' predator meat: bear, wolf, mountain lion, and such." Hoke's face brightened. "Say, you'ens ain't got no barbecued mountain lion, do you?"

Crowder shook his head and looked out the window at the small marquis on wheels he had rolled out to the edge of the road. "Raynelle got me to put that sign out there." Crowder broached the question tentatively. "Were you lookin' to hire on?"

Hoke shook his head, and when he did, something dislodged from his hair, tapped down on the counter and bounced to the floor. "I took your sign for a distress signal. Came in to help you out."

Crowder nodded. "We were lookin' to hire a dishwasher. It was mighty neighborly of you to check on us though."

"How's the new rest'rant goin'?" Hoke inquired.

Crowder offered a hang-dog face. "Well, tell you the truth, it ain't goin'. I reckon I got into a run o' bad luck. First, the job with the county road crew and now this barbeque shack here."

"What happened on the road crew?" Hoke asked.

Crowder shook his head. "Well, you know them little ripple bumps you drive over that let you know you're comin' up on a stop sign? I was s'posed to lay some o' them down on Oak Grove Road." Embarrassed, Crowder frowned out the window. "Well, I got that disorder that turns things around in your head—what they call 'dys-lexy.' " He took in a big breath and let it ease out in a long sigh. "I put the bumps in the wrong lane o' the road. Now, the only thing them bumps do over there on Oak Grove is remind people they just stopped at a stop sign."

Hoke hooked a finger over the red bandana and tugged it below his nostrils. Again, something sprinkled down on the counter. It sounded like tiny pebbles.

"Well, it smells good enough. Maybe business is slow on account o' it's so warm in here, you think?" Simultaneously, Hoke pulled the red bandana down from his face and the blue one from his hair. A shower of white grit rained down on the counter like a miniature hailstorm. Both men stared at it for about three heartbeats, then Crowder picked up one of the grains and rolled it between thumb and forefinger.

"That there's some powerful crusty dandruff, Mr. Limberlost. You oughta think on gittin' more fat in your diet. Keeps your head from dryin' out so bad." Crowder's face brightened. "Might be you oughta eat barbecue on a reg'lar basis."

All morning Crowder had been entertaining a wide spectrum of promotional strategies designed to increase his customer flow. And though he had not thought of this particular incentive until now, he considered it a stroke of genius. *Ramp's Barbecue Elixir—the delicious cure for dry scalp.*

Hoke began to brush the debris off the counter; but when he did, more crystals fell from his hair. He tried to look casual about it—as though this level of skin desiccation was common fare for him. *Clunk, clunk!* Two pieces of rock, each the size of a nickel, dropped to the countertop. Crowder stared at these a little harder.

"Had us a little sandstorm up to Frogtown this morning," Hoke said, and immediately blushed with the lie. "You'ens git any o' that down here?"

Crowder looked out the front window at the perfect cerulean sky. He leaned over the counter to peer out the side window, checking the hood of his Plymouth for dents. Raynelle came from the kitchen drying her fingers with a towel.

"Honey, I'm going to have to stop. My fingers are flaring up so bad I—" She stopped short and hid her hands inside the towel when she realized a customer had come in. "Well, hello there, Mr. Limberlost. Did you stop in for a sandwich?" The ring of hope tolled in her voice, so happy was she to see a customer. When her eyes lowered to the bow and arrow in Hoke's hand, the joy slid from her face. "Have you been out huntin'?" she asked, a calculating tone now investing her words.

"General-ly speaking," Hoke said.

"Well, I wish you'd come out to our place and kill that black devil hog of ours, Beelzy-Bubba the Second," Raynelle said, her face now drawn into a spiteful pout. "I won't be sorry to see him turning on the spit, I can tell you."

Crowder put an arm around his wife's shoulders. "Raynelle thinks he's a saber-toothed hog or somethin'. Chases her, if you can believe that. Came in the house one time and chased her up on top o' the stove."

"Now there's a grand do-si-do for you," Hoke observed. "The pig puttin' the human up on the cook stove."

"Ever' damn time I git out the butcher knife," Crowder went on, "or try'n put the sledgehammer to his deranged brain, he breaks loose and busts outta the pen. Only way I can git him to come home is to use Raynelle as bait. When she calls out for 'im he comes a-running juss so he can terrorize her s'more."

"Whyn't you juss shoot 'im?" Hoke asked.

Crowder looked down at his feet and scuffed his shoe on the floor. "Well . . . I cain't keep a gun in the house. I got this dang bang-a-phobia. Daddy had it, too. We cain't be 'round loud noises. Pair that up with Weak Bowel Syndrome, and it spells disaster."

"It's hard on the laundry, too," Raynelle agreed, letting her eyebrows float upward.

Crowder went hang-dog again and turned pitiful eyes toward his wife. "I cain't help it, Sugar-Toes. You know it runs in my family. Juss like your arthur-itis runs in yourn."

Raynelle rose up on her tiptoes and kissed Crowder on his rosy cheek.

"I know that, Honey-Bunny." Her big brown eyes were so full of love for her husband that Hoke felt a lump in his throat that might have rivaled Buster Gooch's oversized Adam's apple. When she turned those big teary orbs at Hoke, he resolved right then and there to help them any way he could. It was obvious now to Hoke that the sign out by the road had not lied. Help was wanted. They just didn't know how to ask for it.

"We had another'n juss as mean," Crowder said. "Juss called him 'Beelzy-Bubba'. Kilt him off with six pounds o' rat poison, but that turned out to be a bad idea."

"What happened?" Hoke said.

"Well, we cooked 'im, but we're purty sure the poison tainted the Brunswick stew. That was the week the health inspector came out here twice. Lot o' people got sick that week. I never could figure how they could trace it back to us, but I think they were right on the money. We gotta warnin' that time."

"I'll tell you what," Raynelle said. "I'm gonna enjoy chopping up that devil-hog for sandwiches . . . if my fingers will let me." She extracted a hand from the towel. Her finger joints were knobby and crooked. "If I can juss get this swelling to go down," she said and hid the hand in the towel again.

"So you'ens' is havin' trouble with finger joints?" Hoke said in a kindly way, trying to help Raynelle believe her joints did not appear so ghastly. He knew how women were about their looks. "I might can help with that."

A vivid scene had washed up on the shore of Hoke's memories. Hoke and his father walking the banks of Frogtown Creek looking for a plant. Making a tea with the roots. His mother's "arthur-itis" had flared up after sewing a custom dress for Big Beulah Babcock's mother. It had been even more taxing than the time Selu had been hired to sew a new canopy for the funeral home's tent.

"That's why we figured we'd hire on a new dishwasher," Crowder said, pointing out the window toward the sign. "For when things git busy . . . if they ever do. Raynelle juss cain't manage it no more. I been doin' most o' the washin' myself since her fingers knotted up on her."

"They's a old Cher'kee medicine for them fingers," Hoke said. "My mama used it. You'ens needs to find some nettle . . . the stingin' kind."

Already the agony appeared to lift from Raynelle's face. "Where can I get some?"

Hoke pursed his lips and stared out the side window. A map of the county materialized in his mind's eye, and he pinpointed the closest stream with a good deposit of rich soil on the flood plain.

"Whatta you'ens say we take a walk down yonder to Cane Creek out past Buster Gooch's place. There oughta be some nettle growin' in that sandy silt bottomland."

"Does it work?" Crowder wanted to know. "I mean, is it really a good medicine?"

"The grandest-ever," Hoke assured him, remembering how his mama had even taken up the banjo sometime after the nettle remedy kicked in.

Raynelle looked like she had just risen from the baptismal waters of the Chestatee River with the preacher's hand still splayed over the top of her head. "That would be wonderful, Mr. Limberlost." Her gratitude fairly lit up her face. She smiled at Crowder. "Honey-Bun, let's fix Mr. Limberlost a barbecue plate when we get back. It's the least we can do."

"He ain't eatin' meat right now, Sugar-Toes. 'Less it's the meat of a predator. You know . . . an animal that chases another'n. It's a Cherokee thing."

Raynelle stared into Crowder's eyes for about four seconds. Then she fixed on Hoke's bow and arrow. Both men could see she was doing some powerful thinking.

"After we hunt up this nettle, the three of us are gonna go out to our place and kill that devil-pig, and we're gonna fix you the biggest predator barbecue feast you ever dreamed of."

Crowder's face broke into a big smile. "That's right! If that damn Beelzy-Bubba the Second ain't a predator, then I don't know what is!"

Raynelle smiled. But as quickly as the triumph of healing nettles and a dead devil-hog had registered joy on her face, so came a worried expression to replace it. Frowning, Raynelle stepped to the pot cooking on the stove. Leaning in close with her face just inches from the bubbling stew, she sniffed, took on a worried expression, and then looked at her husband.

"Do you think there's something wrong with this batch? Something is smelling dead around here."

"That'd be me," Hoke said. "I git that a lot."

Chapter Twenty-Six

**Lake Winfield Scott Recreation Area
Saturday afternoon**

Ott pulled into the parking lot of the recreation area and turned off the engine of his patrol car. Staring out the windshield at the fifteen-foot tall, marble statue that had been vandalized, he tried to bend some logic around all that had happened in the county in the past week to see if it might be somehow connected to this.

He chewed on an unlighted cigar until it was so wet, he decided to peel the paper off and hold the tobacco inside his cheek. This might be the best idea he'd had all year. Bernice had been nagging at him to quit smoking, but he just couldn't give up the cigars. They were free, after all. And they were Cubans! A gift box from L.T. traded hands every time Ott gave a little legal push to one of Voss's questionable land deals.

Duffy was out there on an extension ladder, while two of the park rangers held the side rails as he inspected the damaged head of General Winfield Scott. Ott knew it ought to be a case for the state, since this was a state park operation. In fact, it was just outside of Ott's county, but the Union County sheriff had passed it along to Ott as a favor. After all, Winfield Scott was his great-great-something-or-other.

It irritated Ott to see Duffy already so involved. It would be a lot easier to back out of this from the get-go, but now that a county deputy had climbed up on the damned statue, well . . . it was one more problem for the Lumpkin County sheriff's department.

Or maybe, Ott thought, *Duffy had a reason to jump on this so fast.* He usually did.

It was the largest marble statue in north Georgia, and it had been donated by a sculptor from Blairsville whose great-grandfather had somehow accrued a thousand acres from the land lottery when the commemorated general Winfield Scott had marched the Cherokees off to Oklahoma. People from all over the country stopped here to see the memorial and then stayed to pull a few bream or bass out of the lake that had been named for the general.

The statue had even once been the subject of a segment on the *Today Show*, but that was only because the artist had lost both of his arms in an ultra-light flying accident that involved a quick stop in a pine tree without the benefit of an airbag. Ott had seen the *Today* segment. The handicap aside, it had been embarrassing. That sculptor's hair was as red as the Vanstorys'. When he had demonstrated, on nationwide television, his use of the custom-made chisel that fit into his mouth, he'd looked like a giant pileated woodpecker on amphetamines.

Being related to Winfield Scott like he was, Ott tried to work up some indignation as he assessed the damage to the old general's likeness. When he saw Duffy looking at him, Ott got out of the car and crossed the lawn, threading his way through the fishermen and picnickers who had gravitated to the crime scene.

The closer he got to the statue, the stranger it looked. The head, now hatless, appeared bright red on top, with streaks of red running down the general's face. Ott was already thinking professionally about it. If it was a wig, this might have something to do with a grudge someone held against that woodpecker-sculptor over in Blairsville.

"The hat's been purty near hammered off," Duffy yelled down when Ott was close enough. "Top o' the head, too."

"Hammered?!" Ott said loud enough so the park rangers were sure to feel the bite of it. "You mean like with a chisel? Cain't see why someb'dy didn' hear all that. Betcha a pearl-handled pistol 'gainst a paper peashooter that chis'lin' made a helluva lotta noise."

Moon of the White Tears

Duffy glanced at the contrite faces of the rangers but kept his face neutral behind his dark glasses. "Heavy storm last night, Ott. This jaybird worked out in the rain. I figure that's why the paint was to run like it did."

"Paint?" Ott said, frowning.

"Poured it right on this flat place he carved out the top o' the head."

Ott looked around at the bystanders. He was tempted to make himself look efficient by canvassing the crowd, to see if anybody here had camped last night and maybe heard something. But he knew Duffy would have already done that.

"Anythin' else up there, Duff?" Ott yelled.

"Some scratch marks on the shoulders. Looks like metal hooks. Grapplin' hooks, prob'ly. Some mud on the front o' the coat there. Partial footprints. I cain't make out any tread pattern. Been mostly washed off by the rain, be my guess."

"Well, it'd be good to know the size o' the foot, anyway. Could be important. You get a picture of it?" Ott already knew the answer, but it made him feel competent to ask. And besides, there might be somebody from the newspaper in the crowd. Or some locals from his county. You always had to factor in the voters seeing you in action, Ott knew. Especially if you were a sheriff and if it was an election year . . . which it was.

"I took ten shots with my cell phone," Duffy replied, "and I emailed the pictures to the main computer at the office."

Ott nodded even though he didn't have a clue about new technology. Because he had never gotten the hang of a cell phone, Ott was thinking: *How the hell can you take a picture of something and email it from a danged telephone? That'd be like tryin' to mail a letter by insertin' your envelope into a washin' machine.* "Yep, Duff, that was the best way to handle it aw-right."

There were shards of marble all over the grass. None of them showed any red paint. Ott filed that detail away for the chronology of the crime. The paint had come after the chiseling. That might prove to be important. You never knew.

"You s'pose somebody juss didn' like the hat?" Ott said as Duffy climbed down. Ott moved closer to him to keep any official theories out of earshot of the crowd. For all he knew, the perpetrator was sitting right here at a picnic table chewing on a deviled egg. "And then maybe he put the paint on to seal the wound . . . kind a like you do with a lopped off tree limb."

Duffy, who knew to expect anything from Ott when he was on a case and simultaneously in the public eye, waited patiently through all this. "It ain't got nothin' to do with the hat. The hat was juss in the way."

"In the way o' what?"

Duffy looked up at the maimed statue, the deputy's stoic face matching the general's. "His scalp," Duffy said. He turned back to Ott. "Somebody done scalped the general, Ott."

Ott slipped his hands into his pants pockets and perused the statue. Coins jingled in his pocket, and his breathing whistled through his nose.

"What I was thinkin', too. That red paint looks like blood, don't it?"

"Top couple o' inches o' the head's been chiseled clean off," Duffy said.

Ott winced at the partial decapitation. "Looks like a bad day gittin' outta helicopter for a man a couple o' inches too tall," Ott said. He lowered his voice to a whisper. "Why the hell d'you figure someb'dy to pick on Gen'ral Scott? You reckon it was a Yankee holdin' a grudge? Lots o' Yankee tourists comin' through here."

Duffy gave Ott a sideways glance. "Scott *was* a Yankee, Ott."

Ott's face took on a pout. "He was?!"

Duffy nodded. "He only served in the Civil War for a short time. He was purty old by then. He was mostly famous for the Mex'can War."

Ott sniffed and tried to channel his embarrassment into ethnic anger. "Well, then maybe we oughta be questionin' some danged Mex'cans. Maybe see what they know down at the Mex'can rest'rant."

Duffy lowered his voice to a whisper. "I don't think this is 'bout Mex'cans either, Ott."

Ott chewed on the wadded-up cigar in his cheek and stared at the marble debris scattered on the grass. He ambled closer to Duffy, crunching with each step.

"Okay," he whispered, "what's it 'bout then?"

"Well, it ain't that hard to figure, Ott. Bein' related to 'im like you are, you know Winfield Scott's the one rounded up the Cher'kee and drove 'em out to Oklahoma."

Ott narrowed his porcine eyes and scratched his triple chin. " '*Drove* 'em'? I thought they walked it. What'd he use? A big Cadillac like L.T.'s?"

Ott held a poker face for about two seconds, and then he laughed and lightly punched Duffy's stomach. Duffy was flexed, ready for it. He was always ready.

"I'm juss messin' with you, Duff."

Duffy looked down at his shirtfront where Ott had knuckled him. He snapped the material flat against his lean body and looked up at the damaged marble head.

"This here is tied to them signs out on the highway," he said. "Dwayne's sign, too."

Ott pursed his lips and tried for a knowing look. "How d'you figure that?"

"We got us a common thread here," Duffy mumbled, keeping their official conversation private from the crowd.

Ott put every brain cell into gear and tried to come up with the thread on his own, but it was no go. The spool was empty.

"Well, let's see if your idea's the same as mine," Ott said.

Duffy waited with typical patience. Ever since they were kids it was usually Ott going first all the time.

"You go first," Ott said with a gracious sweep of his hand.

Duffy pushed his hat brim up with a finger, glanced at the crowd, and turned his back to the onlookers. Lowering his voice another few decibels, he said, "We been so busy noticin' what was damaged out in the county, we forgot to take a good look at what weren't. You notice which signs was spared out on highway four hundred?" Duffy flipped up a finger for each subdivision he named. *"Cher'kee Mists . . . Ind'an Hills . . . Sequoya Estates."*

Ott nodded, though he still didn't have a clue. Duffy gave him a few seconds to let the light bulb turn on above his head, but there was no power.

"Ott, they all got somethin' to do with Ind'ans. Looks like our perpetrator treated 'em special. Even that carvin' job down at L.T.'s office showed a Ind'an theme. Like a totem pole. And now this." He pointed to the scalped general. "I'd say it all ties together, wouldn' you?"

"You're dead on with your thinkin', Duff. 'Xactly what I been ponderin'. So we got a Ind'an-lover running wild all over the coun'y? Hell, Duff . . . I mean . . . why does he bother. It's juss some dumb billboards, a few road signs, a coupla posts o' wood, and a marble statue. Why pussyfoot 'round with stuff like this?" He extended an arm toward the general's scalped head. "Why don't this renegade juss burn down the town? I mean, the town is named for the gold rush that run the Cher'kee outta here."

"Think 'bout it, Ott," Duffy said. "He wouldn' burn the town 'cause the town *is* a Cher'kee word."

Ott's cigar tobacco had turned to mush. He wished he had a new one. Not to chew on . . . but to light up and savor a lungful of nicotine soaking into his air sacs. What Bernice didn't know was not going to hurt her.

"You're part-Cher'kee, Duff. Who d'you know would do somethin' like this?"

Duffy narrowed his eyes at the lake's smooth surface. "I'm workin' on that."

Ott pulled his hat down closer to his eyes and turned to face his car, trying to look like he had a full agenda blocked out for the day. He still thought it was a good idea to check in at the Mexican restaurant. While he would be enjoying his chips and salsa, he could casually interview the waiters and kitchen staff and look for any signs of marble dust. It ought to show up nicely against that dark Mexican hair. Ott sniffed and puffed out his chest. Hell, Duffy Hawkins was not the only officer around here who knew how to investigate a crime.

"Well, you work your end of it, and I'll work mine," Ott said. "But you better work on it a little faster than this jasper can tear things down. Our coun'y's startin' to look a little barren. Without the billboards on our roads, it's like a wilderness out there. People are gonna be scared to travel, and that's gonna hurt a tourist town like our'n." He tucked his shirt into his trousers all the way around the wide circumference of his belt. "Well, I'm gonna go git some *fajitas*. You hungry?"

Duffy shook his head. "I wanna talk to s'more people 'round the park."

"Well, don't scare 'em. People might think we're havin' a Ind'an uprisin' or a Mex'can rev'lution." Ott turned for his sheriff's cruiser but stopped one last time. "Oh, anybody call that sculptor in Blairsville yet? Let him know 'bout this?"

"Not till we can first notify next o' kin," Duffy said.

Ott frowned and stared out at the lake for several seconds. "Kin to who?"

Duffy nodded toward the statue. "Gen'ral Scott."

Ott's brow wrinkled like a washboard. "Hell, *I'm* kin to 'im! Notify me!"

Duffy stared at Ott for five seconds. "Aw-right. Here goes." Duffy held on to his poker face. "Gen'ral Scott got scalped, Ott."

"Okay, it's official," Ott pronounced. "Now, go ahead and call that peckerwood rock-whacker and let's see if we cain't git this thing repaired."

Duffy maintained a sober expression, nodded, and then turned away. Ott watched his deputy walk toward the crowd. Duffy's head was slightly bowed, his hand covering his mouth. Ott was about half-sure that Duffy had been messing with him about the phone call. A little counterpunch for the jab about General Scott driving the Cherokees out west in a Caddy.

"I'll be damned," Ott mumbled to himself. "Duffy Hawkins made a joke." He hitched his head and smiled. "First time for ever'thin'."

Chapter Twenty-Seven

**The Ramp home
Cooper Gap
Autumn, 1989**

Without a word Dwayne came inside, slammed the backdoor, marched through the kitchen with his deer rifle slung over his shoulder, and disappeared into the bedroom. Dora Lynn knew better than to say anything to her husband when he came home from hunting without toting something dead. She poked the spatula under the edge of the egg she was frying for her son and pretended not to notice Dwayne.

"What's wrong with Deddy, Mama?" Crowder said. He was sitting at the table holding a big biscuit in both his hands. Muscadine jelly was layered all over it—top, bottom, and sides.

Dora Lynn kept her eyes on the crisp edge of the egg. "He went a-huntin' this mornin', son. I reckon he's come home empty handed again." She looked at Crowder, and her face fell as it always did when she felt she had failed her son. "Honey, the jelly goes on the inside of a biscuit, not the outside."

Crowder's expression mirrored his mother's. He hated to disappoint her, but it was just the way his mind worked about things. The jelly biscuit tasted as good as when she fixed it for him. It seemed prettier his way. But wrong is wrong.

"I'm sorry, Mama. I git mixed up."

Dora Lynn always melted in the presence of one of Crowder's sweet apologies. "It's not your fault, Sugar Plum. Remember, the doctor says you've got that dys-lexy thing, and sometimes things switch places inside yore head."

Having lost his appetite, Crowder quietly parked himself in his daddy's doorway and watched him work with an oily rag. Dwayne had the rifle taken apart into what looked like a hundred pieces, all of it laid out on a newspaper spread on the bed.

"Whacha doin', Deddy?"

Crowder understood enough about guns to know that you didn't clean one if you hadn't shot it. Unless it had rained. But it had been dry for a week. Maybe his daddy had gotten off a shot but missed. Crowder figured there had to be a story in this. Dwayne Ramp always had a good story about why he missed.

Like the story about the time the rain beaded water on his front sight, and the light hit it just right so as to form a tiny rainbow. Dwayne had been shooting at a rainbow trout at the time—an illegal venture, but still fascinating to Crowder. With the optical illusion arcing over the barrel, it looked just like he was dead-on his target. He'd missed the fish and put a hole in his fishing boat and sunk right there in the Chestatee.

Another time, Dwayne had taken a bead on a tom turkey's head sticking up over a log. The bullet whizzed off the log and then ricocheted off an ironwood tree where it made a hard turn and caromed off a beveled rock from which it zeroed in on Dwayne's truck, which was parked forty yards away in a pine thicket. It went through the door and hit Dwayne's lunchbox and perforated the sandwich Dora Lynn had made for him. The irony was that it had been a turkey sandwich. Everybody who heard the story knew there was some moral to it, but no one could come up with it.

"Come on in here, son," Crowder's father ordered. "I'll teach you somethin' 'bout guns." Crowder stepped into the room that he was seldom allowed to enter. He was only six years old, but he sensed some import to this occasion, as though he were stepping over some threshold cobbled into the rites of passage for a young boy.

"Had a ten-point buck in my sights this mornin'," Dwayne said. "Damned near big as a moose. Would'a fed us for the winter and then some." Dwayne lifted his arms in a pantomime of a man squinting down the barrel of a rifle. "So I start my slow, steady squeeze . . . relaxed but deliberate . . . holding my sights right on that sucker's ticker. He's moving slow . . . grazin' on some acorns scattered among the dead leaves on this hillside . . . chewin' and movin' . . . steady-like . . . and I move the gun with 'im . . . steady as you please . . . pullin' on that damned trigger. Seems like I'm pullin' for ten minutes, and still the thang don't go off." Dwayne shifted his gaze to his son and huffed. "Hell, I was still a-pullin' when he juss walked outta sight over the hill. Hell, by then I was so edgy I juss wanted to make some noise, so I let fly with the bullet and hit a poor old buckeye tree, which, when you ponder it, was a int'restin' target to be a-hittin' on a deer hunt." Dwayne shrugged with a hint of embarrassment. " 'Course, then I had to go an' void my bowels on account o' that problem I got with loud noises."

Crowder knew all about that, all right. He struggled with the same inherited malady.

Dwayne picked up a small, intricately shaped piece of metal from the parts of the disassembled Winchester. "See this here? This is what you call the 'dog,' and it controls how easy or hard the trigger trips the firin' pin." He picked up a small metal file and started scraping one edge of the "dog." "I pulled this damned trigger from hell to Sunday, and all I kilt was some time. Time I finish with this, it's gone be what you call a 'hair trigger.' If the wind was to whip up a notch, a little breeze might set it off."

Crowder watched, fascinated, as his daddy completed his work with the file, oiled the parts, and reassembled the gun. Dwayne worked the bolt and held the rifle near his ear as he tested the pull. No sooner had he laid his finger to the trigger than a crisp *click* punctuated the silence in the room. Dwayne made a surprised expression.

"Man! Now that's a light touch!" He smiled with satisfaction.

Crowder watched his daddy open the bolt again and slide a long brass cartridge into the breech. When he closed the bolt, the bullet locked into the chamber ready for action. He mounted the rifle on the wall rack and turned to his son with the sage expression that he saved for moments like this.

"Remember, son, it ain't no use havin' a gun 'round 'less it's loaded. Ain't no burglars or cattle thieves or hog-nappers ever been shot by a empty gun!" He kept his didactic stare on Crowder and pointed back to the rifle hanging on the wall. "But this here ain't a toy. It ain't for chi'ren. That's why your mama and me don' allow you in here 'less one o' us is in here an' we tell you it's aw-right. You un'erstand?"

"Yes, sir!" Crowder chirped up, his voice loyal and obedient.

What Crowder did not understand was how life in this house was going to go on in its normal fashion with that time-bomb rifle up on the wall just waiting for a gust of wind from a door closed too fast . . . or maybe from his daddy popping the top off a can of beer. And what about when his daddy unleashed one of his surprise sneezes that usually rocked the house and caused any birds that happened to be in the yard to take flight in a flurry of flapping.

That night, as Crowder lay in bed, he couldn't keep his mind off of the hair-trigger gun perched on the opposite side of the wall of his room. He imagined something as insignificant as a fly buzzing through his daddy's room, landing on the trigger, and the gun going off. Fly or no fly, it was almost a guarantee there would be a stir in the air tonight. He couldn't believe that—of all nights—his mama had cooked up her special baked beans and bacon casserole. Which was why Crowder found himself trapped in an endless exercise of analyzing the potential trajectory of the bullet as he cowered under his blanket.

As best he could figure, that bullet would be headed through his daddy's wall and straight for the kitchen. Crowder could see it catching the inside curve of the stew pot sitting on the stove and getting slung toward the wall where the frying pan hung. That would be about the right angle to whang it off the heavy iron and glance it toward his room, ripping through his wall, punching through his Kermit the Frog wall poster, and then gouging right through the footboard of his bed to plow up his brisket and explode his skull like a ripe watermelon left out on the interstate.

Lying in the dark, Crowder broke out in a cold sweat and listened to his teeth chatter as he prayed. The night dragged out interminably. After finally climbing into his chest of drawers and squeezing in with his clean underwear, he managed to close his eyes around 3 a.m., but his nerves were so frazzled he knew he would never again get any sleep in this house.

When his daddy's predictable reactions to the bean casserole commenced, Crowder's prayers made a subtle shift from "Please, God, protect me" to "Well, God, I'll be up there directly," and he just lay among the underwear resigned to his fate.

It was around 4:15 when the sounds from his daddy's room turned dangerously ominous. Once or twice, he mistook the muffled rumbles of gas for the gun itself, and so he seemingly died several deaths that night. Crowder, fully prepared for the end, clapped his hands over his ears and waited for the angels to come get him. It was his fervent hope that no guns were allowed in heaven.

Even with all this foreshadowing, when the rifle finally went off around 5:45, Crowder's stiffened body went into a paroxysm of terror and lost control of its functions. When his mama came in and found him stuffed in the drawer, he at first thought he had died and gone to hell; for where else would a boy see his mother so cruelly tortured by having a clothes pin pinching her nose so tightly. As it turned out, she had worn the clothes pin all night. Now it would serve her doubly well for the time she would spend on the load of soiled laundry Crowder had provided in one fell swoop.

As she cleaned him up in the kitchen by lamplight, Crowder checked himself all over for a wound and found none. Slowly, he came around to the reality that he was still alive. Curious, he studied the kitchen for signs of ricochets. Crowder had been right about the stew pot taking the first hit after the bullet punched through the wall, but it must have taken more of an orbit inside the cookware than he had predicted—that or his dyslexic thinking had turned it around in his head. The bullet ended up whining out the front parlor where it killed the family cat, Ruffles, a gift from his Aunt Bernice.

For the next two years Crowder underwent a sort of small-town therapy, an arrangement conceived by the Baptist preacher, who thought himself well qualified for the task due to his lifelong struggle with flap-a-phobia, that rare but devastating fear of flags rippling in the wind.

As for Crowder, not much came of the sessions. It looked like he was stuck with bang-o-phobia for life. Any loud noise was his nemesis. He could not attend public performances where spontaneous applause was likely to break out. As an adult, he earned a provision on his driver's license that he could not drive a car with a predilection for backfiring. Besides his daddy, he was the only person in the county who did not attend the Fourth of July fireworks celebration at the high school ball fields.

But like the philosophers say, there's always a plus side to every predicament. Like the old saying about the man whose house burned down, and everything he owned was destroyed in one winter's night. The next morning as he poked through the ash and debris where the kitchen had once stood, he found the pack of frozen weenies he had opened the night before in preparation for his supper. Though a little crispy on the outside, they were thoroughly cooked where they had been covered by an inverted fry pan that had fallen from the wall.

In Crowder's case, it was his wardrobe that benefitted from his psychological malady. He probably owned more pairs of undershorts than any other boy in the county.

Chapter Twenty-Eight

**Ambrose House
North Chestatee Street
Saturday night**

For the seventh time in an hour, L.T. Voss, cruising in his big silver Cadillac, approached Ott's house and slowed. Sneaking around in that monstrosity of a car was something he did a lot, and he never caught on to how absurd it looked. About as subtle as an aircraft carrier floating down Yahoola Creek.

Once again, he let the car creep along at a quiet coast as he strained to see through Ott's living room curtains. Since Ott had a closed garage, L.T. used other clues to determine whether or not Ott was at home.

So far, each time Voss had driven by the house, all the windows had been lit up in the bright yellow of table lamps and overhead light fixtures. This was the telltale sign that Ott's wife, Bernice, had been home alone. Now all the upstairs rooms were dark, and downstairs only the den and kitchen were lighted. In addition, in the den window, a blue glow flickered on the curtain. It was Saturday night, and Voss knew that a special weekend edition of *Eye Witness Police Chronicles* was on TV. Ott was at home.

Voss knew all about Bernice's struggle with nyctophobia through Dora Lynn Ramp, her sister. Dora Lynn had told L.T.'s last wife, Eunice, how Bernice had suffered from childhood with an acute fear of darkness. Its origin, so the story went, dated back forty-four years to a night when her daddy had been on jury duty and was sequestered with the rest of the jurors down at the *Econo-Lodge*.

On that lonely evening, with her parents gone to a meeting at the school, nine-year-old Bernice had convinced herself that a very tall, bald man with a pronounced limp was skulking outside her house, testing all the doors and windows. Her doctor thought at first it was a simple case of gimp-o-phobia—an acute fear of people who limped. But the malady was more complicated than that. As the years rolled by, it became clear that she was a victim of multiple disorders: mono-phobia (fear of being alone) and alto-masculo-phobia (fear of tall men) and alopecia-phobia (fear of bald people).

It was rumored around town that a medical journal had published her unique panoply of fears, but it was never provable to the people who knew her, because the researcher had used an alias for her, as was the common practice whenever publicizing a person's health problems.

Adding to the eeriness of her childhood trauma, that slinking interloper had continually whistled a soft, unsettling melody. She swore to the police that the tune was Frankie Laine's *The Moonlight Gambler*, which brought on the extremely rare frankie-phobia. Naturally, out went all the Frankie Laine and Sinatra albums from her parents' house.

All these phobias were a waste of time and emotional energy, because it was common knowledge around town that Bernice's daddy had been the prowler. Disguised in a beige stocking cap pulled low on his head, he had come home to stock up on whiskey in case the jury should be hung up much longer. To escape the motel, he had been forced to drop from the second floor to the lawn outside, where his left foot landed on a sprinkler nozzle. Of course, he could not admit any of it to the authorities. Nor could he tell Bernice, which would be like announcing it through the newspaper. To his credit, he did try to assuage the little girl's fears, but nothing could shake her from her whistling, limping, tall, bald man scenario, and so the quad-partite condition stuck.

When Ott was late getting in or gone to the Annual Sheriffs' Association Convention in Macon, Bernice was known to stalk through the lighted rooms most of a night with a loaded weapon, listening for any sound outside that did not belong there. Like Frankie Laine or a limping whistler. Her ears were tuned in to hear the slightest disturbance. She would no more turn on a TV under those conditions than throw out food scraps for bears.

This is why L.T. snuck around in his Cadillac. He was not about to walk up to the Ambrose house unless Ott was home. Aside from being a daytime soap opera junkie and a paranoid listener of the night, Bernice was a shooter. Shotgun, rifle, or handgun. She could handle them all. She usually placed in the top three in the turkey shoot that was held each year at Gold Rush Days.

Voss eased his car onto the drive and got out. As he climbed the dark steps to the porch, the noisy insects up in the evening trees made a riotous ratcheting sound. Holding his breath, he tiptoed across the porch and leaned to peer through the window. The image on the TV was blurred through the lace curtains, but the sound was a dead giveaway. Squealing tires, a crash, and two gunshots. Then "Freeze, dirt-bag! Police!" Then two more shots.

Yep, Ott was at home.

Bernice answered the doorbell ring like any normal person might, showing mild curiosity followed by a perfunctory smile. Her overweight cat walked skulking figure-eights around her ankles, buffing her skin with its sleek brown coat. Bernice was holding a small plate filled with dark sugary crumbs and little clouds of chiffon and fibrous bits of fruit.

Damn! L.T. thought. *Bernice's pineapple-crumb delight!*

"Well, hey there, Bernice. I hope I'm not knockin' on your door too late. I just happ'ned to be in the area, and I thought I'd save a phone call tomorrow. Is Ott busy?"

With a grim glare at Voss, she stepped back and opened the door wider. Voss walked in and filled the silence with a hopeful performance of surprise.

"Well, how 'bout that! I see y'all are havin' my fav'rite dessert."

"Were," Bernice said in a dry monotone. She closed the door and lowered her dish to the rug. The obese cat wasted no time in licking it clean. When finished, the overfed creature looked up at Voss and licked its lips with cruel delight—an expression apparently learned from Bernice.

Bernice gestured with her chin toward the den. "Ott's in there a-watchin' the weekend recap of *Eye Witness Police Chronicles*." She turned her head and attempted to holler over a fusillade of canned gunfire. "Ott!" She pronounced his name like *"ought."* Whenever she talked about how Ott *ought* to do this or that, it sounded like she was stuttering.

"Ott!" she yelled again. "It's L.T.!" When Bernice looked at Voss again, she shrugged. "He's done seen it before. It's just reruns from the last month. So, I don't see as it matters. I guess you can go on in. I've got some dishes I need to wash up."

When L.T. entered the den, he saw Ott rapt before the TV screen, sitting in his armchair, still wearing his uniform and badge, his stockinged feet propped up on the low coffee table, his gun and holster looped over one wing of the chair back.

"Evenin', Ott! Catchin' up on some crime-stopper techniques?"

"Well, hey there, L.T." Ott gave Voss his guess-what-you-just-missed smile and slapped his belly. "You must'a heard Bernice made her pineapple-crumb delight." He pointed to a smeared baking dish on the table. Right on cue, like salt poured into a wound, the bloated cat jumped up on the table, buried its head in the dish and began a systematic cleansing of the bowl. As busy as the animal was, it took the time to angle gloating eyes up at L.T. "You're 'bout ten licks too late," Ott teased. "Mr. Fluffs would rather eat *that* stuff than go to a all-you-can-eat tuna bar."

Voss waved it away as if he'd never consider butting in on their dessert . . . or the cat's. "I already ate." He said this with a smile, but he gritted his teeth as he watched the damned cat polish off the last of the dessert crumbs.

Ott's attention was back on the tube. A trooper's dash-mounted video had captured a grainy piece of highway drama. The trooper's back came into view as he approached a van parked on the shoulder of a highway. He stopped, leaned toward the driver, and motioned to roll down the window.

"Watch this," Ott said. "This is a hoot." A wicked grin spread across his face.

The driver's muscular arm whipped out of the van window like a boa constrictor and locked around the trooper's neck. In an instant the van roared away with a trail of black exhaust pluming out the back. The trooper's legs moved frantically trying to keep up until finally his legs flopped around like a ragdoll's. Before it was too distant to see, the driver released his captive, and the trooper hit the pavement like a sack of tomatoes. The van lifted slightly when the rear tires bumped over the trooper's legs.

"Ooooh!" Ott breathed, cringing. "Bet ya a barrel o' bacon 'gainst a shattered shinbone he don' never git that close to a driver again." Ott shook his head. "Man! Ever since I seen that, I swore I'd never put myself within a arm's length of any jaybird I pulled over." He turned a dead serious eye on Voss. "Tell you what . . . you can learn more 'bout sheriffin' on the TV than a dozen o' them law enforcement seminars."

L.T. imagined an arm reaching out of a car to lock onto Ott's considerable ballast and that arm tearing right out of the driver's shoulder socket when he accelerated. L.T. just smiled and nodded like he did about most things that came out of Ott's mouth.

"Say, Ott, you gotta minute we can talk?" L.T. pulled two, fat Kentucky cigars out of the box he had brought in. "Thought maybe we could sit on your porch. Fire these boys up and enjoy a little palaver." He ceremoniously laid the box on the table, and Ott's eyes widened. Ott had barely put a dent in the box Voss had recently given him down at the

Sizzling Skillet. The addition of this box could keep him in twice-a-day, *Kentucky Elite* euphoria for a month.

Mr. Fluffs finally abandoned the big dish and moved to Ott's bowl, which had very little to offer. Still the cat covered every square centimeter of the bowl's interior. L.T. was pretty sure this thoroughness was done for his benefit.

"Yeah, sure," Ott said roundly and pushed himself up. "Let's go out on the porch an' burn some t'backy so maybe Bernice won't catch wind of it." He gestured toward the TV. "I seen all this anyway."

The evening was beginning to cool. The smell of honeysuckle sweetened the air. The insects in the tree canopy had settled into a pattern that swelled in waves and then ebbed and swelled again. It made an endless rhythm like fluctuating river rapids up in the trees.

Still in his socks, Ott took the porch swing, and L.T. leaned against the railing with his back to the street. Ott pushed the swing into a tiny arc, but when the chain began a repetitive squeak, he braked the action and tried to match his expression to the earnest demeanor of his sheriff's uniform.

"What's on your mind, L.T.?"

"You reckon them Vanstory boys'll be behind bars very long?" L.T. asked.

"I don' see as they's got any way out o' this mess . . . 'specially with this crackerjack, black A.D.A. we got now. Them boys must'a had a hunerd-thousand dollars in materials in that lab. The judge ain't gonna like that worth a rat's ass. Possession's one thing, but manufacturin' and distributin' gits the hot end o' the stick."

"Are all three brothers likely to do time?"

Ott pushed his lips forward and squinted at L.T.'s stake in this. "I reckon one's as guilty as the others. Why d'you ask?"

L.T. handed over a cigar, struck a match, and held the flame steady for Ott. Ott got it going, removed it from his lips, and held it sideways as though admiring a work of art. L.T. lit his own cigar, and their smoke rose and commingled into a single cloud that the light breeze carried off into the night.

"You know, Buster Gooch has been interested in the Vanstory Farm for some time now," L.T. said around his cigar. "Says it's the perfect site to start up an emu farm."

"A what?"

"Emu. It's like an ostrich. Good tender meat on those birds. Buster says the terrain over at Vanstorys' has got a strong resemblance to their Australian habitat. Says he could turn a profit on it in two years and after that it's all butter and icing."

Ott shook his head in wonder. "What the hell is this coun'y comin' to?" He laughed a single caustic note. "E-moo. Sounds like a Hereford doin' business over the Internet."

"Thing is," Voss continued, "be nice if those boys were locked up so long, they couldn't make their mortgage payments for three months runnin'. You know they had to second-mortgage the farm to pay legal expenses. I figure all their available cash went into the meth lab, and they were plannin' on recoupin' that from sales."

"And then some," Ott said. "Fella down at the GBI said them boys stood to make over two million with what all they had to sell."

"Well, I talked to Ernest Dowdy down at the bank, and he's ready to let the property go to the highest bidder once he makes claim on it after the mortgage default."

Cocking his head to an analytical angle, Ott studied Voss closely. "What's your connection in all this, L.T.?"

"I convinced Ernest that I would be that highest bidder."

Ott produced a devilish smile touched with admiration. "And how'd you go 'bout doin' that?"

"I explained to him how I like rewardin' such a pre-arranged sale by payin' in cash. That way he can mark down in the books whatever price he sees fit. The rest can go into his pocket. Told him he oughta think of it as Ernest money, if you follow my thinking."

"So, it's you aimin' to branch out into this e-moo business?"

L.T. shook his head. "Buster Gooch owns a big piece o' land up on Frogtown Creek. 'Bout four hundred acres. I've had my eye on it for three years. I got big plans for that place for the finest gated community in the state. If I can pick up the Vanstory place and trade that off to Buster for the Frogtown tract, he'll be tickled pink, and I'll be tickled green."

"I hope this Frogtown land o' his ain't buttin' up against Limberlost's property. If it is, I can smell a war brewin' in the forecast . . . b'tween you and Limberlost."

Voss snorted. "Damn that ol' Hoke Limberlost. I'm gonna find me a way to snatch up that jaybird's property, too, if it kills me."

"Well," Ott laughed, "it might . . . or he might. That ol' part-Cher'kee coot is more'n half crazy. Thinks he's the last o' the great redskin warriors. That or the Archbishop o' the Holy Frog. I believe ol' Limberlost worships that land o' his, and I ain't talkin' 'bout on Sunday. Reckon it's the Ind'an blood that does that."

"Tell you what," L.T. said and pointed at Ott with his cigar, "if he does try an' kill me, you just remember all these cigars you been puffin' on. I'm countin' on you, Ott. If I ain't dead, we'll get *him* behind bars, too, and wrap up the whole Frogtown shebang and give it a proper name."

Voss scowled. "Who the hell wants to live in a place named for a frog?"

"What is it you plan to do 'xactly with this Frogtown property?"

L.T. widened his hands in a measuring gesture. "Well, it's gonna be like a resort area. A village. Classy shops, private homes, a big lodge for public performances like music concerts and plays and such. Olympic sized pool, stables and horse trails. I can see walking trails and bicycle paths, bridges crisscrossing the creek, tennis courts on that wide section of floodplain, and a golf course cut outta the side of Crow Mountain. And here's the kicker: a big platform restaurant hanging out over the waterfall.

Come the end of a day, you could sip a martini and puff on your cigar right there thirty feet above the roar of the water. Now picture that with some spotlights floodin' up through the trees. Maybe different colored ones. I'm even thinkin' bout havin' a light down at the bottom of the falls in the pool. Man, I get antsy just thinkin' about it."

"Sounds like a helluva hullabaloo. I can see you put some thought into this, ain't you? Big money . . . both goin' in and comin' out. You might juss end up a billionaire, L.T." Ott cocked his head and let his eyebrows peak over the bridge of his nose. "Now tell me again exactly what I'd git out o' this b'sides a coupla boxes a cee-gars?"

L.T. looked out into the dark. The insects up in the trees were grating away like a convention of clockmakers winding up their goods. Voss pushed his lips into a tight knot and dipped his head to one side like a man about to reveal his best kept secret.

"Well, I'll not be needin' too many investors, but the ones I do take in, I want 'em to be people I can trust." He gave Ott an approving nod. "People like you, Ott."

"Well how much would it take to git on board this money train?"

Voss wrinkled his face and shrugged. "Oh, pretty much whatever you wanted. Hell, you put in, say, ten thousand, and that'd likely grow to a hundred inside o' two years."

"A hunerd thousand?" Ott said and started pushing the squeaky swing again.

"Yep," Voss replied. " 'Course all this hinges on gittin' that Vanstory property."

For a long time, neither man spoke. They worked on their cigars and let their imaginations run toward financial bliss. There was no traffic out on the road, only the occasional dog barking out in the night . . . and Bernice clacking dishes together in the kitchen.

Ott stopped swinging, folded his arms across his chest, and crossed his legs at the ankles. "Betcha a bailsman bond 'gainst a bucket o' bricks it would go hard on them boys with Judge Ricketts were they to attempt a escape out o' the jail."

Voss looked at Ott quickly and began nodding. "I imagine it would."

Ott smiled and tipped his head to one side. "Be plumb stupid to try it."

"That's one thing them boys are known for," Voss said. "Bein' stupid."

"That's juss what I was thinkin'."

They sat for another long time without speaking. Now the ratchety clicking of the katydids became a soundtrack to accompany the daydreams of what all that money would bring to them. For Ott it was the crank of a come-along as he eased a new bass boat off a new trailer into Lake Lanier behind the new lake house he had always wanted. For L.T. it was the tumblers of a vault ticking. For as long as he could remember he had wanted one of those wall safes that could be hidden behind a framed picture. He could even see the painting—a night scene of the tree house restaurant hanging out over Frogtown Falls.

Bernice came to the screen door and stood silhouetted against the light in the front hall. Ott casually lowered his cigar and flipped it behind into the yard. Seeming not to notice Ott's surreptitious removal of evidence, she squeezed a kitchen towel on each finger and stared out at the night. Mr. Fluffs rubbed up against her calf, and Voss could see remnants of the pineapple-crumb delight still clinging to the fat cat's whiskers. He could swear the damned animal was sneering at him.

"Ott?" Bernice finally intoned, "you oughtn't be out in this night air in your socks like that. You juss got over that chest cold last month. What are the two o' you talkin' about anyway?"

"Juss talkin' a little bus'ness, Bernice. I'll be in d'rectly."

"Are you smoking a cigar?"

Ott smiled as he held up empty hands. "I am not." Ott winked at L.T.

"You get on in here right now or I'm a-lockin' this door. I'll not have you sick again. I'd just as soon have you die of pneumonia right here on the porch 'cause I cain't be a-waitin' on you all day when you're sick. I got my soap operas to keep up with." With that, she disappeared back into the house.

Ott made a face that he would not have dared had the porch light been on. He pushed himself up from the swing and marched dutifully toward the door until a thought struck him and he turned back to L.T.

"You hear 'bout the statue up to Lake Winfield Scott?"

"Yeah. Heard it from Lydelle down at the *Skillet*. You find out who did that?"

Ott stuffed his hands into his trouser pockets, pressed his lips together tightly, and shook his head. "I'm workin' on a coupla diff'rent angles. Might'a been someb'dy with a grudge ag'in' me. You know, General Scott's a relative o' mine. Hell, it could'a been somebody I arrested anytime in the last sixteen years."

"What about that awning post of mine?" L.T. said. "When's that gonna be replaced?"

"Ott!" Bernice barked from the kitchen.

Ott put on a scowl, curled his upper lip, and mouthed, *Ott!* —giving the performance a decidedly Bernician look by showing his incisors and lowering his eyebrows to a vicious angle.

"G'night, L.T.," Bernice yelled. Her voice traveling through the house had all the warmth of a judge's gavel. When she appeared at the screen door again with the cat in her arms, L.T. stood.

"Well, reckon I'll be gettin' on home," Voss offered. "Ya'll have a good evenin' now."

"What's left of it," Bernice said.

Ott rolled his eyes, turned, walked through the door past his wife, and lumbered down the hall. Bernice and Mr. Fluffs watched Voss amble down the steps. When he turned at the bottom, they were still watching him.

"Bernice, next time you make up some of that pineapple-crumb delight, you be sure and give me a call. I'll get over here at a decent hour."

Bernice said nothing. Mr. Fluffs's snarky smile seemed to say, *I'll save you a hairball.*

L.T. strolled out to his Cadillac, all the while listening behind him for a sound on Ott's porch. When he did not hear the front door close, he began a soft whistling rendition of *The Moonlight Gambler* and introduced a subtle limp to his left leg. He couldn't help but smile, but he didn't dare laugh until he'd locked himself inside his Caddy.

Chapter Twenty-Nine

Crow Mountain
Sunday, late morning

A light drizzle swirled in the air. The winds carving through the gaps around Blood Mountain wove together into a turbulent pattern of erratic shifting currents, bending the branches of the oak first one way then the other. Joey sat on the rock behind the cabin and, holding the jar between his gloves, lipped the penultimate asparagus spear and began chewing. The sweat lifted off his skin, cooling him, only to be replaced by tiny beads of mist. The sky was the color of wood ash.

Even shirtless in this humid weather, his body was like a flame beneath his skin. His workout on the heavy bag had been brutal, his shoulders still burning from the last three-minute assault on "Booger." That's what he called the bag now. He wanted to always remember what it felt like to lie beneath that mass of inert weight. Never again, he swore, would he allow himself to be so compromised.

Now it was like a bad dream. Right in front of Angie LaFarge, he had practically offered himself up for sacrifice as the centerpiece of a human sandwich. It might have been funny had *he* not been the meat—one lean strip of bouncer between a slab of tough sourdough on bottom and the Pillsbury Dough Boy on steroids on top. He picked up a stick and hurled it as far as he could out into the maw of the valley.

"Shit," he whispered. The word sounded so much like the wind in the trees that he could almost feel the world out there making a similar assessment of him.

A car was working its way up the mountain, whining in first gear. Joey stood, pulled off his gloves, picked up his shirt, and walked to the front of the cabin and waited.

The ladybug Volkswagen appeared and cruised into his little turnout behind his car. Budge filled the passenger side of the VW, and the woman named Lily cut the engine and pulled up the emergency brake. Smiling, she rolled down her window.

"You must live on top of the world," she said, her dark eyes shining like smooth orbs of onyx throwing back glints of sunlight. "This is beautiful. Is that Blood Mountain back there in the mist?"

"Yes, ma'am," Joey said, and pulled on his T-shirt. He walked to Lily's window and bent down. She was so strikingly beautiful that he could not look at her for long. The backseat was filled with sleeping bags, foam pads, and a tent still in its box. "What brings you folks up here?"

Budge was busy sorting through several pages of paper in his lap. He wore khaki hiking shorts and a multi-pocketed safari shirt.

"You ever try to use this map service off the Internet?" Budge said and held up one of the pages. When he tapped his huge index finger to a typed line, it was like watching an elephant trying to use a calculator. "See that right there where it says 'turn left and go point-two miles'? That was through some lady's backyard. It may as well have said to turn left at the hog pen and watch out for the clothesline." He folded the papers and stuffed them into the glove compartment.

Joey opened the door for Lily. "I was about to fix some lunch. Would you two like something? My landlord gave me some ground venison. I can make some burgers."

"Ooh! Venison!" she chirped. "I'm in! And I guess Budge is a given."

Budge casually raised a hand a few inches. " 'Given'!" he announced.

Lily stepped out and turned, admiring the view in every direction. She wore faded jeans, a burgundy, long-sleeve pullover shirt, and white high-top moccasins with borders of blue and black beads. The shirt sported a burnt-sienna, stylistic drawing of a buffalo—a primitive rendering like a painting from an ancient cave . . . except that the buffalo was more three-dimensional than flat. It had the mountain range of her breasts to thank for that. The mist of rain beaded her dark hair like a veil of tiny pearls.

Joey knew that she worked nights at *The Skin Tight Club*. She certainly had the body for it. Somehow, it was hard to imagine her bestowing her wholesome smile on ogling middle-aged men saturated with alcohol.

Budge had one knee up against his ear trying to extricate himself from the cramped space of the front seat. His face was the color of a ripening fig. With a grunt he finally managed to climb out. The VW sprung up several inches like a non-aquatic beetle coming up for air. Once he had arched his back and stretched his thick arms to the drizzling sky, Budge closed his eyes and settled himself with a long sigh.

" 'Those who expect to reap the blessings of freedom, must, like men, undergo the fatigues of supporting it.' " When he opened his eyes, he bounced once with a silent laugh and started for the front porch where Lily held open the door. "Thomas Paine," he murmured as he passed by Joey.

When they were gathered inside the cabin, the rain fell harder. Joey opened the windows, fired up the woodstove, and pressed out five patties from his ice cooler. Soon the sizzle in the frying pan, the smell of meat cooking, and the sound of rain tapping on the leaves outside had the effect of consecrating the interior of the cabin as a safe harbor. Lily looked around at the walls, interested in everything—especially the craftsmanship that had gone into the building. Budge gravitated to the window in the back and took in the limited gray view.

"That your heavy bag out there? It's getting wet."

Joey turned with a deer-burger balanced on his spatula. "I forgot all about it."

"I'll get it," Budge said.

Lily stood at the bookcase, her head tilted ninety degrees to read the titles. "Are these yours?"

Joey shook his head. "My landlord's." He watched her pull one of the books from the shelf. "But he says it's okay if I read them."

She replaced the book on the shelf. "And have you read any of them?"

Joey shrugged. "Just the field guides. I've been getting interested in birds."

Lily approached the stove and watched Joey flip the burgers. "By the way, I like Angie."

Joey looked at her a little too quickly, and then just as quickly he turned back to the frying pan. "Yeah," he said noncommittally. He laughed quietly, realizing why Lily had thought of her. Joey's left hand was on Angie's weapon of choice—a frying pan.

Lily put a little mischief in her smile. "Something going on between you two?"

Joey continued to push the meat around in the pan. "I've known her since we were in the fourth grade."

"And?" Lily goaded.

He looked at her and couldn't resist the friendly gleam in her eyes. "Okay, I've been in love with her since we were in the fourth grade."

Joey peered out at the rain and frowned, wondering why he had shared something so personal with Lily, whom he hardly knew. And just as curious was the tacit understanding that she would not repeat his confession to anyone . . . not even to Budge.

"And how does Angie feel about that?"

Joey shrugged. "The other night . . . that was the first time I'd seen her in sixteen years."

Lily smiled. "Let me guess. All that time you've been a loyal absentee lover?"

Budge had dropped the duffel of sawdust on the back porch, and, brushing the rain from his shoulders, he stepped inside just in time to hear the tail end of the conversation.

"Depends on how you define 'lover,' " Joey replied and flipped a burger as casually as he could.

Budge leaned on the counter. When he spoke, his voice carried the melody of Thespian fervor.

" 'The magician, the enchanter, that changes worthless things to joy, and makes right royal kings and queens of common clay.' " Lily and Joey looked at him and waited. Budge took a last swipe at the rain on his shaved head. "Robert Ingersoll. It's from a lecture about love."

Lily laughed and held her smile on Joey. "You know . . . my radio in the bug is broken, but I never missed it on the ride up." She opened her hands toward Budge as though introducing him for the first time. "This morning I heard from Oliver Wendell Holmes, Yogi Berra, Pope John Paul the whatever, and Popeye the Sailor Man." Her smile widened to show a perfect set of teeth. "Hey, Big-boy, what was the one you recited when we passed that sweet potato crop?"

"I yam what I yam and that's all that I yam," Budge said in a croaky voice. He may have sounded like Popeye, but in his new khaki hiking outfit, he looked like the entire Atlanta Falcons defensive line crammed into a single Boy Scout uniform.

Lily laughed again. "You gotta give him credit. His repertoire enjoys a wide range."

They sat at Joey's little table and ate and watched the fog roll through the valley as Lily talked about her grandparents, who had lived just a few miles west of Blood Mountain on Cane-Tuck Creek.

Joey chewed his burger and studied her dark eyes, her black hair, and the sharp angles of her cheeks. "Are you Native American?"

She offered a beatific smile. "My grandmama was full-Cherokee," she said.

Budge had finished off his three deer-burgers and was keeping close watch on Lily's slow progress with her one. "Lily can make a fire without a match. Does it Indian style, twirling a stick in her hands."

Joey nodded, sipped asparagus juice, and watched the two of them—trying to figure out the nature of their relationship.

"So," Budge said, "you got no electricity up here? No phone?"

Joey shook his head. "My landlord, Hoke, he built this place and lived in it for thirty years until his truck started having trouble climbing the mountain. He can still make it up the hill sometimes . . . just not every time he tries." He looked around at the cabin walls. "I've gotten where I like it. These candles give me pretty much what I need at night. It's peaceful." Joey pointed to Budge's water glass. "That water you're drinking is hand-cranked from a well."

"All very quaint," Budge said, "but it still makes it hard to contact you if I've got work for you."

Joey's teeth had partially sunk into what was left of his burger, but he retracted them, set the burger on his plate, and stared at Budge. "You'd hire me again?"

"Depends on your learning curve. If you learn from the other night, bingo, you're a better bouncer. If not, you're a liability. And it depends on your dedication."

Joey laughed in wonderment and then turned dead serious. "I was born to be a bouncer, Budge. No one was more born to it than I."

Budge conceded this with a nod. "Born to it . . . but will you go the distance?"

Lily, who had been cutting her burger with knife and fork, stopped sawing and looked at Joey. "Budge had an apprentice once and invested a lot of time in him. Free of charge. Eventually, he took a job with a software company."

"Nothing wrong with software," Budge added. "Just made me feel like I was spinning my wheels." He pushed his plate aside and leaned his thick forearms on the table. "It's an art, you know. Like anything else, when you reach a certain level, you want to pass it on . . . strategies, techniques, style, timing. The apprentice has got to be the right person."

Joey pushed his plate aside, too. He waited until Budge met his eyes.

"I will not quit you. I'll stick till you tell me to go. You've got my word on that."

Lily propped her elbows on the table, made a hammock of her fingers, and rested her chin on the backs of her knuckles. She smiled at Budge.

"Well, my jumbo-sized friend, I believe you have found the courier of your legacy."

Joey offered his fist across the table. Budge looked at it a moment then reached across with his own and they tapped knuckles. The contact was so light and delicate that an air of intimacy enveloped the ritual.

"Stick like glue?" Budge said, looking into Joey's eyes.

Joey did not blink. "Epoxy."

"Cross your heart and hope to die?" Budge added, still poker-faced.

"Cross my heart and liver and pancreas and adrenals," Joey replied in kind.

Budge pointed his chin at Joey's unfinished burger. "You gonna eat that?"

Joey made a be-my-guest gesture with his hands. Lily laughed as Budge pulled Joey's plate closer.

"This is one of Budge's redeeming traits, Joey," she said. "Makes me wonder if he's part-Indian, too. Nothing goes to waste in this man's kitchen."

They watched Budge consume every speck and morsel on the plate. Then Lily looked around the room.

"Is it hard keeping your food fresh in a cooler?"

Joey shrugged. "I just pick up a bag of ice every time I'm out. My landlord says come November, I won't need to buy anymore till late spring. He says while the rest of the people in the northern hemisphere refrigerate their food in little boxes indoors, I'll be living in a little box indoors while the outdoors will be my refrigerator."

"I like your landlord already," Lily said and continued to scan the cabin. "Angie would like your place, Joey. Very romantic!"

"Yeah?" Joey cocked his head to one side. "You seem to know her pretty well for having just met her once . . . and that for about five minutes."

"That's Lily's gift," Budge said, chewing. "Lily can see into your marrow."

Keeping his face neutral, Joey sat back in his chair and studied Lily. Her hair was so black it made the whites of her eyes appear incandescent.

"So, can you see into this big guy's marrow?" Joey said, nodding toward Budge.

"Oh, sure," she said. "He's all glass, freshly wiped down with *Windex*. That's one of the reasons we're such good friends. I know I can trust him."

Budge had finished with Joey's plate and now scavenged morsels of meat off Lily's. He gave Joey a shrug.

"It's platonic, in case you were wondering," he said and shrugged again. "We don't plan to mess up a good relationship with the carnal factor."

Joey felt a sudden wave of empathy for Budge, knowing the big man must surely have feelings for this raven-haired enchantress. What man wouldn't? Budge probably hung on just to be near her—to enjoy whatever intellectual intimacy was possible.

The rain rattled the leaves outside the windows, and for a time the three of them sat listening to its soporific patter. Then Lily got up, bent and kissed Joey above his eyebrow. When she straightened, she put a hand on his forehead as though ensuring that the kiss would remain in place. Then she walked to the open backdoor and looked out into the gray void of the valley.

Joey touched his forehead and leaned toward Budge. "What was that all about?" he asked quietly.

Budge hitched his head to one side. "She does that to me, too . . . I have no idea why." Budge looked at Lily standing motionless against the backdrop of fog. "In the big picture of things," Budge said from the side of his mouth, "I think maybe Lily is the last goddess from Olympus. Probably the goddess of higher thinking." He pointed a thick finger at Joey. "You and I? We're lungfish who have just crawled out of the sea, not even sure if we're supposed to be sucking water through our gills or air through our mouths. Still, all we can do is the best that we can."

Joey waited, pretty sure of what was coming. He could feel the moment of edification gathering like charged molecules of stratospheric water piling up in a thunderhead. Budge raised his chin theatrically and assumed a voice not unlike that of Laurence Olivier.

" 'Thus the best human intelligence is still decidedly barbarous; it fights in heavy armor and keeps a fool at court.' " Budge sighed at the inalienable truths of the world. "George Santayana," he added. Then he sighed again and gestured toward the frying pan. "Any more burgers, Captain Epoxy?"

Chapter Thirty

Peachtree Battle Memorial Park
Atlanta
Spring, 1980

It was the kind of day that made you aware of the air you were breathing. There was a taste to it, an effervescence—like the spritz of carbonation leaping from a freshly opened can of ginger ale. The sun sparkled in the grasses around the playground, and, in the shallow swale of the floodplain, daffodils had sprung up like old-fashioned telephones coated with melted butter.

Lily and her mother, Kayla, walked toward a vacant bench that looked out over the creek. Lily's eyes were on the flowers. Kayla watched the children on the swings, pumping and squealing as they stretched their toes trying to touch the sky. As dangerous as it appeared, with the wild abandon of the children's radical arcs on the swing set, Kayla wished this kind of freedom for Lily. Just once she would like to see her daughter cut loose and leap or twirl . . . anything that resembled a lark. Lily was more apt to sit and speak in earnest to a shield bug—which, Kayla supposed, could be considered a lark . . . only an odd one.

Lily paid no attention to the laughing children. She stared down at the ground, watching her feet sink into the wild ground ivy that sent its pungent scent into the air like the vapor trail of a minty jet. Looking back behind her, Lily paused, and Kayla wondered if the girl were able to see the invisible essence of the mint as it diffused into the air. Or was she apologizing to the plants for stepping on them? Kayla never knew what went on inside her daughter's head. Lily bent, picked up a stone and studied it.

"Did you find a special rock, Sweetie?"

The pensive little girl looked up and nodded. Her eyes were fairy tale eyes—so big they could capture the heart of the vilest ogre. Kayla suspected Lily was going to be one of those truly rare and ravishing females that graced the covers of *Cosmopolitan* and *Elle*, and she felt strangely guilty about the envy that crept into her chest when she thought this way. She wondered if other mothers fell into funks over their gorgeous nine-year-olds.

"What's special about this rock, Sweetie?"

Lily held the stone up for inspection, as if the answer were obvious. "An Indian used it, Mama. To smooth out the inside of a wooden bowl."

Kayla put on her patient face and let the melody of her words soften the question. "Now, Lily, how in the world can you know that?"

Lily held the stone out at arm's length, and Kayla dutifully took it, smiling but fearful.

Lily smiled back. "Can you feel it?" she said. Her black onyx eyes widened even more to match the unfettered joy radiating off her flawless face.

Kayla held the cold stone for a few seconds and concentrated . . . on what, she could not say. It was a rock. Period. Though she herself was part-Cherokee, Kayla was not privy to such mystical interpretations. She handed back the rock.

"Would you like to try the seesaw today, Sweetie? I can get on it with you."

Lily shook her head, hugged her arms to her stomach, and turned. Her attention remained on the creek for half a minute.

"Can I sing to the creek now, Mama?"

Kayla's brow tightened. "Sing to it?" She knelt to her daughter but had no words.

"You can sit on the bench while I sing, Mama. Can I go down on the sand?"

This was why Kayla had brought the book in her bag. It usually went this way. Lily was in total control of her nine-year-old agenda and that usually involved sitting by herself for hours. Sometimes it was staring at a tree's trunk, as if she were watching it grow. Or waving her hand like an orchestral conductor, leading a patch of clover through a silent symphony. The most disturbing incident was the time Lily had removed all her clothes and used them to dress a tangle of vines she had said looked cold.

"Just don't get too close to the water, Sweetie. Promise?"

Lily climbed down the bank and stood with her heels together on a chunky flat-topped boulder. Kayla watched from the top of the bank for several minutes, but Lily did nothing except watch the brown water glide by. Kayla tried to remember if she herself had ever stood so still for so long. She marveled at her daughter's self-discipline.

Lured by a bed of deep green moss and its vantage over the creek, Kayla sat and pulled out her book—the one she had found on the bestseller display . . . and in the nonfiction section, for heaven's sake. She had never before ventured outside of a good romance novel, preferring those about female protagonists traveling alone and abroad.

She turned the book over and looked at the photo of Dr. Arabelle Davidovich. The tingle stirred inside her again—the same little jump-start she had felt in the bookstore. She read the woman's bio for the third time and flipped the book over to admire its title. *Broken Vows, Wounded Heart: The Woman's Ascension into Blessed Aloneness.*

She had not bought it for its title, even though the dust from her divorce had not yet settled. It was the photograph of the author that had caught her eye. Kayla was starting to wonder if her divorce had taken less of its initiative from Chad's infidelity and more from the growing suspicion that she was showing signs of being a latent lesbian here at the ripe old age of thirty-nine.

Kayla looked up to check on her daughter. As far as she could tell, Lily had not moved a hair. Kayla listened, but she could not hear Lily singing. If she was, it was a whisper; but neither was her mouth moving. Kayla admired the perfect flare of her daughter's calves and the smooth sun-browned skin that covered them. The square shoulders that were wide for her age. The deep black of her hair. Kayla knew that her daughter was going to fill out into something spectacular one day, and Kayla wondered if she would know how to prepare Lily for the attention those looks would draw. Men would be fluttering around her like moths congregating around a flame. And might not women be drawn to her, too? Kayla began to wonder if lesbianism was hereditary. If so, she had to rethink everything she remembered about her own mother.

The sun was low in the trees when Kayla awoke. The air had turned cool, and the rush hour traffic stalled at the east end of the park. She sat upright, and the book slid off her stomach onto the moss. As the haze of sleep left her, a pang of panic moved in to take its place, and her eyes searched the creek as she stood.

Lily was standing exactly as she had been, and for a crazy moment Kayla recalled a movie she had seen in which aliens had sucked the spirits out of children in a village and left their young bodies paralyzed in the pose they had been found—like a yard sale of hollow statuettes. Kayla listened for a few seconds, but there was only the burble of the creek.

"Sweetie? Are you about ready to go home?"

Lily's head partially turned, but Kayla could not see her face. The little girl turned back to her original pose and said something in a low conversational tone. Then Lily hopped down from the rock and climbed up the bank, and for a moment she looked like a common child all done playing at a creek.

"Aren't you cold, Lily?"

"No, ma'am."

Kayla stared at her daughter's vibrant face and thought about how someone had once told her that parents don't really get to see their children grow up because, ironically, they see them every day. Kayla gently pushed the hair from Lily's forehead. She could swear her daughter looked older than she had seemed just hours before.

"Did you sing to the creek, Sweetie?"

Lily shook her head. "It wasn't my turn . . . I forgot."

Kayla's hand combed the lock of jet-black hair again and let her hand rest on Lily's forehead. "What do you mean? Whose turn was it?"

"The creek told me all about the fighting. A man hid down there and spent a whole night partway underwater. He suffered so much that he cried most of the night."

Kayla frowned at the creek. "What man, Lily? Did you see a man down there?"

"It was back during the fighting. It was one of the men in the gray clothes. He was bleeding right here." Lily touched a finger to her stomach. The sadness in her voice matched the tragic slant of her eyes.

Kayla knelt, putting her face on the level of Lily's. "Is this like the time we were at the airport, and you asked that nice old lady not to board her airplane?" Kayla kept her voice carefully tempered to a clinical tone, so as not to upset her daughter. She had never told her about the plane crash.

"No, Mama. This is from the other end. It already happened."

"What do you mean . . . 'from the other end'?"

Lily shook her head. "I can sing to the creek next time. It will be my turn then."

Kayla rose and took Lily's hand, and they didn't speak anymore as they walked the length of the park to its west end. When they climbed the hill and stepped onto the street, Kayla stutter-stepped and paused to read the metal plaque standing erect at the curb. Raised black letters against a silver background.

Battle of Peachtree Creek. Johnson's troops marched east of this site to attempt a flanking maneuver on Sherman's . . .

Turning away from the sign, Kayla looked out over the park and tried to imagine cannon fire and smoke and Confederate soldiers moving down this hill toward the creek. It was difficult to assign such a chaotic story to this idyllic scene. She looked at Lily, who had picked up a cone of seeds fallen from a tulip tree. She was at the edge of the hill picking away the seeds one at a time and letting them spiral in the air down the slope like tiny helicopters. Kayla joined her and quietly stood beside her daughter until all the seeds had been sown. Then she knelt again and turned Lily to her with both hands on her shoulders.

"You're going to do something very special one day, aren't you, Sweetie?"

Lily beamed. "I'm going to do lots of things, Mama."

Kayla smiled. "That's good, Lily. You can't have too many interests in this life. There's always room to slip one more flower into the vase. My mother used to say that."

"But there's one important thing," Lily added. "I know what I'm going to be, Mama, when I grow up."

Kayla laughed. At thirty-nine, she was wondering what to do with her own life. Her little girl looked so sincere and certain.

"You do? That's my smart girl."

Lily looked into her mother's eyes, and this time Kayla thought her daughter's smile might be the courageous smile of a saint. "I'm going to be a waitress at a cocktail bar, Mama."

Chapter Thirty-One

***Walmart* Shopping Center entrance**
Sunday, just before twilight

"I am *Inâli*, Black Fox of the Blue Holly clan. Black Fox speaks to the Elder Fires Above and asks for the sacred ones to—" Hoke shook his head. This prayer was starting to feel a little stilted. He didn't talk this way to Verdie or Joey, and so he wondered if the spirits above might nail him as a hypocrite. He cleared his throat and started again. "It's Hoke. I wanna ask you'ens to watch over me, guide me, give me strength and cunning. All o' that. But I 'specially need a steady aim with my bow. I cain't be missin' that first shot. It's gotta be dead-on, or I'm a cooked turkey."

He tied the bandana of red—the warrior's color—across the blue one already in place on his forehead and gathered smoke from his small fire with scooping motions of his hands. Sweeping thin wisps of gray toward him, he ran his hands along the contours of his arms, chest, face, and legs . . . not touching, but floating his hands an inch above his clothes and skin as though anointing himself with a holy ether.

Just twenty yards away from the trees where he hid, a smattering of cars streamed along the curving entrance to the *Walmart* parking lot that sprawled over a dozen acres. It was the largest piece of pavement in the county, and each time Hoke looked upon it he imagined the earth beneath choked, colorless, and sterile, with not even a worm down there in that darker-than-dark grave.

Kneeling in the thicket of pines that separated the *Walmart* lot from the entrance to the *Blue Ridge Amalgamated Mine Tours*, Hoke added a stick to the fire—just enough to keep the flame alive—for the fire was not only a part of the ceremony, it was a tool to ignite the flaming arrow he would soon launch.

He peered out from the trees at the giant wooden miner that someone had carved out of huge sections of white pine and pieced together in a rather pitiful attempt at homespun sculpting. Ever since *Blue Ridge Amalgamated* had erected it, Hoke had hated the idea of it. The damned thing looked like a three-way hybridization of Paul Bunyan, Richard Nixon, and Mr. Gumby.

Almost twelve hours earlier at the crack of dawn, using his grappling hook candelabra, he had scaled the monstrosity and secured to the gold miner's hat four balloons filled with kerosene. He was getting fairly adept with statues, preferring wood for its traction but marble for its lack of splinters. As he stared out at his target, he picked at the one remaining barb of wood worrying his left thumb.

The timing on this was critical. He wanted the coming inferno to enjoy a contrasting backdrop of night sky. There was nothing like the high drama of a giant blaze in darkness. A daytime fire couldn't hold a candle to that. And he did not want the lot completely deserted. People needed to witness the blaze. It would take only a few rubberneckers, he knew, and then cell phones would be tinkling ring tones all over the county. There would be a mob of spectators within minutes.

It was twilight minus six minutes and counting.

Hoke loaded an arrow to his bow string and then laid the bow flat on the ground. There was a red mark of bloodroot dye smeared on the belly of the bow for each coup he had counted—from the Byron T. Metcalfe sign to Voss's blood-sucking totem and the highway billboards and then finally for Winfield Scott's crunchy scalp. Hoke allowed himself a moment to bask in his evolution as a renegade warrior.

The business with the highway signs had begun as a whim. He had just gotten tired of looking at them, that is, except for the ones that raised awareness about the native people, who, in his opinion, still owned this land. Now his forays had evolved into a grander theme. Though he had considered it, he didn't hold out much hope for rounding up all the whites and driving them to Oklahoma. So—for the present, at least—he would settle for these inanimate victims.

Nothing was more symbolic of the white man's trespass on Cherokee lands than this gargantuan gold miner towering over the *Walmart* entrance. The mine itself was only a tourist attraction now, but in its heyday, it had represented the pall of white industry choking the native land. It was gold that ultimately had sent the Cherokees packing for Oklahoma—that debacle befalling them even with Chief Justice John Marshall throwing all the weight of the Supreme Court behind the Cherokees' right to hold on to this gold-infested land. But the Georgia militia had had a different idea and gone against the ruling. At the time, no one held Georgia accountable . . . not even the President.

"Andy Jackson," Hoke hissed and spat off to one side. "That damn, fork-tongued devil of a politician with a poisoned heart!"

He picked up the BB rifle and seesawed it in his hands to hear the reassuring sound of the little pellets tumbling like tiny crystals of ice inside the magazine. He set the rifle down and checked the thin cloth binding on the arrow to make sure it was snug. He chuckled to himself. If he had not practiced with flaming arrows at home, this night would have turned out to be a fiasco. For a moment he cringed, imagining his fiery shot arcing into a passing car, that car ablaze like a meteorite rolling down the bypass, the panicked driver launching his flaming vehicle over the guardrail into the reservoir a quarter mile down the road.

There were three things Hoke had learned about flaming arrows. One: Use an extra-long arrow with the cloth tied near the tip. If you didn't, when you came to full draw with the thing lit, the flame would scorch your bow, not to mention charbroil your fingers.

Two: Use as little cloth as possible, just enough to ensure the flame stays lit during flight. Otherwise, the weight is too much. On his first attempt at home, he had wrapped cloth seven times around the shaft—seven being a sacred number to the Cherokee. When he had tried the shot with a full draw, the arrow had traveled a pathetically weak arc, as if he had launched it from a flimsy rubber band. He had been aiming across his front porch at a dampened hay bale he had set up on the driveway. The sluggish arrow foundered and set his porch railing on fire. Three slats had caught before he got a bucket of water to it.

And three: Aim high. A flaming arrow presents a lot of drag.

He felt proud of this list—knowing that, in a sense, he had replicated history. His Cherokee forebears had faced the same riddles of physics and solved them, though probably not for the purpose of igniting a giant wooden gold miner.

Hoke checked the sun. Not long now. He took up the rifle again and walked on his knees until he had gained an unobstructed view of the balloons on the miner's hat. Sitting back in the pine needles he propped his left elbow on his knee and sighted over the barrel. *Pow*, he mouthed, with a little onomatopoetic pop from his lips.

He had practiced with the BB gun—a three-dollar find at the 400 Flea Market—enough to know that it was not a precision instrument. But he had a hundred BB's. Who could miss a hundred times? Well, he didn't like the sound of that question, so he gave himself a little extra incentive with the solemn promise that if he couldn't pop those balloons in ninety-nine tries he would use the hundredth BB on himself.

He couldn't recall ever hearing about a suicide by BB gun, but he had no doubt that it could be accomplished. And if not, at the very least, a BB wound would probably be as bothersome as the splinter worrying his thumb. It would still teach a lesson.

The sun touched down on the tops of the trees across the intersection. The moment of truth had come. He cocked the lever repeatedly to pump air into the chamber and quickly set up for his aim. He could hear the faint leak of air from the faulty chamber.

Putting the front sight just above the red balloon, Hoke took a deep breath, let it out, and gently but firmly squeezed the trigger. After the initial *pfwytt* of the shot, he froze and listened. Nothing happened. Then from across the bypass he heard a faint *plink*. He was pretty sure he had hit the sign above the front door of the pharmacy across the intersection. He pumped the rifle again.

This time he aimed for the yellow balloon, which was located between the red and the green. If it was windage where the error lay, he might hit one of the two on the side.

Pfwytt!

Rather than pop, the red balloon ruptured, and kerosene spread all over the miner's hat. Now that he had the windage figured, he hit the green balloon on the next try. Kerosene dripped off the hat brim onto the miner's torso exactly as Hoke had hoped. It took three more shots to puncture the two remaining balloons and with that done, the statue looked like a miner caught in an isolated thundershower.

Now the tricky part. Expedience, stealth, and accuracy all at once. Hoke had to launch the flaming arrow without being seen. It had to be done soon while he had enough light and before too much of the kerosene evaporated from the statue. He unscrewed the lid on the jelly jar half filled with kerosene and watched the traffic for a time. When a lull came, he carefully poured the kerosene onto the cloth wrapped to the end of the shaft. He held the bow and arrow before him and closed his eyes.

"*Inâli* asks the Elder Fires Above to guide his arrow." Before he lowered the arrow he decided to once again include the blue-collar version of his prayer. "Let's nail that sucker, boys."

Feeling the tremble of war surge through him, he lowered the arrow tip to the small fire. The soaked cloth greedily took the flame with a *whoof!* The bow groaned as he drew. His focus was absolute, as his eyes riveted to the mute miner's wooden face.

Thwang!

As the burning missile arced through the air, Hoke knew by instinct that the aim was good. But the sound was wrong. In his peripheral vision he saw a dark object tumbling away from him over the pine needles.

"What the hell?" he whispered.

Checking the statue, he saw that the head and hat were ablaze with a dancing flame so brightly orange that the miner could have been a cousin once removed from the red-headed Vanstory boys. The arrow—now engulfed in flame—jutted from one ear.

Hoke frowned and rubbed the back of his neck, wondering what had jumped into the pine needles when he had shot. When the rawhide thong that always hung from his neck fell into his hand, he looked down at the bare cord—the one old Mingo had given him so long ago. The necklace had broken, and the fox ear was gone. He guessed that the bowstring had caught it, and a little wave of panic buzzed through him. Crime scene evidence!

Quickly, he stomped out his little fire so as not to be seen. Then, by the light of the flame rising off the miner's upper body, Hoke scrambled across the ground on his hands and knees looking for his talisman, but after a few minutes he knew he had to give it up. It was time to run away to fight another day.

Chapter Thirty-Two

**Lumpkin County jail
Sunday evening**

"I'm goin' to the can, Uncle Ott."

Ott lowered the newspaper an inch and peeked over the *Letters to the Editor* page at Crowder. The boy just did not look convincing in a deputy's uniform, but what could Ott do? Crowder was Bernice's sister's boy and in debt up to his ears since the "death by barbecue" shack had been closed down by the health inspector just that morning. Ott shook his head, wondering how any idiot could serve a pork sandwich with a quartz arrowhead hidden in the meat. It was just about par for Crowder's luck that the customer who bit into it was the violin teacher for the health inspector's daughter.

Crowder closed the book he was reading and walked to the hallway. When the bathroom door bumped shut, Ott jerked open the desk drawer before him and rifled through it looking for a pencil.

Finding none, he crossed the room and took the short pencil lying on the desktop next to Crowder's book. The boy had been taking notes on a legal pad. Ott turned around the book's cover to read the title: *Herbal Medicines of the Cherokees*. Ott's curiosity was piqued. He flipped the cover to find written on the inside: *This here is Hoke Limberlost's book. Don't forget to give it back.* The inscription appeared to be written in green paint.

"Zzzhheee-muh-nini," Ott muttered as he shook his head. "What now? From highway department idiot to barbecue cook to temporary deputy sheriff to medicine man." He slipped the pencil into his shirt pocket, re-crossed the room, and took the bracelet-sized key ring off its nail inside the shotgun cabinet. He was back at his desk reading the paper when Crowder returned and poured himself another cup of coffee.

"I think my bladder must'a shrunk," Crowder complained. "Prob'ly from all the stress o' runnin' a barbecue joint."

Watching Crowder stir sugar into his coffee, Ott knew that his nephew would never pass the written exam required of a sheriff's deputy. At Bernice's insistence, he had hired the boy right away, but only as a night watchman. Night duty was about all Crowder was ever going to see, and Ott didn't care to tell him about the connection between caffeine and urinating. If the boy cut down on coffee, he'd never stay awake for his shift. The only thing dumber than Crowder, Ott figured, was Crowder asleep.

"You read these letters in the *Nugget* 'bout the highway signs bein' vandalized?" Ott asked. "Seems most people ain't sorry to see 'em go."

Crowder set down the freshly poured cup of coffee on his desk and sat. "Mama likes them signs. Says they help cut out noise pollution. She goes to a yoga class down in that trailer park at the south county line . . . the one behind that big sign o' Jimmy Dale Roper's Jeep dealership. She said if it weren't for the sign, they wouldn' none of 'em be able to med-er-tate."

Ott tried to imagine Dora Lynn Ramp twisted into a yoga knot and humming chants, gave up on that, and turned his thoughts toward Duffy's theory about Indian-related signs.

"There a picture on that sign o' Jimmy Dale's?"

Crowder thought for a moment, then began nodding. "Yeah, there's a big green four-by-four Jeep Cherokee." He snorted. "Mama . . . she don't understand. It don't really cut out any noise. I mean, the noise has gotta go somewhere, don't it? It juss bounces back at the cars. Way I see it, them signs cut down on noise in one place and juss double it som'eres else."

Ott kept his face blank and said nothing. He had no wish to attempt an edifying conversation with his nephew about physics and sound waves, because, number one, Crowder was dumb as a brick, and, number two, about the only thing Ott knew about science was how to turn on *Eye Witness Police Chronicles* from the sofa by the magic of the TV remote.

When Crowder stuck his nose into his book again, Ott stood, folded his newspaper, and slapped it against his leg. "Reckon I'll go and donate this newspaper to the pris'ners."

Crowder looked up with a surprised expression. "You think them Vanstory boys can read a lick?" Without waiting for an answer, Crowder began searching the floor around his feet. "Did you see a pencil over here, Uncle Ott?"

Ignoring the question, Ott exercised the limits of his technological know-how at the jail by pushing the wall button, which tripped the buzzer and the dead bolt. Walking into the cellblock, he upgraded his slow waddle to a more sheriff-like amble.

Haymer and Mose were stretched out on their beds, but Garland stood facing the back wall as if there were a window there. Which there wasn't. Shifting his weight from leg to leg, he looked as though he were climbing an endless flight of invisible stairs but getting nowhere.

Haymer's eyes were fixed on the bunk above him, where Mose's snoring revved and idled like a chainsaw with a fouled carburetor. The only features these boys had in common were their orange jumpsuits and their flaming red hair, the combination of which was somehow disturbing to Ott.

"Any o' you boys wanna read the latest issue of the *Nugget*?"

Garland stopped his climbing and turned. "We in it?"

Ott nodded. "Under the arrest reports." He held the paper through the bars, but Garland only stared at Ott. "Maybe you can look at the pictures. There's one o' Beulah Babcock in here a-twirlin' 'round at the contra-dance. If you ain't never seen a tornado b'fore, that picture might be the closest thing to it."

"That ain't our meth lab, ya know," Haymer said from his bunk. "Juss 'cause it's on our farm, don't mean it's our'n."

Ott smiled his yeah-and-tonight-all-you-boys'll-be-receiving-Swedish-massages-after-supper smile. "Save it for the judge, Haymer. You want the paper or not?"

When Garland turned away and started up his weight-shifting rhythm again, Ott tossed the paper to the cell floor. Haymer sat up and swung his stockinged feet to the cold concrete.

"Listen, Ott, we been a-hearin' sounds out there at night on the farm," Haymer began in a confidential tone. "We didn' know what it was. At first, I thought it might'a been the horses got out. But it weren't that. Then I noticed the door to the ol' tool shed keeps gettin' left open. I figure some jasper's been sneakin' in there at night and makin' drugs." He shook his head as he pondered the floor. "It's a wonder we didn' find it b'fore you did."

Ott smiled his indulgent-grandfather-listening-to-a-whopper smile. "I see you boys been engagin' in some creative thinkin'. I hope this ain't leadin' up to a story 'bout your horses tryin' a git a edge at the racetrack by brewin' up some speed."

Garland sat down on his bunk and glared at the wall opposite him. He set one jackhammer leg into motion like it had its own motor and was about to throw a rod. Ott had never known anyone with so much energy. If ever he got Garland assigned to road clean-up duty, Lumpkin County was sure to make the Governor's Pristine County Program.

Ott sorted through the keys on the big iron ring and opened the lock. The metallic *clack* brought around Haymer's and Garland's eyes like a dinner bell.

"You boys juss rest easy now. I need ta have a look-see at this door." Ott pushed the door open and swung it back and forth on its hinges, timing the rhythm to syncopate between Mose's snoring. The action of the door was quiet and smooth, no rust. Ott stood on his tiptoes and inspected the top hinge. Then he crouched to check the lower one.

"This door been givin' y'all any trouble?" he asked of no one in particular.

Garland ceased his manic leg motion, lowered his eyebrows, and frowned at the door with his mouth open. He was clearly perplexed. Haymer narrowed his eyes and watched Ott like a hawk.

"We ain't really been usin' it all that much, Ott," Haymer said in a flat tone.

Ott propped his fists on the roll of fat that bulged like an inner tube above his belt. Still staring at the door, he cocked his head, pursed his lips, and finally waved his hand at the door in a dismissive manner.

"Looks aw-right to me. Plenty o' oil on the movin' parts." Then he looked at one hand and rubbed his thumb against his fingertips. "Guess I better wash up."

He ambled over to the cell's dirty sink and began scrubbing, using his wide silhouette to shield his pocketing of one of the toothbrushes lying on the stained porcelain. The brush went into his left shirt pocket and from his right shirt pocket he slipped out the chewed-up brush he had brought with him from home—the one he had dipped in tuna oil and given to Mr. Fluffs to gnaw on.

"Ever'thin' 'bout your stay here at the jail goin' satisfact'ry for you boys?" Ott asked over the sound of the running water. "Gittin' enough to eat? Enough water? Toilet paper?"

The two brothers frowned at Ott's broad back. There were no towels in the cell, so Ott flung his hands semi-dry, turned, and smiled at the Vanstorys.

"Well, thanks, boys," Ott said. "Glad we could have this little chat." Twirling the big ring on his fat fingers, he strolled out of the cell as only a sheriff could. He closed the door with his shoe as he continued to flap his hands in the air, careful not to touch the door again, which had not closed far enough to engage the lock. "Say, you boys wanna hear a good one I heard down at the barber shop?" He stepped away from the door and leaned his forearms on the flat horizontal piece that ran the length of the front bars. His chubby arms barely fit through the spaces. Jingling the keys in front of him, Ott angled his eyes at the ceiling like a man trying to recall the details of a story. "Okay," he began, "how come the chicken was to cross the road?"

Haymer spat on the floor and looked away. Garland sat very still, staring at Ott's keys. Then he let his eyes drift casually back to the unlocked door. Mose's snoring caught a snag, releasing a gigantic hiccough before finding its rhythm again. It was as close as Ott was going to get to a response, so he forged ahead.

"Okay, so . . . why'd the chicken cross the road?" Ott repeated, letting the question rise in pitch before delivering the punch line. He waited a beat, trying to get the timing just right. When he opened his hands, the keys dangled like the centerpiece of the universe. "To show the 'possum it could be done."

When the brothers showed no reaction to the joke, Ott let go with a laugh. Through the slits of his eyes, he could see Garland's stare still fixed on the unlocked door.

Surprising everyone, Mose spoke up. "You know what we call 'possums out our way, Ott?"

Always ready to savor a good joke, Ott lifted both eyebrows expectantly.

"Lum'kin Coun'y speed bumps," Mose said, following the punch line with two, mouthed, bumpy sounds from his inflated cheeks.

Ott laughed and shot a now-*that's*-a-good'n index finger at Mose. "Well, you boys get some rest now. See cain't you git on the judge's good side next week."

Ott walked to the back of the cellblock to the door that could be accessed only by a key from either side. Sorting through the heavy key ring he found the proper key and opened the door enough to stick his head out.

"Ah!" he breathed. "Startin' to cool off fin'lly. Gonna be a nice evenin'."

As he let the door close, he inserted Crowder's pencil into the jamb so that the lock would not engage. Then he walked back to the cell where the Vanstorys languished.

"Well, boys, me an' my night watchman will head over to the *Skillet* an' pick up some pork chop plates for ya. Y'all hold down the fort while we're gone."

Just before Ott turned to go, Garland's eyes flicked back to the cell door, and for a moment Ott thought Garland was going to jump the gun and try the door while Ott was still standing there. Garland wet his lips with snaky darts of his tongue and started up vibrating both his legs. He looked like a two-cylinder engine pushed to its limit.

When Ott stepped back into the front office, the cellblock door behind him closed. Crowder was at the coffee maker topping off his cup, but he turned when Ott made a big production of testing the door to the cellblock. He slipped the iron key ring over his wrist like a bracelet. Then dusting off his hands as if he'd just completed an impromptu repair job, Ott strolled out to the center of the room, stopped, and slapped a hand to his rounded belly.

"What you say we go down to the *Skillet* an' git us the pork chop special?"

Crowder stared hard at his uncle. "But there ain't nobody else here to keep a eye on things, Uncle Ott."

Ott shrugged. "Well, these boys ain't et yet, an' it'll be a handful for even the two o' us to carry their supper back. I reckon the jail can sit tight for a hour." Ott jangled the keys on his wrist. "We'll take these along with us . . . juss to be safe. Come on now, son. Let's go eat."

When Crowder headed out the door, Ott flipped off the lights, knowing that the Vanstorys would see the dark of the office through the crack at the bottom of the cellblock door. When the two officers reached the parking lot, Ott veered toward the back corner of the building.

"Lemme ask you something first," Ott said as he slipped the jailhouse key ring off his wrist and buried it in a trouser pocket, where it would make no sound. "Walk back here with me, Crowder."

At the rear of the building was a waste lot where dog fennel, pokeweed, and spindly sumacs were trying to grow in the bare red clay. It was a typical back lot where, during construction of the jail, a dozer had scraped away the topsoil and left it in a useless state. Ott led the way past the small chain-linked enclosure that housed the cooling and heating system for the building.

"I'm thinkin' on buildin' a trainin' site back here," Ott explained in his I'm-thinking-about-the-future-of-the-department voice. "Like a obstacle course. Pull-up bars, climbing wall, things to jump over and crawl under . . . stuff like that. Place for the staff to get a workout and hold a edge. Whatta you think? Would that be a good spot right there?" Ott pointed.

Crowder frowned. "Looks aw-right to me, Uncle Ott."

"Well," Ott said, sneaking a peek at the backdoor. He put a hand on Crowder's shoulder and the two of them sidled behind the heat pump so that they were out of sight of the doorway. "Let's juss you an' me stand here a minute and think on it."

Crowder was feeling a mite peculiar about all this, but he made no objection. He *was* the deputy, after all, and Ott *was* his boss. They stood there like a couple of lawn statues, listening to the air conditioner fan whir. After a minute, Crowder started to mention the pork chop specials waiting on them, but Ott shushed him with a finger to his lips.

Ott's timing could not have been more perfect. In the dead quiet of the back lot, a crisp *tip-tap-thump* sound came from the area of the backdoor. Like a thin piece of wood falling on a strip of metal. Or, more precisely, like a small pencil dropping onto the aluminum threshold of a doorway and taking its third bounce off the eraser.

Before another five seconds had passed, the backdoor opened and three figures moved out into the twilight—dark phantoms floating soundlessly across the lot, their silhouettes distinct against the scrubby lot. Leaving the door ajar, there was just enough glow from the cellblock fluorescents to show off the orange of their jumpsuits. To gain the element of surprise, Ott raised his gun straight up into the sky and fired off a round. Crowder grabbed his gut as he spiraled downward into his childhood fear of loud, unexpected noises.

"Juss hold it right there, boys!" Ott commanded from a shooter's stance. He kept his eyes on the three frozen figures and barked out of the side of his mouth. "Git your weapon out, Crowder. We done stumbled onto a jailbreak."

Crowder straightened. "I don't carry a gun, Uncle Ott, remember?" He began a stiff, backward walk toward the backdoor. "I'd better go an' pay a visit to the bathroom again, Uncle Ott."

"Hang on there, son. You'd best stay with me till we got these boys locked up again."

Crowder's face took on a tortured scowl. "There ain't no waitin' on this, Uncle Ott."

"Oh, all right!" Ott barked. "Go on then!"

Crowder walked toward the door like a heavy man crossing thin ice. When he found the door open by a quarter inch, he leaned down to see what was jammed under it.

"I'll be doggoned!" Crowder said. "That's my dang pencil!" After slipping it into his pocket, he waddled inside, and the door closed behind him with a crisp *click* from the lock, leaving Ott alone with the three brothers.

Ott gave them his master-chess-player's-checkmate smile. "Well, now," he crooned, "what we got here?"

With hands raised above their heads, the Vanstory brothers stood with their backs to Ott. Ott couldn't see their faces, but he could imagine them. Haymer, mad as a scalded cat. Garland, speed-filing through his meth-soaked brain for a way out of this. Mose perfecting an explosive popping sound with his mouth, inspired by the discharge of Ott's pistol.

"You boys didn' think I saw what you made in there, did you? Convertin' that toothbrush into a jimmy for the lock. I saw that very thing on *Eye Witness Police Chronicles* a coupla weeks ago." Ott pointed to the door. "Y'all can juss turn 'round and march right back through that door. I'm gonna be right behind you, so don' do nothin' stupid . . . again."

The three prisoners shuffled in a line to the backdoor. Haymer tried the handle, but it merely rattled with its hardware.

"It's locked," Haymer reported.

Ott dug his free hand into his trouser pocket. "Here ya go," he said and tossed the heavy ring of keys to Haymer.

Haymer jangled through the collection of keys. "Which one is it?"

"They're picture-coded," Ott explained.

"Well, I cain't see nothin'," Haymer complained. "It's too dark."

Ott fished in his other pants pocket. "Here . . . use the little penlight on my personal key ring. Then, look for the one with Bobby Darin's face scotch-taped to it. See . . . it's a code . . . you take his initials . . . 'B' and 'D' . . . an' that stands for 'back' and 'door.'" Ott put on his gloating smile. "Little somethin' I picked off o' *Eye Witness Police Chronicles*."

Haymer's face scrunched up as he took the smaller, plastic key ring with the penlight. "Who the hell is Bobby Darin?"

Ott made a little derisive snort at Haymer's ignorance of the arts. "Fellow that sang 'Mack the Knife.' 'Member that'n?"

Mose started thrusting his chin forward in a steady rhythm like a chicken strutting around a barnyard. Then he snapped his fingers in time.

"Oh, the shark's tooth—" he began singing, doing a pretty good impression of Bobby Darin.

"Shut up, Mose!" Haymer interrupted.

Mose stopped singing but kept up the finger-snap accompaniment until Haymer shot him a harder look.

"What about this'n . . . the darky with the curly hair and mustache?" Haymer asked as he shone the tiny light over the keys.

"Chuck Berry," Ott said. "Stands for 'cellblock.' That one opens all the cell doors."

Mose struck a pose with an imaginary guitar. "Deep down in Louisiana close to New Orleans—"

"Mose!" Haymer barked.

Mose dropped the invisible guitar and quieted. He wilted like the tail of a scolded dog.

Haymer continued sorting through the keys. "How 'bout the fellow with a raccoon on his head?"

"Davy Crockett," Ott replied. " 'D C' stands for 'deputy's cruiser.' " He pointed past the building to the parking lot where a lone patrol car shone under the security light. "Like that'n right there."

Mose stood up straight like a soldier. "Born on a mountaintop in—"

Haymer slapped his hand over Mose's mouth, so that "Tennessee" came out like "Dinnathee."

"Haymer!" Ott growled. "Juss find Bobby Darin an' open the danged door!"

When the proper key was found, the prisoners filed through the door and let themselves back into their cell. Ott followed, the backdoor behind him closing with its telltale *click!* He slammed the cell door on the Vanstorys and the lock caught securely with a loud *clang!*

"That oughta hold you boys for a while," Ott purred with satisfaction. He reached through the bars with his palm cupped like a shallow bowl.

"I'll take those keys now, Haymer." He smiled. "Betcha thought I'd forgot, didn' ya?"

Haymer approached with a hang-dog expression. "Nah . . . you couldn'a been sheriff all these years if you wasn't smart as a whip, Ott." He dropped both key rings into Ott's waiting hand. The sheriff pocketed the small plastic ring and slid the iron ring onto his wrist again.

Ott smiled. "You got that right!" He watched Garland and Mose mope and sulk as they sat on their beds. "I guess you boys know this attempted escape will mean things'll go bad for ya in the courtroom."

Haymer approached the door with his hand extended in a friendly way. Reaching through the bars, he offered to shake.

"No hard feelin's, Ott. We know yo're juss doin' yore job."

Ott considered Haymer's open palm for a moment, and then he shook. "Glad you feel that way, Haymer."

Haymer looked almost teary-eyed as he held Ott's eyes with his own. "You been fair and courteous, Ott. We won't forget it." He gripped Ott's wrist with his left hand and squeezed compassion into the moment.

Ott tried to look like he was holding back tears, while he was actually holding back a laugh at how easy it had been to manipulate these idiot brothers into an attempted escape. "Well, boys," he said, "you might could cut down your prison time a little bit, if you showed some remorse to the judge. Do you think you could do that?"

Before any of the Vanstorys could reply, Crowder came rushing out of the front office. "Uncle Ott, I think the *Walmart* is a-burnin' up! I could see the flames from the bathroom window." Come on, I'll show you!"

Crowder started back toward the office. Smiling at his prisoners, Ott gave a little one-fingered salute from his eyebrow, turned, and walked out of the cellblock.

As soon as the door to the office had closed and the automatic lock tripped, Haymer began to chuckle quietly deep in his chest. When Garland and Mose looked at him, Haymer held up the larger ring of keys and let it dangle from his finger like a Christmas ornament. In unison—as if they had practiced this for years—the three of them buried their faces in their pillows and laughed so hard that tears were soaking into the linens.

Ott and Crowder stood on the front lawn and peered in the direction of the Walmart. The fiery spectacle was visible through the trees, as an orange fireball blazed in the distance. The flames appeared to be jumping fifty feet high. A logjam of cars blocked traffic on the bypass. Crowds of people ran through headlight beams toward the conflagration. A siren blared from the top of the hill.

"You better git down there," Ott said and pointed at the car marked *Sheriff*. "Take my cruiser." He dug out his keys and tossed them to his nephew.

Crowder looked like he had swallowed a pinecone. "Well, whatta I do when I get down there?"

"Help d'rect the traffic and keep people outta the way of the fire department. I'll go inside an' git on the radio, see if I can locate Duffy."

When Ott sat at the dispatcher's desk and turned on the radio static, he heard Crowder start up the cruiser outside and drive out of the parking lot like a seasoned officer. Looking over the radio's dials and knobs, Ott tried to remember how a person called out on the new-fangled thing. As he pondered this, he heard another car start up in the lot. It, too, roared out into the street and then was gone from earshot.

Frowning, Ott stood, walked out the front again, and stood on the lawn. Staring at the lot, he tried to understand why it looked so empty.

"That dang deputy's cruiser is gone!" he declared to the night. He tried to think if any of the other deputies were due to go on duty at this time, but he just couldn't pull up the schedule from memory. After walking back inside, he went on to the cellblock door and opened it. "Boys? We might be a little late gittin' those pork chop specials to you! We got us a problem down at the *Walmart*!" He waited and listened. The cellblock was quiet as death. "You hear me, Haymer?"

He listened for as long as he could hold his breath . . . which was about seven seconds.

"Haymer?"

Nothing.

"Garland?"

More nothing.

"Mose?"

Most nothing.

Ott marched angrily to the Vanstorys' cell. It was empty with the door wide open. "Goddammit!" he hissed, closed his eyes, and leaned his head into the bars.

Chapter Thirty-Three

Cane-Tuck Creek Farm
North Lumpkin County
Autumn, 1983

"Lily-Honey! It's time to come in. We'll be leaving soon."

Though her grandmama's old log cabin was only fifty yards away, Lily's mother sounded miles from where Lily was tucked under the roots of the big sycamore that leaned over the creek. Outside her secret room under the root ball, the creek rippled, carrying flotillas of red, gold, and cinnamon-colored leaves. The muted autumn light reflected off the water and illuminated the collection of arrowheads and pottery shards she had lined up in the sand.

She began arranging the artifacts into the seven-pointed Cherokee design that had, through her dreams, allowed her access to a former life as a Cherokee maiden. "Otter"—that was what they had called her. On three different occasions, she had fallen through the haze of sleep into her Cherokee dream past.

The first dream had taken place on a mountaintop, which would be about the last place anyone would expect to see an otter. But there it was . . . seated on a large boulder that overlooked a yawning green valley. Like a queen perched upon her throne, taking in the vast breadth of her realm, she seemed to be searching for someone in the distance. This dream-picture of a waiting otter was a technicolor scene she would never forget.

The second dream had taken place here at the cabin. That was the day she had seen a real otter here by the sycamore pool. The sleek creature had speared into the creek from the bank, diving into the dark water beneath the sycamore. It had been winter, and crenate plates of ice had clung to the shoreline. By the time Lily had climbed down to the water's edge, the otter was gone; but she could still smell its musk.

She fell asleep right there by the water and dreamed of a fox coming to the pool and sniffing the pile of leaves that the otter had dredged up from the creek bed and urinated on as a boundary marker. And in the strange way of dreams, Lily knew that—to the fox—that musk had smelled like "home."

The third dream was the most profound, for in it Lily had been informed that she, herself, was the otter. The first two dreams had been presented to her through a mirror. She had been watching reflections of herself in those dreams.

"Lily-Honey! Come on now! We have to go!" Her mother's voice seemed a thin and meaningless sound trespassing into her dream memories and spreading through the valley like the distant drone of a chainsaw gnawing at a tree.

Lily closed her eyes and listened to the song of the creek, knowing that, among all that had happened since the Cherokees had once been the only people to live here, this song was unchanged. She let herself go light until she imagined herself floating, rising above the dimension of time, and slipping through its portal back into her dreams. When she opened her dream-eyes she was standing on the sand, her feet bound in beaded moccasins and her simple dress of deerskin cinched at her waist by a twisted thong of tanned deer hide. Her braids of hair were tied in strips of otter pelt.

Still in the dream, she peered over the creek bank and across the cornfield to the log house, which now looked freshly hewn from debarked tulip tree logs. Smoke curled from the chimney. Her Cherokee dream-mother pounded corn under the extended roof out front, the rhythm of her work steady and tireless. Her dream-father labored in the field, cutting the brown stalks of corn one by one and stacking them.

When Lily called out, both her parents stopped their work and looked at her. They remained unmoving in this mute triangle for several heartbeats until both the mother and the father raised an arm and pointed to the mountain where the Cherokees and the Muskogees had once met in battle . . . the place called "Blood Mountain."

Lily turned to see why they had pointed. In the distance a stranger made his way toward their farm. He wore a blue sash that held a woven-cane quiver of arrows on his hip. In his hand he carried a bow. As he approached, though he moved with the limber grace of youth, she could see that he was much older than she. And he was a fox-man, part-gray fox, part human.

Long before he reached her, Lily knew that *she* was his destination. And so, she waited, rooted in that natural Cherokee mindfulness that, today, is called "patience." When the man stopped on the far bank of the creek, she saw how very handsome he was, even with his silver hair and wrinkled skin. He stood straight as an arrow.

When he told her his name, she frowned. The dream had not provided her with a command of the Cherokee language. She said the name aloud, trying to memorize it.

"E-Nolly? What does it mean?"

"Black Fox. I am of the Blue Holly Clan," he explained to her. "I have traveled a great distance to find you."

"And how *did* you find me?"

He pointed to the mountaintop. "From up there. It is the grandest-ever view."

She knew this to be true, for it was from that summit she had seen glimpses of all her lives, past and future and sideways. Her final future life—the one in which she hoped to attain her ultimate *raison d'etre*—came to her in flashes, like teaser previews of a coming blockbuster movie. But one part of that incarnation was clear. This fox-man would be standing beside her in that final day of days.

A strange word formed on her mouth. It was a gift of the dream.

"*Tsi-ya*. I am called '*Tsi-ya*,' " she said. "I don't know what it means."

"It means 'otter,' " he informed her. "You are Otter Woman. I am not here to stay, *Tsi-ya*. I am here to tell you that we must wait for another life. The Elder Fires Above have granted me this visit . . . to let you know that our time is near."

"And when that life comes, will we be Cherokee or deer in the forest or fish that swim in the creek?"

It will not matter," he said. "Whatever we are, we shall be like this." He raised his hand and crossed two fingers so that they intertwined like mating snakes.

"I did not know you would be so much older than I," she said.

He looked off to the sun dipping into the west and he smiled. "Well, it is not easy to get this timing right. Maybe next time, we shall be born under the same star."

"We are going to love each other with the passion of fire, aren't we?" she said.

He smiled and pointed to a little sycamore sapling rising from the creek bank. "Like the tree's roots love the earth and water. Like its leaves embrace the air and kiss the sunlight." He stood quietly, his eyes roving over her as if to remember every detail. "I must go now."

"I will wait for you, *Inâli*," she called, surprised at the perfect pronunciation she had delivered. Now she felt as if she had known his name for all her life. "It will be a grand life," she called to him.

"The grandest-ever," he yelled back, his words as clear as the notes of the white-throated sparrow on a frozen winter morning. Then he continued on the journey back to the mountain and then further to his lonely campfire in the night sky—the bright little point of light known to all Cherokee as the "fox star."

Chapter Thirty-Four

The Sizzling Skillet
Monday Morning

Verdie set down ice water for L.T. Voss and Buster Gooch. She was doing her best to keep her eyes off Buster's Adam's apple. Ever since grammar school, he'd had the look of someone who had partially swallowed a big warty toad, and when he spoke, the poor creature made upward lunges as though trying to jump out of that skinny neck. As Buster had grown, so grew the toad until it had begun to seriously complicate the man's profile.

"Morning, gentlemen," she greeted in her unique British accent. "Coffee, Buster?" She rattled down L.T.'s usual cup of black and wondered if scalding Buster's imprisoned amphibian with extra-hot brew might be his salvation.

"Juss some t'mater juice for me, Verdie." She pretended to write in her order pad, but she could not completely block out the toad-rodeo bucking in her peripheral vision.

When she returned with the tomato juice, Dwayne and Dora Lynn Ramp sat down across from L.T.'s table. "Well, Dora Lynn," Verdie said. "Is your stove broken?"

"It's Dwayne's birthday," Dora Lynn said proudly and winked. "We're pullin' out all the stops and doin' the town, Verdie."

"Well, happy birthday, Dwayne. Dare I ask which one it is?"

It went like this for several minutes until, behind her, Verdie heard Hoke Limberlost's name slip out of L.T.'s mouth. Like a veteran aviator locking into "automatic pilot" for the task ahead of her, Verdie held her cordial expression on the Ramps and dropped into double-listen mode for the conversation at the tail section of the airplane.

"If you think you can contest that line," L.T. was saying, "I'd like to get a surveyor out there and see just how much land we're talking about. Hell, his house is damn close to that line. Might be I can get him to just move on out the valley."

Dwayne Ramp rambled on. "I'm leanin' toward the oatmeal, Verdie. You got some bran buds you can mix into that for me? That's the way Dora Lynn fixes it for me at home."

"We been spittin' back an' forth 'bout that line for twen'y-six years," Buster carped, "but I ain't any too fond o' lawyers. I'd juss as soon let the damn property go to kudzu as hire one o' them buzzards. But I'll tell you this. My deed goes back a helluva long ways—back to the land lottery when the Cher'kees was drove out—and, sure as Sunday breakfast, it shows that old pile o' rocks as the line. Now tell me 'bout the Vanstory place. Is this gonna be a sure thing, you reckon? I'll need to order those emus ahead o' time. I hear it usu'lly takes a month for d'liv'ry."

Dora Lynn cupped a hand on Dwayne's arm and patted him like the flutter of a one-winged butterfly. "Dwayne, you eat oatmeal most ever' morning, Honey. This is your birthday! Let's order something special! What about an omelet?"

"It's in the bag, Buster," L.T. assured his client. "I can have the whole thing wrapped up under my name inside o' two weeks. The day after that, it's yours. Order those emus, son. But we are gonna have to sit down with a lawyer. You know we got to, if it's to be legal. Can you do that?"

"I'm juss tryin' to stay on the doctor's orders, Dora Lynn," Dwayne explained. "Hell, a omelet has prob'ly got more cluster-oil than a greased pig. If you ain't got the bran buds, Verdie, I'll have some prunes on top. But let me mix 'em in. I like knowin' where they are. Are they pitted?"

"What 'bout them horses?" Buster pressed. "They part o' the deal? Vanstorys are crazier'n hell, but they know their horses, by God. They got a Morgan I had my eyes on."

"All we use is corn oil, Dwayne," Verdie said.

"That got cluster-oil in it?" Dwayne said, raising an eyebrow.

Verdie frowned and looked at Dora Lynn, who offered an embarrassed smile.

"He means 'cholesterol,' Verdie."

Back at Voss's table, the realtor made a scoffing laugh. "You're gonna mix horses and emus on the same farm, Buster? How's that gonna work?"

"Why not?" Buster argued, a little defensive now. "I know a feller up near Blairsville who runs a bait shop and sells atomic parts on the side. So what about that Morgan? I'm gonna need some way o' gittin' 'round the farm to round up them critters. They say you cain't do it from a motorized vehicle. The sound o' the engine is too much like a pack o' snarlin' dingoes. Puts the animals under a lotta stress. I read a mag'zine article 'bout it. They's this emu expert who says emus suffer from bein' too 'emu-tional' under certain conditions. That's what he calls it. Stunts they's growth and—" Buster snapped his fingers. "There goes your dang profit."

"Well, Dwayne-honey," Dora Lynn crooned. "It *is* your birthday! Maybe you could have whatever you want just one day of the year. I don't think your doctor would mind."

Dwayne looked at his wife as if she had suggested ballet lessons for him. "Well, what if juss one day o' foolish eatin' takes off one day o' my life. What if I died on a We'n'sday and my winnin' card at the church bingo came up on Thursday? How would that be?"

Dora Lynn frowned and stared at her glass of water. "Honey, why would it matter? You'd be gone. You'd never even see that winning card."

"Well, that's my point, Darlin'. Would you rather see me die bingo-rich or bingo-poor?"

Behind Verdie, Buster seemed to have settled down. He sounded less emu-tional.

"I want that Morgan, L.T. It's gotta be part o' the deal."

"Okay, look," L.T. said, "the horses go up for auction on Tuesday. Winslow Mooney will be the auctioneer, and he owes me a favor. I'll take care of that for you."

Verdie heard Voss unroll a large crinkly paper on the table.

"Now look right here, Buster. I believe this line just might run right through Limberlost's cabin."

"Well," Dora Lynn was saying, "I'm gonna have an omelet. Verdie, can I get that Texas-style you make? Onions and green peppers?" She patted Dwayne's hand. "You can have some of mine if you want to."

"I cain't eat onions for breakfast, Sugar. You know that." Dwayne looked beseechingly at Verdie. "Can you herd all the onions over to one side, Verdie?"

The map behind Verdie suddenly rolled up, and a rubber band snapped, making a hollow smack on the tube of paper. "Actually, Buster, I think that Morgan is too good for the Vanstorys. Hell, it *ought* to be yours. Just like that Frogtown valley *ought* to be mine. I think this whole deal is gonna work out for the best for both of us. Sorta like our destiny."

"What about the cluster-oil, Verdie?" Dwayne drilled. "Can you put that on the same side o' the omelet with the onions?"

Dora Lynn looked stricken. "So you want me to have all the cholesterol? What about *my* winning bingo card?"

Behind Verdie, L.T.'s voice dropped to a whisper. "Auctions can put some terrible stress on an animal, if you want my opinion. I think we'd be doing the horse a favor if we could avoid that and get it outta there early."

"We have that no-cholesterol egg product?" Verdie explained. "We can make an omelet with that."

Dwayne's face wrinkled. "Fake eggs? Where'd them come from? Fake hens?"

"Well, I can talk to Ott," L.T. said. "We'll see what he can do for us. I might oughta order a mess of Kentucky cigars first."

Dwayne was giving the ersatz omelet a lot of thought. "The way I heard it at the hospital, it ain't so much about if there *is* cluster-oil, Verdie. It's which kind. Doctor told me there's good cluster-oil and there's bad cluster-oil and my bad cluster-oil is winnin' the game."

"Dwayne, for goodness sake. Do you think one omelet is going to kill you?"

"Well, if it does *and* it's one day before I was to get that winnin' bingo card, it could be the worst day of my life."

Dora Lynn lowered her forehead into her hand and hid her eyes. "Verdie, just bring us one omelet to share. I'll eat the bad cluster-oil and Dwayne can eat the good." She looked up and gave Verdie a cryptic arch of her eyebrow. "You have a special spoon for that, right? So I can pick out all the bad 'cluster-oil'?" She intoned the phrase "cluster-oil" in the same tremulous way a parent might use "boogieman" to get the attention of a mischievous child.

"We have a spoon for each, Dora Lynn," Verdie announced confidently. "One for good and one for bad. I'll bring them out with your meal."

When Verdie brought out L.T.'s two over easy with ham and Buster's fried egg sandwich, she briefly saw the rolled-up maps and deed they had been poring over. L.T. looked up at her with venom in his eye.

"Verdie, you know I didn't order potato chips."

Buster tilted forward as though the weight of his Adam's apple had become too much to bear. "I'll eat 'em," he said and began plucking them off L.T.'s plate.

Chapter Thirty-Five

Frogtown Creek
Monday late afternoon

Hoke was sitting by the creek behind his cabin watching a kingfisher hold vigil over the pool where the stream widened to an oval shape. The bird was perched on a birch branch, alert but, Hoke thought, a little fidgety. Relaxed on the sandy beach, Hoke was leaning his back against a slanting stone, and, in the hour that he had spent there, the bird had made only one dive . . . and that, an unsuccessful one. Since Hoke had arrived there before the bird and because he had been as motionless as the stone, he knew the kingfisher was unaware of his presence.

In times like this—when he held the secret of stillness over an animal of the wild—Hoke felt his four-sevenths Cherokee blood surge through his veins. It was even more exciting than making a raid on a road sign or a statue, because this act by the creek was timeless. Without even closing his eyes he could imagine he had been retro-transmitted seven hundred years into the past, before Columbus had opened up the floodgates to the pale-skinned usurpers who had trespassed upon the North American continent.

Then, wanting to see more than the beauty of the creek and the hemlocks and the birches and the avian fish hunter, he closed his eyes. He wanted to resurrect the image of the otter girl who had come to him in his dream last night. It was the seventh time he had dreamed of her. With seven being a sacred number, he now knew this girl to be someone of critical import to his life.

She was lithe and graceful and remained so even as she transformed from child to adult and from otter to human. Though she swam to him with great purpose, the current she fought would not relent. Somehow—through the ineffable logic of dreams—Hoke knew this current to be *time* itself.

So stunning was the otter woman that when he had awakened that morning, he discovered a great hole had opened inside his chest. He felt this same hole now as he opened his eyes to the creek.

The kingfisher leapt from the branch and flew upstream, its rattling call as boisterous as a string of tin cans tied to the bumper of a newlywed's car. Wondering if a red-shouldered hawk or a kestrel had intruded into the kingfisher's territory, Hoke lifted his eyes to scan the crepuscular sky. Though no predator was in sight, the crackle of paper could be heard somewhere behind him.

Peering over the rock, Hoke watched a short man in a straw fedora move irritably through the underbrush. The man appeared to loathe every plant he encountered, and Hoke pegged him for a city boy—someone who did not know poison ivy from a pole cat. When the little man stopped and rotated a large, unrolled paper around as if to orient it, he alternated darting looks at the paper and at the land around him. He was more fidgety than the kingfisher. When his head came around sufficient to reveal a profile, Hoke recognized the scoundrel. It was that greedy real estate hog, L.T. Voss.

When Voss approached within twenty yards of Hoke's cabin, the realtor crouched and selected his steps more carefully. Every few seconds his head jerked up to check the cabin, but, when he wasn't doing that, he seemed to be looking for something in the brush. When Voss fell headlong into a tangle of fetterbush, Hoke realized what the man was probably doing, for he had tripped right over the rock cairn that marked the southern line of Hoke's property.

Gathering himself into a compact silhouette, Hoke began the slow, meticulous advance of the Cherokee stalker. His body adopted its own set of rules about speed and fluidity until his movement was virtually invisible, slower than a snail's ooze across the glossy top of a rhododendron leaf. Looking through the leaves of the shrubs, Hoke kept his eyes trained on Voss. When the pudgy little man mounted the pile of stones and consulted the paper, Hoke stood stock-still and watched as Voss sighted down a compass toward the cabin.

"I know what yo're up to, you damn thievin' weasel!" Hoke whispered under his breath. As soon as he had uttered the words, the angelic face of the otter woman materialized in his mind's eye. In this picture she had one eyebrow raised in mild rebuke. Otters were in the weasel family, Hoke remembered. He amended the epithet on the spot. Glowering at the sneaky realtor, Hoke whispered a revised accusation. "I know what yo're up to, you damn thievin' maggot."

Voss's head ducked down out of sight. When it bobbed back up, his teeth were clenched and his face a smoldering red beneath his hat brim. Moving away from the cairn, Voss began an odd, waddling walk toward the clearing beside Hoke's cabin. There he dropped something heavy enough to pound a deep bass note into the earth. It was the thump of a heavy stone. Voss returned to the cairn, went down again, came up red-faced, and duck-walked back to the clearing.

Hoke felt his warrior spirit fill his veins like fire. He knelt and pulled the red bandana from his pocket and tied it over the blue one already snug against his forehead. Red for war. He went down on all fours, skirted the fetterbush, and peered through the weeds at two large stones lying well inside his clearing. L.T. was relocating the cairn!

Retracing his path, Hoke picked up two cantaloupe-sized stones near the creek and, when L.T. hauled off another load from the cairn, Hoke tiptoed in and laid his stones quietly on the old pile. When L.T. returned, Hoke was back at the creek bank, prying two more stones out of the earth, timing his silent forays perfectly so that as L.T. carried away one rock, Hoke deposited two.

After thirty minutes of this, L.T. was huffing and puffing so hard that Hoke was able to orchestrate his timing completely around the rasp of L.T.'s labored breathing. When the counterfeit cairn in the clearing had grown to a dozen stones, Hoke changed his ploy. Now he stole from the new pile to return stones to the old, this time carrying three stones to L.T.'s one.

After another twenty minutes of this, L.T. stopped and let the stone he was carrying tumble to the ground. "What the hell?!" he exclaimed, abandoning all stealth. He stood with his fists propped on his hips as he stared down at his less than satisfying collection of rocks in the clearing. His face shone with sweat, and the front of his white shirt and blue sports jacket were covered in dirt and moss and stick-on seeds.

Voss checked his watch, glared at Hoke's cabin for a few seconds, and trudged through the undergrowth toward the road like a man bringing up the rear of a funeral procession. Hoke waited until he heard a car start up and begin the climb for the gap before standing and removing the red bandana. It took only three trips to return the rest of the rocks to their original site.

It was dark when he finished, and he stood for a time listening to the night sounds as they came alive in the valley. The tree frogs peeped and chirped and a few katydids warmed up for their coming nocturnal symphony. A screech owl warbled.

The slow crunch of a vehicle out on the gravel road drew Hoke to the front of his cabin, where he made his way into the laurel grove beside his driveway. There he hunkered down and waited. He had not been in place more than a minute when the car parked just a few yards down the road. A car door opened and quietly closed. Soon a man strode into view and turned into Hoke's dirt drive. The visitor's gait could not be called stealthy, but neither was it casual. As the man passed him, Hoke caught a glint of light reflecting off a badge pinned to the man's shirt.

Duffy Hawkins stopped at Hoke's truck and leaned to look into the bed. From there he moved to the shed roof that hung off the side of the house where Hoke kept his tools. A flashlight clicked on, and Hoke watched the narrow beam of light sweep the workbench in a slow methodical pattern. The light lingered at the gas tank and acetylene torch and then clicked off.

Duffy walked the animal-painted steppingstones to the front door, knocked, waited, and knocked again. "Mr. Limberlost?" he called to the empty house. Duffy turned and splayed his hands on the sides of his gun belt, looking out into the night and—as it seemed to Hoke—directly into the stand of laurel.

Hoke held his breath, closed his eyes, and willed himself into the shape of a crooked laurel trunk. The standoff seemed an eternity. He knew that Hawkins was part-Cherokee, and so Hoke wondered about the deputy's capabilities of night vision. When Hoke dared to peek out at Hawkins again, the deputy was examining the hay bales that Hoke used as archery targets. Then, like a blessing from the Elder Fires Above, Duffy's footsteps passed on out the drive back to his patrol car, which fired up, U-turned, and cruised out of the valley.

Hoke remained inside the thicket to think through all that had happened, but he had barely lined up the events for inspection when another car came down his road and turned into his driveway and parked. This driver walked past him with earnest deliberation, banged on the cabin door, and, getting no answer, stepped to the center of the yard.

"Hoke!" The voice carried a distinctly British accent. "Are you out there?"

Hoke straightened and slipped out of the shrubs. "Verdie? Is that you'ens?"

"It is I. Is that you?"

Hoke approached her silhouette. "I reckon it's both o' us."

Verdie walked toward his voice and bumped into him, noticing right off that Hoke smelled nice . . . which, in actuality, meant: he didn't smell bad. "How in the world can you see out here, Hoke?"

Another car came bumping down from the gap, stopped at the end of Hoke's driveway for a few seconds then turned. Its headlight beams swung across Hoke and Verdie in the front yard, and the car braked just several feet away.

"I ain't seen this much traffic out this way since that chicken truck turned over and ever'body in the coun'y was chasin' after a free meal," Hoke declared.

"Excuse me!" a female voice yelled to them. "I might be lost."

Hoke walked to the driver's side of the car with Verdie just behind him. "Consider yourself found, young lady. Where're you'ens headed to?"

"Do you know where Joey Gallatin lives?"

Hoke nodded. "Reckon I do. He rents from me." He pointed up the hill. "You'ens is doin' juss fine. Juss keep on right up this here hill. It's the only thing up there resemblin' a house. 'Bout a half mile. It'll be on your right."

"Thank you, sir. I'm an old friend of Joey's."

Hoke laughed again. "Well, I don' know 'bout the 'old' part, but Joey would be the lucky one in this arrangement." He offered his hand through the open window. "Any friend o' Joey's—" They shook. "Name's Hoke Limberlost. O' the Blue Clan o' the Cher'kees. Been livin' in this here valley all my life."

"I'm Angie. It's nice to meet you, Mr. Limberlost." She peered past him at the road climbing up the mountain. "A half mile, you say? Does it get very steep?"

Hoke stepped back and eyed her car as though sizing up its muscle. "You'ens oughta make 'er up juss fine. Keep 'er in low gear. When you git up there, be sure to step out back and take in the scenery. It's the grandest-ever view in the coun'y. 'Course you might have to use yore car lights to see it."

"Thank you. I will." She waved, smiled at Verdie, backed out of the drive, and started up the road.

Hoke and Verdie watched the taillights climb the hill and disappear around the bend. The valley fell into black again, and they listened to the car labor up the mountain.

"Why is it you never married, Hoke?" Verdie said. "You seem to enjoy women. You know how to speak to them."

Once again, the perfect face of the otter woman crystallized like a hologram hanging before him in the darkness. He had vowed never to speak to a living soul about his sacred dream, but something in Verdie's kind voice turned like a key inside his chest, and he felt the door to his secret of secrets open by just a crack.

"Fact is, Verdie, I got me somebody."

"Well, Hoke!" she said, surprised. Even more astonishing than this admission of romance was the strange bubble of jealousy that rose from her heart. "I'd say she's the lucky one in *that* arrangement."

"Well," Hoke said. "How 'bout you'ens, Verdie? Ever git married?"

"I'm still waiting on the right man."

"Well, I admire that," Hoke said, nodding. "Do you'ens have a clue what he'll be like?"

Verdie looked off into the night and saw the images of her traumatized childhood flicker before her like a vintage film. Her father being pummeled by the neighbor's twelve-year-old son after the accidental coupling of the boy's pure-bred Corgi and Mojo, Verdie's *Heinz 57* mutt. Then there was the day her brothers got beat up by the girl in the wheelchair at the church Easter egg hunt. And she remembered her own foibles, like the times she herself was chased out of her outhouse by a territorial wren.

"He'll take care of me," she said softly. "Nobody will hurt me as long as he is around. He'll be strong. And kind. And very intelligent. And deductive." In her mind, the image had begun as John Wayne, but it quickly segued into a cross between Ralph Nader and Hulk Hogan, the wrestler. Verdie cleared her throat. "Hoke, I need to talk to you about L.T. Voss and Buster Gooch."

Inside the cabin, before Hoke had set down a cup of ginseng tea before her, Verdie had related most of what she had overheard at the diner. By the soft candlelight in the kitchen, she watched his face at each turn in the story, trying to judge the degree of wrath or retribution he might be considering; but his face betrayed nothing as he set the kettle back on his stove.

"Now I know you needed to know about this, Hoke, but what I need to know is what you plan to do about all this. I can't have you torching off L.T. at the ankles or carving him into a tick or chiseling off the top of his head or setting him on fire."

Hoke stared out the dark windowpane, as though he could see all the way to the Vanstory Farm. "So ol' Buster has gotta itch for that horse farm, does he?" He set down his cup and pointed at Verdie. "Ain't Buster the one got some kind o' allergy to somethin' or other?"

"Cats," Verdie snorted. "He asked Beulah Babcock to go with him to the Sheriff's Benefit Dance two years ago. Beulah said when Buster came to her door to pick her up, he turned pale as a turnip when he saw her big gray Persian. They'd barely left her driveway when he started having trouble getting air. She said that he was holding his throat and making a horrible face and that his Adam's apple got bigger, if that's even possible. Buster jumped in his car and tore away, leaving Beulah standing in her driveway, and that was that. Beulah said she would have followed him and strangled him if she thought she could have gotten her fingers around that lump in his throat. She'd made a new organdy dress with a white lace collar for the dance, so she walked to the dance alone and never forgave Buster."

Hoke stared into Verdie's eyes and considered carefully what he was about to ask. She started to drink again, but, instead, she narrowed her eyes and slowly lowered her cup to the table.

"What are you thinking, Hoke?" Verdie whispered.

He chewed on the inside of his cheek and studied her. "Verdie, where do you'ens stand on cats gettin' kilt out at the Animal Control?"

Chapter Thirty-Six

**Ocahayhalahatcheecola, Florida
August, 1952**

The rail-thin mother leaned forward like a winded draft horse and pulled the three Radio Flyers that were coupled together in a train. Strapped into a makeshift harness of discarded electrical wires padded across her frail chest and shoulders with strips of brown corrugated cardboard, she struggled with a fierce determination against the drag of the rattling caravan through the sand.

Most of the heavy items were piled on the first wagon: the foot-pumped sewing machine, the rusted Dutch oven, and the broken iron brazier she used for broiling. Behind that, in wagon number two, came the gray metal washtub filled up with their skillet and cooking utensils, a galvanized bucket, and two sections of black stovepipe. Finally came the three-wheeled caboose with rolled-up blankets, three small sofa pillows, and three brown paper sacks holding the few items of clothing they owned.

Luther was only six, but he took up a position at the back end with his tiny hands clenched to the rim of the last wagon, where he lifted up the corner missing a wheel. His little sister stumbled beside him, and he had to keep getting after her about trying to crawl inside the caboose for a ride. She cried constantly, and the grating sound of it was like a savage worm in his ear trying to bore its way into his skull.

One of the dark secrets of Luther Voss's young life was that sometimes he wanted to put Lucy into an abandoned refrigerator and shut the door on that razor-edge whine forever. Luther looked up at his mother.

He wondered if she would even notice if he collapsed in the dirt road from heat exhaustion. Or would she notice if he murdered his sister?

"How much farther, Mama?" Luther called out.

Over the din of rattling cargo and rusted axles and sibling whimpering, he thought he might have heard something scrape out of her throat, but it could have been just a clot of phlegm, because she spat off to one side and never broke stride. He looked down at his shadow riding the ruts in the road like a dark slithering reptile. The sun on his back was hot as a slab of heated iron. The fecund air coming off the swamp was so thick it seemed like one more impediment to their progress, something they had to push through. Even if there were no hills on this God-forsaken panhandle backroad, the stench of swamp gases knew how to apply its own hostile gravity.

On the road up ahead, two flattened armadillos reflected the midday sun with their lingering pâté of squished grease. *Possum-on-the-half-shell*, his mother would call them whenever she came upon one fresh enough to cook. Just yards away in the forbidding, jungle-like sloughs, a foul ether bubbled up from the mud from decayed plants and rotting turtles snagged on neglected trotlines. There were alligators out there, too, and Luther knew the taste of this delicacy as well as most children his age knew the flavor of *Sugar Frosted Flakes*. Personally, he didn't care for the toughness of gator meat, but he held the *live* animal in some degree of complicit regard for the part it might possibly play in shutting up his sister, should he convince her to go wash up her teary face at the edge of a swamp where a bull gator sunned on a log.

The shadows of mossy oaks covered the road up ahead, promising at least a brief respite from the blazing sun. Luther's feet were hot and blistered, and his back hurt from leaning down to lift the wagon. Lucy was sobbing now, but her misery elicited no brotherly pity. Luther had learned long ago to narrow down his sympathies for his own survival and no one else's. So he prayed for himself. Prayed for a rest from this death march.

But his mother was like a machine. The more he watched her, the less he could imagine her stopping. Ever.

But she did stop. Luther dropped the corner of the wagon to the sand, straightened his spine, and followed his mother's hollow stare to the battered trailer sitting off the road in a small clearing where the palmetto had been cut back to make a notch in the forest.

"Is this it, Mama?" he said.

Her only response was to lean into her harness again and angle off toward the trailer. Luther helped the caboose make the turn, and then, when the caravan stopped, he studied his new home. It looked a lot like the last one except that this one listed on its base where a sinkhole was opening up to swallow one end. That was all right. He didn't need to live level. At least this home might have an indoor bathroom . . . an assumption he made based upon the lack of a visible outside privy.

His mother squirmed out of the harness and let the wagon tongue drop, the muted sound in the sand like a psalm of joy to Luther's ears. Red welts crisscrossed her shoulders where her FSU tee-shirt sagged at its frayed collar. Lucy sat down and scooped sand with the empty *Vienna Sausage* can that she kept with her few toys. She was still crying.

"Luther T.," his mother droned, "git in there and check for rattlesnakes."

From the second wagon Luther pulled out the Sam Snead Signature five-iron club that served as their snake-handling tool. Wielding the long club, he climbed the crooked steps and pushed hard on the door as it scraped across a linoleum floor inside. Before he went in, he turned to his mother and waited for her lifeless eyes to meet his. With him on the front stoop, they were on the same level, but Luther somehow felt taller, and he supposed that was because of her perpetual stoop.

"Mama, one day I'll buy a big piece o' land for us. I'll build you a house with shiny bright windows and air conditionin' and a 'lectric stove."

She held a dull expression on her face. "Uh, huh . . . may as well include a maid and a butler and a bingo pot of six million dollars. Go on in there and see 'bout snakes, son. Then you and your sister git out to the swamp hammocks and see can you fetch up some dry sticks for a cookfire."

"We eatin' snake again?" Luther asked, but she did not answer. He watched her rummage through the first wagon for their yard sign—their last remnant of family tradition, which was a cypress plank with their surname routed in cursive. The board was painted brown and the letters yellow. *Voss*, it read. Though Luther didn't remember it, his mother told them the sign had been nailed to the mailbox post of their ranch-style house in Wakulla before the bottom had fallen out of the economy and she had lost her job at the potato chip factory.

Though he could not remember the house, he did remember the little sample bags of chips she used to bring home. Plain, ruffled, barbeque, and a hot, spicy version called "South of the Border." Since all her money had gone into the mortgage payments, they virtually lived off of potato chips, though she did not know that after that first year of a nearly all-chip diet, Luther, in a daily ritual, had walked into the woods and thrown them out for the feral pigs, one of which he hoped to skewer with the pointed iron rod from a bird feeder he had stolen from a city park.

He never got near a pig. Speed-wise, a four-year-old boy carrying a heavy spear was no match for a wild pig. The upshot of all this was a lifelong loathing for chips and a longing for pork.

On rare occasions, a bag of *Crispy Cheese Twirls* figured into his diet by way of a school classmate or neighbor who was gullible enough to listen to Luther's story about a sister who was dying from lack of dairy products. The fact is, Luther had discovered a serious fondness for this food group. And, furthermore, so had Lucy. The little girl cried for them so hysterically that Luther's mother gave in to this war of attrition and proclaimed that all the *Cheese Twirls* they might acquire were reserved for Lucy.

While Luther fitted the sections of bite-proof stovepipe around his legs, his mother picked up a piece of broken brick from the yard and began hammering the sign into the front wall of the trailer. It was a bad idea for two reasons: one, it put any snakes inside on guard; and two, posting the Voss name to this tilted rattrap was like wearing a badge of shame. The school bus would run by here for all the world to see his living conditions. The stigma would rebirth throughout his young life like a recurring virus.

He opened the door on its crooked frame and marched inside in his clunky armor, ready to knock the head off anything that slithered, rattled, or hissed at him. He didn't care if it was an alligator. He just wanted to hit something.

Chapter Thirty-Seven

Crow Mountain
Monday night

Joey heard the car outside. By the sound of the engine, it was not a Volkswagen bug. Nor was it Hoke's rattling, modified Pinto. Hanging in the middle of a pullup on the rafter, he waited, listening for the sound of the gearshift to engage reverse when the driver realized he had taken a wrong turn. When the engine shut off, he dropped lightly to the floor, set the open can of asparagus in the cooler, and checked his wristwatch. Twenty minutes to midnight. He blew out the candle.

When the car door slammed, he walked to the front door and waited. After footsteps stopped outside his door, three quiet knocks broke the silence in the house. Always favoring the advantage of surprise, Joey opened the door quickly as the fourth knock was attempted. He heard the knocker's knuckles scrape against the wood.

"Ow!" she said.

Joey slowly straightened from his fighting crouch. "Angie?"

By the glow of the relighted candle, they sat at the table, and Joey extracted the splinter from Angie's finger. After dabbing on antibiotic, he sealed it with a strip of tape.

"It's so dark here," she said.

"No electricity."

She looked around the candlelit room. "Do you like living here?"

"I do." Joey watched the angles of her face catch the candlelight as she turned.

"Is this sort of like *Rocky IV* or *V* or whatever? Where he goes to Siberia and trains in a freezing barn?"

Joey shrugged, and Angie gave him a suspect look.

"You didn't see the *Rocky* movies, did you?"

He shook his head. "Not good to watch those Hollywood fight movies. Gives you a false sense of the reality of combat."

Angie nodded and looked around again. "Where do you go to the bathroom?"

"There's an outhouse outside." He pointed. Just down a short trail."

She fixed her gaze on the metal bucket standing by the sink. "How do you shower?"

"Cold water sponge bath."

"What about when winter comes?"

Joey pointed to the woodstove, still warm from supper. "Hot water sponge bath."

"What about drying your hair?"

Joey leaned and opened the stove door, where a few red coals glowed in the gray wood ash. "Hair dryer," he said, pointing into the stove.

Angie nodded as she smiled at the room. "Well, I have to admit. It's you. There was always something Spartan about Joey Gallatin." Her smile widened and, to Joey, the room seemed to brighten. "Maybe you should have been a monk."

Joey did not smile. "I don't think monasteries have bouncers," he said and looked deep into her eyes. He considered telling her that he had already lived the celibate life of a monk . . . that he had loved her since the fourth grade and along with that came the attendant devotion, the meditation, and the denial of feelings for all other females. Complete celibacy. Instead, he said, "Angie, I'm doing exactly what I'm supposed to be doing."

A look of concern tightened her face. "What if you get hurt?"

He shrugged. "People get hurt," he said, hearing the double meaning in it only after he had said it. "Car accidents, slipping on ice, dropping a grocery bag on a toe." He almost added, *and unrequited love.*

Angie looked around the room. "No telephone?"

Joey shook his head.

"No cell phone?"

He shook his head again.

"It's just that I wouldn't like thinking of you up here all alone and hurt. Nobody to help you."

Joey gave her a reassuring smile. "I'll be fine."

She stared at him as though she were accepting a truth of life that she had been incapable of grasping until this moment. "Yes, I believe you will," she said quietly. She stood and walked to the window at the back of the cabin, toward that "grandest-ever view" that Mr. Limberlost had promised. There was nothing to see out there at this time of night, but still she felt some kind of cosmic privilege at standing before the imagined vista.

When she turned back to Joey, the moisture filming her eyes picked up the candle's glow like a light unto itself. "You followed your heart, Joey," she whispered in the dark room. Now tears were brimming in both her eyes, but she looked strong, deliberate. "I didn't. I sold out for a marriage with an attractive formula attached to it: the right house, the right part of town, a BMW, money." She huffed a quiet laugh through her nose. "You were always true to yourself, Joey."

I was always true to you, he thought.

Angie returned to the table, sat, and tilted her head to one side. "But why a bouncer, Joey? I mean . . . aren't most bouncers real big and heavy?"

When she kept staring at him, he could see that she really wanted to know. Resting his forearms on the table, he threaded his fingers together and lightly rubbed the tips of his thumbs, one against the other.

"I guess you've heard the adage: It's not the size of the dog in the fight—"

She narrowed her eyes and nodded. "It's the size of his teeth?" she said, guessing at the finish of the axiom.

Joey smiled and shook his head. "That's *Little Red Riding Hood*." He cleared his throat to deliver the end of the saying in a dead earnest voice. "It's the size of the fight in the dog."

She frowned and sat again. "But why bouncing for you, Joey? You're smart, disciplined, talented—"

Joey leaned forward on his forearms and thought about his answer for a time. "It's the ultimate arena to test who you are . . . what you are. One on one . . . no rules. Your tools are not just your fists and your skill at handling your opponent. It's how you decide the course of action that is loyal to who you are."

Slowly, Angie began to nod. "So . . . it validates you. For you, I think . . . being a bouncer is . . . completion."

Joey rose and lifted her from the chair in one motion. He pulled her so close to him that he could feel her body mold to his from knees to chest. She was warm and fit him like a favorite pair of jeans. As he had done a thousand times in his dreams, he lowered his head to her and opened his mouth as she performed the perfect mirror image. Their lips met with the softness of a waterfall's mist touching the skin.

He felt no embarrassment when he hardened like a fencepost. She pulled him closer, the muscles in her body trying to match the message in his loins, until the give and take of their bodies was like a prayer whispered to them from the great chasm of eternity that waited ahead of them. The painful past for each, in that moment, was but the blink of an eye.

Only for want of air did they pull away, their eyes locked in the profound fusion of their souls. Joey thought that the taste on his lips was the sweetest he had ever known. As if reading his thoughts, Angie ran her tongue along her upper lip, and she made a quizzical smile.

"Is that asparagus?" she said.

Chapter Thirty-Eight

Vanstory Farm
Monday late
Six minutes before midnight

Just seconds after she had lifted the yellow crime scene tape so that Hoke could drive under, Verdie was beginning to have second thoughts. When she got back into the passenger seat, the car started down the long drive and immediately began to bounce and lurch and jounce, like a ping pong ball trying to roll off the back of a warthog.

"May-ay-b-be . . . we-e-e . . . sh-should . . . ha-have . . . bro-ought . . . your-r-r . . . tru-uck," Verdie said, somehow still maintaining her English accent.

Even with Hoke riding the brakes, inching through the washouts, Verdie's Ford Fairlane was bucking like an off-kilter washing machine on the spin cycle. He stopped, leaned over the steering wheel, and tried to scout the dark road ahead.

"Didn' have much choice, Verdie." Hoke jerked his head toward the backseat. "We'd'a never got all these cats to stay put in the bed o' my truck."

For the hundredth time, Verdie turned to the backseat and fretted over the chaos of sixty-nine cats scrambling around on her upholstery. And the smell was beginning to get to her.

"I didn't know cats got carsick," she said. "We should have put down some newspaper."

Hoke nodded. "It ain't too merciful on the nose, is it?" He let off on the brake and started forward again, turning hard right to negotiate a particularly bad ditch running diagonally across the road. The car lurched left then right, making the Ford shimmy like a drenched dog shaking off water. Despite the unwelcome aroma, Hoke was feeling his warrior mode shift into high gear. Who would ever have believed he'd been on one of his eco-forays allied with a waitress who sounded as if she were British royalty . . . that and a slew of mewling cats rescued from the road to euthanasia?

Verdie, now with pity shining in her eyes, was still looking at the cats. "Poor things. Do you really think they'll be all right on their own out here?"

Hoke snorted. "You'ens ever try to teach anythin' to a cat, Verdie? Hell, they's born knowin' all they need to know. I knowed a cat lived in the bathroom of a hardware store for two years. It weighed forty-two pounds, but nobody knew it was there till the 'lectrical wiring had to be replaced. The damn cat was nestin' up in the ceilin' above some particle board an' livin' off o' mice and *Mir'cle-Gro*." He turned to check on the cats. "You juss 'member . . . these poor lil' thangs was headed for the cat holy-cost." He turned his head to give Verdie a sharp nod. "An' you'ens an' me are the ones who set 'em free!"

The car hit a jarring bump, and the oil pan clanged on a rock. Hoke winced and then looked irritated.

"Them damn Vanstorys don' know a helluva lot 'bout maintainin' the back entrance to a farm, do they?"

Verdie, who now seemed inured to the destruction of her car for the sake of sixty-nine condemned cats liberated from the county's animal control shelter, was holding back tears as she watched the confused creatures climb up into the back window looking for a way out. She'd never thought to ask anyone how cats were euthanized. As she pondered this, she pictured these cats marching unwittingly into a gas chamber designed to look like a big can of tuna. Then she imagined tiny electric chairs and a cruel cocker spaniel warden asking if there were any last statements before the juice was turned on. From there she moved to firing squads, scaled-down gallows, and cat guillotines.

"How do they do it, Hoke?" She couldn't bring herself to say the word "euthanize" in the cats' presence.

Hoke spewed air from his lips and considered the washed-out roadbed. "Shoot, it's juss a scrape or two with a dozer then you juss spread a few loads o' gravel."

Verdie stared wide-eyed at the cats. She was horrified by this new image and was sorry she had asked. But now that she knew, she forgave Hoke all his damaging work with the crowbar on the backdoor of the animal shelter. She might have initiated this mission herself if she had known the cruelty of the county's extermination methods . . . not to mention a slipshod burial under gravel.

Hoke looked at Verdie and arched one grizzly eyebrow. "You'ens feelin' aw-right?"

"Quite!" she returned and nodded eagerly down the road. "Drive on, Watson! The game is afoot!"

Hoke squinted at her with a question in his eyes.

Verdie smiled and shrugged. "I've just always wanted to say that."

Chapter Thirty-Nine

**Vanstory Farm
Tuesday morning
Four minutes after midnight**

"This must be it," Angie said and pointed. A battered hand-painted sign was nailed to a tree. It read: *Vanstory Proppity—Keep Owt!* Another sign stood upright on a post, this one new and lettered in stenciled print: *Auction Tuesday 10 A.M.* Joey braked the car and stared at the police crime tape stretched across the driveway.

"Why is it so important that you get in there *tonight?*" Joey asked.

Angie unfolded an auction brochure. "Maryanne—my boss—is going to a book fair in New York today, and she needs to know if somebody from the stable ought to attend the auction. She needs two animals who will take to Western saddles, and she'd rather not ship from out of state."

"And you're qualified to inspect?"

"I am."

Joey nodded. "She has a lot of confidence in you. You must know a lot about riding."

Angie leaned across the seat and nibbled on Joey's earlobe as she whispered into his ear. "You ought to know, cowboy. You were doing some pretty hard riding yourself tonight." She ran her hand along his thigh and darted a wet tongue into his ear.

With that encouragement, Joey got out and lifted the tape to its limit and motioned Angie to drive under. "Better cut the lights," he said as she inched past him.

Joey got behind the wheel again and took the car just far enough that it could not be seen from the road. He pulled into a turnout and parked behind a flatbed trailer stacked with plastic barrels. When he cut the engine, they both looked down the long sloping pasture toward the barn and listened. Nothing moved on the farm. A few crickets sawed in the grass, and down in a hollow a whippoorwill declared its name with insistent redundancy.

"So why are the horses getting auctioned off?" Joey said.

"The owners are all in jail. Drugs, I think." She looked out the window for a time. "It seems pretty quiet, doesn't it?"

Joey surveyed the farm, but he had other thoughts working in his head ... points of logic ... like the consequences of traipsing through a police-cordoned crime scene in the middle of the night. But he could not take the trespass as seriously as he knew he should. This night was magic. If Angie had expressed an interest in bidding on fish, Joey would have driven to the bottom of Lake Lanier for her.

"Let's walk from here," he said. "We'll need to be quiet. Might be somebody staying at the house ... keeping an eye on things."

They tiptoed down the dirt drive, and though Joey entertained real reservations about what they were doing, he could not throw off the feeling that, on this night, he and Angie were the only two people in the world. The night air was like a tonic seeping through the pores of his skin. He felt electric and full of energy. Above them, the sky was studded with stars. For the first time in his life Joey felt that he had a firm grip on the doorknob to the best of all possible destinies. Angie had stepped back into his life. And Budge was a mentor with no equal. Joey's new residence on the mountain had captivated him. He felt as though he had been introduced to a new world entire, one that had been hidden from him in childhood. And along with this world had come a hospitable tour guide named Hoke Limberlost.

"This is fun," Angie whispered, and then giggled as she pinched Joey's arm. "Kind of like Bonnie and Clyde."

Joey decided not to mention how that partnership had ended in a blaze of automatic gunfire riddling a stolen Ford sedan that ended up looking more like a colander than an automobile. When Angie laughed again and ran ahead, Joey had to break into a trot to keep up with her.

Chapter Forty

Across Cane-Tuck Creek from the Vanstory Farm
Tuesday
Six minutes after midnight

"At the risk of bruising the celebrated pugilist's ego, may I have a try?" Lily said. There was a little tease in her voice, but Budge was still clinging to a shred of male dignity. "I thought every man knew how to make a fire," Lily said, taking the matchbox from him.

While he had burned up scores of matches, she had been watching the moon rise behind the pines on the ridge. Lily had been patient with Budge and was patient still, but now she feared he might exhaust their supply of matches.

"The wood's wet," he explained. "And there're only two matches left."

She shook the box next to her ear, its meager rattle like a farcical fanfare to male impotence. Lily pocketed the matches, unfolded a pocketknife, and began shaving away the wet outer rind of the sticks they had gathered. After a few strokes on each piece, she would test the dryness of the wood against her cheek then carefully arrange it with the others that she had stacked onto a miniature shelf she had constructed. It looked like a Plains Indian burial scaffold made for a mouse. She winked at Budge, struck a match, and held the flame in place beneath the shaved wood. The flame took and built and flourished, and now she added on damp sticks to dry.

"One match," Budge said in a flat tone.

Lily smiled. "These wet sticks ought to catch soon enough," she counseled. "But we're going to need more wood." She picked up the matchbox—now with a last match inside—and shook it. The single stick inside rattled boldly, like an anthem to female authority. "For tomorrow morning," Lily announced and handed the box to Budge.

Budge was tight-lipped as he stuffed the box into a pocket. He stared out into the night and began to nod until a humble smile stretched crookedly across his face.

" 'Next to God, we are indebted to women, first for life itself, and then for making it worth living.' " He turned to Lily. "Nestell Bovee," he added, naming the speaker of the quote. Budge pursed his lips and squinted one eye. "Bet you he took Mrs. Bovee camping, don't you?" When Lily said nothing, Budge looked up at the stars and shrugged. " 'Course, I didn't have a knife."

Lily looked down at the fire, and the light played across the smooth skin on her face like water rippling in moonlight. When she looked up at him, there was a smile on her face that would have given Mona Lisa fits.

"Bet you Mrs. Bovee took *him* camping," she said.

Budge laughed and looked out at the broad meadow across the creek. "So, your grandmother owned all this? How did she manage it all after your grandfather died?"

"Better than when he was alive. Grandpa Henry was a moonshiner. She couldn't get him to lift a hoe around the garden, but out here on this creek he just about worked himself to death making homemade liquor. He operated his still somewhere right around here." Lily pointed across the creek at the lush meadow now overgrown. "That's the Vanstory place. They had an orchard right there. Grandpa Henry made his whiskey from the Vanstorys' apples. He'd trade . . . whiskey for apples."

"Very symbiotic," said Budge.

"Grandmama used to let me sleep out here on starry summer nights like this, whenever I came up for a visit." Lily stared at the water as if it had spoken to her. "I used to have some wonderful dreams listening to this water."

"Do you remember any of them?"

"All of them," she said and in the privacy of her thoughts exhumed the conversations she had enjoyed with the handsome Cherokee fox-man whom she had adored in a previous incarnation. "Nolly" . . . that had been his name. Or something like "Nolly." The old warrior had been tall and strong, always wearing a blue sash tied around his buckskins. He was the love of her life. Of all her lives. How fortunate she had been to find him, if only in dreams.

She pointed across the creek. "Sometimes, I used to sneak over there to steal an apple from the orchard. I'd pretend it was a magic fruit and if I ate it—seeds and all—I would find my one true love." She left out one word: *again*.

"And?" Budge asked.

" 'And' what?"

"Did you find him?"

A serene smile lifted the corners of her mouth. "Not in this life."

Budge studied the meadow beyond the creek. All that remained of the orchard was the skeleton of a single crooked fruit tree a hundred yards away. It stood in the grass like a lone sentinel guarding the memories of Lily's childhood. The moon had cleared the pines now, and its beams gilded the branches of the orchard tree in metallic gold.

"I'll bet *that* wood is pretty dry," Budge said pointing at the dead tree. "We oughta go break off some of its branches."

Lily beamed. "Just like the old days. I haven't snuck across the creek in ages." She looked down at her high-laced moccasins. "Give me a minute to take these off."

Budge surprised her by turning around and squatting like a sprinter stepping into the starting blocks. He patted his back.

"No need, my lady. Hop on." He patted his back again.

"Ah-h-h," Lily cooed, "my shining knight on a white horse."

Budge produced an equine flutter of air from his lips. Then, deep in his throat, he nickered.

Lily jumped and straddled his broad back, her hands clasping the slopes of his thick shoulders. Budge cupped his meaty hands under her feet like stirrups and marched off for the water. After his first step into the creek, he hesitated. Already the water level was just an inch below his crotch.

"Whoa! That's cold!"

Lily hitched herself up higher and shifted her grip to Budge's boxy chin.

"The die is cast, big boy. And I think I'm the one supposed to say 'whoa.'"

She spurred her heels into his ribs and made a *chick-chick* sound with her tongue against her molars. Budge nickered again and sloshed ahead.

Chapter Forty-One

**Buzzard Knob above the Vanstory Farm
Tuesday morning
Eight minutes after midnight**

"Let's just lay here an' listen," Garland said as he stretched out on the rock with his brothers. "Make sure there ain't nob'dy down there."

They lay on a flat outcrop of granite and peered down into the dark valley that cradled their farm. A whippoorwill was cranking out its monotonous call somewhere below in the hollow. When it stopped, Mose—as was his unconscious habit with any interesting sound—mouthed a whispery rendition of the bird's call. He did this four times until he felt Garland and Haymer staring at him. Mose glanced at them, closed his mouth, sniffed, and then looked studiously at the farmhouse.

"I still think we shoulda kept drivin'," Haymer said. "That car was the perfect cover . . . a deputy's cruiser. What cop is gonna pull over another'n?"

"Yeah, but we need some clothes," Garland insisted. "We ain't gonna fool nobody in these damned, orange citrus suits. "B'sides, ol' Ott would figure this'll be the last place we'd come to. Plus, he ain't got that many dep'ties, and I cain't see how he'd spare one to stay out here when he knows he oughta be out lookin' all over the coun'y for us."

Garland nodded, trying to look confident about his assessment. He ran his tongue across his teeth and thought about the stash of meth he had hidden above the rafter of the outhouse. He hadn't told Haymer or Mose about this secret supply.

Mose nodded. "Hey, you know what? There oughta still be some pork barbecue in the 'fridgerater. And a whole mess o' that tater salad. I say we go on down. I'm 'bout half starved. After all, it's our damn house, ain't it?"

No one moved as they weighed their options. But now Haymer was thinking of the *Dr. Duke's Bovine Udder Cream* they kept in the tractor shed, where they sometimes penned up the milking cow due to its propensity for teat-rash. Haymer had started using the lubricant on his feet to titillating results and had sorely missed this pleasure during his recent stay at the county jail.

Though Haymer had not yet objected to the idea of going down to the house, they all knew that his word was the last one on any plan they would make. A screech owl made its loopy call behind them. Far off in the direction of highway 19, a truck sputtered flatulently as it downshifted on the grade from Hester Gap—which had the temporary effect of making Mose forget about barbecue long enough to rhapsodize over the industrial-size cans of *Beanie-Weenies* stored in their pantry just five minutes away. He ballooned his cheeks and mimicked the sound of the distant truck.

"What if Ott is figurin' on us figurin' he wouldn' put a guard out here," Haymer posited. "That damn Duffy Hawkins could be down there right now."

For a while the brothers considered this added peril. Haymer was picturing the chief deputy sitting in their dark kitchen with a shotgun balanced across his knees. Garland wondered if the deputy might have already found his cache of meth in the outhouse, maybe even used a little to get hyped up for the possibility of a shootout. Mose was getting worked up over thoughts of Duffy taking liberties with that barbecue and potato salad.

"Then again," Haymer said, the edge of reason working its way into his voice, "Ott might be figurin' that he knows we're figurin' that he's figurin' on surprisin' us, and so he figures why bother with the whole damn thing."

They were quiet again. Mose turned his head to Garland, and they exchanged frowns.

"Or," Haymer continued, his voice now case-hardened with logic, "Ott figurin' on us figurin' that he's figurin' we're figurin' on what he's figurin'."

Garland lowered his head into his hand, closed his eyes, and pinched the bridge of his nose. "That's too much damned figurin' for my head," he whined. "Let's juss go on down there."

Haymer studied the valley for a time. "Aw-right. We'll go." But Haymer's decision lacked his usual ring of certainty, and so no one moved.

The moon was just into its third quarter and now painting the meadow below with a metallic glow. In the forest where they hid, the sea of shadow beneath the trees was dappled with bright steppingstones of lunar green. It had the ominous look of a minefield. Still, no one made a move to start down the hill.

"Wait a damn minute!" Haymer whispered. "Look at that!" He was pointing off to the east end of the property. A pinpoint of orange light flickered there like a twinkling star that had dropped out of the sky and landed in the meadow. "Looks like a fire," Haymer said. "That's down at the creek, ain't it?"

The three of them squinted at the distant speck of flickering light. With their flaming red hair, they could have passed for Irish setters frozen on point before a quail they had sniffed in the brush—except that their mouths hung open and, in truth, they looked less intelligent than hunting dogs.

"Shit!" Mose hissed. "Bet you that fire is that damn Duffy Hawkins warmin' up that barbecue. Prob'ly thinks nobody can see 'im down there at the creek." Mose pushed himself up to his feet, and the others followed. This was an unprecedented variation of the pecking order. "I hope he ain't heatin' up that tater salad," Mose whined. "It's better when it's cold."

"Hold on a minute, Mose!" Haymer called out in a whisper. "Let's talk about this some more."

Mose stopped, and the three brothers held another council. "Hawkins ain't dumb enough to build a fire on a stakeout," Haymer said. "Prob'ly a lightnin' bug congregation or somethin' of the sort. Besides, looks like it's across the creek where the old Cher'kee cabin was."

Garland pulled on the sleeves of his jumpsuit. "I'm sick o' these jailhouse coveralls. I say we git down to the house and git our own clothes and stock up with what we need. Mostly, we're gonna want guns and food and money and the old flatbed Ford."

All the while he was saying this, Haymer could almost smell the *Dr. Duke's Bovine Udder Cream.*

"Quit your droolin', Mose," Garland snapped. "No barbecue for you till you git that truck runnin' for us. Can you do that?"

Mose's face traded misery for indignation. "Is the sky blue?" he asked rhetorically.

Garland sniggered. "As a matter o' fact, it's black right now if'n you don't count the stars."

Mose's face darkened. "I didn' mean 'right now,' pea-brain!"

Garland dropped his smirk and pretended to be interested. "Oh-h-h," he breathed on a down-sliding note. "Say, Mose, are you asleep?"

Mose's thick brow lowered over his eyes. " 'Course I ain't asleep, BB-brain!"

Garland altered his voice, raising it a few notches to sound like Mose. "I didn' mean 'right now', flea-brain!"

Haymer stared at his brothers for a time, wondering how all of them had avoided being arrested until now. His inclination was to preach to his siblings and drive home the point that they needed to be more careful now that they were fugitives from the law. But he could see that Garland was feeling too smug to listen. And Mose still had barbecue on the brain.

"Let's go, boys," Haymer said, and together they began their descent into the Valley of Vanstory.

Chapter Forty-Two

Vanstory Farm
Tuesday morning
Twelve minutes after midnight

The headlights from Ott's sheriff's cruiser illuminated the yellow, crime-scene tape like a sideways lightning bolt caught in a photograph. L.T. hesitated with his hand on the door handle.

"You gonna snap that tape or not?" Ott said.

"What'd you eat for supper tonight, Ott?"

Ott frowned, and his face wrinkled like a bulldog's. "Why?"

L.T.'s face went stoic. "I gotta tell you. Somethin' in this car stinks to high heaven."

Ott, a little annoyed at the inference, reached across to the glove compartment and opened it. It was like opening an exhumed casket. The reek of something putrid filled the car.

"Lord, God!" Voss gasped. "What in the hell *is* that?!"

"Evidence," Ott replied and extracted a plastic bag with a dark triangular relic sealed inside. "My chief deputy found this down at the entrance to the *Walmart* where the wooden miner got torched. This and the remains of a campfire." He let the bag dangle between his thumb and finger. "Smell like anybody you know?" Ott quizzed, wearing his who's-the-smartest-sheriff-in-the-county smile.

L.T. stared at the mystery object. "Man, that smell is so powerful it comes right through the bag! How does it do that?! What is it?"

"Don' know yet," Ott admitted, but I gotta idea who b'longs to it. Gonna hafta send it to a lab in Atlan'a to pin it down." Ott shook his head ruefully. "Hard to build a case on smell alone, you know."

"How the hell do you stand it?" L.T. mumbled through the hand pinching his nose and covering his mouth.

Ott put on his I've-been-around-the-block-a-few-times smile. "It goes with bein' sheriff, L.T. You see stuff like this. Smell it, too."

Grateful for a little fresh air, L.T. got out of the cruiser and took a double-fisted grip on the yellow tape and tried to break it. When his face turned the dull red color of a rhododendron blossom, he tried tearing it with his teeth. After a full minute of this, Ott got out and dug his folding knife from his pocket. The horse in the trailer nickered softly, and Ott felt a flicker of gratitude that the pitiful creature was still alive.

"Damn, L.T.," Ott laughed, watching Voss sit down and wipe the back of his neck with a handkerchief. "You might oughta start gettin' more exercise. Are you aw-right?"

L.T. got his breath and glared at Ott. "Lemme see you break the damn thing."

Ott was surprised at the challenge, but he could see that L.T. was serious. He folded up his knife, put it away, wrapped the tape one turn around each palm, stretched it taut, and strained until he felt his eyes bulge. The tape didn't even give a quarter inch. As he redoubled his efforts, a tiny wet sucking sound imploded under Ott's shirt collar. It was like the dull pop of a drumstick pulled out of the thigh of a baked chicken. Ott's face collapsed with pain, and he lowered his right shoulder as his left hand cupped over the joint.

"Goddammit! I think I tore that rotator-cuff-thing again." He kicked at a tuft of cane grass rising out of the road. "Shit! I tore that thing at last year's dance tryin' to spin Beulah Babcock." Ott glared at the tape and cursed. He considered shooting it with his sidearm but thought better of the idea of sending a pistol report through the valley. Crowder was at the Vanstory farmhouse watching over things, and now Ott knew first-hand about his nephew's reaction to the sound of gunfire.

With his shoulder hurting like it was, Ott wasn't sure he could open his pocketknife again. "Hell, let's juss git in the car and run the damn thing down."

Which is what they did. Ott could have sworn he felt the momentum of the car falter for a moment just before the tape snapped. When the horse in the trailer behind them stumbled and whinnied its complaint, Ott stepped on the gas. He was in no mood for equine critiques on his driving.

When they had pulled into the hardpan yard between the house and the barn, Ott turned off the motor, leaving the headlights on. He frowned and rolled down his window.

"Where in the Sam Hill did all these danged cats come from?"

There were cats scurrying across the yard to and from the barn, cats prowling the porch rail at the house, and cats bolting into the grass at the edge of the meadow. A brindle cat was walking the oval lip of a large metal water tank. Two tabbies were perched on the engine cover of the Vanstorys' tractor in the shed near the outhouse. Several more hunkered down on the roof of an idle flatbed truck with weeds growing high around the dry-rotting tires. A calico's head stuck out over the outhouse eave like a gargoyle. A black cat with white socks stood poised in the open loft door of the barn. When a big gray jumped up onto the hood of Ott's patrol car and stared back at him, Ott stiffened in his seat and rolled up his window.

"Git!" he yelled through the glass and flung his fingers at the windshield. The cat continued to study him with feline indifference. Finally, conceding his defeat in the standoff, Ott got out and stood with one foot on the doorframe as he banged on the roof of his car. The cat offered a snarky smile and casually hopped up on the cruiser's roof and then on to the top of the horse trailer.

Looking around the farm for a deputy car, Ott felt his mood begin to sour. The house was dark. The yard was either too dry to show fresh tire treads or else he was just too poor a tracker to find them.

"Where the hell is Crowder?" he growled.

L.T. got out, walked to the back of the trailer, and jerked open the slide bar that locked the gate. After lowering the ramp to the ground, he made the *chick, chick* sound in his cheek that he'd heard from mounted cowboys on TV. The horse did not move.

"Crowder!" Ott yelled.

There was no answer. There was only the shuffle of hooves from the barn and the light *clickety-click* of claws as the cat on the trailer scampered across the roof and leapt to the barn loft.

"This is what happens when you give a damn job to a nephew," Ott muttered and marched off toward the house.

Meanwhile, L.T. was tiring of his standoff with the horse they had carted here. "Get on out of there! Hyah! Hyah! Back up, you old bag o' bones!"

L.T. waited for the used-up creature to back down the ramp, but the horse appeared unenthusiastic about the plan. Voss walked to the front of the trailer and waggled his fingers through a slot in the aluminum frame.

"Go! Giddy-up backwards! Hyah!" He even tried the backwards version. "Hayh!" When that brought no results, he banged his fist on the metal. "Ow!" he yelped and whipped his hand back and forth from the wrist. Glowering at the stubborn horse, he kicked at the trailer frame and felt a bright pain announce itself in his big toe. "***Ow!***" he screamed much louder, this time in an oddly feminine pitch. "Git on outta there, you mangy mule!" This he growled in a decidedly masculine timbre, trying to counterbalance the embarrassing girlish shriek that had slipped off his tongue.

L.T. peeked through the aluminum slats and saw only the dark silhouette of the motionless animal. He stepped up on the trailer tongue and pumped it with his legs, rocking both the trailer and the cruiser. The uncompromising horse stood its ground.

The porch light came on, and Ott came out of the house and stood at the top of the steps rubbing his shoulder. "That damn Crowder is in there asleep on the Vanstory's sofa. I thought he was dead." Ott shook his head and spat over the porch rail. "Finally had to bang a fry pan against the woodstove to wake 'im up." Ott shook his head in regret. "Prob'ly a mistake. The boy made a bee line for the privy out back."

L.T. bent at the knees and applied his weight to the trailer tongue again. When the trailer came to rest, Ott laughed.

"Whatcha tryin' to do, L.T.? Shake the horse outta there?"

"This is a damned ornery cuss for a horse. It don't wanna come out. You know anything about horses?"

Crowder emerged from the back of the house tucking in his shirt and squinting at the porch light, trying his best to look like an officer on duty. On his hip he now wore a black holster that carried a gun that had been a regulation sidearm in the department thirty years ago. What he did not know was that the pistol was unloaded. When Ott made an official jerk of his head toward the trailer, Crowder shuffled over to the ramp.

"The horse ain't dead, is it?" Crowder asked. "It looks dead!"

L.T. stepped down from the trailer tongue and glared at Crowder. "How could it be dead? It's standing up."

Crowder looked up at Ott, as though all explanations had to be directed to his uncle. "They sleep standin' up, don' they? I figure they can die that-a-way, too."

Ott and L.T. stared blankly at one another for a few seconds, until Ott closed his eyes and shook his head. "He's Bernice's sister's boy," Ott said, as if that explained something. In fact, he wasn't so sure that the boy wasn't on to something about a horse's angle of repose.

L.T. took hold of an aluminum slat and shook the trailer from the side, making it groan and sway from tire to tire. When the trailer came to rest again, the horse exhaled in what might have been a sigh of boredom.

"It's alive aw-right," Crowder said.

"It appears you two don't know a helluva lot about horses," L.T. said, "but I'll ask anyway. Either of you know anything about getting a horse to move backwards?"

While Crowder scratched his head, Ott squatted with hands on knees and peered into the dark of the trailer. "This here a boy-horse or a girl-horse? Maybe we could coax it out with t'other sex."

"I don't know what the hell it is," L.T. said. "For all I know it's a transvestite."

Crowder turned to Ott with his mouth agape. "They got transvestite horses now?"

Ott stepped back for a view of both car and trailer, squeezed the flaccid skin under his chin, and pivoted his head back and forth in thoughtful increments. "How 'bout we leave the trailer gate open, slip the cruiser into "drive," and put the pedal to the metal. That oughta squirt that flea-bag right outta there." He looked at Crowder. "Kindly like that time your Uncle 'Lonzo accident'ly off-loaded that new refrigerator down at the red light."

"Yeah," Crowder said, "that might work." Then his face sagged with the certainty that he would be doing the stunt-driving for this equine delivery. "Now, why is it we're doin' this again, Uncle Ott?"

Before Ott could decide on a proper version of their clandestine mission, a young woman marched out of the tool shed beside the house and headed right for them as though she were about to read them their rights. So confident and deliberate she seemed that neither Ott nor Crowder thought to pull a gun. The sound of her footsteps in the yard had the effect of a hypnotist's charm swung on a chain. Slack-jawed in her spell, the three men stared at her.

"You can't take a horse off a trailer that way!" she announced. "You'll break a leg!"

The young man who followed her into the yard snapped their senses awake. Crowder was the first one to get his gun clear of his holster. He kept opening and closing his fingers on the grip, wishing now he had washed his hands after eating the barbecue from the Vanstory refrigerator. Ott was still searching for his own weapon around the generous circumference of his waist.

"Y'all better iden'ify yo'selves," Ott said officially. "I'm the Lum'kin County sher'ff, and you're on restricted property that's part of a crim'nal investigation."

Ott gave up on finding his gun and hooked his thumbs on his belt. This is what deputies were for, after all. L.T. crouched in the shadow of the trailer and tried to hide his face. Crowder held his gun in one hand leveled at the approaching man. With his other hand he tried to shade his eyes from the glare of the porch light.

"Don' I know you, son?" Ott said, squinting at the male half of the intruders.

"Joey Gallatin, Sheriff. I rent Mr. Limberlost's cabin up on Crow Mountain. I won't pretend we're not trespassing, but we mean no harm being here. We're just checking on some horses that are scheduled for auction. We're wanting to know the quality of the animals to see if we should come back for the bidding."

L.T.'s head bobbed up from the back of the trailer. His indignant expression failed him as soon as Angie brushed past him and squeezed into the trailer with the horse. She touched a hand to the animal's rump and stroked along the flank as she sidled up to the bewildered creature's head and whispered soothing reassurances.

The four men watched as she backed the white horse down the ramp without protest, her hand gripped to the halter. Angie combed the coarse forelock from the horse's eyes and patted the big flat cheek.

"Whoa now, girl. You're okay now."

When Angie turned, there was fire in her eyes. She glared at Ott and then at the squat man lurking in the shadow. When she turned her gaze on Crowder, the deputy lowered his gun as if he had been outmatched by heavier artillery. Which, in his case—with his pistol unloaded—could have been a slingshot.

"This horse is blind," Angie said. She ran her fingers along the accordion ribs of the horse's emaciated body. "And it looks like she hasn't eaten in a week."

Ott swallowed. This girl was good. It had been exactly seven days since L.T. had picked up the nag from the slaughter pen over at the dog food plant in Alto. Ott glanced at L.T., whose face looked as pale as biscuit dough. When Ott felt a swirl of current at his feet, he looked down. A black and white cat—its back arched and tail erect like a whip antenna—was leaning into his legs as it walked figure-eights around his ankles. He wanted to kick at it but something about the woman's judgmental eye said "no." He mustered his I'm-the-sheriff-and-you're-not smile and met Angie's gaze.

"Kindly a odd time to be appraisin' animals, if you ask me."

Before Joey or Angie could answer, there was a crash inside the house. It sounded both wooden and metallic, like a wooden crate full of tools had been dropped. Crowder tightened his sphincters and leveled his gun at the front door. Crouching, he looked to Ott for a cue.

"Who else is here with you?" Ott said to Joey.

Joey nodded toward Angie. "It's just the two of us, Sheriff."

Ott pursed his lips and considered the house. "Prob'ly one o' them damn cats." He met Crowder's glassy eyes and jerked his head in the direction of the house. "You better go on in and check it out."

The skin on Crowder's forehead tightened. "Alone?"

"You was in there alone b'fore I got here," Ott said.

Crowder faced the house and licked his lips. "Yeah, but it's diff'rent when you're alone in an empty house that ain't really empty." He nodded at the front door.

Ott fluttered air through his lips, causing the horse to fishhook its neck to face his direction. "You ain't afraid of a cat, are you?"

Crowder shifted his weight from leg to leg but did not go anywhere. "What if it ain't a cat? What if it's them Vanstorys come back?"

Ott snorted, and the blind horse perked up her ears. "They ain't *that* stupid."

Crowder's face wrinkled like a balled-up rag. "Well, that's why you tol' me to stay out here, Uncle Ott . . . in case they showed up. You said they was dumber'n mud."

Ott made an impatient wave of his hand. "Them boys ain't within fifty miles o' here, son. But if it'll make you feel any better—" Ott dug a hand into his trouser pocket. "Here. Why doncha take this bullet and load up?"

Crowder's face took on a frown to such a degree that it appeared his face was melting. "You mean my gun ain't loaded?"

"Well, hell, son, I figured that's the way you'd'a preferred it, considerin' your medical condition."

"Uncle Ott," Crowder mewled, "just 'cause I got the bang-a-phobia, don't think I wouldn't be willin' to sacrifice a pair o' regulation deputy trousers in order to protect myself!"

When Crowder held out his cupped hand, Ott tossed to his nephew a single cartridge. "Now, go on in there and see cain't you git the drop on the cat that's makin' all that noise."

Crowder opened the loading gate on the revolver and slipped in the lone bullet. Much to Ott's amusement, Crowder did not know enough about guns to manually advance the cylinder and put the cartridge next in line to be struck by the firing pin. Crowder just closed the loading gate and crept stealthily up the steps to the front porch.

When the deputy got to the door, he pivoted smartly to one side and pressed his back into the clapboard wall beside the doorframe. He held his handgun in both hands now, the barrel pointing straight up beside his cheek. Ott figured it was something the boy had learned from cop shows on the TV.

When Crowder gave a smart nod to his uncle, Ott—bewildered—returned the signal simply to prod the boy into action. Crowder swung through the door following his outstretched weapon, his seemingly armless torso disappearing into the dark of the front room.

"Lord, help us," Ott muttered, shaking his head. "I believe he was better at makin' poisoned Brunswick stew than bein' a crime-fighter."

"Sheriff," Angie said, the tone of her voice reminding Ott of Bernice. Without realizing he had moved, Ott found himself standing at attention with his heels together. "Is this the quality of horse being auctioned off tomorrow? Because if it is, you should consider canceling the sale and inviting agents from ASPCA and the Humane Society instead. And if you don't . . . I will."

Ott cleared his throat and tried to ignore L.T., who was making some kind of frantic hand signals that Ott did not understand. "Listen here, Missy," Ott said, pointing a chubby finger at Angie. "I'll be askin' the questions 'round here. I got a mind to cart the two o' you off to my jail tonight. Do you un'erstand the ser'ous nature o' trespassin' on a crime scene?"

"Sheriff," Joey said. "We didn't mean any—"

"Joey," Angie interrupted, her eyes locked on Ott. "What do you think brings a sheriff out to an abandoned farm in the middle of the night with a horse that's blind, malnourished, and has one hoof in the grave? There's something going on here."

Her question hung in the silence of the night like a dark light bulb lowered from the heavens by its infinitely long electric wire. Everyone waited to see if it was going to blink on or be a dud.

Hoping to feel strength in numbers, Ott gestured toward Voss and toward the house where Crowder was probably squaring off with some vermin in the Vanstory kitchen. "Well, Missy, not that we gotta 'xplain the sheriffin' bus'ness to you," Ott began, "but it juss so happ'ns we juss confiscated this abused animal, and we stopped off at the closest place we could find to feed it." He nodded toward the barn. "L.T., whyn't you see if you can find some oats or hay or some other kind o' horse chow in there?"

L.T. slunk from the shadow of the trailer and started for the barn. He had not gone six paces when he stopped.

"Ott? Looks like there's a car in here. This your nephew's Ford?"

Ott walked to the entrance of the barn. Deep in shadow was a car that was neither Crowder's nor the Vanstorys'. He flicked on the tiny penlight on his key chain and saw a light-blue Fairlane with a big, fluffy, Persian cat for a hood ornament.

"That looks like Verdie's car . . . from down at the *Skillet*," Ott announced. He shone the dim light around the interior of the building and, when a movement caught his eye, trained the faded beam back on the car. A head now appeared at the driver's seat. "Verdie?"

By the time Ott reached the car, Verdie was poring over a map she had unfolded across the steering wheel. "Let's see," Verdie mumbled, her finger tapping the map. "I must have taken a wrong turn about right there." She looked up. "Oh, hello, Ott," she said cheerfully. "What capital luck! I'll bet you can give me some directions."

Ott stared down at the map and frowned. "That there's a state map, Verdie. It don't show the dirt roads."

"Well, there you are then," she said in her British lilt, sounding somewhat relieved. "There's the rub."

"What is it you're lookin' for, Verdie?" Ott leaned in and panned his flashlight beam across the backseat, which was covered in an angry, multicolored sea of feline hairs and dotted with little volcanic islands of cat vomit.

Thinking quickly, she replied, "I've been out looking for my cat."

With a skeptical arch of one eyebrow, Ott locked eyes with her. "That right?" He raised both eyebrows and gave her his I-believe-I-got-you-now smile. "What color is it?"

Verdie was not about to let her Holmesian mind be outsmarted by Ott Ambrose, who thought more with his eyebrows than his brain. "It's a mix. Gray, black, tabby, brindle, calico, rusty-orange, and white."

Ott watched her eyes closely. "That right?" he purred. "What's its name?"

Verdie swallowed. "Jack," she said. "After Jackson Pollock." It was the first name to pop into her head that seemed feasible for such a multi-colored cat.

Ott pointed at the cat on the hood. "I guess that ain't your cat settin' right there?"

Verdie leaned out the window and squinted as if she had not seen it. "No." Then she looked around the barn. Cats were everywhere crisscrossing the hay-strewn floor. Every stall had a horse's head hooked over its gate as though mesmerized by the ebb and flow of felines. "What is this, Ott?" Verdie asked. "A cat farm?"

Ott stepped to the back open window and leaned in to take a closer look at the back seat. As Verdie awaited Ott's verdict about the ability of one cat to shed so many hairs while at the same time delivering up a Guinness Book record of heaving up its cat biscuits onto the upholstery, the night seemed to hold its breath.

"When's the last time you cleaned out your car, Verdie?"

Verdie's agile mind went to work, but before she could answer Ott's question . . .

Boom! The sound echoed all through the valley like a thunderclap.

Eight things happened almost at once: One, Ott straightened and crashed his head on the top of Verdie's window frame. Two, in trying to extricate himself from the vehicle he unthinkingly pushed off with his injured shoulder and grunted so loud that Verdie thought he had been shot. Three, Verdie screamed, the shriek somehow coming out British. Four, the horses in the barn whinnied and banged their gates, setting up a racket like a loaded-down timber truck rumbling across a wooden bridge with loose nails. Five, the nag, still in Angie's grip, reared and lifted her off the ground. Six, Joey got to Angie, sliding on his shins as he caught her across his arms, just as she was coming down for a nasty landing on her back. Seven, the blind horse bolted and, in its panic, bounced L.T. Voss like a basketball off the front of Verdie's car. And eight, the cat L.T. landed on yowled like an old phonograph needle skittering across a vinyl record.

"What the hell?" Ott said, trying to sound collected. "Was that a gun?"

By the time Ott located his handgun and got back to the yard at a fast waddle, Joey was standing with Angie still draped over his arms. Ott was breathing hard when he leaned in to look at her.

"She git shot?"

"No," Joey said. "The sound came from inside the house."

Ott held his weapon trained on the front door and moved up the stairs onto the porch. Then his worst fears were realized when Crowder stepped out from the house onto the porch with his hands held above his head. There was blood trickling down one side of his face.

"Th'ow down ya gun, Sher'ff, or your dep'ty here gits a hole in his nice new dep'ty shirt."

"Why not the trousers?" Crowder mumbled. "They're aw-ready ru-int."

Behind Crowder a big meaty hand emerged from the doorway. The hand was holding an old Smith and Wesson .38.

"That you, Mose?" Ott said, lowering his gun.

"It's me, Ott. Now, th'ow that police-popper out toward the tractor shed, and ever'body git yore hands up."

Ott tossed his weapon and immediately regretted it for two reasons. One, wrong arm. A pain cut through his shoulder as if a red-hot dagger had been plunged deep into the joint. Two, only now did Ott remember that the gun in Moses's hand was the very gun that Ott had reluctantly assigned to Crowder for the night's stakeout. Which meant, it had to be empty. Unless, of course, Mose happened to have some old .38 ammo handy somewhere in the house and had reloaded the weapon.

Mose eased out onto the porch, the gun in his right hand, a charred and liberally sauced shank of barbecued ham in his left. He tore off a huge chunk of meat with his teeth, and dark red barbecue sauce drooled down his chin like a red mustache and goatee trying to complement his fiery red hair.

L.T., Verdie, Voss, Joey, and Angie stood off to one side in the main yard with their arms raised.

"How bad're you hit, Crowder?" Ott said, already dreading the moment he would have to tell Bernice about her wounded nephew.

"Well, I ain't been shot, far as I know," Crowder declared. "But I cain't see out my left eye, Uncle Ott. Hurts 'bout like a yeller jacket stung me right on the eyeball."

Mose laughed and held up the saucy haunch of pig. "I hit 'im with this here ham hock. It would'a been a lot worse for 'im, but your damned dep'ty has been eatin' on the job, Ott. Must'a lightened up this head-knocker by ten pounds." When he smiled, his cheeks dimpled with two large parentheses.

"Well, I can tell you right now," Crowder complained, "there's too damn much vinegar in that sauce. Man, that smarts!" He wiped at his eye with his shirtsleeve and then jabbed a thumb back at the house. "Uncle Ott, it was a drawer full o' silverware hittin' the floor we heard."

Mose ramped down his gloating smile to a modest grin. "My bad!" he said. "I's tryin' to find a spoon for the tater salad."

"Well, who the hell got shot?" Ott asked.

Mose pointed the chunk of meat toward Crowder. "When I knocked 'im in the head, your dep'ty here clicked his trigger 'bout three times till he finally managed to shoot the damn tater salad." Mose was working himself up to be indignant. "That's 'who the hell got shot'!" He poked the gun toward Ott, who was trying to cradle his injured shoulder. "What the hell's the matter with you, Ott? You ain't shot, too, are you?"

Ott made a sour face and massaged his shoulder. "May as well have been! Think I tore my damned rotator cuff again!"

Mose shook his head ruefully. "Appears to be a hard night for taters." As he continued to gnaw on the barbecued pork, Mose worked his way down the steps to the yard and sidled toward the tractor shed, where he located Ott's gun with his foot. Picking up the Glock, he tossed the empty Smith and Wesson into the weeds.

"Hah!" Mose laughed. "Y'all just got suckered by a empty gun!" He leaned back against an oval, metal water tank and resumed his attack on the barbecue. So voracious was his chewing that he did not hear the thrashing in the grass behind him. Everyone else heard it though. It was something big. Ahead of it, six cats were flushed from the grass and shot across the yard.

"What the hell?" Ott muttered under his breath. His best guess was a big draft horse or a cow . . . maybe a bull . . . until he saw that it wore a khaki shirt and shorts and carried a bundle of sticks under one arm.

Now Mose heard it, too, but, expecting that one of his brothers would show himself at this opportune moment, he did not bother even to turn his head to the sound.

"Ain't this a purty picture, brother?" Mose crowed out of the side of his mouth. "I'd say realtor Voss is on the losin' end o' this deal, and ol' Ott'll be losin' his next election once word o' this little party gits out." Mightily pleased with himself at taking this group single-handedly, Mose laughed and took a bite of the barbecue again.

Budge, stopping right behind Mose, assessed the situation in a flash. Behind him Lily emerged from the tall grass and stepped beside him with her own load of dry sticks. They made quite a pair—a giant Boy Scout and Miss Universe, both making a home delivery of firewood in the wee hours. They were about the last thing anyone there would have expected to come wandering in out of the night.

"Whoever can surprise well must conquer," Budge said pressing the tip of a straightened index finger into Mose's right buttock.

Mose stopped chewing, straightened from the water tank, and wrinkled his brow. "That ain't you, is it, Haymer?"

"Nope," Budge replied.

"Garland?"

"Nope," Budge said again. "Hold the Glock by the barrel and hand it to me slowly."

When Mose surrendered the gun behind him, Budge leaned to his ear. "John Paul Jones," he said, giving the proper credit to the quote.

"Howdy, Mr. Jones," Mose said. "I's Mose Vanstory."

At that moment, Haymer walked out of the tractor shed. "Drop the shooter into the water tank, Big 'un." Haymer's voice was calm and calculated. "I don' rightly see how I can miss somebody big as you, but if I do, I'll prob'ly hit the purty lady with them fancy moccasins."

When Budge dropped Ott's Glock into the tank, the gun *clank*ed against the inside wall of the metal container and then *clatter*ed against the bottom. Haymer stepped into a pool of moonlight in the barnyard. He was barefooted, and the skin on his feet glistened like quicksilver. They appeared to be covered by a film of oil.

"Haymer?" Mose said, frowning, "how come your feet are shiny?" Mose cocked his head, closed his eyes, and sniffed. "Ain't that *Dr. Duke's* I smell?"

As Haymer eased around Budge and Lily, Joey could see that the weapon the man held in his hands was nothing more than a caulking gun. It was a bluff! It wasn't even loaded with a tube of spackle. Joey casually walked across the yard toward the water tank.

"Where the hell d'you think you're goin'?" Haymer said, scowling at Joey.

Joey leaned into the tank and picked up Ott's gun. When he straightened, he held the weapon down by his leg and pointed at the ground.

"Budge?" Joey said, keeping his eyes on both Vanstory brothers, "you got anything in your cornucopia of quotes that might be appropriate for turning the tables on an opponent armed with a caulking gun?"

The calm in Joey's voice was like a death knell to Haymer and Mose. Haymer visibly sagged, and the impotent caulking gun fell to the ground. Mose continued to work on the barbecue ham, but his chewing took on a decidedly defeated rhythm.

Budge cleared his throat. "There is that in us which can turn defeat into victory," he said. He leaned toward Verdie and started to whisper into her ear, but she surprised him by speaking first.

"Ah . . . Edith Hamilton, if I am not much mistaken." She produced a literary smile.

Budge's eyes were like two shiny quarters, and his mouth remained open for several seconds. Then he broke into his own smile and nodded.

"Right," he whispered in awe.

Behind the house the outhouse door opened, and Garland Vanstory hurried out at a fast pace with a manic grin stretched across his face. His teeth and eyes glowed like they could set off a Geiger counter into a paroxysm of ticks. Stopping in the yard, he constantly shifted his weight from leg to leg as he held what looked like a short double-barreled shotgun in both hands down by his hip, the muzzles pointing directly at Joey.

"Th'ow that gun down, hot shot!" Garland barked. "Th'ow it right back into that livestock tank."

Joey did as he was told. The gun arced into the tank and disappeared into the metal receptacle with hardly a sound of impact. Garland moved toward the tank, keeping his weapon tucked close to his belly, making it difficult to be seen. As he reached down into the tank with one hand, he smiled at Ott.

"Dumber'n mud, huh? Well, lookie at what I found in the outhouse, Ott." Garland cackled as he held out the makeshift weapon with which he had fooled everyone. It was two short cardboard spools, both emptied of their tissue. He tossed them to the ground, where they bounced with light, hollow tapping sounds on the hardpan of the yard. "Kid," Garland chuckled as he sneered at Joey, "reckon you'll be the only man in hist'ry ever to be backed down by double-barreled toilet paper tubes."

Garland laughed again as he groped for the gun in the tank. Then a change came over his face, tightening first and then going slack—like a shriveled prune rehydrated in a pot of hot water. Garland took a startled step back as Hoke Limberlost rose from the dark bottom of the tank. Ott's gun was in his hand.

The angular Glock looked like a futuristic anachronism in his wrinkled, sun-browned hand. No one spoke or moved. Hoke waited to see if there were to be any more tables turned before committing to having the upper hand. When no one popped out to challenge him, he scissored his legs over the edge of the tank and backed away for a better look at the participants of this midnight tableau. That was when he saw Lily . . . by moonlight.

His eyes traveled the length of her, savoring her long raven-black hair, the flawless olive complexion of her virtuous face, the bottomless depth of her ink-dark eyes, the perfect hourglass silhouette of her body, the beaded moccasins laced up her long-tapering calves, the impressive collection of firewood under her arm.

"Great Elders Above," Hoke whispered. "*Tsi-ya*! It's you."

Lily dropped her firewood and took two tentative steps toward Hoke. "Nolly?"

Hoke studied her face as though he were seeing his entire life projected on the screen of her skin. "Close enough, I reckon. It's *I-nâ-li*," he explained. "I am Black Fox of the Blue clan."

"And I am Otter Woman. . . of the Wild Potato Clan."

Everybody's mouth hung open, riveted to the ineffable drama unfolding before them. Verdie's lips trembled, and her eyes welled with tears over the romantic vignette playing out in the yard. Mose seemed especially interested after hearing something about wild taters.

Ott closed his eyes, took in a deep breath, and then smirked at the maudlin theatrics. "Yeah, and I'm Wyatt Earp o' the Dodge City clan," he muttered to no one in particular. "Now how 'bout handin' over that gun, Hoke?" Ott started across the yard in a confident swagger.

Chapter Forty-Three

Vanstory Farm
Tuesday
1 A.M.

"Aw-right, boys and girls!" Ott announced in his I'm-back-in-charge-again voice. Even before he reached Hoke, he held out the hand of his good arm. "Better let me take over now, Hoke."

Hoke casually brought the gun around to bear on Ott, who stopped as if he had come to the end of a tether. Ott's big smile inverted to a questioning frown.

"You ain't forgettin' I'm the sher'ff, are ya?" Without waiting for an answer, Ott propped his hands on his ample hips and chuckled. "I doubt you even know how to use a modern shooter like that."

Hoke ratcheted the slide to seat a bullet into the chamber. The crisp metallic sound got everyone's attention. Then Hoke raised the gun to point at the sky.

Boom!

"Oh, Lord," someone moaned in a pitiful voice. All eyes turned to Crowder, who stood near the porch. He was bent forward with both his hands pressed to his abdomen. Turning stiffly, his body rocking from side to side like a penguin frantically searching for the Southern Cross constellation, he got his bearings and started for the outhouse.

Hoke gestured with the gun and backed Ott away two steps. "You juss keep your distance there, Ott," Hoke said. "I ain't so sure where ever'body stands in this little parley. He took a step sideways toward Lily and seemed to settle in there like a fox snuggling up to a vixen in her den. "Let's juss see cain't we sort it all out a bit." Lily's hand slid into the crook of Hoke's arm, and the two of them stood so close together as to appear as one.

"You smell good," Lily whispered.

Hoke blushed, and, in that moment, he understood the reason for his having lost his fox ear talisman on the *Walmart* battleground. It was destiny, pure and simple. To meet the Otter Woman was to complete who he was, and now he no longer needed the necklace. It was precisely what old Grandfather Mingo had told him so long ago. He patted Lily's hand and waved the gun in a line that connected the Vanstory brothers to the water tank. "I want you three boys to slip into that there empty tank where I can keep a eye on you."

Because Mose would not let go of his barbecued pork, it took both brothers to lift him inside the tank. Even with Garland's surplus of meth-induced energy and with Haymer's red-faced anger, they had to deal with Mose's body in sections. First a leg, then a shoulder, and so on.

"Man, this is 'bout like tryin' to lift a dead cow into the kitchen sink," Garland grunted.

Mose took offense as he hung over the edge. "You ain't never had to lift no dead cow, and you know it, Gar!"

"It was a simile," Budge said and walked to the struggling trio. There he took a wider stance and began rubbing his hands together in preparation for lifting a heavy weight. Garland gnashed his teeth as he strained with the weight of his gargantuan brother. Haymer's face had darkened to the purple of a ripe muscadine. But Mose still tottered on the edge. Finally, Budge bent at the knees, got under Mose's massive body, and heaved him up and over. The bottom of the tub buckled, and the walls sloped inward a few inches from the warping of the floor, but, otherwise, the vessel held up.

Once ensconced in the tank, Mose took a bite out of the barbecued pig's leg and watched with interest to see what would happen next. He looked so content, he might have been in the house watching *Wheel of*

Fortune. Budge picked up Garland by his waist and inserted him feet-first into the tub. He did the same with Haymer. Then he stepped back and crossed his python arms over his chest.

" 'Rub a dub dub, three fools in a tub, and who do you think they be? The butcher, the faker, the methamphetamine maker. Turn them out, knaves all three.' "

In the dead silence that followed, every person there stared at the hulking giant in khakis who quoted nursery rhymes.

Budge assumed his edifying, NPR tone of voice. "A variation on the James Orchard Halliwell English version from eighteen forty-two."

Hoke waved the gun toward L.T., who had sidled closer to Ott. "Now let's git the rest of the crooks in there with 'em, why don't we."

Stricken, Voss touched his stubby fingertips to his own chest. "Me?" he croaked.

"You'ens been swindlin' folks outta their land for too long, you damn snake. And juss cause you'ens is Ott's buddy in crime, you'ens ain't above the law. You'ens was over to my place tryin' to move my boundary marker. I know all 'bout you'ens wantin' to trade properties with Buster Gooch. What I don' know is what you'ens is doin' out here tonight with the sher'ff."

"Perhaps I do," Verdie said in her best Sherlock Holmes tone of humble discovery. "My theory is they want to switch a blind, malnourished mare for one of the healthy horses in the barn."

Ott and L.T. snapped their heads around to Verdie as if they were puppets jerked by the same string. Ott had on his I-don't-have-a-smile-for-this smile.

"My guess," Angie said, "would be that big Morgan in the first stall."

Hoke smiled at Ott. "That's one way to make sure you git what you want outta a auction. I'm bettin' that Morgan is for Buster Gooch. That horse and this Vanstory land here would be juss about right for that emu farm he's always talkin' 'bout. An' I'm bettin' you'ens' been talkin' 'im outta his Frogtown property. Am I right?"

Voss opened his mouth, closed it, and looked at Ott.

Ott raised both arms to shrug but immediately regretted it. He grabbed his right shoulder as if he had taken a bullet. When the pain abated, he one-handedly pulled up his trouser belt and sniffed with authority.

"Me and L.T. juss confiscated that poor animal. Found it juss a hour ago a-wonderin' 'round the north end o' the coun'y. It looked so hungry we thought we'd stop by here to feed it." Ott took a shot at a never before rehearsed People-for-the-Ethical-Treatment-of-Animals smile.

Hoke snorted. "And the two o' you'ens juss happ'ned to be out cruisin' 'round at midnight with a horse trailer," Hoke said. He huffed a false laugh and shook his head. "There ain't but two people I can think of who would let a animal suffer like this and they's both standin' right here by the cookie jar with crumbs on they's faces."

Ott tried for his you-got-no-idea-how-demanding-it-is-to-be-the-sheriff smile. "Then we seen a blue car pullin' in here," Ott continued, "so natu'ally we come in to investigate." Ott bucked up with sheriff-like deliberation. "Verdie, there, is stickin' her nose somewhere it ain't s'posed to be. She's been known to do this b'fore."

"That's right," L.T. said with enthusiasm. Now he was suddenly animated, pointing in three different directions at once. "We saw Verdie pull off the highway and pull in here. Then she hid her car in the barn. There ain't no tellin' what she's up to and what she'd say after she done it. She spreads more gossip in this town than the women at the beauty parlor."

Verdie's lower lip began to quiver. Taking the light from the crescent moon climbing higher into the starry sky, two tears shone at the corners of her eyes. When she closed those sad eyes, the droplets crept down her cheeks like glow worms on a slow retreat from insult.

Budge clenched his teeth, and the tendons in his jaws hardened like angle iron. Thrusting his hands into the pockets of his khaki shorts, he strolled across the yard with his head down and his lips thoughtfully pursed, as though he were working out a problem. When he stopped and spread his feet, he was so close to Ott and Voss that the two men arched their spines to lean away from him. Budge raised one hand in a measuring gesture, showing an eighth-inch gap between thumb and index.

"I'm about this far away from stuffing you two clowns into that horse trailer, hauling you out to the interstate, and hooking you up to an eighteen-wheeler with a faulty exhaust." He swept his hand toward Verdie. "I suggest you apologize to this lady post-haste."

There were about two seconds of dead quiet, and then both men began spouting off platitudes of remorse like overzealous mourners at a funeral. With all this going on, Verdie sniffled once and wiped at her eyes. Her mouth formed a small circle of surprise as she stared at Budge. She couldn't help but let her teary eyes roam over the muscular terrain of his massive body. Here before her stood the ultimate protector. Nice looking, too. And so erudite.

Hoke beckoned to Ott and L.T. with the gun barrel. "Whatcha say we git all the birds of a feather into the same nest. Both o' you'ens, climb into that tank with these other jaybirds."

While Ott and L.T. wrestled their way into the tank, Budge pulled a forest green bandana from his back pocket and offered it to Verdie. Through her tears she smiled up at him.

"Thank you, sir."

Budge lifted his meaty hand and gently brushed a lock of hair that had fallen over Verdie's eye. "Anybody ever tell you . . . you look like Julie Andrews? Sound like her, too." His hand gently cupped the side of her face and remained in place, feeling to Verdie like a plate of protective armor perfectly molded to her cheek.

With her teary eyes lit up by a full-voltage smile, Verdie slowly shook her head. "Oh, dear . . . I don't think anyone has ever said that to me." A look of surprise washed over her face, and her smile widened a notch. "I do sound a little like Julie Andrews, don't I?" The film of tears on her eyes caught the moon's argentine glow, and her hand came up as though feeling for an aura radiating around Budge's reverential face. As he had done to her, she touched her palm to his cheek. "Oh, dear," she purred again.

"I saw *The Sound of Music* seventeen times," Budge confessed.

Verdie blushed and gazed out at the dark scrim of mountains rising around her, and for an unguarded moment she considered bursting into a Julie Andrews song. Already she was adjusting the lyrics to fit the situation. But something entirely different spilled from her lips.

"Do you like detective novels?"

Budge frowned and shook his head. "Not the current ones. Only the pre-twentieth century paradigms. The modern private eye genre is too rife with smart alecks for my taste. Everything's got to be a cute quip, you know?"

"Conan Doyle?" Verdie ventured.

Budge narrowed his eyes and smiled. "Absolutely. Holmes is the ultimate." He nodded toward the barn. "You reminded me of him a little bit . . . that idea about switching the horses. Very astute." Budge pursed his lips and looked out into the night. "The Case of the Purloined Pony." He looked at her and raised his eyebrows. "What do you think?"

Once again, Verdie let her eyes travel the length of this fascinating man—from his big, hairless, cannonball head down to his size-seventeen hiking boots. She imagined this hulking man beating the tar out of everyone from her past who had ever harmed her or her skinny brothers or her thin-as-paper father.

"Lordy, Lordy," she said, "just look at you." She smiled. "Is it 'Budge'?"

"You can call me 'Randall,' if you want."

Verdie canted her head, and her smile spread into her eyes. "I like 'Budge.' "

With the Vanstorys, Voss, and Ott waiting obediently in their galvanized prison, the livestock tank took on a gamut of mythological symbolisms. It was the lost lifeboat from Noah's ark, the one containing those doomed species the future world would never know. It was the bottom rung of Dante's Inferno, where the most heinous of creatures charbroiled for eternity. It was Pandora's Box housing five men and a ham hock. It was Louis Pasteur's worst nightmare of a Petri dish spawning the vilest diseases of mankind.

"Now, what 'bout you'ens, son?" Hoke said to Crowder. "Still got a cravin' to learn the Cherokee herbs and become a medicine man?"

"It's for certain I ain't cut out for this dep'ty job, Mr. Limberlost." Crowder eyed the tank. "I hope you ain't considerin' stickin' me in there, too. There ain't hardly room."

"Can always slip one more rose into the vase," Hoke said. "My mama used a say that." Hoke canted his head to study Crowder from an angle. "But I figure you'ens to be on our side o' this sit'ation. Would that be 'bout right?"

"Yes, sir. I'd be proud to learn the plant medicines from you. I 'preciate it."

Hoke smiled. "Well, it's took you'ens a while, but I reckon you finally figured out why you put that 'help wanted' sign out on the street."

Lily squeezed Hoke's arm. "That saying about 'one more rose'? My grandmama used to say that, too." She put her cheek to his shoulder and whispered, "You smell so good."

Hoke looked into her eyes. "Reckon I ain't never gonna git tired o' hearin' that." He nodded toward Budge. "What 'bout that big 'un there. He a friend o' you'ens? He sure seems to be a friend o' Verdie's."

Lily nodded. "He's a good man."

Hoke nodded once sharply. "That's good 'nough for me."

"Me, too," said Verdie, who was now attached to Budge's big arm like moss hugging the north side of a tree.

Hoke lowered the hammer of Ott's gun, set the safety, and stuffed the weapon in the waistband of his jeans. "When's this here auction to be?" he asked of anyone willing to answer.

"Tomorrow," said Angie.

Hoke gave Ott a knowing smile. "Well, now . . . there's a coincidence."

Ott jostled his way to the front of the tub and gripped the edge of the basin. "You got any idea the trouble you're gittin' into, Limberlost!? Pullin' a gun on a sher'ff!?"

Hoke snorted. "A sher'ff crooked'r'n a corn snake climbing a flight o' stairs."

Ott kicked the inside of the metal trough, and it rang like the muted note of a distant church bell. "This is kidnappin'! I'll have you in the federal pen, you ignorant, part-Injun lunatic! I'm the sher'ff, by God! My name is known all over this state. Hell, this here," he swept an arm in a wide arc across the valley, "this oughta be called Ambrose Coun'y. My family built this coun'y. And don' think I don' know who's been tearin' down the countryside, you stinkless jasper. I found that piece o' dead whatever-it-was that smelt 'xactly like the way you used to stink! We're gonna prosecute you for vandalizin', plus I'm gonna sue you personal for scalpin' the Winfield Scott statue up at the park. General Scott was my kin, and I figure the mental hardship on me is gonna be worth close to a quarter-million dollars. Betcha a quart o' quarters 'gainst a court order you're gonna have to sell ever'thin' you own to pay up on this lark you've been on."

L.T. squirmed his way to the front of the tank to stand beside Ott. "And I know it was you who mutilated those awning posts out in front of my office. That's good for defamation of character. By God, I'll sue you for your Frogtown property!"

Hoke scratched the side of his face with his fingernails and let his eyes angle off toward the moon. "You'ens don' leave a man with much else to lose, do ya?" He turned back to Ott and Voss, and the calm on his face was like a force pushing the sheriff and the realtor deeper into the tub.

"Damnit, Ott!" Haymer yelled. "Git off my feet!" He cradled one of his *Dr. Duke's* cream-slicked feet in one hand and with the other pushed Ott into L.T. Both men stumbled into Mose, who swatted at them with the leg bone of his barbecue snack. Garland's motor idled on super-octane as he cackled at the brawl in the making. Hoke pulled out the gun, clicked off the safety, and raised it to the sky.

Boom!

The commotion in the tank quieted. But a low moan issued from the outhouse. "I wish y'all would stop shootin' out there!" Crowder yelled in a pitiful, pleading voice.

Hoke lowered the gun, glared at his prisoners, and began shaking his head. "I think I see where this here situation is needin' to go," he said and pointed at Ott. "So, your family built this coun'y, you say?" He shifted his eyes to Voss. "You go 'long with that, Mr. Rock-Stealer?"

"Well, yes!" L.T. said. "The Ambroses were stalwart pioneers and politicians and lawmen and—"

Hoke held up a flattened hand to stop him. Then he turned to Mose. "How 'bout you'ens, big'un? You'ens go 'long with that?"

Mose wiped sauce from his face with his forearm and frowned. "Well, hell, us Vanstorys been purty damn important to the coun'y, too."

"Hell, yes!" Garland blurted out. "Our family was the first to make a moonshine worth drinkin' 'round here. Our great granddaddies marched off to the Civil War and fought for this land. You juss think where we'd be right now if they hadn'."

Haymer turned to Garland and said quietly, "We lost that war, Gar."

Garland's eyebrows knitted together. He opened his mouth, closed it, and then tapped out a little paradiddle with his fingers on the side of the tank. Before long the simple four-four beat evolved into a complicated jazz tempo. Garland closed his eyes and got into the rhythm until Haymer laid his hand over Garland's and the drumming stopped.

"Haymer?" Hoke said. "Wanna take a shot at the million-dollar question?"

Haymer looked up at the stars with a philosophical cock of his head. "Well . . . I'd say *Meadowdale* is got this coun'y to where it is. I mean . . . without the chicken processin' plant—"

Boom!

Hoke lowered the gun from the sky. The men in the tank remained crouched and frozen.

"*P-l-e-a-s-e* stop that!" Crowder cried from the privy, his voice edged with a keening whine as if he were calling from the bottom of a well.

"Wanna take a stab at it, son?" Hoke yelled to the ex-deputy in the outhouse.

The quiet of the night gathered around them as they waited for Crowder to proffer an opinion.

"Well . . . as I see it . . . it was the Cher'kees. They's the ones got it all started." Crowder stepped out of the privy and tucked his chin to his chest as he buckled the belt holding up his trousers. "My Uncle 'Lonzo? He tol' me that most o' the roads 'round here was built right over the ol' Ind'an trails." Crowder raised his arm and extended it down the valley. "The Cher'kees lived all over here. Farmed it, hunted it, fished it. Took juss what they needed right from the land but never used it up like we done."

"Oh, great!" Ott murmured. "We git to listen to my idiot nephew do his version of a hour of Public Television."

Hoke was nodding at Crowder. "That's dead-on, son. I 'xpect you got a little Cher'kee blood in *you*."

"Now wait a fried-chicken minute!" Ott snapped. "Take a look 'round this coun'y and show me one damn thing the Cher'kees left behind that's worth a spit. You don' see no Injun schools or Injun *Walmarts* or Injun golf courses, do you? Hell, my great, great Uncle Winfield did 'em a favor takin' 'em out to Okl'homa where all that oil is." Ott spewed a flutter of air through his lips. "Trail o' Tears, hell. It was juss a little stroll out west to a buried treasure. And now they's all sittin' purty out there . . . rich as bankers." He thrust his hand out toward the dark valley. "Cher'kees didn' do diddly out here. There ain't nothin' *out* there. Just look!"

And they did look. All of them. A mist hung over the meadow, and through its shredded veil of gray, the mountain peaks rose up like great black waves cresting toward the star-studded heavens. A cool breeze poured from the north, carrying the first hints of autumn. Ripening persimmons and blossoms of ironweed and meadow beauty. A barred owl hooted from the creek, its song sonorous and sweet. The night seemed to hold its breath.

"Can you see 'em, Ott?" Hoke whispered, his glazed eyes fixed on the dark. "There they go . . . movin' off through the grass toward the west . . . timeless and silent as the land itself . . . men, women, children, and the elders all mixed together . . . the disinherited . . . the banished . . . the forgotten . . . the first people."

Lily pressed her cheek against Hoke's shoulder and squeezed his arm. "That was pure poetry, *Inâli*, my love."

"That was pure hog flop, and you know it," Ott carped. "Ain't nothin' out there in that medder but weeds and chiggers and field mice. Betcha a vein o' gold 'gainst a Vienna sausage them Cher'kees was happy to stretch they's legs, take a hike, and take up in a new place. Hell . . . that walk was good exercise for 'em."

"You like to bet, don't you, Ott?" Hoke said. " 'Betcha' this, 'betcha' that! Makes me think you might 'preciate one o' them Cher'kee casinos. Whatcha think?"

Ott puffed up. "Now see there? That's what I'm talkin' 'bout! If the Cher'kee' had left somethin' like that 'round here, I might be singin' a diff'rent tune. Man, I always wanted to go to one o' them casinos, but

Bernice—" As quickly as it had flared up, Ott's enthusiasm clicked off when he saw Hoke's pensive face blossom with a smile. "What!?" Ott barked.

Hoke walked up to Crowder and handed over Ott's Glock. "Better snap this in you'ens' holster and clean that barbecue sauce off you'ens' face, son. We're 'bout to make you'ens a hero, Dep'ty Ramp. Where's yore car?"

Crowder pointed. "Yonder behind the barn."

"How many handcuffs you got?" Hoke asked.

Crowder looked pained as he considered the calculation, but counting on the fingers of one hand, he emerged victorious. "One."

Hoke nodded. "And I reckon the sher'ff's got a few in his car."

Within two minutes, all the Vanstorys, Ott, and L.T. were manacled. The three red-headed brothers were stuffed into the prisoner cage in the back of Crowder's cruiser, and Crowder got behind the wheel of the car. Hoke leaned to the driver's window to give final instructions.

"You'ens is gonna be famous for bringin' in the Vanstorys, son. Juss take 'em on into the jail, and, if somebody asks you 'bout the sher'ff, you ain't seen 'im."

Crowder swallowed. "You want me to lie?"

"No," Hoke said reassuringly. "Close your eyes, son."

Crowder did.

"Can you see Ott now?"

Crowder frowned. "No, sir. I cain't see nothin'."

"Well, this is the time o' night I want you to remember. When somebody asks 'bout Ott, you juss think 'bout this moment right now. You juss tell 'em the truth."

With his eyes still closed, Crowder wrinkled his brow. "Well, what if they ask me did I see him here *at any time*?"

"Son, if they say 'at any time' . . . sounds to me like they's givin' you'ens a choice 'bout what time to consider. So, what I want you to do is to consider this time right here. Now I'm gone ask you again . . . can you see the sher'ff?"

Crowder smiled. "I think I see where you're goin' with this, Mr. Limberlost."

"No," Hoke said, "I don't think you do see. Yore eyes are closed."

Crowder hesitated, his face worrying with a question as he chewed on his lip. "Mr. Limberlost, I need to ask you. What're you plannin' on doin' with my Uncle Ott?"

Hoke turned his gaze to Ott and Voss in the water tank and lifted one corner of his mouth. "Why, we're goin' on a little walk, son. Good exercise. Good scenery. Your uncle said he's always wanted to visit a casino. Juss think of it as a vacation with a hist'ry lesson attached to it." Turning back to Crowder, Hoke patted the deputy on the arm. "Ott'll tell you all 'bout it when he gits back."

Appearing relieved at this news, Crowder started the cruiser and began to back out of the yard with his captives in tow. The three red heads in the backseat gave the appearance that the cruiser's upholstery was on fire. The car began to veer toward the water tank, and Ott began working his way behind L.T.

"Crowder!" Ott called out. "Look out, you idiot!"

The cruiser halted suddenly and idled in place. Crowder craned his head out the window.

"Dammit, boy!" Ott growled. "Watch where you're goin'!"

Hoke approached the cruiser and laid a hand on Crowder's shoulder. "Better open up your eyes now, son," he counseled.

Crowder did. The car pulled away without further incident, except for the cats that parted from its grill like water curling off the bow of a boat.

Ott crossed his arms over his chest, looking fit to be tied as he glared at Hoke. "Would you at least tell me what the hell all these cats are doin' here, Limberlost?"

Hoke's eyes crinkled when he smiled. "Buster Gooch is allergic to cats. He'll never set foot on this land." Hoke pointed at Voss. "Which means you'ens'll never git the deed to his Frogtown property. Juss like you'ens'll never git hold o' mine."

Hoke turned to Lily, who appeared to be enthralled at the manner in which he commanded the situation. "Let's us saddle up, purty lady."

"Where're we going?" she asked, seemingly delighted at the blind invitation.

Hoke fingered the whiskers on his chin as he studied the two men left in the water tank. "Well, they's Cher'kee casinos in Okl'homa, but I reckon a little stroll up to North Car'liner is a lil' more realistic for these fat jaspers."

Joey and Angie stepped beside Hoke and Lily, and the four of them studied the two men remaining in the tank. "I'll saddle up a horse and go with you, Mr. Limberlost," Angie said. Then she looked at Joey. "Want to go? I think we're overdue for a real date?"

Joey laughed. "I've never ridden a horse before."

Angie's mouth twisted into a beguiling smile. "Well, you'll have a good teacher. *And . . .* you'll be with *me*."

"Say no more," Joey said. When he looked back at the two out-of-shape men in the tank, Joey lost his smile. "You think they can make it that far on foot, Mr. Limberlost?"

Hoke shook his head in one sharp movement. "Ain't a matter o' what I think. It's what's gonna happen!"

Ott puffed up. "Now, look-a-here, Hoke Limberlost! I sure as hell ain't gonna—"

Whang-g-g-g!

Hoke had picked up the caulking gun and swung it hard against the water tank, the metal-on-metal collision reverberating like a giant gong designed to send a message all the way to East China. Off in the distance a car's tires screeched briefly on the highway and a loud ***thud*** seemed to kill the engine. In the quiet that followed, they heard the car start up again then resume its journey toward town, this time with its siren blaring in the night. Hoke lowered the caulking gun and grinned at Ott.

"You ain't really got a choice in the matter," Hoke said and let his smile stretch across his face. "Historical, ain't it?"

Budge stepped forward with Verdie, her slender hand nestled inside his giant mitt like a baking thermometer inserted into a rump roast. Together they stood before Hoke and Lily.

"Well," Budge said to Lily, "I started this camping trip with you. Guess I'll finish it with you. You never know when you might need a little muscle." Budge looked hopefully to Verdie. "Could be a memorable first date. Are you game, Miss Verdie?"

"The game is afoot!" she declared. "Count me in."

Budge held out his big fist to Joey. "Captain Epoxy?" he said, his voice carrying the soft timbre of affection. Gently, they tapped knuckles.

"And Wonder Woman," Angie added and bumped her fist against the two men's.

And then Verdie added her taps and nodded toward the water tank. "You'll no doubt need a consulting detective . . . in case these two escape."

In a complete show of solidarity, Lily balled up her hand and made the fist-bumping rounds. "And with the season changing, you'll be needing campfires at night. Otter Woman, at your service."

Then Hoke reached his hand into the tap-fest. The six of them stood with their fists still connected like the hub of a spoked wheel. Hoke looked around at every face in their circle and smiled at his friends, new and old.

"This here is gonna be the grandest-ever do-si-do these old mountains have ever seen. Am I right?"

The sextet of soon-to-be historical reenactors yelled in unison, ***"Right!"***

The collective sound of their voices fairly exploded and expanded throughout the valley. A half-dozen fists shot into the air, and the newly united conspirators started into action like the offensive team of the Atlanta Falcons breaking from their huddle. The game was afoot, all right. Hell, it was *afeet*. Fourteen, to be exact.

Chapter Forty-Four

**Lumpkin County Courthouse
Tuesday, early evening**

"This ain't like Ott," Duffy said, staring out at the town from the top of the courthouse steps. He checked his watch. "*Eye Witness Police Chronicles* comes on in fifteen minutes." Duffy turned and squinted at Buster Gooch. "Ott never misses it."

"Where do you reckon he's at, Duff?" Buster said.

Duffy filled his lungs with air and then let go a long sigh. "Danged if I know. I checked his calendar. He was s'posed to see a chir'practor today over to Gainesv'lle." Duffy shook his head. "He never showed up there. His wife, Bernice, is worried."

"Hell, I don' blame 'er," Buster declared. "They'll prob'ly charge for the visit even though he didn' git nothin' out o' it." Buster gazed up at the big Chinese chestnut tree spreading over the courthouse lawn. He shook his head. "I'll tell you who else is scarce right now. That damn L.T. Voss. I's s'posed to meet 'im out at the Vanstory auction today." When he huffed this complaint, his Adam's apple jumped in his throat like a bullfrog. "I'll tell you what, them Vanstory boys was highly overrated far as they's livestock goes. They wasn't but one damn horse over there, and it looked like they'd dug it up from the grave." Buster snorted. "Hell, they could'a had Black Beauty, Trigger, and Seabiscuit for sale today, but I wouldn'a stayed out there to bid a penny on nothin'. They's cat hairs all over the damn place."

Duffy nodded. "Yep. Scarce on horses, but they must'a had a mess o' cats out there." Duffy was quiet for a moment, thinking. "Found Ott's cruiser out there with a horse trailer hitched to it. What do you reckon that's about?"

Buster narrowed his eyes. "There juss ain't no tellin'."

Duffy squinted at Buster. "You're lookin' a mite swole up, ain't you?"

"It's them damn cats. Throat swells up like: I tried to swaller a softball. Cain't breathe any better'n a cow got his head stuck through some chicken wire. It's why I didn' stick around at the auction."

Duffy couldn't help staring at the bulge in Buster's throat. He wondered how the man could breathe at all.

"Were you wantin' to buy some horses?" Duffy asked.

"Actu'lly, I was wantin' the whole damn farm. L.T. was s'posed to buy it, and me and him was set to trade for it." Buster gingerly touched his throat. "Don' want nothin' to do with the place now. They's more cat hairs out in that medder than fescue. Hell, if you was to try'n cut hay, forgit a bush-hog. You'd prob'ly need industr'al-strength hair clippers."

Duffy stared out into the night and tried to sort out all this information. "This whole thing 'bout Ott . . . and the Vanstory place . . . is startin' to look like foul play."

Buster frowned hard at Duffy and began shaking his head slowly. "Didn' see no chickens out there. Should'a been feathers out in the grass if they was chickens."

Behind them, the courthouse door opened, and Maria Gunlock backed out of the building carrying a briefcase and an armload of folders.

"Evenin', ma'am," Duffy said.

Maria straightened and presented a surprised smile. "Deputy DePuma." Her dark face flushed even darker, and she tried to laugh. "I mean Bronson." She bit her lip and closed her eyes to hide her embarrassment. "I mean Deputy Duffy." The skin on her face seemed about to burst into flame. "Deputy Hawkins," she finally said. She turned to Buster and his mammoth Adam's apple and decided she had better say nothing else.

"Well, I gotta go and see 'bout gittin' me a new Epi-pen down at the drug store," Buster said and nodded to the A.D.A., who, to Buster, may as well have been the Queen of Madagascar for her good looks. "Evenin', ma'am." He shot Duffy an index finger. "You take 'er easy, Duff. Wouldn' worry none 'bout chickens out at the Vanstorys', if I was you. Cats, maybe . . . but no chickens."

In shifting her paperwork against her chest, a few folders slipped from Maria's grasp and scattered on the pavement. Almost before they had hit the ground, Duffy was squatting, picking them up. Maria watched the way he moved with such fluid grace.

"Thank you, Deputy," she said when he stood. "Any word about the sheriff?"

He tried to help her add the folders to the stack she clutched to her chest, but it was difficult due to the tight hold she would not surrender. When the folders slipped again, Duffy's hand reacted by reflex and saved the files, but his fingertips pressed firmly into her left breast. He had a brief glimpse of himself in the reflection of the door glass. His face was the color of a radish. In the awkward silence that followed, Duffy cleared his throat, afraid his voice might surprise him with the wrong octave.

"Ma'am, I gotta hunch 'bout Ott's disappearance. Seems it's got to do with this Vanstory auction somehow. Somethin' ain't right 'bout it."

Maria dropped her voice to a confidential tone. "I agree that there are questions to be answered about the auction. The D.A. has already asked me to look into it, because the auctioneer's inventory did not jibe with the one we took two days earlier . . . unless 'roan' and 'gelding' and 'Tennessee Walker' and 'Morgan' can refer to cats." She shrugged. "We didn't actually find any cats out there, but the evidence was overwhelming."

Duffy nodded distractedly. The files were spreading like a fan against her chest, about to drop again.

"Ma'am, can I carry those for you out to your car?"

This time when the folders fell, Duffy caught them in the air, his hands moving like a magician's as he gathered them in. Again, he somehow inadvertently brushed her breast and, afraid he might be glowing in the dark, he avoided his reflection in the glass. Maria was breathing harder.

"I suppose you'd better carry them," she said and surrendered the few she still held. In the exchange, only their hands touched, but she felt a tingle in both breasts.

They walked to the parking lot, their footsteps resonating on the walkway as if they were the only two people in the county not watching *Eye Witness Police Chronicles*. She took two steps for every one of his. Duffy's tread was like the soft touch of a mountain lion's pads against the staccato taps of her high heels. Ten yards shy of her car, Maria stopped, planted her feet, and waited for the etched-out-of-stone lawman to turn to her.

"Has anyone ever told you . . . you look like Charles Bronson?"

Duffy chewed on his lip and thought for a time. "That's not that new feller workin' at the bank, is it?"

Maria shook her head. "He's a movie star. Very handsome. He played in Westerns and police movies."

Duffy stared right into her emerald eyes and felt a lock and chain loosen around his vocal cords. "I think you're more beautiful than that woman-lawyer on *Law and Order*."

Maria smiled. "Thank you, Deputy."

"I reckon you'll need to be callin' me 'Duffy.'"

They gazed into each other's eyes for a long five seconds. "I'm 'Maria,'" she whispered.

Five more seconds ticked by—a geologic era with tectonic plates crashing, reshaping the world.

"I'm gonna go out to the Vanstory place and look around," Duffy said. "You wanna go?"

"Now?"

"Now," he said. With the auction complete, Duffy knew there would be no one at the Vanstory farm. No one to distract them from the quiet of the valley, the twinkling of the stars, and the murmur of the creek. Unless some of those cats remained out there.

"We can take my car," Maria offered.

Duffy looked at her little Toyota with bucket seats. He was thinking about a less confined arrangement.

"The road into the farm might be rough," he warned. "We can take my truck." Surprising himself, he raised a hand and cupped one of her cheeks. "One thing though," Duffy said. "I don' want you seein' this Charles Bronson feller when you look at me. I want you seein' Duffy Hawkins."

When she nodded, the smooth skin of her cheek caressed his hand. "What about the *Law and Order* floozy. Can you break it off with her? What's her name?"

Duffy stepped close enough to smell her shampoo. "I can't remember now," he said and kissed her.

Chapter Forty-Five

Jinks's Bait Shop and Atomic Parts
Nottely Community, Union County
Tuesday, late afternoon

Hiram Jinks stepped from behind the cash register and walked to the front door of his store for the fourth time to check on the man pumping gas. To Hiram, the man holding the unleaded nozzle looked like something from another planet. Not to mention the clownish little car, bright orange with black spots the size of dinner plates.

Hiram didn't like the looks of the man *or* the car, but he liked even less the way the fellow was stalling for time—pumping in a few cents worth then looking around like he was expecting a flying saucer to land with reinforcements. Hiram was pretty sure the freak was going to try to rob him, so he moved from the door to the window to get a look at the license plate. Fulton County. That would be Atlanta. Well, that figured. Almost anything could show up here out of that place.

Hiram fingered the handle of the old .32 caliber Remington pocket pistol that he had stuck into his trouser pocket. It had been his great grandfather's and had not been fired since a bear had tried to get into the bait box out back. The gun had not much fazed the bear, and Hiram held out even less hope for this bald-headed buffalo of a man outside his store. But at least it would make some noise, and that might get Adele's attention over at the house.

Hiram moved to the front screened door and called out to the man. "I'll be a-closin' in juss a few minutes. Anythin' else I can do for you?"

The gargantuan customer holstered the nozzle back in its slot and came toward the store. Hiram hurried back to stand behind the counter, removed the cash drawer from the register, and set it on the shelf under the counter where he kept the paper grocery bags. Stashing the antique pistol inside the register where the drawer had been, he pretended to read the bait catalogue, flipping through pages and staring blankly at the array of night crawlers advertised by a dealer in Arkansas.

Inside the store the Atlanta man looked even larger. Seeing all this bulk of muscle prancing around in khaki shorts inside his store gave Hiram a sudden and paralyzing fear that he might become more than a victim of robbery. The banjo theme from *Deliverance* played in his head, and Hiram dropped into a cold sweat.

He watched the man browse the aisles and pluck items off the shelves. It took eight trips to get all the goods to the counter, and Hiram's apprehensions slowly gave way to hope as the register started ringing up a profit.

"That there's a lot of *Beanie-Weenies*," Hiram said steadying his voice.

The big stranger nodded. "You Jinks?"

"That's me. Hiram Jinks." Hiram was so nervous, he hardly knew what he was saying. "Friends call me 'Hi.'"

Budge stared at him for a while, trying to determine if the proprietor was trying to pull his leg. Figuratively, of course.

" 'Hi Jinks'?" Budge said flatly.

Hiram smiled. "Yeah . . . well . . . you know how friends are 'bout nicknames."

Budge arched both eyebrows. "Indeed, I do." He pointed with his thumb over his shoulder toward the front of the building. "What's with the name of your store? Atomic parts?"

"Aw, hell, I got me some competition up the road. That *Lake Nottely Quick Stop*? He's got him a two-headed snake in a jar and a albino bat. I had to do somethin'. It's what you call a advertisin' gimmick. Brings people in. And it's the truth, ain't it? I mean, ever'thin's got atomic parts." Hiram popped open a brown paper sack and started stacking cans of

Beanie-Weenies inside it. "Sorta got the idea on account o' that outlaw feller down to Lum'kin Coun'y. You been readin' 'bout that? He's been cutting down all them dumb highway signs he don't wanna have to look at. That and burnin' stuff down. I's hopin' he might come up here and burn this damn store to the ground so I could collect on the insurance, buy some lake property, and start up one o' them Internet cafes." Hiram nodded at the dozen boxes of crackers stacked up on the counter. "That's a lotta saltines you got there, son. I reckon they're to go with the *Beanie-Weenies*?"

Hiram whipped his wrist and popped open another paper sack. "I see you're special fond o' oatmeal, too. Forty-two boxes. I believe that might be a store record for a single sale on a Tuesday."

"It's for some livestock," the burly stranger said. "I didn't see a feed store around."

Hiram shook his head. "You'd have to go into Blairsv'lle for that." He totaled up the sale and ripped the receipt off the machine. The moment of truth. He held out the slip of paper with his left hand and put his right on the butt of the pistol hiding in the register. He was sweating all over now and shaking so badly he was afraid he might set the damn revolver off while it was still in the drawer space. "Comes to two hunerd, forty-three dollars and seventy-eight cents with tax. What kind o' livestock you feedin'?"

"Horses."

Hiram balked, unable to keep his eyes off the man's considerable bulk. "You ride?"

"I tried it for about thirty seconds but gave it up. Wasn't fair to the horse."

When the giant pulled five fifties out of his wallet, Hiram's breathing settled.

"Mr. Jinks, do you know the old logging and mining roads around here very well?"

"Hell," Hiram almost sang from relief, now that he was certain not to be robbed, "my great granddaddy cut most o' the roads through these here mountains. He was a logger his-self. Then my granddaddy . . . he worked for the For'st Service till they started butcherin' up the whole damn place. Then my daddy ran moonshine on all the backroads. Which one you lookin' for?"

Budge flattened a map on the counter and studied it for a few seconds to orient himself. He tapped his finger down just south of Lake Fontana. "Is there any way to get here using the old dirt roads in the forests?"

Hiram looked out the door and studied the garishly painted car. "Wanna stay off the main roads, do you?" he said, and let his hand return to the Remington. When the freak laid another fifty on the counter, Hiram loosened his grip on the pistol, leaned both hands on the counter and lowered his voice. "You're on the run, ain't you, son?"

Budge stuffed the extra fifty into the man's shirt pocket, and Hiram Jinks made a knowing smile and began nodding. "Hell, son, I been known to run a little moonshine up here in these hills, myself, when the bait business slacks off. I reckon I know 'bout ever' road and trail snakin' through Union Coun'y." Hiram looked out at the Volkswagen again, shook his head, and then studied the enormous physique standing before him. "You ain't rightly set up for a low profile, are you?"

Budge turned the map around, and the storekeeper hunkered down on his elbows, his head drooping below his shoulders. "See that turnoff right there?" Jinks said and tapped a finger to the map. "That there is the road up to Trackrock Gap. You can find it 'cause they's a old broke-down, rusted, Studebaker tractor sittin' in the weeds in the right-o'-way."

Jinks hesitated, frowned, canted his head, and pursed his lips. "Well, actually, it's on the left, so I reckon it's in the weeds on the left-o'-way. You turn north there but don' go on to the gap. Take the first fork to the right and then juss keep on northeast for six miles. That's when you'll hit the old wagon ford at Brasstown Creek. From there you gotta sneak over highway sev'nty-six in the dark, I guess."

He looked up at Budge to make sure the man was following him. "You'll pick up the dirt road again juss 'cross the highway. They's a crooked post oak standin' there, bent like a dog's hind leg. That'll take you through some scrub pines and after 'bout a mile you'll come out on Cavanaugh Fields. Then it's only ten miles into North Car'liner." Jinks narrowed one eye like a bandit. "With a lil' luck, the only thing to see you out there is gonna be sportin' either fur or feathers."

Budge tilted his head to Lily's car. "Will that VW make it through the backcountry roads?"

Hiram stuck out his lower lip and nodded. "Hell, maybe . . . if you can straddle a rut a time or two." Jinks shrugged. "And you might wanna git out an' walk a few o' the worse spots . . . let somebody lighter do the drivin', if you know what I mean."

Budge gathered up his groceries and stood staring at the man, giving him a well-practiced bouncer's glare. When he had the storekeeper's full attention, he used his eyes to point to the man's shirt pocket.

"The way I figure it," Budge said, "fifty dollars ought to buy a good case of amnesia."

Confused, Hiram grabbed his special order pad. "That anything like Milk o' Magnesia?" He started to write, but instead he looked up at Budge. "How will I know where to send it to?"

Budge held his stare. "Ever hear of Thomas Carlyle?"

The parallel creases on Hiram's forehead deepened like surgical incisions. He looked northwest out the door. "Used to be a Tom Lyle over on the lake. Opened up a roller skatin' rink, but it didn' catch on. All 'round bad idea, if you ask me. Cain't see mountain folk takin' to roller skatin', can you?"

Budge stood with the bags in his arms as if they weighed nothing at all. " 'Under all speech that is good for anything there lies a silence that is better.' " He nodded once. "*That* Thomas Carlyle."

Hiram's troubled brow gradually smoothed out, and he began to nod. "Oh-h-h-h- . . . amnesia. For a minute I forgot what that meant." He winked. "I think I follow you now." He gazed out the screened door at the gaudy VW bug crouching by his gas pump. "As I remember you was a skinny feller with a head o' curly black hair drivin' a green van, an' I gave you d'rections west and sold you a road atlas for Alabama."

Budge made a little bow from the waist and smiled. "As Charlie Chan would say to his number one son . . . 'Ah, so.' "

The storekeeper returned the bow but offered no reply, as he considered his command of the Chinese language insufficient for conversation.

Chapter Forty-Six

Cavanaugh Fields
Tuesday, twilight

The pines were deep in shadow, but up ahead, where the old road opened into the field, there was a stark contrast of light. It was like a portal. When they emerged from the forest the grainy texture of dusk began settling on the open meadow, blurring the details of everything around them. The air was cool, a welcome change after the hot day.

The two hostages were bone-tired, but there was no talk of setting up camp. Hoke was intent on making it to North Carolina by sunrise. They were taking the journey a piece at a time, resting every five miles, so that neither Ott nor Voss could weasel out of the trek due to heart attack.

Hoke was out front, his keen eyes surveying the trail ahead, missing nothing. His horse—the stout Morgan—seemed to take some pride in leading the procession, for it lifted its forelegs high and put them down with a smart, military snap that would have looked good in a parade.

To Verdie, Hoke no longer seemed an anachronism. It was as though he had slipped through a tear in the fabric of time and found his place in history. He looked twenty years younger. Verdie guessed he had Lily to thank for that.

The lead rope that trailed back from Hoke's saddle to Ott's handcuffs slackened and went taut in a repetitive rhythm that the sheriff could not seem to catch on to. His abraded wrists and stressed shoulder kept him in misery, and his moaning and whining became part of the soundtrack of the journey. It didn't help that Voss was handcuffed to the back of Ott's service belt and stumbling so erratically that he continually stepped on Ott's heels.

Neither Voss nor Ott had been an ideal prisoner. Their weary shuffling steps might have tugged at the heartstrings of a more merciful captor, but Ott's constant whimpering and Voss's frequent snaps of anger had grated on everyone. In the midafternoon, Voss had started begging for ear plugs to block out Ott's carping. When he realized he would evoke no mercy from anyone—least of all Ott—Voss just settled into a weepy state of self-pity. Pretty soon, Ott was crying, too.

And then—when it was close to eight o'clock—everyone had to listen to Ott's incessant complaints about missing *Eye Witness Police Chronicles* on the TV. Hoke's solution to that problem was to let out another forty feet of rope to put the two captives out of earshot.

With the grisaille light settling on the grass, Lily nudged her horse into a canter to gain Hoke's side. There she slowed, took his hand, and laced her fingers into his. They rode this way the length of the field.

Behind these two, Joey and Angie rode stirrup to stirrup, something they had been doing most of the trip. More times than not, when Hoke turned to check on his tribe, these two youngsters were leaning from their saddles, whispering to one another, sometimes their lips locked in a passionate kiss. If they got through this odyssey without a chipped tooth, Hoke thought, it would be a miracle.

Living up to her surname, Verdie Rider looked surprisingly at home on her chestnut gelding, her back swaying in perfect harmony with the stride of the animal, her hips rolling with the gait. She considered the equine mass between her legs a reasonable training seminar for the inevitable tryst coming her way, for she had decided she would receive Budge to her bedroll the next time they stopped to rest. It was the most natural decision of her life. If Sherlock Holmes could have his Irene Adler, then Verdie should be able to have her "Budge."

As for Budge, who drove behind her in the VW, he stared serenely out the windshield at the Julie Andrews-silhouette of Verdie Rider and dredged up from memory every quote he had ever memorized on beauty, destiny, and devotion. Whenever he temporarily stalled and could think of nothing new, he resorted to falsetto lines from *The Lonely Goatherd* and *My Favorite Things*. He even came up with a new arrangement for *Edelweiss*—substituting "mountain laurel" as the botanical object of affection. It didn't have the same lyrical flow, but the rendition was touching.

They climbed over the crest of the hill and descended to lower ground, where a whippoorwill began its plangent heralding of night. Katydids ratcheted in the trees, the sound like a great ocean wave swelling and crashing against a shoreline of dry sticks. Above the treetops the stars were pinholes in black velvet, rotating in a slow spin that read like a code unlocking the secrets of the universe. The moon lighted their way.

Bringing up the very rear of the entourage, stretching for almost a quarter mile behind the procession, a long sinewy tail slithered through the grass. Lined up perfectly, nose to tail, came the trailing line of cats emancipated from the Animal Control shed.

In addition to the original sixty-nine, volunteer cats from every farmland they had traversed had abandoned their stations and joined the march. Now there were hundreds of them. Felines of every color. Long hair, short hair, scruffy, and sleek. Their little paws padded the earth quietly, as their tails flicked side to side with the rhythm of their gaits. Every now and again, two might switch places and then switch back again, looking for all the world like a cat's rendition of a do-si-do.

But the grandest-ever do-si-do was the journey itself. Two fat-cat white men stumbling along behind a handsome couple of part-Cherokee guides. With every leg of the march, these two black-hearted, white jaspers suffered from any number of ailments: foot blisters; handcuff abrasion; rope burn; skin chafing where their chubby legs rubbed one another below the crotch; muscle fatigue; chigger bites; heat stroke; yellow jacket stings; poison ivy rash; trickling rivulets of sweat that ran down their bodies to soak their socks; hunger and thirst; lack of sleep; cold temperature at night; and general depression and psychological defeat. And, of course, for Ott it was the irritation of knowing that he was missing *Eye-Witness Police Chronicles*. That and his suspicion that Mr. Fluffs was somehow involved in this surreal feline hegira that followed them through the mountains.

Every now and again, Hoke circled back on the Morgan and rode alongside the two suffering men. "You'ens boys enjoyin' the scenery and the exercise?" he would ask.

Ott and Voss just glared at him. Neither one would shed his pride long enough to ask for mercy.

But Ott was not above throwing out a threat now and then. When he worked up enough steam, his words spat out like little balls of fire.

"They'll be a reckonin' for all this, Hoke Limberlost. You can count on that. An' then it'll be me a-smilin' at you through the bars of a federal jail. An' it ain't juss the courts you'll have to answer to. One day you'll have to face Bernice and 'xplain to her how I got my uniform all tore up. She's the one who'll have to sew it all back up." Ott shook his head. "Don't envy you that little face to face encounter." Ott chuckled to himself.

Hoke assumed a look of Thespian regret. "Why, Ott . . . do you mean to tell me that this little jaunt through the woods is taking its toll on you'en's clothes?"

Ott pulled at the side of his trousers so that Hoke could see the damage. "Ever' time you take us through them damn devil briars, I get a new tear in my pants! My socks are tore up from scratching the chigger bites on my ankles! When we go through the pine thickets, them damn low branches that're dead tear at my shirt! I even got tears in my skin on both arms from scraping against some damn tree bark that felt like razor blades!"

"Black cherry," Hoke explained.

"An' my sher'ff's hat's got tears all over it from those damn trees with thorns from hell attached to 'em."

"Devil's walking stick, honey locust, and hawthorn," said Hoke in his edifying tone.

Ott wasn't finished. "Look at my damn shoes! All tore up from them sharp rocks in that boulder field back yonder." As he plodded on, Ott tried to show all the tears on the sides of his leather shoes.

Hoke hitched his head, and his eyes slanted with a kind of cold remorse. "That there's a lotta tears, aw-right, Ott. We just might have to give a name to this little hike o' ours." Hoke laughed. "Ain't this juss the grandest-ever do-si-do?" Still laughing, Hoke nudged the Morgan with his heels and galloped back to the front to join Lily.

Ott turned an angry face to Voss. "What the hell did he mean by givin' this torture-walk a new name?"

Voss chirped up with a haughty laugh. "Well, I guess you asked for that one, Ott. Complainin' about all the tears in your clothin'."

"So what? What's that got to do with a name?"

For the next few paces L.T. just gloated at Ott. "Trail of tears. Git it?"

After trudging a few more steps, Ott looked madder than a wild boar brought down by a chipmunk. Looking straight ahead, he did not talk anymore for hours. The two white men slogged on across the wilderness, the only two in the whole entourage who were not immersed in bliss.

Epilogue

By the time the moon was halfway to its apex, the dark forest appeared to be touched by a silvery tint, where the argentine light dappled the ground amongst the deep shadows. The cold was bracing, and so Joey and Angie rode double on the bare back of Joey's bay, sharing body heat as well as the warmth of affection. And, of course, the fire of passion that smoldered inside them. In quiet whispers they reminisced over their days in grammar and high school, recalling their memories of one another as seen across the distance of Joey's unrequited love.

Hoke and Lily doubled up on the Morgan, with Lily sitting behind the cantle of the saddle, her arms wrapped around Hoke's wiry torso, her cheek pressed into his back between his shoulder blades. As they rode through the stunning, nocturnal light, they taught each other the Cherokee words that they had picked up along the course of their lives.

Even as they traveled through a land seemingly too dark to recognize, Hoke enchanted her with the Cherokee names of all the valleys, knobs, ridges, streams, and gaps as they passed through them. Her favorite was Otter Cheek Creek, and she made Hoke promise they could come back there in daylight one day. Which they would.

Hoke did not have the heart to tell her that it had been named for a Dutch preacher from the late 1700's. This pious man had been well known as a pacifist and proselytized the principle of "turnin' da otter cheek." He had died right there by the creek after turning his other cheek to a stout log of hickory in the hands of a fat German fur trader who coveted the preacher's wife.

Verdie tied the reins of her roan to the back bumper of the VW and rode with Budge in the bug. Budge kept the car running slowly in second gear so that he could hold Verdie's hand without the interruption of shifting gears. They talked of literature and philosophy and the general state of the world. Budge was fascinated at the tribulations of Verdie's childhood and admired her climb out of poverty to become so erudite and compassionate.

For her part, Verdie felt more secure than ever she had before in her life. As they bumped along the forgotten backroads of Appalachia, she subtly probed the different parts of Budge's body in a sort of clinical assessment of each muscle group, knowing that every fiber of biceps and abs and lats and pecs was now dedicated to her protection. She felt like a freshly minted silver dollar tucked away in a felt box and nestled inside a vault at Fort Knox with the entire United States Marine Corps standing guard on the parapets.

After a time, these six pairs of lovers traveled in the quiet of contentment, soaking up the peace of the autumnal night forest and the hypnotic twinkling of the stars above the colorful tree canopies. Occasionally, an owl *hoo-hoo*ed from the bottomlands and a gray fox barked in response to the kissing sounds of a flying squirrel. Once, off to the west, a chorus of coyotes sent their looping yowls and yammering across the mountains as if they were celebrating their first-place trophy in the Call of the Wild Championships. When the symphony faded it left an eerie edge in the air, as if to remind all two-leggeds that there was much more unknown than known in this world.

Each of these human travelers felt the gift of completion and understood the uniqueness of their joint confluences with their destined soulmates. It would bond them forever as the truest of friends. Blood brothers and sisters all.

As the travelers, horses, and bug disappeared into the Snowbird Range and began the precipitous work of paralleling the Nantahala Gorge, unknown to each of them, the long line of cats quietly veered off to the east and made its way toward the North Carolina coast. If the legend be true, it is said that they were bound to board ships by following rats up the catenary curve of thick nautical tie ropes that held vessels fast to the docks. They wanted to find another land entire.

They had heard of India, where cows were sacred and never harmed, and so they, too, sought a similar sanctuary, where all things feline were revered and protected. There had to be some place, they believed. There were rumors of possibilities: Catagonia, Calicofornia, Catoslavokia, Greenlion, and Lynxembourg. And if those did not pan out, there were the teaser countries like Hungry, Turkey, and Grease.

No one knows for certain how many cats made it to such idyllic destinations, but this, of course, would warrant another book by some industrious researcher willing to delve into the international records of cats, if such a thing exists.

As for Ott and L.T.? They did eventually recover from their ordeal and—after five or six years of mopping the floors and sweeping the parking lot of the big casino in Cherokee, North Carolina—they returned to Lumpkin County with little or no fanfare.

Ott and L.T. never spoke of their experience to anyone. Not even to one another. They never ate together again at *The Sizzlin' Skillet*. Ott never again wore a badge. Bernice had divorced him after the first two years of his absence. This, on the grounds of abandonment. She never remarried, but there were strange rumors about her relationship with Mr. Fluffs. Ott could find no work anywhere, so he became a politician. Not being very successful at that, he sometimes volunteered at the landfill in exchange for rummaging around for any item he might need at any given time.

L.T. could not find his footing in real estate again. All of his holdings had been sold for back taxes to the highest bidder. On one of those properties, a massive factory had been erected by the *Quick to the Lip Potato Chip Company*. Ironically, L.T. hired on there as a sales representative and traveled all over the Southeast trying to accrue new customers as he filled vending machines in gas stations, motels, and rest stops.

It was part of his job to carry sample packets of every flavor of chips and to partake of them with a prospective client as a gesture of good will and faith in the product. As would be expected, he gained weight and lost all self-respect. Eventually, and paradoxically, he just disappeared. His therapist's best guess was that he had returned to Florida to deal with early childhood issues. Lumpkin County never saw him again.

Dr. Crowder Ramp, the county's first ever holistic healer/librarian, became well known for the care and attention he paid to the citizens who checked out books at his library, often helping them to heal from whatever maladies plagued them.

When he and Raynelle had purchased the Limberlost properties and moved into Hoke's old cabin up on Crow Mountain, Crowder had devoured Hoke's library and become quite the practitioner of Cherokee herbs. He provided this service for free, because the librarian job paid pretty well for just standing around inside the quietest work venue in the county and gently stamping due dates on book check-out cards.

With less laundry to deal with, Raynelle had time to pursue her own passion: genealogy. Through her studies, she discovered that Crowder had a great-great-grandfather who had sired an illegitimate child with a Cherokee maiden with whom he was deeply in love. The maiden's name was either "Crow Woman" or "Deer Woman." The records showed both names at various times. It was confusing.

If her child was a boy, they had planned to name it "Crow." If a girl, "Deer." When the baby emerged, it was physically equipped like a male, but its mannerisms and speech and hand gestures were clearly female. So, they named it "Crow-Deer." This was Crowder's great-grandfather and namesake. He was the county's first mixed gender citizen and was well thought of throughout the mountain community. Now that Crowder's lifestyle was devoid of loud noises, he, too, enjoyed a similar kind of respect from the citizens of Lumpkin County. Raynelle made a fortune on the Internet researching people's ancestry.

Moon of the White Tears

After being appointed temporary sheriff in Ott's absence, Duffy Hawkins won the next election in a landslide victory over Ricky Earl Babcock, Beulah's brother's boy. Ricky Earl had been a tray washer and table wiper and floor sweeper at the *Chicken Palace* out on the bypass. He had run on the slogan: *Let me clean up the county like I cleaned up after you at the Chicken Palace*, but the cleverness of the line backfired on him when people took offense at the accusation that they might have been less than well-mannered while they devoured their meals with their children at the Palace.

Duffy and Maria Gunlock exchanged vows and became man and wife right after the election. Maria kept her maiden name—the one she had reverted to after her divorce from Darren—and Duffy supported her in this choice. Together they worked as a force for the law such as the county had never before seen. Criminals did not stand a chance. Arrest and prosecution was as sure a thing as summer days and chigger bites. Duffy took them down. Maria sent them up. It was that simple.

Three years later, though he had operated the sheriff's office with spotless efficiency and rid the county of countless meth labs, chop shops, and credit card scams, Duffy tired of the job. Sheriffing had lost its appeal due to all the red tape of state regulations and the favors he was expected to dole out to the mayor and county commissioners when their kin fell afoul of the law.

In that same month, Maria gave notice to the district attorney's office and hung up her yellow legal pad. She started wearing jeans, a plaid shirt, navy-blue running shoes, and a short-waisted leather jacket with straps on the sleeves, just like the one worn by the guy who lost the game of "Chicken" in *Rebel Without a Cause* and made the swan dive in his jalopy off the cliff. With her hair now neatly woven into cornrows on top and a single thick braid in back that reached below her shoulder blades, Maria looked like an actress who might have played an offbeat private eye in her own TV series.

To the surprise of everyone, Duffy and Maria formed Lumpkin County's first private detective agency. As full partners they shared in all the work fifty-fifty: research, investigations, interviews, stakeouts, tailing by auto, tailing by bicycle, tailing by horseback (and, in one interesting case, tailing by emu), case record keeping, phone duty, and office cleanup, which included the bathroom. They were a crackerjack team. But more importantly, Duffy and Maria were the closest thing to happily-ever-after that Lumpkin County had ever seen.

Hoke and Lily disappeared into wilderness somewhere in the Smokey Mountains, apparently living a primitive lifestyle in the manner of their Cherokee forebears. They never made contact with outsiders, and no hikers or hunters or birders ever reported spotting them. So, there is nothing to report on them. Except that in the first six years after their disappearance, fourteen gigantic billboards disappeared from highways 40, 19, and 441. No traces of the signs were ever found.

Budge and Verdie opened the *221 B Baker Street Bed and Breakfast* outside of Blowing Rock, North Carolina. The *"Four B's,"* as it was dubbed by the locals, offered a wonderful reading room full of books on every subject. One alcove was dedicated to Arthur Conan Doyle, and Verdie offered Friday night programs on the genius of Sherlock Holmes.

The *Four B's* boasted the finest workout gym in the state, albeit a small one to fit their theme of "Think big, act with deliberation, but leave a small footprint." Budge provided personal coaching and maintained the grounds. Yet, he was never out of earshot of Verdie, as he considered his primary mission in life was to protect her. Conversely, Verdie's mission was to feel protected. It was a case of perfect symmetry. Complete symbiosis. Pure adoration on a two-way street. Budge still kept the VW bug that Lily had gifted him, but he repainted it sky blue with honeybees swarming all over the surface. **BBBB** was painted on each door to identify the car as the official *Four B's* shuttle service.

Joey and Angie gravitated to Wyoming, where she took over as head wrangler at a horse ranch in the shadow of the Medicine Bow Mountains. Joey earned a job as bouncer at the *Red Rock Bar* and at *Hole in the Wall Saloon*, alternating nights with them. In both venues, he dealt with tough cowhands twice his size and weight and quickly earned their respect for the gentlemanly and efficient manner in which he subdued and disposed of troublemakers.

Joey and Budge kept in touch through hand-written letters, and once every couple of years, they visited for a week, one family traveling to the other's home for a vacation, the direction of the journey flipping each time. During one of those reunions at Blowing Rock, Hoke and Lily came wandering out of the forest on foot behind the *Four B's*. After their four-day visit, they disappeared into the woods the same way they had arrived.

As the years went by, the numbers in the gathering increased with a new baby for each family. Budge and Verdie produced a beautiful little girl named "Sherly," whose variation on the spelling of her name was a tribute to Sherlock Holmes. Joey and Angie ushered into the world a determined little boy, whom they named "Buck," simply because at his birth he came out kicking like a green mustang just roped out on the prairie. Hoke and Lily produced a veritable tribe of little fox-boys and otter-girls.

Buck and Sherly would one day find their own common destiny, both romantically and adventurously, but that, of course, is another story for another time.

THE END

About the Author

Mark Warren is a teacher of Native American survival skills in the Appalachian Mountains of north Georgia, where he lives with his wife, Susan. He is a lifelong student/historian of the Old West, a composer/musician, and an archer.

Upcoming New Release!

BY AWARD-WINNING AUTHOR
MARK WARREN

A COPPERHEAD SUMMER

When the mother of 12-year-old Tyler Raintree secretly buses her son off to summer camp to hide from an abusive father, two of Camp Itawa's veteran counselors become more than teachers to the boy. Stoney St. Ney and his Cherokee mentor, Bobby Whitehorse, must serve as bodyguards as well as play the role of private detectives. When the boy is snatched out of camp by the mob-affiliated father, Stoney and Bobby venture into the big city to "track down" the family to ensure that mother and son are safe. When the trackers "re-abduct" Tyler and his mother and return to Itawa, the father and his hired thug come after them. The odds usually favor the mob in such situations, but Stoney and Bobby are on their "home turf" in the deep forests of Southern Appalachia.

**For more information
visit: www.SpeakingVolumes.us**

Now Available!
AWARD-WINNING AUTHOR
MARK WARREN

For more information visit: www.SpeakingVolumes.us

Now Available!
ACTION/ADVENTURE WESTERNS BY SPUR AWARD-WINNING AUTHOR ROD MILLER

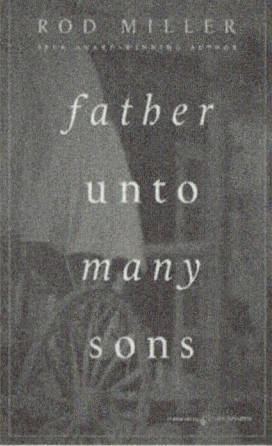

For more information visit: www.SpeakingVolumes.us